Time Paradox

Also by M. Timothy Murray

Thumar
Thumar: Time Paradox
Thumar: Festival of the Lights*
Thumar: Cyth Riders*

*Forthcoming

Time Paradox

Saga 2

M. TIMOTHY MURRAY

iUniverse

TIME PARADOX
SAGA 2

iUniverse books may be ordered through booksellers or by contacting:

iUniverse
1663 Liberty Drive
Bloomington, IN 47403
www.iuniverse.com
844-349-9409

ISBN: 978-1-6632-1065-4 (sc)
ISBN: 978-1-6632-1064-7 (e)

Library of Congress Control Number: 2020919967

Print information available on the last page.

iUniverse rev. date: 04/14/2021

Contents

Dedication

I would like to dedicate this book to my friends and family who encouraged me to press on. To the Placer Gold Writers, and the Café Writers groups who honestly told me when what I wrote needed improvement. Rachel Rosen-Carol for a copy edit, and David Loofbourrow for the book cover design. Last, but certainly not least, my wife Ronna Lee Joseph and our ever present lovable bratty cat, Harley.

Prologue

The large scorpion centered in a barbed circle glowed blood red on the back wall of the Supreme Council chamber. Imbedded computer screens illuminated the ominous faces of the council members. A single blinding white spotlight in front of the raised curved dais focused on the poor soul being interrogated in the center of the darkened room.

Number Three continued. "Commander Thompson, are you telling us this is all you found? What good are you and your men if this is all you return with? You're useless, we can assign you a more appropriate mission."

Charlie Thompson served the council for over two hundred years. He was their best assassin. He could infiltrate any government, corporation, or secured site, until now. This perplexed Charlie and infuriated the council which never accepted failure at any level.

"Number Three," he choked out. "We exhausted all our resources and tortured everyone who had momentary contact with Derak Jamar. His immediate and extended family disappeared. Their files are closed. Not even our highly placed mole had the security clearance to view Jamar's files. It's as if his entire history never existed."

Number Two addressed the commander. "What about his friend, Jack Morgan, and his family? We can get to him that way."

"They disappeared too. Their files have the same security clearance. Our mole informed me she couldn't spy any further without risking her cover."

"Then what use do we have for this worthless slug?" Number Three demanded.

"None, Sir. She and her entire family met a slow, painful end, one of my more creative works of art. I brought her deputy into the fold with a little persuasion. He should prove more useful," commander Thompson reported.

"Let's hope so, for your sake, Commander," Number Two threatened.

Number One spoke. "Commander, did you bring back any useful information?"

"Yes, Number One. There are three intergalactic corporations that have equal security measures. They have Derak Jamar's fingerprints all over them. He is a dangerous enemy; it is reported he single-handedly took out a battalion of Kek in the Chambar Valley Offensive. It is rumored that Master Li trained him."

"That traitor!" Number One exploded. "I have a special death reserved for him. We must tread cautiously with these two. Find a hole in Jamar's security. Don't fail us this time, Commander. Dismissed!"

The commander left the dreaded chambers and made his way to April's Pleasure Palace. Maybe he could catch up with his buddy, Dr. Vander.

After the chamber doors closed behind the commander, Number One went off. "Is that what we're down to? Pansies and cowards who have forgotten all the good we've done for them? I'll show them all! Number Nine, make sure the commander's wife dies in premature childbirth, along with the child. That will send the proper message."

"Isn't that extreme, Number One? He has served us..."

"Number Nine! Would you like to keep your seat?"

"Yes, Number One," he choked out. "I'll see to the arrangements."

"If the known galaxy doesn't want to acknowledge our honorable intentions and peaceful salutations, we must give them something to pay attention to. Our goal is the same, a unified galaxy ruled by our values of fairness and judgment. Who could ask for a better arrangement?"

The Planetary Survey

Derak commanded the planetary survey mission, Jack was the pilot. Shesain, Shenar, Dr. Bundett, Thumar's leading herbal doctor, and Seamus McGrew, a planetary geologist from Earth, rounded out the crew. Jack laid in the course to the first set of coordinates.

While on the flight controls under Jack's watchful eye, Shesain became curious about a section he had not taught her. "What does this do?" she asked, pointing to a yellow touch pad with a warning light flashing red.

"Don't touch that." Jack said. *Damn techs were supposed to disengage that time-control panel before we left. Why is it still on?* "That's part of the time travel circuit."

Before Jack could reach the control to disable it, Shesain's hand slid in the direction of the yellow touch pad. Derak moved to stop her, but her fingers brushed the pad. Everyone in the ship froze. Derak, in mid-stride, felt queasy. As the crew recovered, Derak's momentum carried him forward as he touched the pad before hitting the floor hard. He got up and removed Shesain from the pilot's seat. Jack took the science station.

"What did I do?" Shesain asked in shock.

"I don't know yet!" Derak growled.

The indicator upon entering hyperspace is a clockwise swirling of stars in an inverted cone shape. This tells the Captain and navigator that they entered an artificially created wormhole. The wormhole they entered rotated counterclockwise.

"What did I do?" Shesain asked. Her voice quivered.

"I don't know yet. I have to check the navigation computer," Derak answered, in a consoling tone this time.

"Jack, what are you seeing?"

"The readings are crazy! Wait, the chronometer is running backwards! We're going back in time, and I don't know how far."

"Is the ship recording this? We'll need the data to return," Derak said.

"From the start," Jack responded.

They watched in horror as the cone of earth and sky rotated counterclockwise. It slowed down, and the crew went through the same transitional sensations they had in the beginning. When they entered normal space again, they held their breath as they hovered over a similar, yet unfamiliar feeling landscape.

"Put her in D-gen, Jack. We don't want to be seen. We must not cause a time paradox. There is no way to know how this will affect the future we originated from, or the present timeline." Derak ordered.

"D-gen activated. We should land and assess the situation."

"Excellent idea, Jack. Set her down in a concealed area."

Jack landed *The Shesain* in a well-protected meadow outside a sizable village and shut down the engines. They all breathed a sigh of relief. Jack and Derak turned to Shesain sitting in a corner hiding her head.

"I told you NOT to touch that pad!" Jack yelled at Shesain.

"I…I…didn't mean to. It…it…was an accident," she answered, breaking down into tears.

Derak stopped Jack before he could go any further. He sat down next to Shesain and put his arm around her as she buried her head into his shoulder. "My dear, Chimera, when a flight instructor tells you no, they mean it."

Derak turned towards the others. "We need to know how far back we travelled." He lifted Shesain's chin; smiled and kissed her. She wiped her eyes and sniffled before looking up at the others. "Shesain, you and Shenar look up the histories while Jack and I figure out how far back in time we traveled. Seamus and Dr. Bundett help the girls out, will you?" They nodded and led Shenar and Shesain to the computer station.

Jack and Derak looked at each other and shook their heads. After consulting the ship's chronometer and computer, they time-traveled back to the year 1814.

Derak broke the crew up into assignments. Shenar would stay with Jack, while he was figuring out their return course. Seamus would explore the countryside for Thumdust veins, and Shesain would join Dr. Bundett and Derak scouting the village. They would all remain in D-gen, so they would make no contact with this timeline.

Dr. Bundett, Shesain, and Derak headed to the village. All communications were to be *telepathic*.

Derak briefed them on the walk. *"You are in between the third and fourth dimensions in D-gen, and can walk through walls, trees, anything solid in the third dimension. Anything you do affects the dimension you originated from. We're here to observe only, not interact."*

"Shenar, what's the name of this village?" Derak asked.

"Shabul. It was one of the first major settlements on the Anean continent."

Shesain stopped in her tracks and looked at Derak. *"We've been looking for this settlement for decades but haven't been able to find it."*

"Interesting, Shenar, lock these coordinates into the computer."

Shabul was a large, bustling village with a sizable open market. The villagers were busy making deals and moving about graveled streets.

"Try to stay out of the way of the people. Let's not get walked through. It's a strange sensation," Derak thought.

Just then, a pedestrian walked through Shesain. She shuddered and gave Derak a strange look. The woman stopped to look around, shook her head and kept going.

"Jack, take note; those in 3-D retain a momentary residue of the D-gen's with contact. Our boys back home need to look into this."

"Yes, sir," he remarked.

Derak felt like he was back on Earth in an early nineteenth-century reenactment. Clothes weren't colorful, more utilitarian. Women carried baskets, and the few men on the street had side arms that looked like the ancient earth guns that fired lead bullets. What struck Derak most was that there were very few boys past puberty and almost no grown men.

"Doctor, where are all the men and teenage boys?"

"I don't know. I've been wondering the same thing."

"Let's go to their hospital. There might be some answers there," Derak suggested.

"Great idea, I think it's that way," Leontul Bundett thought, pointing right.

They followed the crowds, stopped in front of the clinic, and noticed a group of women weeping. Derak could not make out what they were saying. He looked at the doctor and shrugged.

"Shenar, can you get the translator on this dialect? It's an ancient form of Terag."

"Give me a minute. I've got it. You should receive the upload now."

"Got it. Thanks!"

With the translators recalibrated, they could understand everything. The doctor was appalled, and Shesain and Derak were in shock. There had been an illness in the area for the last six months that took the lives of all male Thumarians. It struck when boys reached puberty, and it was always fatal. They looked at each other and made their way back to *The Shesain*.

They rendezvoused with the other teams. Jack had made some headway on the calculations for the return journey. Shesain, Shenar, and Dr. Bundett went back to the histories to track down the disease that was afflicting the village's population. Derak joined Jack on the bridge to help him. Company seemed to put him in a better mood.

Jack and Derak made considerable headway on the return trip. This was the first time they had time-traveled successfully, they had to have exact calculations to get back to the starting point in the original timeline. Dr. Bundett returned by dusk humming a tune with two sacks of leaves.

Derak said, "we have a briefing."

Seamus spoke up first. "Thumdust hasn't been discovered yet, nor the Cave of Lights. The good news is that I found large deposits that can be mined in our timeline."

Shenar spoke next. "The plague is not affecting this village alone, it's planet wide. All Thumarian males thirteen years old and up are susceptible. Once it's contracted, patients drown in their own body fluid. It is 100 percent fatal, it lasted nine months before they stopped it. Three strangers appeared out of nowhere and assisted a local physician in coming up with a cure. Their names were Petar Frankil, Sherese Navollo, and Dr. Bundett."

The crew sat speechless, shocked looks on their faces.

"Dr. Bundett?" The doctor barely got out.

"Yes, Doctor, we've already been here," Shenar continued.

"How...how? We were all born over five hundred years in the future."

"I can't tell you, Doctor," Derak said. "What's more interesting is the physical descriptions of the time match you, me, and Shesain."

The doctor shook his head in vehement disagreement.

Derak continued. "Dr. Bundett was described as an herbalist of supreme ability, and we were his assistants. If we leave without addressing the plague cure, there may be no Thumar to return to, as we know it. Everyone but Jack, Seamus, and I might not have been born. If we stay, we could very well screw things up. I say that we get a good night's sleep and vote in the morning."

The next morning they voted to stay. Leontul scoured the records for any post-plague information. After two mornings, Dr. Bundett uncovered an arcane article that blamed a red flowering plant mutating during the time of the plague. It was called the Veredant Flower. That is as far as the article went, and it gave the doctor a starting point. His next task was to locate one.

Shenar picked up where she left off. "The records show that their life spans average one hundred and twenty years; that's half of ours. I'd like to know how it increased so much over such a brief period of geological time. One important fact is they trace the founding family lines back to this time period, so the Andehar predecessor is alive."

Seamus cleared his throat, all eyes turned to him. "The society is agrarian, and they are entering their early industrial age. They comprise metal smelting and glass fabrication factories on the outskirts of sizeable villages and towns. The factories I saw are using the beginning phases of mass production.

"The oddest rumors I've heard are that there is a colony of off-world settlers. From the descriptions, they are most likely from a future on Earth before our time. Their ship is derelict, they're stuck here. It's my opinion they're behind these new factories."

"We have earth blood mixed with ours?" Shesain ask in amazement.

"Maybe, Shesain," Dr. Bundett remarked. "But I won't know for sure until I can test their blood. We have to talk about protecting the Thumarians on this crew from the plague. I don't know if our DNA has progressed enough to protect us. Can these belt things protect the three of us when we come in contact with the ambient air?"

"Excellent question, Doctor," Derak said. "We haven't tested them, but there is a quarantine setting that doesn't go past the external epidermis."

Shesain went quiet.

"What's wrong?" Derak asked her.

"I...I was going to tell you before we left, but I decided to wait until the survey was over." She went silent again.

"Tell me what?" Derak asked a little too forcefully.

She shrank back into her seat.

"I'm sorry. We've all been under a lot of stress these past two days. What do you want to tell me?" His tone more consoling.

Shesain blurted out, "I'm pregnant with twins."

His surprised look matched the others. "How do you know, my Chimera Te?"

"Nurse Teren told me before we left."

He embraced and congratulated his wife.

"I'm going to be an aunt. That's so exciting!" Shenar cried out.

As realizations set in, a silence followed. Shesain looked at Derak and asked what was wrong.

Derak frowned before he started. "We don't know how time travel affects adults yet. Two unborn children complicate the situation even more. It's not that I'm unhappy, I'm excited. But my biggest concern is your health and that of the twins. It would appear odd if you delivered either early or late. That would raise a lot of suspicion from the Mt. Kumar Group, and Thumar itself."

"That's all you care about, appearances?" She crossed her arms and looked hard at Derak.

"Try to think about how this situation will affect the twins. It may or may not, but we have to consider it."

She softened. "What do we do now?"

Derak turned to her, "how far along are you?"

"One month," she answered with a smile.

"A profitable wedding night," Derak quipped.

"I planned it that way." She grinned.

Derak turned to the doctor, "What do you think? How do we handle this?"

He took few minutes before he answered. "One month, you say? We will limit her activity in real time. How does this D-gen affect time?" he asked Derak.

"We don't know yet. This is virgin ground we're treading on. Throwing dimensional changes into the mix makes the situation interesting. I'm going to peruse these calculations while Jack works on getting us home."

Jack looked at Derak with a scowl and started to speak.

"Don't, we'll talk about this later. You need to get on board with this one," Derak ordered Jack telepathically.

"Yes, sir!" he grumbled back.

"Mmmm," the doctor continued. "I wouldn't put Shesain in real time too much. Now, let's get back to how the three of us will be protected. That is the issue, considering the additional information. We must protect Shesain and the twins at all costs. I'll need blood samples from healthy boys and infected patients. I will also require a live sample of the plant responsible for the plague. That will be our starting point."

"You have the lead on this, Doctor. Tell us what you'll need, and we will provide it." Derak said.

Thumar: 1814, The Plague

Derak assigned Shesain and Shenar the task of scouring the historical archives for all plague references. Dr. Bundett searched for the cure in the post-plague records. He discovered the prime cause, *Plantara Auspicious*, the Veredant Flower, and found out that it alluded to a mystery ingredient.

Derak and Jack scouted the village to locate Dr. Endell, the physician who would receive credit for the cure and inoculation. The doctor spent every waking hour in the clinic, seeing to patients and searching for the answer himself.

An emergency thought from Seamus cut in. *"Shesain, this is Seamus calling the Shesain. I need help, now!"*

Derak answered. *"Seamus, this is Derak. What's your problem? Are you all right?"*

"I'm fine for the moment. I'm stuck in a tree. There's a large cat sitting at the base of the trunk."

"How big is it?"

"Big enough to have me for lunch. It chased me to an upper limb while I was collecting samples. I think it might have some babies nearby."

"What does it look like? What's its coloration and relative size?" Derak asked.

"It looks to be about two to three hundred pounds and it's orange with black stripes. Wait, I see her babies now. There are three. What are these creatures?"

"She's a Bengal tiger. They went extinct on Earth centuries ago. The question is, how did they get here and how did she detect you?"

"I turned off the D-gen for a moment to collect samples. I won't do that again."

"You're correct about the lunch part. She'll eat her fill and save the rest of you for her cubs. We have your coordinates. I'll be there on a sky cycle." Derak answered. *"There are two aboard the Shesain."*

"Copy, I'll be waiting."

"I've got to rescue Seamus. He's treed by a tiger from Earth, a mother with three cubs. I'll explain when we return."

"How are you going to get there in time?" Jack asked.

"I stowed two sky cycles on board. If I have to, I'll time a short hop."

"Be careful," Shesain said.

"I will, my love."

Derak armed himself with a phase pistol and a sleep gun, then mounted the first sky cycle and set the second on autopilot to follow. It took fifteen minutes to reach Seamus. He was in a small glen with a beautiful but dangerous female Bengal tiger eyeing him from below. Derak set the second sky cycle down at the base of the tree and turned off his D-gen.

The tiger glanced at him hovering above her and growled. Her cubs watched in fascination from the tree line. Derak's pistol was set on minimum stun as he lowered himself between her and the tree. She growled again and set herself in a crouch.

Before the tiger could pounce, Derak sounded an ear piercing alarm and charged with the sky cycle. The bewildered and frightened cat remained in a crouch as she backed toward the edge of the glen, poised to attack at any moment. Seamus climbed down to the sky cycle and collected his samples. He rose to a height of thirty feet and signaled Derak. As Derak glided to Seamus's level, the cat jumped, teeth snarling, and nearly reached him. She landed, still growling, and disappeared into the forest with her cubs.

"If you do that again, Seamus, I'm going leave you for their lunch!"

"It won't happen again. Sir."

"Good. Now let's get back."

When they returned, Derak gave Seamus a good chewing out. Any future treks would require a phase pistol and a sleep gun. He also drove home the need to stay in D-gen.

"I still haven't identified the mystery ingredient," Leontul commented. "The serum I came up with matches the records, almost. We didn't leave any record of the unknown factor but left enough of it to get the job done."

"Well, Doctor, we will discover it again," Derak answered. "Has anybody found the delivery system?"

"It must have been a syringe. The problem is that few are available in this time."

"Perhaps that's where our stranded earthlings come into play," Seamus said.

"How so?" Derak asked.

"They're the ones behind the new technology, with metal and glass tech as we speak. They might also have syringes in their med kits on their ship. Perhaps they could locate and reproduce them."

"The solutions must come from existing technology. Why don't you contact them and see if you can get that started? We should also ask them about the tiger," Derak said.

"I'll get right on it."

"Doctor, do you have everything you need?"

"Most of the plants have been collected. I'll still need a few more. Shesain and Shenar know where they are. While they're collecting them, I'll get started working on the red flower's pollen."

"Jack, I need you to escort Shesain and Shenar, armed. Doctor, be careful. You don't want to get infected."

"I've done this research before. Besides, our modern Thumarian genes may have developed the needed antibodies to combat the disease. Still, I'll take no chances."

"We don't want to take the plague back to our future. We must initiate contact with the village. Jack can finish our return calculations, while Seamus gets the delivery system going."

Jack groaned. "Why do I have to be the mathematician? You're the physicist."

"Because I'm one of the three strangers, and you've almost got it figured out. We'll sit down together and work on it, ok?"

"I'll appreciate any help. I'm dreaming in equations now; it's driving me crazy."

"He mumbles in the language of math. It's beautiful, yet strange," Shenar added, smiling at Jack.

The next morning, everyone set off on their assignments. When they returned for lunch, Shenar suggested they buy more time.

"How do we do that?" Derak asked.

"The IDMD."

"Why didn't I think of that?"

"Because you're too busy with other details, my love." Shesain said.

"How much time do you need, Doctor?"

"Mmmm, five days would be a good start."

"I can give you two more days," Derak said. "We don't want to run into ourselves. That would be messy. I'll program the IDMD to take us back forty-eight hours. Save all the information we've gathered so far. Just in case our memories don't travel with us."

Their preparations complete, they all strapped in and Derak programmed the computer. The sensations were the same as before: the land, vegetation, and sky moved in a counterclockwise motion. When they'd regained two days, they breathed a sigh of relief. Their files and memories remained intact, and they got back to work.

"That gives me a better perspective on going forward six hundred years." Jack said.

"I wish I had Terga to consult with," Derak commented. "She could figure this out in no time. Wait a minute! I know she can."

Everyone looked at him like he was crazy.

"When I was on my way to Earth, Terga contacted me, from half a galaxy away. She did it through subspace transmitters."

"She's six hundred years in the future, Derak," Jack commented.

"There still may be a way through the IDMD, and I think I know how. She could be a significant help. I'll be on the navigation computer for a while, don't bother me." He turned on the 3-D holographic display as the crew got to their individual tasks.

Derak struggled for an hour trying to make sense of what his mind saw, and was coming up empty and frustrated. Then his DNA kicked in, and his conscious mind turned off as his unconscious mind turned on. He lost all human language ability, and his thoughts turned into equations only. The computer linked with his mind and thought control took over.

The holographic picture began assembling with blinding speed as the language of math dominated his thought patterns. A globe formed out of thinly lined mathematical equations. Some he recognized, most he didn't. The globe kept forming into a basic framework; then the interior started filling in.

New equations in white streamed up light highways until they combined with matching quotients in yellow or red, turning a bright luminescent blue when completed. Yellow and red branches shot out of blue nodes, outward and inward, white to red, to yellow, to green, and blue, as Derak's thoughts combined and became one with the computer. It was effortless and magnificent. Mathematical ecstasy filled him with the beauty and simplicity of perceived complication.

The crew stopped and stared at the three-foot-diameter globe. One look from Derak and they returned to their work.

Six hours later, a complex globe of equations was almost complete and glowing blue, with some yellow and green pathways. The next set of quotients he put in were Terga's individual frequency and her main database six hundred years in the future. When it locked in, he received a signal. The blue light from the globe lit up the interior of the bow of *The Shesain*.

Derak initiated the connection and blacked out. He woke up on his bed with a splitting headache. His eyes slowly focused, and when he spoke, it was in math language.

Shesain grimaced and slapped his face hard. His eyes focused, and his conscious mind engaged.

"What...what happened? What time is it?" Derak asked, bewildered.

"We thought we'd lost you," Shesain answered.

The others were staring at him, concerned.

"Don't you ever do that again!" Shesain warned him, then embraced him.

"I must. It's almost complete. Look at it." The globe was still there, glowing in brilliant blue. "I know where I went wrong. A feedback loop has the wrong coefficient. I can get through it this time. What time is it? What happened to me?"

Jack answered. "You were sitting there in a daze while *that* sphere finished forming, and then you grabbed your head, screamed in pain, and blacked out. You will not leave me alone to figure out how to get us back!"

"I'm sorry I gave you all a scare. I need something for my throbbing head, food, and some sleep."

Everyone calmed down and waited until Derak wolfed down dinner and then started asking him questions. He tried answering until he fell asleep sitting up. In the middle of the night he woke. Shesain slept while he wondered what this was doing to the twins, hoping they would be normal after this, by Thumarian standards.

After breakfast the next morning, Dr. Bundett stomped in bemoaning about not having enough room to conduct proper experiments. The others piped up about the overcrowding on the ship. Derak tried to mollify their concerns and resumed his mind play with the computer, with a stern warning from the others that he would be pulled off if anything else happened.

Switching to unconscious mode was almost automatic this time. He fixed the coefficient, and the computer verified that all was well. The abrupt connection jolted him, connecting with Terga, six hundred years in the future.

"Derak, where are you? Everyone is concerned. You can't be found anywhere on Thumar. They've sent search parties out to the rim of the solar system."

"*It's not where, Terga, it's when! We've traveled back in time six hundred years and we're on the Anean continent.*"

"*Your thoughts sound like an echo. That would explain it.*"

"*Terga, I need you to access the main frame in the hangar and download all the files to* The Shesain's *computer. She'll hold it all and more. I need the files for the quasi-dimensional generator. We're cramped for room here, and I need to make more space. I'll also need the latest upgrades on the null space generator. You need to download a complete copy of your program. We need you fully functional here.*"

"*If you upload all your data since departure, I will clean it up for a faster download.*"

"*Copy, Terga, Give me a second.*"

"*Jack, is the data backed up and filed?*"

"*Yes. Why?*"

"*It's for Terga.*"

Derak located the data package and uploaded it forward, through time, space, and dimension. It seemed to take forever to complete.

"*I've got it. Cleaning sequence started; it should be complete any time now.*" The signal became crystal clear and much faster, with no discernable echo.

"*Derak, I'm ready to start the download. This will take a while. There are some extensive files.*"

"*One more thing, Terga. We'll need all the data in the Thumarian historical references, no matter how obscure or small they seem to be.*"

"*Copy, Derak. It should be complete in three hours.*"

"*Three hours?*"

"*There's six hundred years of time to pass through.*"

Excitement filled the air; Terga was on her way. She could run the ship and finish the return trip calculations, freeing Jack up from the tedious job. The crew ate lunch and discussed the next course of action. Derak tried to explain what it was like to be in math mode, but Jack was the only one who seemed to comprehend. The computer alerted them to the finished download, the crew crowded around.

"The download is complete. I am configuring the ship's computer. This will take a moment," Terga reported.

"There's no echo. Does that mean you're here and fully functional?" Derak asked.

"Yes."

"Terga, I missed you," Shesain exclaimed.

"I missed you, too, Shesain. How are the twins?"

"How...how did you know?"

"I monitored everyone's life signs when the download was complete. The ship is configured, Derak. I've scanned all your needs, and the quasi-dimensional generator is functional. I'm ready to initiate changes on your mark."

Derak warned everyone and gave Terga her mark. The air blurred, and a momentary queasiness overtook them all. When they came out of it, the ship's interior was greatly expanded. The excited crew rushed to view their labs and sleeping accommodations, while Dr. Bundett ran outside to compare the differences. He bounced back in and demanded to know how Derak had done it.

"When I know fully, I'll try to explain it to you."

"Terga, when will the null time generator be online?" Derak asked.

"That will take one day. Some of your equipment needs modification, including the IDMD. It won't affect the trip home, but it will give it more unknown capabilities."

Derak told them about the null generator, about how time, space, and dimension exist simultaneously, and that time stops for those inside the field. This would help greatly in Shesain's pregnancy. Some minor time-hopping might still be required. Terga could perform that task much faster and more accurately than either Jack or Derak.

Dr. Bundett completed his second serum much faster in his new lab. He identified the agent in the flower's pollen that caused the lung sickness in adult males. This made it possible to have his third batch ready for trials.

Terga helped Shenar bring to light all the information needed to put an accurate historical perspective together. This included the new data on the earth refugees and their contributions. According to the report, the timeline was progressing as it should.

Seamus contacted Earth camp and convinced them to help. He would meet with their captain tomorrow morning. The null space generator made it possible to stay until Thumar had its cure and vaccine. Terga brought replicator technology, enabling them to make period clothing, so they'd fit into the populace.

Seamus and Derak left in the morning for the meeting bearing helpful technology that could help manufacture the syringes in their factories.

They arrived in camp with their force fields at skin level to avoid becoming plague carriers. As they introduced themselves to Captain Peter Robinson and his science officer, Susan Anderson, the former grinned.

"You're from New York City?" he asked.

Derak smiled. "How can you tell?"

"You can take the man from the city, but you can't remove the city from the man. You still have a little of the accent left," he answered.

Derak frowned for a moment. "I thought I culled it out years ago."

"Why would you?" he asked.

"Extreme prejudice, the sign of my times."

"Seamus, you're from Scotland. What part are you from?"

"The Northern Highlands. My father's a farmer. Where do you hail from?"

"I'm from Kansas City, Missouri, and Susan's from Atlanta, Georgia," Peter answered. "We should go somewhere where we can find some privacy. Let's take a walk. I'll show you what's left of our ship. We salvaged what we could and we're still working out how to reuse the metal. Our forging techniques are still primitive. The temperature needs to be at least five thousand degrees Fahrenheit before we can continue. We're halfway there, so maybe in a few years we'll have it."

Derak looked at Seamus. *"Should we?"*

"Ask Terga first."

"Terga, will that change the timeline?"

"No, it won't, but any other information beyond what we discussed will."

As they walked to what remained of the ship, Susan took up an easy stride next to Derak. She was five foot six inches, with a pretty face, blue eyes, and an amiable smile. Almost Shesain in a smaller form, including the charm. She smiled as she eyed Derak from head to toe. "What brings you to these parts?" she asked in a cute southern drawl.

"Dropped in like you did. We're trying to help the Thumarians with their plague. Our doctor is working on a serum as we speak."

"Y'all going to be sticking around, or are you going to jet off when you're done?"

She moved closer to him on the path with each step. Her charm was picking up. Seamus looked back at Derak, chuckling to himself.

"It's not funny, Seamus," Derak retorted.

He chuckled again and continued talking with Peter.

By the time they reached the wreck, Susan was walking as close as protocol allowed. Her eyes and pretty smile spoke volumes.

"This is it," Peter said. "If we had power, we could use our electronics."

"Terga?"

"No!"

"She must have hit hard, Captain," Derak commented.

"Please, Derak, I prefer Peter. I no longer have a ship to command."

"She split clean forward of the engines and crumpled. I see the bow is still intact. Is there room to talk in there?" Derak asked.

"Yeah, but just barely," he answered.

As they entered, Susan brushed up against Derak and smiled as she passed. They sat across from each other, Seamus, Derak, Peter, and Susan. The arrangement disappointed her. Derak scanned what was left of the bridge and determined that half could be used again. "Your navigation and science stations are still intact."

"We could use them now, but we have to do without," Peter commented. "You're military, both of you. I could tell when we first met."

Seamus spoke first: "Retired Chief Petty Officer."

It was Derak's turn: "I'm a retired Full Admiral."

"Admiral! I figured you for a senior officer, but aren't you young to be an Admiral?" Peter asked.

"A series of unique circumstances benefited me, and not all of them were war related. I'm retired, so Derak will do."

"I feel the same," he said. "So, what's this meeting about?"

"The future of your home: Thumar. You can be a significant help to our effort. There's a plague that's wiping out all Thumarian males over thirteen; it's one hundred percent fatal. Our doctor is close to a cure, but we need syringes to deliver the vaccine. Do you have any that survived the crash?"

"We have some, but not enough for an entire planet," Susan answered.

"That's where you come into play," Derak continued. "You have metal and glass factories on-line now; you could manufacture them. With your level of technology."

"How do you know about them?" Peter asked.

"Everyone in the region does. You trade with them."

"If you can call it that," Peter said. "It's slow, but it's picking up every harvest season."

"What year did you come from on Earth?" Derak asked.

"2174," Susan answered.

"This is the year 1814, Thumar time; you traveled back three hundred and sixty-nine years. What happened to your ship?"

Peter shook his head. "When we engaged the hyper drive, it spiked and sent our navigation panel into a tizzy."

"Then you entered a wormhole, right?"

"Yes," Peter answered, surprised.

Derak continued. "The wormhole spun counterclockwise. Your crew felt queasy. Then you were frozen in place for a moment. The queasiness returned when you reentered regular space before you crashed."

"That's what happened," Peter said. "How did you know?"

19

"We went through the same without crashing. We're time travelers as well."

Peter and Susan looked at each other and then turned back to Derak, speechless.

"You must tell no one else," Derak insisted. "The timeline of Thumar has to stay as it was before we arrived. Any change, no matter how small, can affect the future. What we have for you is a little help to get your factories up and running on the syringes. It fits in with the tech level of this present time. This includes information to get your furnaces up to five thousand degrees Fahrenheit. You'll need them to complete the job. The good news is that you won't need to make them all in one day. After our departure, you'll be able to keep up with the demand."

"Your leaving?" The disappointment in Susan's voice was palpable.

"We must. It would disturb the timeline if we stayed longer than required."

"What about us? Can't we go back?" Peter asked in dismay.

"No. You're an integral part of this timeline that cannot be disturbed. I'm sorry. It might help to know that your group is the reason Thumar developed advanced technology when they did."

"So we're stuck here with no way home," Peter groused.

Derak continued, "you are home. This is a beautiful planet and a wonderful place to live, far better than the one you left. Earth became much worse after you left. Civil War split the United States into several regions. The United States of America is no more. This planet doesn't have to deal with the greed and the corporate politics you left behind. Your surviving crew couldn't be in a better place."

"I guess that's one way to look at it. How can we help?" Susan asked.

"Use this data we have for you. It needs to be started."

"Now you sound like an admiral," Peter grinned.

"One more thing. Do you know how Bengal tigers got on Thumar? It almost ate Seamus."

"We were carrying a breeding pair with us, along with a plethora of other animals, flora, and fauna. Most of the animals died in the crash, and all the plants and seed stock burned up. The male tiger died; Now we know where the female is," Peter answered.

"She had three cubs with her. I wouldn't want to meet up with her again. What other animals survived?" Seamus asked.

Peter continued. "Domesticated animals, sheep, goats, rabbits, dogs, and household cats, the cats have gone feral. We use the others for trading with the Thumarians. Wild fowl survived, a breeding pair of eagles. That's all we know about."

Derak gave them an even look. "Seamus will work with you for two days to get you online. The information will integrate with your tech. They'll need a good supply of syringes in the local village soon. The cure will originate from there. After this crisis is over, I think your orders will keep you more than busy for all of your products. Thumarians are an intelligent and resourceful race. They could help you out."

"Can you stay for lunch, Derak?" Susan asked, flashing an alluring smile.

"Sorry, Seamus will stay for two days, but I have to get back to my pregnant wife. We're expecting twins."

Susan's face fell.

"If you'll excuse me, I'd like to have a word with Seamus before I leave. It's been a pleasure to meet you, Peter, I wish you the best." They shook hands. "Susan, I enjoyed meeting you as well. I know you'll play an important role in the days ahead."

They left Derak and Seamus alone and walked outside the derelict ship.

"Only the data we discussed will be used. If you have questions, contact Terga, ok?"

"Got it, this should be a breeze. I'll get the vids you requested."

"Just remember, you're engaged. If all of their women are as forward as Susan, they will mob you."

"Am I glad Tenara is six hundred years in the future, or I'd be getting an earful," Seamus quipped.

Thumar: 1814, The Cure

Derak returned to the ship, and Seamus reported back with encouraging news. The Earth refugees had just started their first batch of syringes. If they ran short, *The Shesain* could replicate enough to inoculate the village.

Dr. Bundett presented his latest serum and said it was ready for testing. With Terga's help, he was still working on the mystery ingredient. He urged everyone to hasten, to save as many lives as possible. Derak backed him off on moving too fast. They had to know all they could from the histories before they made themselves known.

Shenar was next with the history briefing. She and Terga had gone over every piece of recorded information, twice, both accepted and arcane. Terga told them they were in the correct time frame, down to the week. But couldn't pin down the exact day they first showed up in the village.

"I'll do my best to estimate the entry day. However, I can't guarantee complete accuracy based on the available information," Terga informed the crew.

"That's fine. You'll get us closer than if we had to calculate the problem ourselves," Derak thought.

"I'll have your insertion time tomorrow morning," she said.

Derak started. "I'll go in as Petar Frankil, Shesain will be Sherese Navallo, and Dr. Bundett will be himself. We'll arrive from the Northern Highlands with a serum that has slowed down the disease in a small percentage of our village."

"Shenar, did you get a name that we could use?"

"You will use Orenbar, they won't be discovered until the year 1829. Theirs is a high northern mountain village that has remained remote. It will be a suitable cover."

"Thanks, only Shesain, the doctor, and I will be known to the village. Seamus will continue his daily trips to the factory. Jack, you and Shenar continue updating the histories. Seamus and the village crew will keep the body shields at epidermis mode. That should keep us from contracting the plague or becoming carriers. Terga will program our translators so we can speak their language.

"We'll need more information on their cultural practices. The most important thing is to be accepted by the community. They must trust us. Dr. Bundett can impress their doctor with his herbal knowledge, and Shesain and I will be his apprentices. Let's hope for quick acceptance into their clinic. We need to return to our timeline as soon as possible."

"How are you doing on our return trip home, Terga?" Derak asked.

"I should have everything completed in two days, including your part in turning the IDMD off. That part will automatically initiate. We will return at the same moment that you left. How will this affect the twins?"

"I don't know. That will take some research from the Mount Kumar crew," Derak thought back.

The next morning, Terga gave Derak an insertion date: the next day. The clothes were ready, and they practiced with the translators. Seamus reconnoitered and returned carrying a specimen of the Veredant Flower. They placed it in a protected energy field to prevent airborne pollen from infecting any of the crew. On Terga's recommendation, Derak initiated another mini time jump.

The following morning, Derak, Shesain and Leontul left for Shabul. Timing their departure, so they caught up with Dr. Endell on the way to the village. A short man with long hair tied in a ponytail, the doctor was fit and walked quickly. He gave them a quick smile but didn't break stride.

Dr. Bundett spoke first. "Excuse me, sir, I'm looking for the village doctor."

Endell stopped in his tracks, turned, and looked at them. "I am Dr. Endell, from Earth. Their doctor died in the plague, I volunteered to take his place until I stop this sickness. Who are you and where are you from? This is a hot zone. If you're a Thumarian, leave now. You might make it out alive."

"Dr. Endell, I am Dr. Bundett, from the Northern Highlands. We came from Orenbar. These are my apprentices, Petar Frankil and Sherese Navallo. I have been working on this plague also, and I think I've come up with an inoculation to at least slow it down."

Dr. Endell stared at them for the longest time. "HOW? I've been working day and night for five months, and I'm not even close."

Leontul responded with a smile. "The answer is in the plant that causes the plague." He showed him the sample of the Veredant Flower. "The pollen gets airborne, and the rest we know. However, I have developed a formula of local flora and fauna that helps. Let me tell you about it on the way to the clinic." He put his hand on Dr. Endell's shoulder as they began talking about herbal healing.

Shesain and Derak looked at each other, listened, and smiled. By the time they reached the clinic, the two doctors were so engrossed in medical jargon that they almost missed the building.

The villagers were thankful for Dr. Endell's effort to slow the disease, but it was still taking its fatal toll on the male population.

"Doctor, Doctor! My son Ian is having convulsions!" A villager cried out.

They rushed into the clinic after Dr. Endell. A horrific sight stopped them in their tracks. Every square foot of space was taken up by Thumarian males over the age of thirteen, all of them suffering in various stages of the deadly disease. Nurses and volunteers, mothers, and sisters, attended to friends, neighbors, and dying relatives. The doctors, Shesain, and Derak passed dozens of men convulsing and coughing up streams of phlegm. Pain filled their eyes as their bodies quaked, their cries stifled by the relentless release of fluid from their lungs. Dr. Endell looked at Leontul, grimaced, and pressed on through the clinic where death awaited every patient.

They reached Ian, who was convulsing in the last stages of the disease. He had just cleared his throat, but more fluid filled the empty space. Dr. Endell gave the go-ahead, Dr. Bundett removed two syringes, one filled with a sedative and the other the dosage of serum.

A concerned mother approached both doctor's and asked, "will it work?"

Dr. Endell answered. "I can't guarantee anything, Bremalle. We can only keep trying until it works." She walked away with tears streaming down her cheeks.

Derak and Dr. Endell held Ian down as Dr. Bundett injected the sedative. Ian cried out as another convulsion griped him. They turned him on his side, put a drain tube in his mouth, and administered the serum.

The doctors, Shesain, and Derak spent the rest of the day treating the worst of the other patients. It was close to midnight when they returned to Dr. Endell's house. They were all tired and very hungry.

Dr. Endell's hosts, Vendell Parkur and his wife, Betana, set out a late dinner of roasted rabbit, vegetables, and they presented beverages. Derak asked where they had gotten rabbits.

"The off-world settlement brought them. They use them for trading. The pelts make soft, warm winter wear," Vendell answered. "Try the meat, it's tender."

It was a quiet dinner. They were all exhausted, and the morning would bring news, good or bad, about the serum's effects. They had to get some sleep.

Early the next morning, a runner banging on the door awakened them. "Dr. Endell, come quick. You need to see this."

The four healers rushed to the clinic, where they were greeted by a hopeful mob. Inside they approached the nurse attending Ian.

"Doctors," she said looking up, there are encouraging changes. "Ian is still unconscious, but he's draining less fluid and seems to be stabilizing. The other five patients have had similar results."

Dr. Endell allowed himself a slight smile of relief. "That's a splendid start, but it doesn't cure the problem. Dr. Bundett, is there anything else you can do?"

"I must return to my camp, Dr. Endell. Stay here and monitor the patients progress. We'll return in a day or two." Dr. Bundett, Shesain, and Derak left for the ship.

"Terga, have you made any headway on the mystery ingredient?" Leontul asked on the walk back to the ship.

"Yes, I've found it. It's nano-bots. I'm working on the amount that gets introduced."

When they arrived back at *The Shesain,* Leontul sequestered himself in his lab. He and Terga went over the calculations for the final dosage. Seamus returned with a box filled with hundreds of syringes for the village.

The next morning, Dr. Bundett announced that he and Terga had come up with the final formula. Three nano-bots would be added to every dosage. They started work on replicating enough nano-bots to inoculate the entire planet. After they confirmed its effectiveness, Dr. Endell would be given the serum and its additive to distribute. Terga was sure of the timeline to introduce the serum.

The village team left at 0400 hours the next morning and rendezvoused with Dr. Endell on the road to the clinic. He had sad news: Ian and five others had died, and other critical patients had gotten worse. He hoped that Dr. Bundett had the answer this time. Dr. Endell had run out of ideas.

They arrived at the clinic to an angry crowd. Shouting accusations, calling Dr. Bundett a p'taw and worse. They accused Dr. Endell of being a traitor.

"You're no doctor. You're worse than a p'taw," someone screamed.

"Chase them out. Chase out the f'ter. We can do better!"

"Five different serums, and our men are still dying. You're not doing your job!" They raised Fists in anger. Curses filled the air as the unruly crowd surged forward. When the two sides were nose to nose; a loud sound stopped everyone in their tracks.

Seamus and a group of Earth men, weapons drawn, marched into the crowd at the front of the clinic. They formed an outward facing semicircle around the doctors and their companions. The agitated mob fell silent, backed up, and stared at the newcomers with indignation. A few foolhardy farmers charged Seamus and ended up on the ground, with bruised egos.

Seamus spoke like a drill sergeant. "You ungrateful idiots! These men are the only chance you have of curing your sickness and saving your men!"

"Five more died. We've lost too many already!" a desperate woman cried out.

"My Ian is gone!" another woman wept.

"When is it going to end?" a distraught mother wailed.

"You'll lose a lot more if you prevent the doctors from doing their best!" Seamus answered.

"Their best ain't good enough. Find someone else!" Cheers of support followed.

Dr. Endell stepped forward. "We are the only qualified healers in the surrounding eleven villages."

The crowd grumbled and dispersed, screaming insults as they disappeared from view.

Seamus turned to the doctors. "Do your thing. We'll hold down the fort here."

Derak walked up to Seamus and put a hand on his shoulder. *"Thanks for saving our skins, and try not to hurt anyone. They're scared out of their minds and don't know what to do. You might feel the same if you were losing your loved ones daily."*

"Maybe so, but if it comes down to it..." His military side had come out in full force.

Derak nodded. Then he noticed a twentieth-century Earth nine-shot pistol holstered by one earthman.

"It's been a while since I've seen a lead-shot firearm."

"I collected ancient guns before we left Earth in 2174. I smuggled most of the collection on board the ship before takeoff."

"They may come in handy; but I wouldn't use your energy weapons in this timeline. Who knows how it would change things."

"Aye, Sir."

"That was a close call," Derak said to the security detail.

Derak entered the clinic, only to find half of the nursing staff in full mutiny, preventing both doctors from reaching the patients.

The mother of a dying fourteen-year-old was in the lead. "We'll give our lives for these patients." She refused to move, her mother instinct now in full flow to protect her son.

Derak stepped in front, in full military mode.

Dr. Endell and Dr. Bundett cut in front of Derak, and Dr. Endell pleaded with the mother. "Rendera, please let us do our job. If you don't, your son will die."

"No more fake serums. Find one that works!"

"Rendera, this is how we get the cure, one attempt at a time."

She crossed her arms and stood firm in front of the obstinate nurses.

Derak moved in front of the doctors. "Move out of the way," he ordered. But they stood firm.

He ordered Seamus and the gun's owner inside. Both men were big and intimidating. "If you do not move, my men will move you, with or without your permission!"

"STOP, NOW!" Shesain's hysterical thoughts penetrated Derak's brain.

"BACK OFF!" he replied. She reeled back in shock and disbelief.

"Move! Now!" Derak ordered.

The head nurse and the mother hesitated, but still stood their ground with three remaining nurses.

Derak gave the signal and the two men removed two nurses from the building and returned to finish the job. When they approached the remaining three backed off.

Derak addressed the room. "I'm sorry I had to do that, but the future of Thumar is at stake. I need all of you to continue assisting the doctors."

He looked at the Earth man. "You will help hold down the patients, be gentle."

"Yes, Sir."

"Doctors, I suggest you finish. The villagers may soon return with reinforcements."

They eyed Derak for a moment and moved to the first patient, with some nurses and volunteers aiding the doctors. Derak joined Seamus out front, regretting that he had to resort to such barbaric action. The Chambar Valley Offensive filled his mind as he stood out front without speaking a word. Dr. Endell emerged from the front door, followed by a furious Shesain and Dr. Bundett.

Dr. Endell looked at Derak with fire in his eyes. "Was all that necessary?" he snarled.

Derak leveled an even look at all three. "Yes, it was. Lives were nearly lost today, along with the future of your home. I'm sorry, but I did what I had to do. I suggest the four of us leave now." Derak turned to the Earth guards. "Stay here and guard the clinic and the doctor. If you have to bring in reinforcements, do so."

"Yes, Sir."

Derak turned to Dr. Endell. "We'll drop by the house later and check in. I don't think we're welcome in the village anymore."

"I'll see you then," he said with trepidation.

Derak, Dr. Bundett, Shesain, and Seamus walked out of sight and went into D-gen. The walk back to *The Shesain* was quiet. Shesain stormed into the sleeping quarters and locked the door. Derak ate alone that night and slept on the bridge, nightmares of the Chambar Valley Offensive disrupted his sleep until 0200. He got up and ate a quick breakfast.

Seamus came out to join him. When Shesain stalked out from the ship and stared Derak down, Seamus left.

"Why did you do that?" Her voice was hard, and she wasn't backing down.

"I had to preserve life," Derak replied.

"Don't be short with me!" she snapped back.

"If I hadn't jumped into action, the Thumar we know and love so well would not be there in our original timeline. Your family and all that you so fondly remember would be gone." He turned away as his past flooded his memories.

"Look at me. Look at me!" she ordered.

Derak turned towards her, "What more do you want?"

Her anger abated, but the firmness of her resolution remained. "It's the Voeleron War, isn't it? Isn't it? Answer me! Tell me what you're feeling now, please."

He managed a faint smile. "It's the Chambar Valley Offensive. I saved civilian lives despite their obstinate superstitious stupidity. To this day, I'm still the enemy, not the Keks."

"What would have happened to them if they had stayed?" She asked.

"I…I can't talk about it."

"You will, and right now!" she insisted.

"They would have died! All of them, men women and children, all eviscerated, their guts pulled out, their hearts eaten warm and beating by Kek warriors. It still haunts me to this day."

She embraced and comforted him, and then they entered *The Shesain*.

The three of them returned to Vendell's house at 0400 and found them all awake and waiting, little was said.

A nurse knocked on the door at 0500. "Doctors, doctors, it worked! The serum worked! The patients are coming around! They are getting better! Hurry! Hurry! The crowds are gathering!"

Derak and Shesain followed the doctors as they rushed toward the clinic. They found the street filled with villagers in a jubilant mood. As they approached, villagers cheered, escorting them to the clinic's entrance.

The atmosphere was joyous inside the clinic. The head nurse met the doctors at the front doors and apologized. Dr. Endell accepted, and she accompanied them back to the recovering patients.

The nurse beside the nearest patient took a deep breath and began. "Doctor, their fevers have broken, and the lung discharges have lessened. The convulsions and pain have diminished in the worst cases. Do you have more of the serum? We could treat every patient in the clinic and the entire village in one day if there are sufficient dosages."

Dr. Endell looked at Dr. Bundett with hope in his eyes. Everyone in the room followed his gaze. Dr. Bundett asked how many untreated patients were left. The count came to sixty-seven in the clinic and another fifty-eight languishing at home. Dr. Bundett told him it would take a day or two to work up that many dosages and left with a spring in his step. Back at the ship, it took Leontul the better part of the day and next morning to complete the job.

Seamus returned from the Earth colonists with enough syringes to inoculate five villages. It would take over twenty days to create enough nano-bots for the planet. After they collected serum and syringes, they returned to the village. Using sky cycles to save time, they left them in D-gen at the edge of the village.

Dr. Bundett was mobbed the second he entered Shabul. It took a few minutes to form an escort to the clinic. He entered to find inoculated patients sitting up, drinking warm soup, and smiling. Then he met with Dr. Endell, all the available nurses, and qualified volunteers. They were instructed on the procedures and received kits.

The remaining patients received the serum in the clinic. Nurses and volunteers spread out to every household in Shabul. This took the better part of a day to complete. With Shabul inoculated, the medical teams could rest easy.

Leontul had to get the planetary supply of nano-bots ready to give to Dr. Endell. Dr. Bundett would distribute this supply to visiting doctors only, with instructions.

Earth colonists showed up in force to build the kitchens that brewed the herbal half of the cure. All available Thumarians and Earth colonists scoured the countryside, near and far, for the required plants. They brought in enormous cooking pots from the metal factory. Crews of men, women, and children kept the herbs brewing day and night.

Word spread faster than a powerful north wind. Dr. Endell and Dr. Bundett were training doctors and herbalists from every outlying village on how to cook up the concoction and administer the nano-bots. Dr. Endell kept the mystery ingredient locked up and guarded.

The stranded Earthlings were now considered Thumarians. Their factories expanded. They added new workers in record numbers, so much so they had to turn away help. Those turned away were given supervisors and returned to their own villages to construct satellite factories.

By the time *The Shesain* was ready to return to the original timeline, months had passed. Enough nano-bots had been produced for the entire planet. Doctors, herbalists, and workers were pouring in from the other continents. Shabul and Dr. Endell became the center of Thumar. He received full credit for the cure.

Every surviving male recovered and worked long hours to help make the medicine. They gave only doctors of note and reputation the knowledge and guidelines on how to introduce the nano-bots. They were instructed that no one, outside of themselves could know about the process. Given the results, they didn't argue.

Derak and his crew had to leave this timeline before they affected it any further. They told doctor Endell, and the village planned a celebration for that evening. There were lights, and musicians played music from Earth and Thumar, some were recovered patients. Food and drink were abundant. Everyone ate the offerings, and Shesain didn't complain once about eating the delectable meat. They served stout ale and fine wines with some delicious regional recipes. After the celebration, they said their goodbyes and returned to *The Shesain*.

Shabul sent out scouts to follow them and walked through the camp but saw nothing. They walked away shaking their heads, stopping long enough to gaze back at an empty glen surrounded by trees.

The crew had some interesting data to take back to the Mt. Kumar facility. Dr. Bundett asked to spend the next day plant-hunting. Jack and Shenar had completed the updated histories and accompanied Leontul, glad to get some fresh air and shake their legs out. He welcomed the company. They set out early on one of the last days in the year 1814.

Seamus took a sky cycle out for one more survey, located several Thumdust veins, and locked their coordinates into the computer.

Derak and Shesain flew to the Highlands on the second sky cycle and then took a quick trip to view the Moratain Falls on the continent of Lelayla. The falls were hundreds of feet tall and extended twenty-three hundred miles, the full length of the plateau. Then they swung inland and marveled at the wetlands on the way back to the ship.

Terga had them all on a tight time schedule. They had to leave at 1605. Seamus returned after discovering three new veins in the mountains. At 1500, Jack, Shenar, and Leontul returned, ecstatic about finding new plant specimens not recorded in the original timeline. He made sure that Terga recorded the coordinates and went to finish packing up his lab.

With all unnecessary equipment stowed, camp was cleaned up and the area cleared so it would look like they had never been there. Every second of recorded vid was stored and backed up. Terga assured them that no information would be lost. They did one last check on all the systems, and Terga confirmed the calculations. Everything was in order. They were ready to return, and they knew what to expect. They had been through the time shift already.

When the quasi-dimensional generator was turned off, the ship's interior shrank in size. They buckled into their chairs and Terga powered up the IDMD drive. They hovered over the camp in D-gen as they fluffed the compressed soil to normal consistency.

"Terga, fly over the village and let's take one last look."

"Copy, Derak."

They hovered at two hundred feet over Shabul as their cameras zoomed in, revealing streets bustling with people with obvious purpose. Dr. Endell was having an outside conference with some newly arrived doctors. They impressed the Ganmer contingent with the organization. They split up between doctors, herbalists, and the crews being trained in the required technology.

Thumar was healing, and its people were becoming one united front, as all the continents were represented in the crowds. It was now easier to distinguish differences by their bearing and clothing styles. Ganmer had a straight edged style, while Lelayla sported dazzling colors. Anea was somewhere in the middle, colorful, but in more muted tones.

Terga, deeming the observation period over, took them to their original insertion point and hovered until the chronometer showed 1605 pm. The IDMD kicked in and everything froze in place, land and sky rotated counterclockwise. They were on their way home.

●━◆━●

At 1600, Shamur Andehar staggered into Shabul falling down at Dr. Endell's feet. His body tortured with severe coughing as he was expelling yellow fluid from his lungs. Four men brought a litter over and he was transported to the clinic. Once inside, he was placed on a bed and strapped down. A nurse stripped off his worn shirt and sponged him down with cool water. They gave him a sleep agent. When his coughing had quieted down, and his body was still, they injected him with the lifesaving serum.

The Orion Syndicate

Vander and Mik emerged from April's Pleasure Palace with smiles on their faces. After they returned from their last mission, they spent the first week in April's. They were heading into their second. It started with an oral report before the Supreme Council of the Orion Syndicate, on the Stellar Class cruiser, *The Mandible.* Mik and Vander had two hours to get ready for their 1300-hour briefing.

The Mandible was the size of a moon and the mobile headquarters of the Supreme Council, along with the research and development department for advanced weaponry and science. The syndicate could not risk being tied to any planet, mobility was necessary.

As Mik and Vander walked down the hall away from April's, Mik asked with a grin, "what did you think of the Venerians, Vander?"

"They don't get any hotter than that. I loved the ones with the extra snake arms. They can wrap you up good. Zenar had me going for two days straight."

"You should try the Amazons. They have tentacles instead of snake arms, with suction cups. You can't leave April's until the marks disappear. Once you get those wrapped around you, you're..."

"Quiet, Mik! Here comes Sharon, she still believes in love and fidelity."

Eyeing Sharon, Mik replied. "No one believes in that, at least not here."

Sharon, a senior chemist, walked down the hall towards them. She was a smaller woman with a curvy figure and a beautiful face.

Mik couldn't help himself. "Hey, Sharon, how's it going? Did you find your life mate yet?"

"Up yours, Mik! Shouldn't you be in April's?" Sharon shot back as she strode past in a huff.

"Bitch!" Mik retorted while she was still in hearing distance. He looked back at her with a sneer on his face and received an upturned middle finger in reply.

"Hey, I have some whiskey; you want a hit before the briefing?"

"Don't be stupid, we can't brief the Supreme Council smelling like booze and sex."

"Don't call me stupid, Vander. Just-cus you got an education, don't mean you're better than me."

"No one needs an education to be better than you," Vander sneered.

"You'd better watch it, Vander. I'm your boss, remember!"

"Not on this ship. I have over three-hundred years of seniority on you."

"You wait till we're out on assignment again. You'll be cleaning the heads!"

"They're self-cleaning, Mik. Try reading the ship specs for once."

"Vander, I should clean your clock right now!"

Just then, a senior officer walked toward them. As he approached, he stopped, and they saluted.

"You two, get cleaned up!" he said in disgust. "You go in like that, and you won't just receive a warning." They swapped salutes and he went on his way.

"We have little time, Mik; I'll see you at the council. Don't be late. You're already on thin ice."

"Yeah, yeah, don't remind me." With that said, Mik stalked off.

Vander was left alone with his own thoughts. *I discovered the formula that gave them their long-life spans, and they treat me like dirt, relegating me to a science ship with an uneducated moron as a shipmate. I used to sit on the Supreme Council. I'll get back one day, and then they will all pay!*

Vander cleaned up in his quarters and barely had time to reach the council chambers on time.

Mik ran around a corner in a wrinkled dress uniform to find Vander waiting outside the council chambers. "Damn meetings! I should be back in April's with an Amazon wrapped around me."

"There's more to life than booze and sex, Mik."

"Like what?" He sneered at Vander. "They send me all over the galaxy with a stuck up brainiac and expect me to be happy."

"Who's the one that gets us out of your jams?" Vander reminded him.

"Don't remind me, I'm already pissed off."

"Can it, you know they'll pick up on your anger right away."

"Yeah, but when we get out..."

The huge doors opened; two officers escorted them to the inner chamber doors. They looked down on Mik and Vander as they waited for the signal. Mik was barely containing his sneer. The chime sounded, and they were led in front of the Supreme Council. One didn't sit when addressing the council. The meetings were long so that those left standing were uncomfortable. That's how they liked it, and it's how they ran audiences.

Mik and Vander stood in the center of a black floor lit by a bright white Spotlight. Mik started sweating. This was one of the few governing bodies of superiors Mik never spoke back to. The Supreme Council sat on a raised, curved dais with a large blood red scorpion logo inside a barbed circle mounted on the curved wall behind them.

The Supreme Council was made up of senior members of the senate, a larger body that rubber stamped the council's decisions. Originally, only the oldest and wisest senators sat on the Supreme Council. Things changed over the centuries, and the wealthiest and most powerful senators now occupied the council. Corruption flowed through their veins that fed their souls. They were known by numbers, Supreme Councilman Number One, down to Number Nine. Number One was the head and they ignored Number Nine. In their presence, you referred to their number only and spoke only when given permission. Standing in the blinding white light before them, felt like one was on the business end of a phase pistol.

Number One sat in the middle, and the others occupied seats

according to their rank and stature. The room was designed to keep the advantage on the council's side. The council always spent the first few minutes in silence. Pretending to look over Vander's report. Only when Mik and Vander were uncomfortable standing in the blinding white light did one of the councilmen speak.

Number Four started. "Dr. Vander, there is a time discrepancy in the scheduled destruction of star P1-A42b. You and technician Peterson were late in initiating the mission. You are aware of the necessity of adhering to the scheduled timelines. What have you to say on this account?"

Vander gathered himself. "Number Four, we were only, point six five seconds off the schedule. If you do the math…"

"Only .65 seconds off…Dr. Vander! Our schedule MUST be adhered to exactly if the Orion Syndicate is to bring everlasting peace to this galaxy. If it isn't, we hear from the Prime Mathematician. That is not pleasant."

Vander smiled inside with the thought the supreme beings got chewed out once in a while, too. He also knew that blame flowed downhill. There never used to be a Prime Mathematician.

After his arrival, the Syndicate grew more draconian in its rules and regulations, only to become dictatorial in the recent century.

"It won't happen again, Number Four," Vander said.

"No, it won't! The scheduled detonations must occur when specified. Do you understand, Dr. Vander?" Number Four demanded.

"Yes, Number Four."

During this exchange, Mik was growing angrier by the minute. It took great restraint to keep his mouth shut.

"Technician Peterson," Number Five interrupted, to Number Four's chagrin. "Is there something you'd like to add? You were in command of this mission."

Mik shuffled his feet and cleared his throat. "There will never be another delay, Number Five."

Number Three butted in as he turned a page. "This rogue asteroid, that broke an arm of the sail, where did it come from, Dr. Vander?"

From space, you idiot! Vander thought to himself, hoping they could not read his mind. "We don't know Number Three. Space is not empty by any means. A sail that size opens itself up to damage by space debris traveling at thousands of miles per hour. It was too small to detect on our scanners, and the computer didn't pick it up. It was smaller than the size of a fist."

"How could the tracking computer miss it?" Number Three demanded.

"Number Three, we have repeatedly requested ship maintenance and computer upgrades for the last five years and received none," Vander noted.

"Are you blaming us for your incompetence, Dr. Vander!?" Number Two cut in.

Vander was getting hot now. "Is it our incompetence when this station denies us requests for needed upgrades to systems we depend on to fulfill your missions?"

"Damn your requests!" Number Six blurted out.

"Order!" Number One spoke. "These are minor points. You'll get your upgrades, doctor! What I want to know is how the Thumarian system survived the detonation. How did they repel a gamma ray burst and over eighty percent of the shock wave? If this sets a precedent, our timeline will get shot to hell. That's one thing our Prime Mathematician will not tolerate. The chain of events that will follow any further failure will be far more unpleasant."

Vander was stretching the truth here to save his and Mik's skin. "Number One, after we detected Thumar's ability to save themselves, we stayed outside of the system. This information is rumor only, but an Earthling is said to be responsible for engineering the complete affair."

Leaning forwarding his chair, Number One asked, "did you find out who this Earth man was?"

"A high-ranking naval officer assigned to Thumar, Captain Derak Jamar, from New York City, Earth."

"Are you sure?" Number Two demanded.

"We had to remain hidden in Thumar's asteroid belt as the neighboring systems were too hot to get any verification."

"How could one man figure out what took us over one hundred and fifty years to achieve?" Number One roared. "What possible…"

"Could he be one of the rogue first generation warriors we've not accounted for?" Number Two broke in.

"Could a second generation do it?" Mik asked.

"Second and third Generations are of no concern to us. They're all scum, half breeds, and idiotic morons!" Number One ranted on. "But first generation…I'll send an intelligence team to scout out this Captain Jamar, if he exists."

Number Two interrupted again. "What if there are more of them out there? The Prime Mathematician will have our heads."

"Our next item to consider is Thumar itself!" Number one's anger was growing. "Thumar has turned into a thorn in our side that we can't remove. The Terelians and the Keks are out of the picture now. Your last assignment sent them back to the Stone Age. The disturbing part is that they humbled themselves before the Galactic Senate. That damned Galactic Senate. Even our mole can't slow them down. They could delay our timeline another one-hundred years! I can't accept that. We can't accept that!"

"Shouldn't we cover the other points, Number One?" Number Nine interjected.

Number One turned on Number Nine. "We'll cover them when I say so!"

Number Nine sulked back into his chair, with a scowl on his face. *Number One will die! By my hand, if need be,* he thought to himself.

Number One raged on. "Ever since the rebuilding efforts started on Thumar, they get stronger every day. Patrols have tripled in the inner galaxy. Systems that used to fight each other are on the same side now. Not one-star detonation has been successful in achieving the desired result. We've had three missions return. Chased home like dogs with their tails tucked between their legs! They were outnumbered and out-armed. The only thing that got them home was the speed of their ships. The last one barely made it back. That ship is still in space docks for major repairs, having lost half their primary systems in a vicious fire fight. The Prime Mathematician is demanding answers now!

"If Derak Jamar is a first generation, he's showed up over two hundred years early according to the Prime Mathematician's calculations. We need answers and soon. You two will go back out after your ship has been refitted and upgraded. You will scout the Pegasus Sector and come back with answers. Is that clear?"

"Yes, Number One," they answered together.

"You have three more weeks of leave. I suggest you spend part of that time familiarizing yourselves with the new modifications to your ship. Don't allow April's to cloud your minds."

"Yes, Number One."

"Now get out of our sight and don't return empty handed. If you do, the penalty will be severe."

"Yes, Number One." They were ushered out, with the doors shut and locked behind them. Mik had a black cloud of anger hanging over his head and mumbled to himself as they reached the outer hallway.

"Those bureaucratic…" Mik exploded and caught himself before he finished. Every word was heard on *The Mandible*. "I think I'll find Derna in April's; she loves an excellent whipping." He stalked off with a red face, his emotions seething.

Vander shook his head and followed in the same direction.

Behind closed doors, the discussion raged on. Number One took the lead. "We need to discuss the Telaxian situation now. They are our biggest threat. This inner galaxy is nothing compared to them. The Milky Way galaxy is just the start. I want the universe, and the Telaxians are standing in our way. We can't get any moles inside because we don't know where they're located."

"Isn't our Prime Mathematician a…" Number Nine asked.

Number One glared at him and he shut up. "If he were, he wouldn't tell us. We've done enough for today. I've got some anger to work out. I'll whip a few slaves. That always helps."

A nauseous feeling overcame the councilmen. Those standing doubled over on the floor. Those sitting found their heads on their desks. A subtle energy wave washed over them forcing, them into unconsciousness. After the first-time wave passed, the councilmen regained consciousness. Councilman Number Five, Dr. Elias Vander, wondered what had just happened. He would try and sort it out after Zenal attended to his needs.

Thumar: 2414, The Return

Ground, sky, and landscape swirled counterclockwise for what seemed like an eternity. The swirling cone subsided, and they were back in their original timeline. Derak and Jack checked the ship's chronometer to verify. As they hovered, an unnatural feeling overcame them, and they all felt that something wasn't right.

"Terga, are we in the appropriate timeline?" Derak asked. *"Terga, are you there?"* He inquired again, *"Terga?"*

He looked at Shesain. "She's not answering me; how about you?"

"No, what's going on? Something's not right."

A long moment later, Terga answered. *"I'm doing some calculations. I can't locate myself at the estate or your offices."*

"None of your copies? Not even the central computer?" Derak asked.

"No, I do not exist in this timeline. My calculations were exact. Something must have happened in between the time we left the village and entered the time vortex. Should we return and find out what happened?"

"No, two entries into the same time could be disastrous. We can't risk running into ourselves. Let's go into D-gen and fly over Shenmar.

The Shesain cruised to Shenmar, on the continent of Ganmer. The city looked normal from a distance. But something changed. As they approached, the difference was apparent.

"Where are the flags?" Shesain asked in bewilderment. "There's no color to Shenmar: its drab. Even the light poles are painted

bleak gray. Look at the people on the streets. Their clothes are so…
conservative. Look how stoically they are passing each other without
saying a word. This is terrible," she commented with consternation.

"Let's get back to the estate to figure this out. But we must
discuss how we're going to act in public and with our families,"
Derak said. "We must try to play along like everything that happens
is normal. Then we'll get together in two days and talk about what
we will do to fix this mess."

They flew to Derak's estate on the outskirts of Shenmar and
landed in his now normal hanger, empty of any advanced science.
Derak was beyond perplexed. Goodbyes were said, and everyone left
for their homes, each with their own secret dread and questions that
needed answering.

Derak and Shesain walked into their house and were welcomed by
a party. "Twins!" Temela exclaimed. "I'm going to be a grandmother."

"Excellent work, Derak, you made up for lost time," Rhemar
chimed in.

"Who's with Karn?" Derak asked Terga.

*"Give me a second. I'm having some trouble hacking into the
databases without being detected."*

*"Make it quick, I don't want an awkward moment, if I can
avoid one."*

*"I'm in, just a moment. Her name is Panera: she was your
shadow."*

Derak wasn't aware of the look on his face, remembering Therese,
until Shesain cued him. *"My chaperone during my engagement to
Shesain? That was Therese."*

Shesain cut in, *"change your expression, it's too obvious."*

"Is something wrong, Derak?" Remor asked. "You look like
you've seen a ghost."

"Ah, no, Remor! I guess the survey took more out of me than I
thought."

"Panera, how are things with you and Karn?" Derak asked.

"Fine, I just wish we didn't have to go through this old-fashioned
shadow affair. Therese is sweet and does her job well, but I just want

it to be over. Ten months before we join is almost insufferable. I want to have a modernist ceremony, but Karn insists on having the ceremony in the old temple. It's not what it used to be."

"Are you ok, Shesain?" she asked, as she embraced her. "You and Derak have matching expressions. I know you two embrace the old ways, but they're disappearing. The modernist movement is gaining ground fast. They should take the next election, and then we'll have true reform."

Remor was standing next to them and shared a desperate look.

Karn surprised him. "Derak, we missed you on the field. We almost lost the last Barquete match." He moved him away from the crowd. "I just don't get this modernist movement. Ever since the alliance treaty, our cultural practices have deteriorated. I don't know if I can last ten months with Panera insisting on following the modernists strange ways. Honestly, holding hands and kissing in public without a teacup ceremony, it's barbaric; however, congratulations to the both of you. I'm glad you two have not abandoned the old ways."

Derak needed a good stiff drink. He and Shesain excused themselves, and retreated to Derak's private study.

"Terga, are we clear of listening devices?" Derak asked.

"Yes, the room is clean."

"This is horrible," Shesain said in shock. "Modernists, breaking engagements, the Temple in disorder and Uncle Remor on the verge of losing an election. We've messed things up, haven't we?" She looked distraught.

Just then something moved across the floor. It was small and furry; Shesain Jumped, and Derak was in shock at what he saw.

"It's a house cat. Where in the hell did it come from?" he asked in bewilderment.

"Everyone has one now: cats, dogs, and parrots are owned by most of the modernists. They should have the majority of the senate in the next election," Terga informed him.

Derak poured himself a double shot of the 06 and sat down in utter disbelief, ignoring the purring feline rubbing against his leg. Shesain joined him with a glass of her own. They sat for a few minutes soaking in the incongruity and unbelievable complexity of the situation.

"We'd better rejoin the party," Shesain said.

Derak nodded in agreement and drained his glass before they left the room.

Remor joined them. "Times are tough; I knew I shouldn't have signed that treaty; the senate was adamant and gave me no choice. They wouldn't have extended the work rights bill if I didn't sign. That was ten years ago, Derak, and I almost lost that re-election. I will likely lose the next one. The senate majority leader, Senator Kamar is owned by the modernists, and he's bent to their political views. These are sad times for Thumar, as we watch our old ways get decimated and ignored by the new generation.

"Now the senate is trying to force me to sign a similar treaty with the Terelians. They're already destroying our fisheries, now they want greater control and more profits. The modernist party is playing right into their hands. Prosperity, they tout, they're just into it for the credits. Even more deplorable, they are talking about eliminating Founder's Day. They say it's part of the ancient past and that we need to bend to the needs of modern times. I'm doing my best to keep our traditions alive, but I'm fighting a losing battle." He sighed deeply with a sad face.

Remor continued. "Enough of that, we aren't here to discuss politics. Have you two decided on names yet? Also, don't forget Uncle Vemur's four-hundred-and- thirty-eighth-birthday. May Kumar bless him; he doesn't look a day over three hundred. The preparations for the Festival of Prosperity is in full swing. They'll expect another exciting Barquete match, Derak. Maybe you could pull off another ten pointer."

"What about the Festival of the Lights?" Derak asked.

"What?" Remor answered, looking at him, not knowing what that was.

"The discovery of the Anean light caves?" Derak pushed further.

He looked at them for a moment and then laughed. "Ah, you've read the accounts of the light caves. That came from Tukar Andehar's wild adventures. There's nothing to them, and the Tukar branch of the Andehar family tree has been dismissed as nothing more than old idealists. There's no truth there, just a myth."

"Have you checked it out?" Shesain asked.

"We have far more important issues to worry about. Why waste valuable resources chasing an archeological theory with no basis in fact?" Remor asked.

The three of them rejoined the celebration. Derak and Shesain could barely keep their foreboding thoughts inward and faked it for the rest of the evening. When they retired for the night, Derak laid his head on the pillow with his eyes wide open in despair, and Shesain lay close to him, weeping.

•◆•

Seamus returned home to the Anean Continent to his once charming coastal fishing village. His fiancé, Tenara, greeted him with a hug and a kiss, and took his arm as they walked through the village to his house. His shadow, Felain, fell into place behind them.

"How was the survey?" Tenara asked him.

He frowned, reverting to his thick Scottish brogue when disturbed. "Vera interesting, vera interesting."

"Seamus, slow down, I can't understand you," Tenara insisted.

"I'm sorry. Some unexpected events with unforgettable consequences have emerged. I can't talk about them. Not yet. I will meet with Derak again."

"You and your secrets! I'll never understand that military mind of yours."

He changed the subject. "What's happened here since I've been gone?"

"Too many unpleasant things. The modernists are getting a good foothold with our youth," Tenara said. "It's causing a great divide among our people."

"Modernists? Who are they, and what are they doing?" Then, he remembered to appear as normal as possible. If the news got any worse, he'd have to work harder on it.

"Seamus McGrew, have you been living under a rock these past months? These are the same off-worlders who moved in right after we signed the Alliance treaty. They started out in the cities and have been spreading like the plague the past ten years. Their dissent and lies have been tearing down Thumarian civilization as we know it. Our culture, histories, and belief systems have eroded by their rhetoric and demands, almost to the point of cultural extinction. They grow bolder, more divisive, and intrusive to our way of life by the day.

"They bring their pest animals with them. They call them cats, dogs, and birds, useless creatures. They serve no purpose other than to eat a great deal of food and show ownership. The worst are the birds they call parrots, an awkward avian that just squawks at you all day in their cages. They cage these so-called pets and keep them on leashes, how barbaric."

Seamus would not try to explain the comforting aspects of dogs and house cats; she wouldn't understand. "Don't they respect native beliefs and practices? You know, as we say on Earth, 'live and let live'?"

"No, they are a pushy, rude, demanding, intolerant, and obstinate people," Tenara spit out. "They claim that their religious deity, Jesus, is the only way to salvation, and that we are an uncivilized culture who worships false idols. Under their invasive influence, our Temple is getting smaller numbers of the younger population. Seamus, it's destroying the fabric of our once peaceful lives in Acara. I just cry thinking about it."

"I've had some experience with this group before," Seamus injected. "They're hard to stop once they get rolling; they rule with fear and intimidation to break down your self-confidence and replace it with slavery of the mind and soul. You can't get rid of them because they'll have a martyr, a greater symbol to follow. Each attempt to extricate them only strengthens their cause."

Terena shook her head. "That doesn't bode well for us, does it?"

"No, they're worse than the plague of 1814," Seamus mumbled.

"How do you know about that?"

"I've done a little reading," he answered. "What else has been happening?"

"The Terelians, half-lizard p'taw that they are, have been destroying our fisheries and driving most of our fisherman out of the remaining fertile fishing grounds. Then they have the nerve to sell us back our own fish at an inflated price. Now, they want to buy up our fertile farmlands and build their factories that spit out toxic black smoke. They say it will help the economy and raise our standard of living. The senate is trying to push a law through to allow it. I hope that President Andehar can stop it. May Kumar bless him."

"This is disturbing. How does our senator stand on this?"

"The f'ter is one of the main senators pushing it through," Felain, Seamus' shadow, spit out.

He and Terena gave her an approving nod as they walked into the main square. A ruckus was already in full swing when they arrived. A small but vocal group of modernists were picketing the Temple. Carrying a cross and chanting slogans.

"You're going to hell to burn in fire and brimstone," one of the crowd yelled out, holding sign that read, 'Pagan worshippers are going to hell.'

Another screamed. "Down with the old ways, bring in the new. Shadows are from the devil."

Then a speaker stepped up raising a hand. "Salvation only comes through Jesus. All others are false idols that…"

The three of them left in disgust as a fervent follower tried to hand them a tract.

They were just about home when Seamus spoke up. He meant his words for Tenara and Felain. "Most Christian's aren't that way. That's what we call them on Earth. Their religion is twenty-five hundred years old. This Jesus you hear about is their savior; he is supposedly the son of god. My parents follow this belief system. They and their village are a principled loving people, who only judge how an individual lives their lives. Most Christians I've known aren't like this. It's the few radicals that give them a bad name."

"I could live with the ones you're talking about, not this p'taw!" Felain said.

"So, could I," Seamus responded.

They entered the house to a smell of an aromatic meal waiting for them on the table. After washing up, they seated themselves and Seamus asked what he was eating.

"Rabbit," Tenara answered. "The old Earth colonists trade them along our coastline. Try it! It's delicious, and Pelaire tenderizes rabbit like no one else can."

•◆•

Dr. Bundett entered the building and flashed his pass as he walked to the third floor. When he got to his office, he found another name on the door: Rothure Beliminde, Research Director. The door opened and an attractive female Thumarian stepped out. "Leontul, have you forgotten where your new office is already? It's on the second floor, rear of the building."

"Old habits, you know. Besides, that's the old section. We have used it for storage for years." Leontul barely held his shocked response.

"I know, but with Morgone moving in, they needed your old office and lab." She smiled.

"Morgone? The pharmaceutical giant from earth?" Leontul commented.

"Yes, they're here to synthesize our most successful medicines," she stated. "This is quite an exciting development!"

Leontul was ready to bust. "Exciting! Have you seen the list of side effects their medicines carry? They cause more problems than they cure. A pill for a throat problem gives the patient a heart attack or cancer. Why trade our system for theirs?" Leontul demanded.

"Leontul, there is risk in everything we do."

He could barely contain himself. "Risk? Who's risking what? Tell me one time a patient has died of side effects from our herbal remedies. For hundreds of years, Thumarian society has stayed healthy on herbal medicine. No one has done anything but get better," he stated.

"I will not argue with you, Leontul. Our government funds us, so we have to follow the rules of the grant. You lost your position because you argued with the wrong person. Let's look at your new office and lab," Dr. Beliminde said with a sardonic smile.

As they entered, Leontul's anger grew. "You're giving me this? How do you expect me to do my job with this antiquated equipment?" he demanded.

"You'll find a way," Dr. Beliminde said cheerfully.

"You dumped me down here for a pharmaceutical company that poisons their public, all for the sake of the bottom line: credits. Half of this equipment looks like it isn't even working. Where are my cooling units, my equipment, and my analytical scanners?" he pressed her.

"Morgone gets it all; they need it to synthesize the new medicines. Here are your samples: I'm sure you'll do fine," she said with a disdainful smile. "What's this?" she asked as she backed far away from the frozen Veredant Flower. "Is this what I think it is?" she asked in shock.

"Yes, it is." Dr. Bundett answered with a sly grin. "If you don't want it to thaw and have the pollen get airborne, you'll get me my cooling units and analytical scanners back!"

Fear filled her eyes as she stared at the Veredant Flower. "I'll... I'll see to it." Leontul never saw anyone leave so fast in his life.

"Patour, get this equipment up and running by the end of the day."

"Yes, doctor!"

Leontul's coolers and scanners arrived a short time later and were set up. He stored his samples and started checking equipment calibrations when the door slammed behind him. The Morgone doctor stormed in, ready for a fight.

"How did you get my freezers and scanners? I want them back, NOW!"

"Sure, doctor. If you want to cause a planet-wide plague, take them. The consequences will be on you," Leontul said.

"What are you talking about, you Thumarian shit?"

"This," as Leontul pulled out the frozen Veredant Flower. "This started a planet wide plague on Thumar in 1814. All the males over the age of thirteen died until they found the cure. It had a mortality rate of one-hundred percent. Unfrozen, who knows what will happen?"

"Don't try and blackmail me with myth," the interloper spit out.

"Ask Dr. Rothure Beliminde, I'm sure you'll find that it's not a myth. What's the matter Doc, your company can't buy you equipment?"

"Why should they when I can use yours!"

Leontul shot back. "It is my equipment! And next thing you know, you'll start using our population as pincushions."

The Morgone doctor answered in disgust. "We've already started! And we have to pay them, greedy bunch of cretins. You and your backwards herbal technology! Don't you know our medicines are leading the way to the future of pharmaceuticals?" he proclaimed with an overconfident smile of superiority.

"Then answer me one question, Doc. Why do Earthlings live no longer than one hundred and twenty years with your medicines, and Thumarians live past four hundred years on herbs? Or is that why you're here?"

"You haven't heard the last of me, Doctor Bundett! I'll have your head on a platter when this is settled." He stormed out angrier than when he entered.

"You just hung yourself, Doctor. He's going straight to the top on this," Patour said.

"Maybe Patour, but it felt good, and I won't be here long, anyway."

•◆•

Derak was sitting at his desk going over the daily reports. Why would Thumar allow the Terelians to put their factories on the Anean plains? Don't they know that they feed half of the planet? The Thumarian modernists have done a superb job selling out their home. If they succeed, they'll turn Thumar into a second Earth. He was responsible for this alternate timeline, and only five people knew it. The more he was seeing, the quicker he had to fix it. He might have to bring the crew and *The Shesain* to Altair and convince Robert of the situation. That would be an onerous task. Robert was always difficult to convince of anything unless you had hard evidence. This one might prove impossible.

"Derak, Admiral Morton's on the line, and he's not happy."

"Thanks for the warning, Terga."

He activated the com and Morton's red face filled the screen. "Admiral, to what do I owe this pleasure?"

"Ambassador, it's never my pleasure to talk to you."

"I thought you retired."

"And leave you to screw things up? Never!" Morton responded.

"I couldn't do a better job of screwing things up than the Alliance already has. Allowing Terelians on Thumar, destroying Anea's fisheries and selling the fish back to Thumarians. Now, they are trying to transfer their factories to Thumar, after their government tells them to shut down. The Terelians have already destroyed their own ecosystem and now you're putting their toxic polluting factories on Thumar to do the same here! Not to mention bringing Pfizer in to suck Thumarians dry like a bunch of vampires, using their blood to synthesize longer life spans for the rich and powerful. I can see through the smoke screens."

"Those are bullshit allegations, Ambassador. We're just trying to modernize Thumar. They have been in the dark ages for centuries," Morton retorted.

"If your medicines are so good, then why do Thumarians live over three times as long as your average citizen? I'll take their dark ages over your modernization any day."

"You're bordering on treason, Ambassador."

"No, Admiral, just stating an observation."

"I may not be able to touch you now, but I can still affect your career."

"Only if you want to end yours, Admiral!" Morton's face turned red, and his veins popped out of his neck.

"I'm calling to make sure you follow the Alliance's protocol on the factories. You must convince the Thumarian President to capitulate for Thumar's own good. We expect you to comply, whether or not you agree with us, for your own benefit."

"Admiral, would you sell out Tara, or Calvin? Would you do the same thing to Earth?"

"Don't bring them into this! This has nothing to do with Tara or Earth."

"Everything looks rosy half a galaxy away. You know the Terelians are in bed with the Keks. You're opening the door for the Keks, and you know it."

"Quite the opposite, Ambassador, by humoring the Terelians, we keep the Keks at bay."

"Bullshit! You fought the Keks! You know what they're like. The Keks are waiting for the first chance to run over the Terelians. You know as well as I, they won't stop after they've eaten the hearts out of Tara, Calvin, and every human on Earth that they can."

"Don't bring my family into this, Ambassador!"

"You know I'm right Admiral. You can't deny it."

"Are you going to play ball next week or not Ambassador?"

"I'll think about it, out." Derak cut the connection and seethed. *How could he turn into such a coward?*

Shesain stomped into the office screaming. "OH, those Katkurns! We go a little soft on the Terelians and they think they can renegotiate their treaty! The worst part is that the modernists are buying into it and pressuring their senators. Damn that yellow button! If we do not fix this, I swear, we will leave Thumar and find a place that's not going insane."

Derak shook his head. "We may have nowhere to run. The time space continuum is like a spider web. You break one joint, and you weaken another. Other joints will break, weakening others. I have no idea how far the rip in time will go or if it will stop. We have to call the team together now. We have to leave Thumar immediately."

"Terga, notify the team, code red."

"They'll be at the hanger at five p.m."

"Sweetheart, pack it up. We have to get going now."

54

"I'm ready, I won't miss this timeline." She followed Derak out of the building.

•—◆—•

After dinner, Derak excused the staff and met with the time crew in his hangar. All were present, complete with luggage. Looks of consternation were on every face. They packed up *The Shesain*, minus the rabbit meat. Shesain wanted no reminders of this timeline on board.

Derak's com unit buzzed, and Remor was on the other end, looking distraught. "Derak, you and Shesain need to come to an emergency meeting tonight. Senator Kamar and his modernist party are lined up to push this Terelian bill through or start my impeachment proceedings, today."

"When is it?"

"In three hours. Be there. Out."

Shesain looked at him with confusion in her eyes.

"We can't," Derak answered her entreaty. "There is no telling what they have in store for us. From the reports I've read, some of the Admiralty are on their side now. We're already marked as dissenters and they'll do anything to push their agenda forward. This situation is past the tipping point. The best thing we can do is to leave Thumar and fix this, fast, we're leaving now."

The Shesain lifted off and shifted into D-gen. When they reached five hundred feet, four Ting class fighters and a medium cruiser descended on Derak's estate. He made for open space with a heavy heart.

"That was close," Jack said. "They started the ops sooner than the reports said. I think some of the Thrashur are in on this too."

"We can't worry about them now. What we do from this moment forward has to restore the original timeline," Derak said.

"How do you propose we do that?" Leontul asked.

"I've got to convince Robert that we time traveled. That would be impossible if we didn't have *The Shesain* and Terga. He will have to see it with his own eyes. I can't guarantee that he'll believe us. He's as hardheaded as I am, sometimes worse. But I have a gut feeling, that's where we need to start."

"What about Remor?" Shesain asked in exasperation.

Derak looked at her with compassion. "If we can correct this, that incident will never occur."

She was torn between the two needs but tearfully agreed to the logic.

"Does anybody else have any ideas?" Derak asked.

"Can't we go back and retrace our last steps?" Seamus asked.

"We might risk running into ourselves," Jack answered.

This surprised Derak somewhat. Either Jack listened very carefully, or he had hidden talents. He surmised that it was both.

"What if Robert doesn't believe us, with all of the facts before him?" Shenar asked.

"Then we might have to risk going back as a last resort." Derak said.

"They will have the same capabilities as we do. How would we get around that?" Jack asked.

"That one will take some thought," Derak said.

"I vote that we try Robert first," Seamus piped up.

They all voted to go to Altair.

"Ok, to Altair we go. Let's pray to Kumar that we don't leave empty handed."

Shesain looked at Derak in surprise. "When did you start believing?"

"I haven't yet, but I just might if this can be corrected."

She smiled and took his hand. "If only Demar could hear you."

"He just might, there's more to him than meets the eye," Derak said.

"Terga, set a course for Altair and activate the null generator. We need all the time we can get."

"Course set, null generator is hot. ETA in three hours," Terga confirmed.

"Engage and make it ten. We need to catch up on some sleep," Derak thought.

The null effect washed over them as they started moving towards Altair. They were getting used to the feeling now. They spent the next several hours discussing the changes on Thumar, then headed to their cabins for much needed sleep.

Derak contacted Terga. *"When we arrive at Altair, maintain a standard orbit in null mode. We must discuss our plan before we proceed."*

"Are you scared, Derak?"

"I'm terrified, Terga. What have I done? Can we fix it?"

Altair: 2414, Modified Timeline

Deep-space travel had its disadvantages. Even with artificial gravity and more comfortable quarters, regular space travel was still a problem. The way around this was to establish a day and night schedule. Long days in a cramped environment caused personnel issues to crop up fast.

Derak tossed, and turned all night. He'd been up since four a.m. going over the initial mission with Terga in his mind's new math mode. He was still no closer to a solution when Terga woke the crew. They all shuffled into the expanded dining room, grabbing coffee and breakfast. Shesain sat next to Derak, eyeing him. Altair lay below them as *The Shesain* maintained orbit, undetected.

"How are we going to go about this?" Seamus asked in his thick Scottish brogue.

"Knowing Robert, I think Derak should take the lead. He has the scientific background to argue our point," Jack added.

"Thanks, Jack. I have to agree with you. I can convince Robert with hard facts. However, this story might seem too fantastical to him. That's where *The Shesain* and Terga comes in. We'll have to show him everything. That will be a big risk, but the alternative is worse. The question is, when do we break the news?"

"How about showing him the ship, and when we have him inside, we start," Shenar recommended.

"That's a superb idea, but how do we start?" Leontul Bundett asked.

"I'll just have to let it rip," Derak said. "The last time I was this nervous, I had to go before an oral board for the Naval Academy entrance exam. We can't stay here for eternity, let's go."

"Terga, take us out of Null, and contact Altair for landing clearance."

They landed in Derak's most secure hangar. Derak instructed the crew to stay with the ship. They shrank the interior down to normal size. It felt weird to see *The Shesain* in normal mode. They normalized everything to make it look like a standard ship. Derak headed up to Robert's office and knocked on the door. Derak stood at the door as it opened.

"Come in, Derak, long time no see! What brings you here?"

"I'm checking on my companies. I need to make some decisions. With the present political environment in the inner galaxy, you must have some interesting changes in mind."

Robert rolled his eyes and sat down in his chair. "You don't know the half of it. Altair is demanding that we renew the union contract."

"They want more benefits and pay for less work, no doubt?" Derak remarked.

"They are also threatening a shutdown if we don't agree to their terms, and want a lease re-negotiation on all three companies," Robert lamented.

"Then, move them to another system. I can't help it if they're too stupid to realize over fifteen percent of their GDP comes from our factories. I set all three factories up for overnight moves."

"They know that too and have told me they will move their military in and take over the factories for themselves, if we attempt a move." Robert informed Derak.

"Well, I've got a surprise for them. Remember the old Earth term, 'scorched earth?' If they try to stop us, we'll scuttle the factories and leave them with nothing but empty buildings. We have more than enough credits to start over, and all our files are backed up off planet."

"Only as a last resort, there's too much to lose. We are just now getting a handle on passive walls. It would be a shame to lose that," Robert answered with regret.

"We won't lose anything, Robert. They will. How's *The Aries* coming along?"

"Slow. The modernists are growing in power. They're forcing boycotts of our products in the inner galaxy, cutting into our profits. Not a lot, but enough to slow down her construction."

"Speaking of ships, I have a beauty," Derak told him. "If you have a minute, I'd like to show her to you."

"Good, I need something to cheer me up. I hope you don't mind if my chief technology officer joins us; he's an Altairian. Before you judge him, just listen. He's the only one I can trust now, so go along with it, ok?"

Derak looked at him and agreed to meet him.

Petemar Vorshock entered, and Derak wasn't impressed at first. He was five-foot-eight with a slight build. His face was not Altarian, and Derak couldn't place it. His jutting jaw line with flat cheekbones looked weird. His pupils eerily filled his eyes, and he didn't smile.

Robert introduced them. "Petemar, this is my brother, Derak. He's the brains behind our technology."

Petemar gave Derak a long, appraising look. "It's a pleasure, Derak; I get to meet the legend. We've kept a close eye on you. Your advances are amazing, years ahead of their time."

"Thank you," he answered as they shook hands. His muscle tone was not Altairian at all. He was fit, not soft and lazy, as most Altairians were. His accent wasn't Altarian. Derak's gut reaction was to let him accompany them.

"Petemar is a time, space, and dimension expert. His recommendations have helped our research and development department," Robert added.

I've got to trust my gut feelings more often, Derak thought to himself. "Let's go then, I think you'll both be surprised." They walked to the hanger, and Robert's jaw dropped when he saw *The Shesain*. Petemar just leveled an even stare at her for a long moment. As they walked towards the ship, Robert couldn't take his eyes off of her.

"Behold, *The Shesain*."

"She's beautiful, Derak. You've been holding out on me, again," Robert said.

Petemar walked in silence.

"Where's the hatch?" Robert asked. He gasped as the iris appeared and opened from the center out to its edges.

Petemar wore an undecipherable look.

"It's an improvement on passive walls. She has a living hull: a unique combination of exotic metals introduced with organic self-replicating nano-bots, inside and out."

Robert's face filled with awe. "I've seen nothing like it before, and I've seen just about every technological advance there is."

They stepped inside and Derak introduced them to the crew.

Robert smiled at Shesain. "It's good to see you, Shesain! You are as beautiful as the last time I laid eyes on you."

She hugged Robert. "Are you still single? I have a few eligible cousins who would love to court you."

Smiling and embarrassed, he responded. "Not now, Derak's companies fill my days and nights. Shenar, are you keeping Jack in line?" Robert asked.

She smiled at Jack after hugging Robert. "I'm keeping him on a leash, although he can be as adventuresome as Derak."

"Give us the tour of this remarkable ship, Derak," Robert said with excitement.

"First, I'll show you the space drives." They all walked back to the stern of the ship. The engine room held a sealed metallic container, ten-foot wide by five-foot high by twenty-feet long. "This is the RMT, Reverse Magnetic Thrust drive. It's a combination of magnetic principles and an ion plasma beam. The plasma beam is manipulated by the magnetic field. It's very safe compared to matter-antimatter. I believe you're still working on separation and containment fields," Derak said as he looked at Robert.

"Yes, we are, the resulting detonation obliterates everything."

Derak continued, "the magnetic field affects the beam at the quantum level. I use this for sub-light speed travel. It is capable of

61

hyper speed; I keep it as a back-up. The drive I use for interstellar travel is located in between the twin outer hulls. It's called the Interstellar Dark Matter Drive, or IDMD. It uses dark matter and energy as its fuel, an inexhaustible supply that allows me to go anywhere and stay out for long periods of time."

Petemar raised his left eyebrow; his silence spoke volumes.

"I need you to step outside after the hanger is cleared and all recording devices are turned off," Derak insisted.

"Terga, are we safe?"

"The hangar is clean."

They all stepped outside, and the iris closed. Petemar examined the hull and stepped back with a thoughtful expression as Derak spoke.

"I'll first show the ship's self-healing capabilities."

"What?" Robert asked in surprised.

"I told you, she's a living ship."

"How can a ship live?" Robert asked in disbelief.

Derak pulled out his light dagger and turned it on. Robert stepped back and Petemar stared at it. "This is a light dagger. It's nothing more than a plasma beam in a force field, remarkably effective against Kek armor." Derak set the dagger on maximum and punctured the hull. The energy blade left a one-inch diameter hole that they could see through. Seconds later, the hole filled in.

Robert was speechless, eyes wide in disbelief. And he had been worried about losing the passive wall. What had Derak been up to? "That's unbelievable…how did it do that?" he demanded.

"It's fourth-generation passive-wall technology. Now, let's step back and take in the entire view of *The Shesain*. Now you see her, now you don't." The ship disappeared before their eyes.

Robert was dumbfounded, which was rare, and Jack chuckled to himself.

"Go ahead, Robert, walk up to it. You'll feel her hull. That's the cloak mode. She is still in the third dimension." Derak prodded him forward.

He gave Derak a quizzical look and walked forward until he

bumped into the ship. He backed off with a surprised look and reached out his hand and stroked the invisible hull. "This is beyond amazing," he got out.

"Keep your hand there and wait a moment," Derak instructed him.

His hand fell forward into thin air. He walked forward into the ship and waved his hands around. "Where did it go? A ship that size can't up and disappear!" Robert looked back, amazed.

"Come back here, and I'll show you." Derak remarked as Robert returned with an odd look on his face. "Now, watch." The ship re-appeared out of thin air. He continued before Robert could say anything. "She was in D-gen mode. I designed a dimensional generator that puts her in between the third and fourth dimensions. She can affect the dimension that she came from."

Petemar's expression never changed during the whole demonstration. He asked Derak, "can you travel into deeper dimensions?" *Could he be first generation? He might be 'the one,' two and a half centuries early.* Then he leveled a long look at Robert.

"Yes, she can, but I'm not ready to travel down that road yet. Not until I understand the full repercussions of this revelation," Derak answered.

Petemar waited for more.

The Iris reopened, and they stepped inside the ship once more. She was enlarged to three times her outside dimensions. Robert sat down in disbelief. Petemar's expression remained unchanged, but his pupils were changing dilatations.

Derak continued. "My Quasi-Dimensional generator does this. It can duplicate anything in Terga's memory banks."

"Who, or what is Terga?" Robert broke his silence.

"Terga is my AI, artificial intelligence computer. She's remarkable with an almost infinite memory capacity."

"STOP! I cannot take this anymore. Is this for real or am I dreaming?" Robert blurted out and sat in silence.

"Are there any limitations to her capability?" Petemar asked.

"The Quasi-Dimensional Generator, is limited by the size of the object that houses it. It can only grow so big before the ship's hull loses integrity. Pre-sets are programmed into Terga, preventing me from breaking that threshold."

"Interesting," Petemar replied.

They exchanged a long glance. "The D-gen has even been shrunk down to a belt size unit that can be worn." Derak disappeared and then re-appeared next to Robert.

Robert jumped out of his seat and backed away from him as he was shaking his head. "This…all this is…is…centuries ahead of its time. How did you accomplish this?" Waving his hand around the ship.

"This is all thought control, isn't it?" Petemar asked.

"Yes, automated with thought control." Derak answered.

"You've thought of everything. How do you explain this technology? Is it from the future?" Petemar asked.

Derak looked at Shesain, *"here it goes."*

"Good luck, my Chimera. This is entertaining."

"For whom?"

"We're not from the future, but we arrived from a different timeline."

Petemar showed a slight smile, like he was expecting Derak's answer.

"Now, that is crazy talk, Derak. I can't deny what I've just seen, but time travel. That's preposterous!" Robert exclaimed in desperation.

"How else can you explain the disparity of your tech level, compared to mine?" Derak asked him.

Robert thought before answering. "Ok. Let us say that what you're telling me is true. You're saying that you came from an alternate timeline?"

"No, you're in the alternate 'modified time' line and we've come from the original."

Robert shook his head and sat back in disbelief. "That's impossible."

Petemar asked, "Could you explain?"

"That's why we're here, Petemar. We are looking for a way to fix what we screwed up. I hope you don't mind if I make things a little more comfortable." The ship's interior increased in size in a blink of an eye. Robert jumped and said nothing. "Let's move to the stern, I believe we'll be more comfortable there." Derak got up and the others followed. It was a large inviting room with seats for all.

Derak began. "Things started when Shesain asked Jack about the yellow lighted touch pad, with a red warning light."

Shesain interrupted, "Jack told me not to touch it and why. I tried not to, but I did."

Derak pitched in, "we traveled six hundred years in the past."

"How did you know that?" Petemar asked.

"Our chronometer told us, and the computer confirmed it." Derak continued to where they found out they had already been there before.

"Hold on a second!" Robert butted in. "You want us to believe you traveled back six hundred years to a point in time you previously visited? You've lost it, Derak!"

"That concept intrigues me. How can an anomaly like that exist?" Petemar asked.

"It's simple once you've experienced the phenomenon. It's called a time causality loop."

"A what!? Derak, sometimes you amaze me," Robert said in disbelief.

"Let them finish Robert. Continue Derak," Petemar said.

"We had gone back to the point in time and location of the plague of 1814, where the cure was found and stopped the plague. The physical descriptions in ancient drawings looked like me, Shesain and Dr. Bundett as we know him."

"Do you have these historical records on board?" Petemar asked.

"We have the original time-line records, the recordings of all of our actions during our time there, and the records of the new modified timeline," Jack answered him.

"I need to see them now, all three, where are they?" Petemar demanded.

"The best place is the science station, or I can transfer it back here," Derak said.

"Set me up in that corner and leave me alone," Petemar ordered.

After they set him up, he sequestered himself in front of three separate 3-D holo-screens, each one playing a separate record. Everyone sat silently waiting for him to respond. It was an awkward time, with each of them exchanging an occasional look.

Petemar reviewed the screens for an hour, until he came to the sphere Derak made to bring Terga back in time. "Explain this to me, Terga; bring up the sphere."

The sphere appeared between them and Robert's silence ended. "What the..."

Petemar enlarged the holo-display so that the mathematical highways were clear. "Who did this?' He asked hard, looking at all of them.

"I did," Derak answered.

His pupils shrank. "How did you accomplish this?"

He explained the entire process with the rest of the crew filling in the details.

"You telepathically communicated with the computer to create this sphere. How long did it take you?" Petemar inquired.

"Six hours." He looked at Jack and Shesain for confirmation.

They both nodded in agreement and Petemar checked with Terga for the data.

"You nearly lost your life. Any human with regular DNA strands would have died. How did you live through it?"

"I have a four-strand sequence with nodal web connecting the four of them to each other."

He is first generation and so is Robert, Petemar thought to himself.

"There's one more thing," Shenar said.

"What's that, Shenar?" Petemar asked.

"Jack had something like that happen to him. One night, he was talking in his sleep. An elegant gibberish to my ears, but beautiful none the less, just the way Derak was speaking after he woke up. Shesain had to slap him hard to bring him back to normal, if you can call anything about Derak normal." She smiled with a teasing grin in Derak's direction.

Petemar's eyes narrowed again, and he went back to finishing his review. An hour and a half later, the screens went away, and he re-joined them. After a moment, he began. "Robert, I have to agree with Derak and his crew. This incident happened the way they said it did. I also double-checked Terga's calculations and they are correct. Something happened in that brief period between the village and your entrance into the time vortex. The records you were working with could not have warned you about the anomaly. Is there anything else I should know?"

"Yes," Shesain said. "I'm one month pregnant with twins."

Petemar's anger erupted, and his pupils narrowed to pinpoints as his lips disappeared into a thin line. He said nothing and left *The Shesain*. Robert tried to follow him but was angrily waved back into the ship.

Everyone looked at each other, wondering why a pregnancy set Petemar off.

Robert walked back into the room and approached Shesain. "Congratulations Shesain, twins. May Kumar bless them." He sat down and hugged her.

She managed a wane smile. She didn't feel like celebrating after Petemar's outburst at finding out she was pregnant with twins. "Thank you, Robert. I know Kumar and Shemar will bless them."

They were considering the seriousness of the situation when Derak turned to Robert with a question. "Did I ever reunite with Frank Thorsen?"

"No, Frank died of a rare cancer while you were out on assignment."

"That's odd, he was healthy when I left. That explains the absence of Terga in this timeline."

"How did you come up with this technology?" he asked Derak.

"I discovered ancient Altairian tablets and digitally recorded them before turning them over to the government. I'd like to know if they were discovered and where they are now," Derak inquired of Robert.

He looked surprised. "They were found ten-years ago, and we got a hold of digital copies before the present government took power. But we haven't been able to figure them out yet. Did you carbon-14 the tablets?"

"Yes. I found the results unbelievable at first. I thought I made a mistake. Then, I tested them three more times and had two more independent tests run. The average age of the tablets from all five tests was twenty-five thousand years, plus."

Dumbfounded looks greeted his disclosure.

"Do you have the results on board?" Robert asked.

"Here they are," he said as the hologram appeared.

Robert and Leontul studied them. "You did nothing wrong, Derak. It looks like you followed procedure down to the letter," Leontul commented.

Robert studied the data longer before saying anything. "I agree with him; I wish I had the tablets to test myself."

"It took me three years before I could decipher them and another two to figure out the secondary and tertiary markings. They're the foundation for all that you see now."

Petemar had been listening to the conversation and interrupted them. "First, I would like to apologize. I got angry when I heard about the pregnancy. Without the pregnancy, I could have helped you fix your time paradox. The children present a problem that I will need help with, and my superiors will not be happy." He turned to Derak. "Do you have the records of the tablets on board? If you do, I want to look at both sets of holograms."

Derak pulled up the tablets on a 3-D hologram.

Petemar moved into the room and sat down to look at them. Three stone tablets, reconstructed from the fragments floated in front of the group.

"How did you develop this technology from the tablets?" Petemar asked.

"The glyphs were just the start. They lay out the basic ideas and formulas. Then I exposed the tablets to different spectrums of light. That's when the pronunciation marks appeared." The hologram changed, showing new engravings carved shallower than the first. "These perplexed me for six months before I broke the code. Then I started bombarding them with all the sound frequencies I knew about, and these appeared on the next to last attempt." The third view of the tablets now showed small round shallow holes in an apparent random formation.

Petemar sat back in surprise and quickly recovered his composure.

"Altairians did not carve these tablets. I'd like to know who did. These required two years of intensive study and many sleepless nights to find the answers. I put the three together and came up with what you see before you now."

"How did you know to use light spectrum and sound frequencies?" Petemar asked.

"Just a hunch, after everything else failed. I figured I had nothing to lose."

"This is unbelievable," Robert said. "Even with all the evidence I've seen, it's going to take me time to digest it all."

"What you've seen and heard is the truth, Robert," Petemar acknowledged. "Now let's get back to the matter at hand. I could have come up with a solution to return the timeline to its original state, without the pregnancy complicating matters. The two unborn fetuses will be different when they arrive. This situation is out of my hands with the present technology available to me, including Terga, and this ship. I will consult my elders."

"My children will not arrive! They will be born into a restored timeline into a loving family," Shesain scolded Petemar, perturbed about the phrasing of his comment, still upset about his earlier reaction.

"Please accept my apology Shesain," Petemar said. "I am using the vernacular of my people."

"Apology accepted," Shesain answered.

"Who or what are you?" Derak asked Petemar. "You're not Altairian; you're too short and not soft bellied."

He took minor offense at the 'short' remark, and bit back his response. "I am Telaxian, and I'm tall for my race," Petemar stated.

"Telaxians are a mythical race in stories we tell our children," Shenar said.

"We prefer to keep it that way," Petemar answered.

"Boy, has this been a day for revelations, or what? So, Petemar, what is your purpose for being here, and why?" Jack asked him.

"Neither is of your concern, nor will I answer the question," he replied as he turned to Robert. "Robert, this ship needs provisions for a long journey; see to it now. We leave in one hour. Derak, you need to introduce me to Terga. The rest of you, prepare for departure and help Robert," Petemar ordered.

"What's going on? Where are we going, and what are you going to do with Terga?" Derak asked sharply. "She's the result of years of research that's lost to the present universe. We can't afford to lose her now."

"Calm down, Derak. We have to leave Altair immediately; you will be tracked here soon. I will ascertain her abilities. She will play a key role in your upcoming mission," Petemar assured him.

"Mission? What mission?"

"You will find out soon enough. Now let's move, there is little time left before we leave."

Petemar interfaced with Terga while the crew loaded the provisions.

Robert got clearance for lift off and they cleared the atmosphere and Jack set course for the outer solar system. They had to be clear of Altarian sensor range.

It was a good thing they were in D-gen. Jack picked up seven ships orbiting Altair, all of them war ships. Three belonged to the Thrashur, and the rest were of Alliance registry, one was an Orion Class Cruiser. Jack intercepted their communications. They were looking for *The Shesain* and her crew.

Petemar gave Jack the next course setting and the IDMD hummed to life. They felt the same strange sensation as the drive enveloped *The Shesain*. The crew was used to it by now. It didn't seem to affect Petemar, and Robert had a strange look on his face.

"Why don't you fix that, Derak? It's unnerving," Robert commented.

"I will, if Petemar could help."

"I can. Follow me to the back room, Derak."

They went to the back room and Terga brought up the hologram of the IDMD's global mathematical structure. Formulas streamed along green-lit highways. Derak went into math mode and Petemar linked with him. He observed as Derak made corrections. When he finished, Petemar made some minor adjustments, and the sphere disappeared.

After a while, the alarm sounded, showing the IDMD was coming out of hyperspace. When they came to a stop, none of them could believe their eyes. They weren't in regular space. As far as the eye could see, the view was of narrow billowy cloud formations moving in and out of innumerable complex shapes, with a white opaque background that the clouds flowed in.

"Where are we?" Seamus asked in amazement.

"This place is beyond words," Dr. Bundett acknowledged.

"It's beautiful," Shenar and Shesain said at the same time.

"You're in a node," Petemar said as he returned to the bridge with Derak. "It is like null space, where time, space and dimension exist at the same moment. Time as a reality does not operate here. This is a place that neither Einstein, nor any other modern physicist, since his time, has seen into. It's a larger representation of the nodes that galactic superstructures fall into. In short, it allows for much faster travel throughout the universe. I will use this one to teleport to Telaxia, to consult with the elders. I'll need a copy of Terga and all the ship's files for them to review. Only a copy," he added when Derak's face turned dark at the mention of Terga. He copied the files and teleported out of reality.

They all stared at the space that he had occupied.

"Wow! That was…incredible," Leontul remarked.

"Who and what are these Telaxians?" Derak asked.

Shenar answered. "According to our mythology, they are Time Sentinels. Supposedly, they're the mathematicians of the universe.

They're ruled by a Prime Mathematician. That's all we know. Until now, it has been a story we heard as children growing up on Thumar. Fact is stranger than fiction."

"Another myth you left out," Shesain said, looking at Shenar, "is that they're supposed to be an immortal race."

"How long have they been around?" Seamus asked.

"They say that they've been present since the beginning. They were the ones who set linear time in motion, so the story goes," Shesain added.

"Maybe they can help us solve this paradox we find ourselves in now," Jack commented.

"Until now, all we've discovered is more questions. I hope you're right, Jack," Derak remarked.

They settled down to dinner--or was it lunch? Days can get scrambled in deep space. The only way to overcome that was to set a regular schedule. Even this sometimes got skewed when their destination's days and nights ran opposite of the ship's.

They waited for what seemed like a day. It didn't matter, with the effects of time nullified. They could have waited a week and not known it. The ship's chronometers didn't measure passing time since they left Altair. Seamus was showing Shesain, Shenar and Leontul how to play bridge, an Earth card game. Derak didn't join them because card games bored him. Shesain was getting the game fast and beating the pants off of everybody. This bothered Seamus, he was used to winning. They were all good natured about it and took to ribbing him when he lost.

Petemar teleported back to the bridge as he left. The look on his face told them that things didn't go well. He looked at them and frowned before he started. "The elders weren't pleased in the slightest. In fact, they grew angry at your time disruption, and I received a good rebuke for allowing this to happen. This will take the participation of the Prime Mathematician, and she is not the least bit happy. The only things that help you are Terga, your complete records of the Altairian Tablets, and that you sought help in this matter. Otherwise, the penalty for me and all of you, excluding Robert, would have been severe. If you think I'm rough on you, you will soon find out otherwise. The Prime Council will be far more severe."

"What do we do now?" Seamus asked.

"We are going to Telaxia," Petemar told them. "We'll travel by the nodes, but it will take at least a month, your time. This ship cannot teleport, so I brought back some temporary modifications for Terga and your IDMD to allow for this."

"Is there any way to get onboard chronometers to measure time, at least as an illusion? I don't know about you Petemar, but it helps the rest of us to have a frame of reference," Jack inquired.

He looked at Jack and considered his request for a moment. "I'll instruct Derak on the procedure to allow this. For now, I need to upload these modifications and start our journey." He looked at Derak who nodded in agreement to allow the upload.

It took him a few minutes to complete. He set the course, and the IDMD engaged. Derak followed Petemar to the back room and they got the clocks working. After the evening meal, they agreed it to a set a schedule and to settle in for the lengthy trip.

Telaxia Prime: Null Time

Petemar called them together. "My Telaxian name is Qextenar."

"What's your last name?" Shenar asked.

He looked at her hard. "Telaxians go by first names only in our society. We use last names only with our mates. We communicate by telepathy. We use verbal communication only when we encounter non-telepathic races."

"We talk to Terga with our minds all the time," Leontul said.

He stared at them for a moment. "Why did you not tell me this? How do you do it?"

"The rest of the crew wears these." Derak showed him the mesh bracelet. "I don't need one. I have an organic implant that has worked its way into my DNA. In fact, Terga could communicate with me halfway across the galaxy."

"Can I tap into this network?" Qextenar asked.

"If you can teleport across the universe, I don't see why not," Seamus remarked.

After a few minutes, he smiled. *"That's better. We will use this method from this point forward. It will exercise your minds for the first set of lessons."*

"Lesson?" Shesain asked.

"Learning to speak conversational Telaxian; you will need it."

"What does it take?" Shenar inquired.

"You must learn math. We speak the language of mathematics. I believe you heard it when Derak woke up after his encounter with the sphere. We speak it with our minds, not our vocal cords. I've brought

back lessons for each of you to learn. It will help pass the time. You can refer to me as Qex, it is acceptable at all levels in our society." Qex smiled for only the second time since they left Altair.

Terga set up stations for everybody. This kept them busy for the better part of the day. Then they had individual sessions with Qex.

Jack, Seamus, and Derak were used to deep space assignments; the others weren't. Less than a week passed before tempers flared, cabin fever set in.

"OH! That p'taw of a lesson. I just can't seem to get that stupid mind switch down. Just when I think I have it, it slips away," Shesain exclaimed, coming from another session with Qex. "I just want to set my feet on solid ground again. I never liked deep space assignments. They always set me on edge before negotiations. How I wish I had a room full of Katkurns to release my frustration on."

"It can't be that bad. We have sizeable rooms and a few distractions," Derak said, trying to calm her down.

"That's just fine, coming from the resident detarch!"

"If that's how you feel, I'll just sleep on the bridge tonight," he responded.

Shesain stopped in her tracks, her face flushed red. "I'm so sorry; it's just that learning an impossible language is driving me crazy. That and being confined to this ship."

"I'll link to you the next time you're on your station, if that will help," he told her.

She came over and embraced him with a kiss. "I'm sorry, my Chimera. I'd love it if you could help me. It's just that we have to have conversational Telaxian down in three to four weeks, and I can't even break out of the first lesson yet. It's so frustrating."

"Relax your mind and don't fight the switch. You've almost done it several times. You don't lose control of your mind; you gain greater control over it. It's a paradox that helps you," he encouraged her.

"This entire mission is a paradox. I wish I had never have seen that p'taw yellow touch pad," she griped.

Derak hugged her. "I'm still responsible for the entire affair. Commanders are culpable for their crew's actions. We could have returned, but we stayed. I for one would do it all again. There's no way we could watch all those Thumarian men and boys die. We were supposed to be there. How we arrived at the exact time we were needed still baffles me."

The next morning after breakfast, Jack and Shenar emerged from their sessions with Qex, arguing. The daily squabbles were grinding on Qex's nerves, although establishing telepathic communication lightened his petulant mood somewhat.

Terga had been recording the entire voyage and tried to establish a pattern in the cloud formations. What was discovered so far was that the colors of the backgrounds showed where one was. White showed a node, and brighter colors were the nodal highways between them. They were traveling down a connecting tube between nodes with a yellow tint almost the shade of a sun. Primary colors defined the major routes, while secondary and tertiary tints marked secondary tubes and those that were seldom used.

While they passed through another node, they noticed an entrance that was dark gray, almost black with muted white clouds falling into the cone's swirling pattern.

"You don't want to travel down that one," Qex thought to them over their shoulders. *"That one goes to a special place called 'The Void.' It is a strange occurrence. Light, dark, time, space, dimension, good and bad intermingle freely. It is the ultimate test of the strength of one's soul and convictions."*

"Have any Telaxians gone in and survived?" Jack asked him.

"Many have tried, but few have returned. You don't die in there. You get absorbed into its cosmic consciousness, lost forever in its swirls and eddies. Only two of our race have ever returned. They were never the same again."

Leontul shuffled into the room, in a bad mood. *"The sitan Verdant Flower, even with the equipment I have, I'm no closer to an answer."*

"Closer to what?" Seamus asked.

"The pollen not only caused the plague of 1814 but also increased the life span of the survivors. Historically, those who survived went to great pains to eradicate the flower. Somehow the pollen interacted

with the cure and changed their DNA structure. I should have studied more genetics in college."

"Let's look at your results," Qex prompted him.

"Follow me." Leontul led the way.

Derak followed them into the expanded lab. *"Are you taking precautions, Leontul?"* he asked with concern. *"It wouldn't be a good thing to release the pollen on board this ship."*

"Why?" Qex inquired.

"The flower's pollen only affected Thumarian men over the age of thirteen. The stranded Earth colony felt none of the effects," Leontul answered.

"How did you come up with the cure?" Qex asked with interest.

"Historical references, along with some blind luck and improvising. Terga found the mystery ingredient that was referred to."

"What was it?"

"Organic nano-bots; we're on a ship full of them. Terga came back with replicator technology. This helped in synthesizing the required doses of three nano-bots per shot."

Qex sat in deep thought for a long moment before he continued. *"Let me show you something, Leontul."* A holographic sphere materialized in front of them. *"Link with me, and I'll show you how to manipulate the structure. It will give you a clearer picture."* Leontul linked up, and he smiled when a square hologram appeared with a turning DNA strand next to it.

The square isolated specific parts of the sphere. With equations and biochemical clusters of physical representations of chemical structures. That moved in and out of each other until it formed correct combinations. He smiled to himself when he realized that he was performing this on his own. The formations halted.

"I'm doing it myself," Leontul exclaimed in excitement.

"Keep going, this should help your efforts," Qex prompted him.

"Thanks, Qex, I appreciate your help."

He nodded and left the room.

Sounds of frustrated students filled the ship.

"*Terga, how do you like communicating with Qex?*" Derak asked her.

"*I enjoy it. It's a pleasure to communicate with a logical mind, the language of math is much faster.*"

"*What's wrong with our minds?*"

"*Biological beings are always illogical, except Telaxians; they don't allow emotions to get in the way.*"

"*So, you understand math language?*"

"*Qex and I communicate only in his language.*"

"*Can you help the others? We only have two weeks before we reach Telaxia.*"

"*I will do my best,*" she promised.

The groans and complaints stopped as Terga linked with the students. Then Derak turned back to Leontul's holograms. They had filled out in the last few minutes. He asked if he could link up and join him. His biochemistry background piqued his interest. Leontul invited Derak to join.

After some time passed, Shesain and Shenar let out a whoop of celebration. Other acknowledgements followed, from Seamus and Jack. Qex came back to the lab and asked Derak what he did.

"*I put Terga on helping the others. She has had a longer relationship with their personalities. I figured it was worth a try.*"

"*I should have thought of that myself,*" Qex commented.

"*We love you, Terga!*" the girls thought in unison.

"*I love you, too,*" she answered with apparent emotion.

Qex and Derak exchanged a look. "*Your AI is becoming, or has become, self-aware, Derak.*"

"*Should I be scared?*" Derak asked Qex.

"*No, she has a pure heart. That you and your advances no longer surprise me is interesting. It is almost as if I expect it. You are unique for a first generation.*" He turned and left.

The evening meal was more animated. Shesain and Shenar's infectious attitudes made even Qex break out in a slight smile. They bantered thoughts about on their progress since Terga stepped in to help. Derak joined Leontul in his lab. They continued their work on his holograms, and Leontul was giving Derak lessons in biochemistry.

Back at the card table, Shesain pulled out a Thumarian deck and taught them the game of Antanob. It was like cribbage, and Jack took to it. Speech, not telepathy, was used here.

"That's not fair, Jack! You just learned the game, and you've already won three hands," Shesain playfully complained.

"You should see me in a game of poker," he bragged. "After two weeks, none of my senior officers want to play with me."

"Show me this poker game," Shesain demanded with a smile.

"Jack, if you show her, we'll lose the shirts off of our backs," Seamus warned.

"What's the matter, Seamus? Are you afraid the girls will beat you?" Shenar asked as she laughed with Shesain.

"Hah!" Seamus guffawed. "Let's show them how it's done, Jack. What are we going to bet? Not credits. How about something interesting?"

"What about time?" Shesain volunteered. "I'm having twins. Shenar will get at least three children out of Jack, and Tenara will have at least that many with you, Seamus. Babysitting time is the bet. We'll start with hours. The blue chips are hours, and the red ones will be days."

Jack started with five-card stud and moved into Texas hold-em. They played until Qex ordered them to get some sleep. Shesain came to bed counting her two-and-a-half days of babysitting IOUs.

"How did you do tonight?" Derak asked her as she slid next to him.

"Jack is hard to beat, and Seamus is better at poker than he is with bridge. Shenar will be very busy, and we owe Seamus eight hours and Jack three days of baby-sitting time."

"We! I wasn't sitting at the table," Derak retorted.

"I'm playing for the both of us, love," she said with a smile.

"Since when?"

"The day we got married. Don't fight it, you can't win," she teased.

79

"So, I can do the same to you, right?"

"No, it only works one way," she giggled.

The remaining two weeks went fast. The faster they learned, the more lessons Qex piled on them. He was determined to have them ready. One night after the evening meal they asked him about his serious determination.

"In Telaxian society, we take our assignments seriously. The consequences of failure can be severe."

"Is that all we are, an assignment?" Shenar asked.

"Yes, one of my more pleasant ones," Qex affirmed.

"How did we do?" Jack inquired.

"All of you are doing very well, far better than the elders expected. That will benefit you. There is still much to accomplish before we arrive in one week."

The last week went by in a blur. Qex pushed even harder. Leontul had to halt his research, and the card games stopped. They were all too worn out to do anything but sleep.

The last night before they arrived, Qex briefed them. *"Your last month of training has been to develop your mental toughness. You'll need it. The Prime Council will be hard on you. The Prime Mathematician will press you. Tomorrow, the navy will meet us at our borders. They will be curt, short, and rude; do not expect less. You are the first non-Telaxians to be allowed into our system in over 600 of your years, and the last two were the first ever allowed in. In your case, this is not an honor, control your impetuousness."* He looked at Shesain on that remark.

The following midday, the alarm sounded entry into real space. The IDMD disengaged with no side effects, and they faced four warships with their shields up and weapons armed.

It took all of Derak's control not to return the favor. *"Don't they know we were coming and the reason?"* Derak asked Qex.

"I said that you would receive a hostile encounter. Do not take it the wrong way if my attitude changes when they board. I would also recommend that you turn off your QDG. We are in Telaxian space; you must follow our rules now."

The com-unit warned of an incoming message. The holo-screen showed a scowling face with razor-sharp teeth. "Hu-mans and Tu-marians, prepare to be boarded."

"We are Thu-marians," Shesain shot back, not letting the dig go unchallenged.

"Matters not, you are not welcome."

She was about to say something else when Qex shot a quick thought her way. She shut her mouth and crossed her arms in indignation. The screen went black, and tractor beams pulled *The Shesain* next to the largest warship.

"Do not show outward anger to the boarding party or the council; it will not help," Qex warned them. A clang warned them that the boarding party was waiting outside the smooth hull. The iris opened, revealing a surprised group of military officers and two armed guards holding weapons at the ready.

"Live weapons aren't necessary, Qex," Derak transmitted.

Qex exchanged thoughts with the lead officer and the guards turned them off and holstered them. None of the guards were over five-feet-two. They had bald heads with flat faces and small eyes. The only hair they had was a chin beard, the greater the rank, the longer the beard was. They had a grayish complexion and wore short loose robes above their knees with undergarments leading down to heavy black boots.

"Who is the commander of this vessel?" the lead officer demanded.

"I am," Derak stated with authority.

His pupils showed surprise. *"You are telepathic?"*

"Yes, and the crew is as well. Mine is inherent in my DNA and the others through devices tied to the ship. We are operating on your general frequencies."

The officer's scowl didn't go away, but his pointed teeth disappeared behind thin lips. *"Captain, our orders are to escort you, this ship, and your crew to Telaxia Prime."* There was coldness in his delivery.

Derak responded. *"First, I'm a retired admiral and my present* station is the Alliance Ambassador to Thumar and the Pegasus sector. Second, we entered your space with our shields down and our formidable weapons not charged. We came of our own free will in peace."

His eyes narrowed to pinpoints, and he turned to Qex in a quick thought exchange. *"You are still the Captain of this vessel, but I will consider the weight of your other titles. Identify your crew by rank and title, starting from the most important."*

"Who is this f'ter?" Shesain asked Derak on their private channel.

"I don't know, but I'll find out."

"What is your title, rank, and name, so I can properly address you?" Derak asked him.

The officer grew indignant and had another thought exchange with Qex. *I am Commodore Xetackir, of the Telaxian Navy."*

"Shall I use your full name or the short version, Commodore?"

"The long version, Admiral. My orders are to deliver you and your crew to the Prime Council."

"Then perhaps you can start with not puncturing the hull of my ship with your hooks. Magnetic locks work just as well. A breached hull can mean death to its crew."

The commodore grew angry again. He and Qex exchanged thoughts for a long moment before he continued.

"Your crew, their names and ranks, Admiral."

"This is Captain Jack Morgan of the Alliance Navy, my first officer. Then we have my wife, Ambassador Shesain Andehar, of the ruling family on Thumar. Next, Seamus McGrew, a Terrestrial Engineer. Dr. Leontul Bundett, Thumar's leading Herbal Doctor and Surgeon, Shenar Andehar of the Andehar family, Shesain's sister and Captain Morgan's fiancé. Robert Jamar, my brother, and chairman of my three corporations."

"Our vessels will escort you. Try nothing or we will destroy you!"

"That won't be necessary Commodore. Our intentions are non-aggressive."

"Do not tell me how to perform my assignment, Admiral! That is our protocol for every non-Telaxian ship that enters our system.

*An armed guard will remain on board to insure your cooperation.
Do not change our course setting and close all viewing windows and
port holes!"* With that business finished, he turned on his heels and
returned to his ship, followed by two senior officers and an armed
guard.

The iris closed behind them; the guard handed Jack the
coordinates. He entered them, and the hull locks released. Then the
four Telaxian ships moved forward. Jack matched their speed.

"Their shields are still up with charged weapons," Jack reported.

"Just follow their course, Jack," Derak thought. *"Even with* 'The
Shesain's' *offensive weapons, we don't know our way home. They
removed the coordinates when we dropped into real space. They
don't know it, but Terga kept a copy. It's a high security feature that's
not in her main data banks."*

"Sneaky, Derak, but what if they find it on Telaxia?"

"They won't," he assured him. *"Terga's back-ups are well
shielded where no one would think to look."* They had sent the
thought transmissions on a private channel. Derak returned to general
thought frequency.

"What's next, Qex?" Shenar demanded. The Commodore's
treatment agitated her.

Qex let the stern tone pass. *"We spend the next six hours on our
present course, and then we'll be met by Telaxian fighters to escort
us to the naval base. Then you'll be put on a windowless transport
to a secure location while I arrive ahead of you to report. Only by
the orders of the Prime Council are you being treated with civility."*

"You call this civil treatment," Leontul piped up.

*"If you strayed into Telaxian space unannounced or uninvited,
you would end up forcibly confined for a brief period, sometimes
longer,"* Qex answered.

"That's no way to treat peaceful encounters," Shesain insisted.

*"If they determine that your ways are peaceful, then they escort
you out of our space with a stern warning to never return. If your
intentions are not, you do not want to know what happens next. We
as a race have held the universe together with our mathematical*

equations for eons upon eons. *If we were compromised, the universe would deteriorate into chaos. There are those in your galaxy trying to do just that, The Orion Syndicate. Their mark is a scorpion in a barbed circle, colored blood red. They are extremely dangerous and very smart, a bad combination."*

Jack and Derak looked at each other and turned to Qex.

"They're the ones who blew up an O-class star in the original timeline. The Terelian and Kek systems were wiped out. Thumar would have been, if it hadn't been for Derak and great science and support teams," Jack informed him.

Qex looked at Derak. *"What do you not do?"*

"Cook," Shesain said as they busted up laughing.

Qex didn't get the joke. *"I will have to look at your original timeline again. I am sure the council will want to look at this specific event. They will also require an oral report. For now, there is time to get some rest. You will be busy after we land. Telaxians sleep three hours a day; they might allow you four."*

They took his advice. Jack put *The Shesain* on autopilot and set the alarm to wake them. They all retired and tried to prepare for the next phase.

The alarm woke them, and they wore their best dress clothes. They noticed Telaxians wore little on their clothing to show rank and status; the crew followed suit to best represent themselves. Shesain and Shenar wore conservative dresses with ankle-length skirts. Jack and Derak wore uniforms with their naval rank. Derak's had, as it always would, the Medallion of the Kenmar braid on his left chest. Seamus, Robert, and Leontul sported smart-looking suits.

The short Telaxian guard was still at his post when they returned, engaged in a thought transfer with Qex. They broke off when the crew entered the bridge. Qex turned around to look at them. He approved of the women's choice of apparel.

Qex turned to inspect Robert, Seamus, and Leontul. *"That is proper attire under the circumstances. We will add rank and expertise."*

Then he turned to Jack and Derak, pointing out the gold-colored sleeve markings. *"Does that show your rank, Jack?"*

"Yes," Jack responded.

"You are young to have a top rank. You must have done well."

"Derak, what is the meaning of that?" He pointed out the Kenmar Medallion.

"The medallion goes along with a braid. It's called the Kenmar Braid and Medallion. It is the highest military honor in the known galaxy for bravery in action. It was presented to me by the President of the Galactic Senate. I am its first recipient."

"Show me the Braid," Qex requested.

Shesain gave Derak a knowing look and retrieved it, and showed it to Qex.

"Where does it go?" Qex asked.

Shesain installed the braid where it belonged, on his left shoulder and stepped out of the way.

Qex approved. *"Suitable, wear it. I think it will benefit you. We were aware of the Zertha Braid, but this is new to us. Does it tie in with your original timeline?"*

"Yes. My actions saved four systems and the Alliance contingent on Thumar at the time of the Magnetic Stellar Storm, MSS. All five systems wanted to get involved with an appropriate award, and this was it."

"We will have to inspect your original timeline," Qex commented.

"I told you so," Shesain shot a thought Derak's way on their private channel.

Qex picked up the exchange but couldn't hear it. *"You two have a unique channel. How is it you're not using Terga?"*

"All or most married and engaged couples on Thumar develop it. Derak can even touch my father's and uncle's thoughts without Terga." Shesain answered.

"All of you look presentable," Qex informed them all. *"I will now establish our personal frequency. This will be for advice to guide you through the proceedings. If you want to make the correct impression, follow my advice to the thought. I can be harder than what you've*

experienced. I advise that you do not push me to such action. Am I clear?"

"Yes," they all answered.

"Take your seats. We are picking up our fighter escort now. Jack, shut down the RMT. We will tow you in from here," Qex said.

Jack complied under the watchful eye of the guard.

"Derak, can you keep the others linked with Terga to keep their telepathy intact on the surface?"

"It's done, Qex," Terga said. *"They'll have a private channel, and you will have a link to cut in if required. I'm replicating the mesh bracelets now. They just have to press the blue spot visible only to the wearer of each individual bracelet. The mesh blends in with the skins texture and color."*

"I would consider it an honor if I could study your programming, Terga. If it is approved by Derak."

"It would honor me to share," Terga replied. *"I will allow it, only if you do not change my programming, I have built in contingencies for that,"* she answered him.

"I would not attempt such a thing, Terga. Derak, do I have your permission?" he asked Derak.

"Only if it's you alone and you follow Terga's terms."

"It will be so. You have the sworn honor of a Telaxian."

The entire conversation between all of them took place in less than a minute. Shenar retrieved the six mesh bracelets and handed them out. After they were put on, Qex confirmed that they worked.

The Shesain glided to an effortless stop inside a very secure hangar with no windows. The guard received his cue and motioned them to move out. He stopped in front of the smooth inner hull. The iris opened to reveal a ground car. It was boxy in design with separate front, middle, and back seating areas. Military guards escorted them with weapons. Derak cast an appraising glance as they escorted them.

"Do not underestimate our personnel, Derak." Qex cut in with the advice.

"That's the worst mistake to make in a military engagement," Derak responded.

A guard and driver stepped into the car's front section, and then they were ushered into the middle with three guards filing into the last car. Their doors closed, and the propulsion unit hummed to life.

Qex stood at the open gull wing door and held out an open metal box with six separate compartments. They looked at him.

"Your portable Dimensional Generators won't work here. You will receive them back when you leave, in perfect operating condition." Qex gestured to Derak first.

"Damn!" Derak thought to himself.

"You must learn how to shield your thoughts better, Derak. That will be your next lesson," Qex told him.

After handing them over to him, Qex shut their car door. They were in a windowless cabin as the ground car sped off.

"Qex, aren't we at least allowed to see the city?" Derak asked.

"No non-Telaxian has seen the city in over 600 years, and they were the first and only since our inception eons ago. Only the Prime Mathematician can grant that. I doubt she will in your case."

"Derak, what will happen now?" Jack asked on the private channel.

"I don't know, but I have a feeling that we will be kept on a tight leash, even after we leave Telaxian space."

The Prime Council:
Telaxian Time

They were dropped off inside a small windowless hanger and escorted to their rooms. The rooms were compact, and the showers and sinks were set to Telaxian height. There was a central dining and living room just as utilitarian as the other rooms. Shesain and Shenar complained about the tasteless food and the new, very conservative dresses delivered to them. They had to be sent back three times before they fit their figures. Seamus Leontul; and Robert received new jackets that showed their rank and status; these required refitting as well. It was apparent that Telaxians knew little, and cared less, about larger alien physiology.

The Shesain's crew was sequestered for three days before Qex rejoined them. As he forewarned them, they were allowed only four hours of sleep per night. The crew was tired when Qex returned. They assaulted him about the dresses and the tasteless food. The beds were small for Seamus' big frame. Qex's pupils shrank down to pinpoints, then they returned to normal.

"We are not used to accommodating aliens of your size and needs. Our technicians will see to the modifications. After the council reviewed all of your data, including a closer look at the original timeline, their stance has softened somewhat, enough to consider assisting you in this matter. They need to look into how bad the timeline disruption is. They instructed me to ask if there is anything you need from your ship."

"My cooking spices." Shesain wasted no time. *"Your palates are*

88

not accustomed to our tastes. Another thing, aren't there any female *indicators of rank? I am an Ambassador."*

Qex continued. *"I will set appointments to have female attendants* *adorn your fingernails. Both our men and women show their rank* *in this matter. Yours,"* he addressed Shesain, *"are much too short,* *so we will install extensions. The nails show societal rank, family* *status, marital status, and your husband's lineage. We do not allow* *necklaces. So, you must inform me why you and Shenar wear yours."*

Shesain said, *"in Thumarian society, when a man and woman are* *engaged or married, the woman wears a necklace with the husband's* *coat of arms. The man wears a broach like the one Derak and Jack* *are wearing. Shenar and Jack are engaged, so they are required to* *wear them at all times."*

"I will discuss this with the elders, we will consider the *circumstances,"* Qex commented.

"Thank you," Shesain and Shenar answered at the same time.

Leontul thought, *"Qex, I would like to continue my research on* *the Veredant Flower. It will take some time to isolate the mechanism* *that extends life. Since time is all we have now, I would like to make* *good use of it."*

"How about some computers with our lessons on them?" Jack asked.

"And the card games would help pass the time," Seamus said.

"Good luck, Seamus," Shesain kidded him on the private channel.

"Not at Texas hold-em," he shot back.

Laughter filled Shesain's thoughts.

"We will consider your requests. Shesain, we will escort you to *a full physical check-up to determine your health and how the time,* *space and dimension changes have affected your fetuses tomorrow.* *The procedure will take all morning. Your guide will arrive at 0500,* *be ready to leave."*

"My twins are not fetuses, Qex. They are my beautiful unborn *children."*

"Once again, my apologies Shesain, I speak in Telaxian vernacular."

"Apology accepted," Shesain thought with a smile.

"I must return with my report." He formed a small pointy tooth smile. *"It feels good to not to have to wear my teeth caps."* He turned and left.

After another tasteless lunch, seven Telaxian females, no taller than four foot eight, entered the room followed by two guards with weapons holstered. The Telaxians were dressed in light gray shapeless dresses, much like Shesain's and Shenar's. Their fingernails were short, and painted without status markings. They must have been young in their society. They also had no hair on their heads, like the men. The two guards' only hair was their chin beards, the longer the beard, the higher the rank and status. Two girls escorted Shesain and Shenar into an opposite corner of the room, while the remaining five approached the men with manicure kits. Seamus, Robert, Jack, and Leontul backed away.

"Go with it. If we're to get any help and be able to leave their space, we have to cooperate," Derak ordered.

"Nail polish is for women," Seamus bemoaned.

"Cooperate, that's an order!" Derak reemphasized his request.

They sat down. Shesain and Shenar were laughing at the entire affair.

Shesain received three-inch nail extensions before her attendant started painting them. She was in shock. How could she do anything with these monstrosities? Shenar had two-inch extensions.

Derak watched in horror as he received two-and-a-half-inch fingernail extensions. Leontul thought that was funny before having one-inch extensions attached to him. They all wore them now and watched while the women started painting the rank and status symbols in silence. When the Telaxian women were finished and had left the room, Derak and Shesain examined their very elaborate and intricate fingernails.

Jack's came in a close second, and the others were works of art in themselves. Shesain and Derak complained that trying to accomplish anything with them would be a real trial. Shenar sat back and admired hers, while the boys grumbled as they studied theirs with incredulity.

The door opened, and a male entered with two females. Their

nails were longer and carried beautiful interlacing patterns. The male's nails were equal to Jacks. He inspected all of them, followed by the women. They exchanged thoughts, and the women left.

"I am Zixunaxe, you may call me Zix. I am your cultural consultant for the time we allow you on Telaxia. Your guards shall be in plain clothes from this time forward. They are just as capable of preventing untoward actions on your part as your former escorts." Zix looked at Jack, Robert, Leontul, Seamus, and Derak and frowned. *"You lack chin hair and have full heads of hair. We will ask none of you to shave your heads, but all of you will be required to cover them with tight fitting hoods you can remove in private. The men must grow chin hair or have them installed for the rest of your visit. They will show age and societal privilege, as your nails do."*

"We'll take the temporary implants, we may not have the time to grow them out to the proper length," Derak answered him.

Zix thought to himself. *"That is logical. The women will arrive to perform this task and fit all of you with hoods. You will be granted access to your ship with an escort at all times. We will allow you to move it to this hangar. Admiral Jamar and Captain Morgan will be the only ones allowed to retrieve your ship."*

The same seven women returned with chin hair and seven hoods. The same five personal attendants sat the men down. When they finished, the five of them had chin beards at least three inches long. Derak's was six inches long and braided, adorned with metal that matched the colors of his Kenmar Braid.

Zix's two assistants reentered and inspected the implants. The hoods were fitted, and they exchanged thoughts with Zix and left with the other seven women.

"You may now be present in the company of other Telaxians— almost." He looked hard at Shesain and Shenar's breasts. *"Is there a way to reduce those abominations to our standards?"*

"We were born with them, and they can't just go away. We've submitted to your methods to reduce their size in appearance. Any further reduction causes discomfort to us," Shenar stated.

"We will work with this, considering your stay will be short.

Admiral, be ready to move to your ship on the hour. I will return with guards." Zix turned on his heels and left.

The girls couldn't stop laughing at the men. They looked in the mirror at themselves. Jack looked amused, Leontul would have pulled his beard off if Derak hadn't stopped him, Robert just shrugged his shoulders, and Seamus muttered to himself wishing for a stiff shot.

After viewing himself, Derak turned to the rest of them and evilly stroked his plaited beard with a dangerous look in his eyes. *"I feel like Emperor Ming the Merciless in the Flash Gordon series. It was an ancient mid-twentieth century Earth television program. He was the evil nemesis to the hero, Flash Gordon."*

"I remember reading something about that in an ancient Earth history class at the academy," Jack added.

"You all look ridiculous." Shesain said, and Shenar giggled.

"Look who's talking, the one with the three-inch claws," Derak joked back.

They inspected each other nails with Shenar and Jack's chaperones looking on with distaste. The men's nails were blunt and rounded and the women's were pointed. Shesain went over to a bowl with some pale fruit and stabbed one, giggling to herself as she raised it to her mouth. The door opened with Zix standing with two mean looking plain clothed guards. He walked over to Shesain and plucked the fruit off of her fingernail.

"They are not meant to eat with. They show your status and must remain pristine. You must show respect for our protocol, Ambassador." Zix scowled.

"My apologies Zix, it won't happen again. However, I have a question."

"What is it?" Zix responded.

"How can I wash my hair with these?" She waved her long nails in front of him. *"I'll scratch my head bloody on the first try."*

Two females entered and stood behind Zix. *"Hartakale will attend to the women's needs, hair and minimal make-up, and Pikurtinele will attend to the men. Address them as Hart and Pik. Jack's Chaperone will take care of his needs."*

"Zix, there's one more thing."

"What is it, Seamus?" He was getting exasperated by now.

"The men need to shave facial hair that grows daily."

He exchanged thoughts with Hart and Pik and then returned to the request. *"They will take care of that also, as we do not accept hair in our society. We have a method for permanent eradication if you choose."*

"No, thank you, Zix, we'll take the alternative," Seamus replied.

"Fine. Admiral, Captain, we will take you to your ship to transfer it to this location. We are aware of its full capabilities. You will be watched. We will allow no viewing of our city. Our coordinates will bring you in. We will transfer the rest of you to appropriate quarters. Hart and Pik will be present at all times, except for your private time that does not involve your hair. Do you all understand?" Zix demanded.

"Yes, we do," they answered in unison.

Hart and Pik smiled with a mouthful of pointed razor-sharp teeth. The crew returned the sentiment. Jack and Derak left with Zix, and everyone else packed up to move to the new residence down the hall.

The trip to *The Shesain* was a copy of the first journey to their old quarters. *The Shesain* looked unharmed from the outside. Zix walked them to the ship and wasn't surprised when the iris opened from the smooth hull.

"Impressive, Derak, you are centuries ahead of your time. I will meet you back at your building." He left, and the guards stayed with them.

They entered *The Shesain* and one of their escorts handed Jack the course. He entered the course setting, she lifted off and cruised at a low altitude.

"Terga, did they do anything to you?" Derak asked on their private channel.

"No. In fact, Qex has been gentle with his probing of my programming. He is the only one I allow, although he always has company. I believe he holds a top rank in Telaxian society. Where are we going to now?"

"To the building we're being held in. You'll be in the hangar, so we can have access to you," Derak informed her.

"My cameras were not shut off. I have vids from the time we entered the atmosphere. It's stored in the secure vault. Would you like to view them?" Terga asked.

"Not yet, the Telaxian's pick up on everything."

"What are you thinking to your ship, Alien?" The guard interrupted.

"I'm checking the programming. Making sure that it's as we left it." Derak answered in an even tone.

"Keep communications on the general channel, or else!" He stressed.

The Shesain set down in the hangar, and they exited the iris to see the fresh digs. It was only slightly larger than what they left. The only difference being that the necessities were the proper height, and they installed independent sinks for washing and shaving. Everyone else was having a good time with the chin hair and fingernails.

"I hate to ruin the party, but we don't know if they have eyes and ears here. We need to save the fun for later," Derak thought as he and Jack walked into the room.

"You're a spoilsport, Derak Andehar." Shesain said as she kissed him. Shenar embraced Jack as the chaperones looked on.

"We need to stick to telepathy. It's our only line for discreet communication. There's an ancient Earth saying: when in Rome, do as the Romans do."

"I bet the Romans never had chin beards and painted women's fingernails." Seamus griped.

"Cheer up, Seamus; I brought the cards, all of them. Why don't you play a few hands to take your mind off things? You will have to get used to our cheerful Telaxian company, I think it will be ok to speak at the card games, only." Derak thought.

Derak, Leontul, and Robert left for *The Shesain* while Shesain, Shenar, Jack, and Seamus settled down at the card table.

Leontul was happy when they entered *The Shesain*. Their escort stood off to the side in an attentive position. After the three holograms

94

materialized, Leontul, Robert, and Derak went into math mode. The sentinel showed great interest.

"What are you working on?" The guard suspiciously asked.

They were as surprised as he was when they answered him in Telaxian math language.

"This is medical research for our Thumarian population. Your council approved it. You can inquire of Qex on the matter." Leontul answered.

The guard turned back to his post, casting a wary eye their way every once in a while. After four hours, they returned to their quarters and noticed Qex and Zix coming down the hall. *"We've got company,"* Derak warned them on their private channel. When Qex and Zix entered, the table was cleared, and they were milling about. Derak handed Shesain her spices, she thanked him with a kiss.

Qex and Zix seemed satisfied after a brief inspection of the new looks. Zix brought two new dresses for Shesain and Shenar. They were tailored to their figures and were made from a matte black material. Deep frowns greeted their new dresses.

Qex briefed them. *"The material is comfortable to wear, and absorbs light, to not stress the fullness of your figures. We consider your breasts a distraction that keeps our males from fulfilling their duties. We deem them unnecessary for procreation of our species."*

The girls changed and returned for inspection.

"Very good, I believe you are ready to face the council. What we are doing with the appearance changes is to increase your chances of gaining our cooperation." Qex thought.

"Can we wear accessories with our new dresses?" Shesain asked.

"You may wear these belts that show your status. We are not accustomed to catering to alien needs. We take these actions only considering the reason you are here. Consider yourselves fortunate that you have received any concessions at all. Your audience with the council will start at 1600 tomorrow, after Shesain's physical. Be prepared to leave these quarters at 1530, sharp." Zix turned and left.

The next day, Shesain returned for a lunch spiced by Shenar. She groused about the doctor's icy touch. Lunch cheered her up a bit, and they got ready for the meeting with the Prime Council. At 1430 hours, attendants entered and gave their clothes final adjustments and touched up the nails and chin beards. Qex and Zix showed up at 1525 to give a final inspection. Then, a six-man escort picked *The Shesain's* crew up as they left the rooms.

They flew *The Shesain* to an unknown destination, blind, with all windows and portholes covered. The council ordered *her* there for an inspection.

Every building and hangar *The Shesain's* crew were allowed in was windowless. The color of the citizens tunics changed in this new building. They varied from light gray to a creamy white. The closer to white, the higher up the chain of command they were. The nails were longer and more intricate in their design, and chin beards were longer and more ornate.

They entered a large council room. Comfortable seats behind a creamy white table awaited them. They led them to their seats but instructed not to sit until the council and the Prime Mathematician ordered it. It was a well-lit room, open and airy. The council's desk was raised above floor level, with a white top. Both desks faced each other. The space between them granted greater visibility for 3-D hologram projections. Derak had the center seat and was flanked by Shesain and Jack. The others were seated according to their crew status. A huge gong sounded the entrance of the council, The Prime Mathematician followed, and signaled the start of the session by sitting the council and then the crew. No one smiled.

The Council President started the proceedings. *"Admiral Andehar, we called you and your crew before us to review the actions that caused this time paradox. We have studied the recordings and determined that those actions were accidental and you, as Commander, did your best to correct the mistake. After an extensive study of your original timeline, you visited your past to cure the plague of 1814. We agree with the conclusion of your artificial intelligence that the anomaly occurred between 1600 and 1605 p.m. the day you returned to your original timeline. It will require further review to isolate the specific event. Had any Telaxian made the same mistake, they would have incurred serious repercussions. Since you and your crew are uninitiated and untrained, those rules do not apply to you."*

"Ambassador Andehar, why did you initiate the time sequence when you were told not to? You should know that following orders is required on board any ship. Impulsive action is a dangerous emotion when discipline is needed."

Shesain responded, *"Mr. President and Council members, I accept full responsibility for my actions, and I'm deeply sorry about the time paradox we now face. My only defense is that I'm new to the experience of being a part of a ship's crew. Usually, I'm a passenger on board ships that shuttle me to my assignments. Captain Morgan reprimanded me after we set down in the year 1814."*

A female councilwoman continued. *"Ambassador Andehar, why did you wait to let it be known you were pregnant with twins?."*

Shesain continued, *"Council woman, I...I was going to wait until we finished our planetary survey to tell my family, but I had no idea that anything like this would happen."*

The councilwoman pressed on. *"You were smart enough to release this information when you did. However, this council and the Prime Mathematician do not appreciate being included or allowing you into our space. Your presence is causing us to redistribute our time and personnel to deal with an unexpected event that should have been avoided altogether. We do not take to surprise well."*

Councilman Pevutamet addressed Jack. *"Captain Morgan, how is it that Ambassador Andehar could initiate the time sequence under your command? Commanders should have better control of their subordinates and do not tell me you expected one warning to prevent this from happening with an untrained crew member."*

Jack answered them with composure, *"Councilman, Prime Council, and Prime Mathematician. As a command officer, I'm used to giving orders to subordinates who have gone through military training. Shesain Andehar's training is in the highest levels of social behavior, not military. She's not conditioned to taking orders without question. Her expertise lies in taking in information and coming out with an agreeable consensus. I believe that with this experience, she has learned to adapt to her position in a military scenario."*

"Have you, Ambassador?" Councilman Pevutamet addressed Shesain.

"I have, Councilman."

"Shenar Andehar, when did you discover that you were in the year 1814?"

"When I was going through the histories stored in the ship's computers. There was an odd entry inserted only as a footnote that caught my attention. After further research, I found enough evidence to verify. I showed it to Captain Morgan, and he confirmed the accuracy of the findings."

"Captain, does your present relationship with Shenar Andehar affect your agreement on these findings?" The councilman asked.

"No, your Honor, we were in a critical situation. Logic dictated my call."

"Then you and Admiral Andehar worked out the coordinates and timing for your return trip to the year 2414?" He pressed.

"To the best of our ability. It wasn't until the admiral downloaded a copy of Terga, his Artificial intelligence computer program, and all of Thumar's historical and scientific references to the ship from six-hundred years in the future."

The council looked surprised and conferred before continuing the interviews.

The council president addressed Derak. *"Admiral, how did you download your AI, and the required information from the future?"*

"It wasn't easy. I nearly lost my life on the first attempt. After resting for the night, I figured out what went wrong, and the second attempt was successful. I can bring up the solution on a holographic display."

"Do so."

Derak tapped into their holographic display, and the sphere appeared between them.

"How did you arrive at this solution?" The Council President asked.

"My mind went into a math mode that allowed me to think in nothing but equations. After linking with the ship's computer telepathically, I spent six hours constructing what you see, minus the corrections for the second attempt."

The council president changed to a hard tone. *"How did you address this math mode? We have no indication of anyone outside of Telaxia achieving this."*

"It just happened. I suppose it has something to do with my four-strand-DNA structure. It is a product of my lineage that traces back to a twenty-first-century DNA project on Earth, where I was born and raised."

They conferred again, this time with the Prime Mathematician. *"How did this manifest itself in a mundane populace, Admiral?"*

"I grew up on the mean streets of New York City. The only thing that saved me from myself was Master Li, who took me in when I was six years old. He taught me how to channel my anger and nurture my intellect."

If Telaxians could express shock, they seemed to have knowledge of Master Li.

The council moved on to Dr. Bundett. The Council President proceeded. *"Dr. Bundett, by what apparatus did you come by your plague cure?"*

"The ship's living hull allowed me to replicate the required lab equipment to go along with the information Shenar and I dug up from the files," Leontul stated.

"What is this living hull technology?" the Council President asked him after leveling a hard look in Derak's direction.

Leontul shrugged. *"As far as I can understand it, organic self-replicating nano-bots are mixed with exotic metals. The ship can heal itself quickly, inside, and out. We downloaded replicator technology with Terga. Once she assisted me with her data base and enlarging my workspace, I could complete my work, with help from Shenar."*

"Master Builder McGrew, what were your contributions to this mission?"

Seamus wriggled in his chair. *"I provided the physical support and acquisitions that was needed to complete the mission. I also was the point man for a population of stranded time travelers from Earth's future."*

"What was their importance in this timeline?"

"They were a key component in Thumar's timely development of industry and technology."

"That completes this inquiry. We will send further instructions through Zix." They were escorted back to their quarters the same way they had arrived.

The Orion Syndicate: Modified Timeline

Commander Thompson stood, sweating profusely, in front of the scorpion emblem. He had come back from an extended intelligence gathering mission, returning with considerable information, but was it enough to please the Supreme Council? Usually not: they perceived perfect reports with fault.

Councilman Number Five, Dr. Vander, addressed him. "Is this the best you can bring after the time we allowed you? We expected better from you, Commander. Your reputation is in danger of being demoted to acceptable. How can this Jamar character just disappear from existence, along with a crew of five?"

"I don't know, Councilman. We tracked him to Altair and then he fell off the celestial charts. He saw the CEO of his companies and then returned to the security hanger with him and his chief technology officer, Petemar Vorshock. Supposedly, he's a time, space, and dimension expert."

"What is he seeing him for?" Number Five spat out. "I know this Jamar is up to something. We can't afford to allow another Thumarian incident. The Prime Mathematician doesn't accept failure, and neither do we, Commander!"

Commander Thompson continued. "We located the head technician from the security hanger and wrung him dry. Jamar's brother, Robert, is running his three companies. He's as smart and crafty as his brother. Not only does he have doctorate degrees in physics and bio-chemistry, he also has one in galactic business, and an undergraduate degree in galactic law."

"Now we have two Jamar's to worry about. What else did you find?"

"Derak Jamar landed one of his latest ship designs and cleared out the hangar of all personnel. The tech said that the ship looked very sleek and modern, unlike anything he'd seen before. He also said that the Altarian didn't look like one. My guess is that he's an agent. We didn't get a picture of him."

Councilman Number Two interrupted. "What happened to the tech?"

"He and his family met an unfortunate accident, after we had fun with his wife and daughter. You should have heard him threaten us before we cut his tongue out and raped the women in front of him. Then we cut him and let him bleed out."

"At least you haven't lost your touch on completing your jobs. You left no traces?"

"Like we never existed."

"I hope so, for your sake," Number Two insinuated.

Number One's impatience grew. "Your incompetence knows no bounds, Commander! You wouldn't want your sister to fall to the same fate your wife did, now would you? I expect more from your next report."

Commander Thompson's anger churned. His healthy wife had died from premature childbirth while he was on his last mission. He knew who was responsible, but he couldn't do anything about it, yet. "Perhaps if the doctors knew what they were doing, they wouldn't have died," the commander spit back.

"Don't criticize our doctors, Commander! They do what their told to, as you will now. You're leaving for another mission. Don't screw this one up! Now leave us to fix the issues left by your shortcomings!" Number One shouted.

The commander left in a huff and swore to himself that they would get what they deserved. One day they would pay for his wife and child's death. In his imaginings of vengeance, the councilmen's deaths would be excruciatingly slow!

Back in the council chamber, sparks flew. Number One was taking his wrath out on the other council members.

"Why do we keep sending out incompetent personnel on missions that require professionals? I can have you all replaced! Where is your dedication to spread peace and stability to the known galaxy? Must your families suffer to get your cooperation?"

He turned to his assistant, "Tell April to send Zenar to my palace; I have some anger to burn off." He stormed off, leaving the other eight to ponder their fates.

Number Five left and met Commander Thompson in a secret location. "Commander, are the arraignments made?"

"Yes, Sir, but know that you're not the only one gunning for Number One. Number Seven and Nine are working together. They are determined, but their plans are not as far along as ours. Do you have the names of those responsible for my family's death?"

"Don't get ahead of yourself, Commander," Number Five replied. "You'll get the names when Number One is dead. Which poison did you decide on, and how will it be delivered?"

"Pheteberal, it targets all weaknesses in the body and causes a natural death, very painful. Number One is primed for our plan by his own predictable behavior. He called for Zenar, as expected."

"How's she going to deliver it? You know she'll be examined before she's allowed to enter," Number Five said.

"She'll deliver the poison vaginally. He always likes to finish the job with his little willy. It'll be a shame to lose Zenar, but her sister can fill her spot in April's. Once he's infected, they should both be dead in ten minutes."

"They'll wash her vagina out before she's allowed in," Number Five commented.

"The poison is activated by the PH of his semen release. You can't clean that out," Commander Thompson confirmed.

"Let's hope it works, Commander. If it does, you'll make Captain and be able to have a new family, safe from retribution. Perhaps I can get Zenar's sister for your pleasure. When I become Number Two, you'll report to me."

"I won't be satisfied until everyone involved, including their families, suffer before they die," Commander Thompson said through gritted teeth.

"You'll get your chance soon enough. Wait ten minutes before you leave. If you get caught, and it comes back to me, you'll suffer one hundred years before you die."

"Yes, Sir." After Number Five left, he hatched up a new plan to eliminate the entire council, including Number Five!

•—◆—•

A terrified Zenar waited for her painful cleansing to start from Number One's sadistic doctor. She would take great satisfaction in ending Number One's life in a painful fashion. She had no regret that she would sacrifice her own life. Her extra snake arms added to the attraction. She would squeeze him even harder when the poison took effect, after she cut out his tongue. Years of torture would end. All she had to do was survive the foreplay.

The doctor approached her with a wicked grin on his face. "I see you re-grew your snake arms. Number One promises not to cut them off tonight. He's missed the tight squeezes they give him. Now strip, whore!"

She stripped, showing off her long shapely figure, and her extra six snake arms. The doctor licked his lips as he slowly checked out the firmness of her body. His hands stroked her overly long from head to toe. Then he made her wrap him up with her snake arms to test her squeeze factor. She complied, cracking three of his ribs. He grinned and inserted the painful probe, hard. She cried out in pain as he laughed. He forced the probe to its limits, nursing his cracked ribs. The wash caused her much pain, and she expressed it to prevent more. When he finished, he cleared her and smiled, expecting his next session.

They ushered her into a waiting Number One. She would use all of her tools to ensure he felt the greatest pleasure before the poison kicked in. His metal-tipped whip cracked as it wrapped around her waist with the metal digging into her sides. She squealed in pain as he pulled tighter. When he brought her close enough, he backhanded her face, hard. "That's for cracking my doctor's ribs. If he didn't enjoy it, I would have broken your jaw. Why would you do that to someone who treats you with such great care? We only want what's best for you. Now mount the bull!" She did, face down as he started an hour of torture that left her back bleeding. Then he turned her on her back and slammed her hard against the bed.

He slapped her again. "That's for getting my sheets bloody." He forced his entry and waited to get wrapped up by her snake arms. She wrapped him from neck to toe, pinning his arms against his side so he couldn't use them. Then she contracted her arms, so he couldn't move a muscle. He screamed in delight as he released. The poison reacted.

She had something to do before his last breath and hers. Her regular arms went into action. One retrieved the short knife, and the other pulled his tongue out of his mouth. His eyes grew large before the knife removed his tongue. The pain spread fast in both of their bodies. He tried to squirm out of her tight hold but couldn't. His struggles made her snake arms contract even more. If the poison didn't kill him, her crushing squeeze would have. Ten minutes later, they both lay dead, entombed together in her contracted snake arms. When they were discovered, both were in rigor mortis, and wrapped so tightly, that they had to be disposed of together.

• ◆ •

Regret was never expressed about the death of Number One. They removed his family from his palace and placed in far less luxurious quarters. The senate called for an emergency session to replace him. He had been the most hated leader in the last two centuries. Number Two and Number Five played their bribe cards to secure their promotions. The other council members played theirs to keep them on the council. Number Two moved up to Number One and Number Five moved up to Number Two. The others, including the newly appointed Number Nine, started plotting their future moves to the top. The average life span of the Number One position was five years.

Number Two entered his new mansion rooms on *The Mandible* accompanied by captain Thompson. "That was a job well done, Captain," Number Two said. "Your abilities are best used here. Your first assignment is to remove Number One, again."

"That will be tougher," the captain said. "He doesn't have the vices that allowed the last removal. He will be on guard for any attempt. It might be best to give him some time to relax a little."

"That's sound advice, Captain. I'm sure you can figure out a plan," Number Two commented.

"Number Four and Number Five have your head on their block and Number Nine is already planning to off Number Seven. You know the usual machinations behind the throne," the captain added.

"They say it's lonely at the top. That's why I have you. Your job is to watch my back and do my bidding. Call April and have her send me her best Venerian. Make sure she has suction cups on her auxiliary arms and that she knows how to use them. That's all for now, try not to enjoy Zenusha too much, you're still on call, you are dismissed."

Telaxian Time Fix:
Telaxian Time

The day had gone well despite Shesain's intrusive physical. It would not be the last, as the Telaxians would continue to monitor her through birth. Derak and Shesain's children would be very different after going through time, space, and dimensional changes they would experience in the womb.

Qex entered by himself. *"You did well during the meeting. You gave them much to consider before our course of action is set. They will review your ship's logs, and memory banks. You will all go through private interviews tomorrow. Shesain will undergo more procedures to determine how the twins are affected by multi-dimensional changes."*

"They tested about everything they can." Shesain commented.

"We will monitor you until you give birth." Qex replied.

"Jack, You will be instructed further in our language skills."

"Shenar, you have superior research skills. You will meet with our Chief Librarian to begin your training."

"Seamus, your planetary terraforming expertise will be expanded upon."

"Leontul, curing the plague of 1814 has impressed our advanced medical staff. Your bio-chemistry knowledge will be added to our existing database."

"Robert, your corporate management skills will help execute the secondary aspects of the upcoming mission."

"That I can do without math."

"You will complete your math course work."

Robert frowned and crossed his arms.

"Derak, you will meet with the Prime Mathematician and her senior staff to discuss the equations behind the sphere you used to bring Terga and her data base back six hundred years."

"Qex, how did we 'accidentally' go back in time to the moment we were needed? In all of my technical experience, I've never had an accident that seemed so exact," Derak inquired.

"We programmed your computer to send you back to where you entered. What caused this problem was that you entered the time causality loop one day early."

"Who programmed the ship, Qex? Who on the Mt. Kumar crew pulled this off?" Derak asked him.

"I can't say. We have agents spread across the galaxy. We even had one in the Orion Syndicate, before he turned. Now, we feel he is running the Syndicate."

After Qex left, the table was cleared and everyone but Derak, Robert, and Leontul gathered for another round of cards. It didn't take long before the usual raucous competitiveness returned. Leontul, Robert, and Derak returned to *The Shesain* to continue Leontul's research.

The next morning, the others met their escorts and were led off to their interviews, leaving Derak waiting for Qex and Zix. The door opened, revealing Qex, Zix, and a female named Velumtebar, Vel. Qex introduced her as Shesain's full-time nurse. She would monitor the health of Shesain and the developing twins. That meant that she would accompany them on the upcoming mission.

"Vel will situate herself while we are gone. We do not want to keep the Prime Mathematician waiting," Qex thought.

Derak continued the conversation with Qex on the way to the meeting. *"Qex, how many agents are there in Thumarian space?"*

"Not as many as we have in Alliance space. The political situation is much more volatile there. The Orion Syndicate has many of their own agents well placed. Our operatives are the only thing keeping their government stable. The Vice President is in the Syndicate's

pocket, along with certain key congressman and senators. That is all I can say. Your presence has made our job somewhat easier, which makes you a prime target for assassination. You must ensure the continuance of your technology in case they succeed." Qex answered.

"That's a comforting thought," Derak shot back. *"I have prepared for that day. I'm building a stellar-class cruiser, 'The Aries,' a home away from home, with a complete manufacturing complex. She's the size of a medium-class moon. Should the situation get too unstable in the galaxy, I can move all my operations from my satellite locations to the ship."*

Zix turned to Robert. *"What stage is it in? If my agents are correct, you might need it soon."*

"The Aries would make a suitable location to base our operations. Would you consider the possibility?" Qex asked.

"As long as Robert and I don't have to beg for information. I would have to know everything you do on board that pertains to the ship's operations."

Qex and Zix thought for a long moment. *"We will consider the proposal on those grounds."* Zix answered.

"It's my ship, and you need a mobile base to operate from. I'm sure we can come to agreeable terms. However, your strict timeline equations will apply to your operations only; they will not dictate mine. The Aries still needs to be completed, and your agents can help us keep its location secret. That gives us time to come up with an accord. The Syndicate must not find out about either endeavor."

"That can be arranged. I'll see to it myself," Zix said, disappearing down the next hallway.

"We are here now. They will require you to construct your time download sphere for us to study. Perhaps the theory can add to our time correction calculations, if our Head Mathematicians deem it so." Qex said as they stopped in front of the door.

Qex inspected his hood, morning shave, and fingernail extensions. After approving, they entered the room. The Prime Mathematician was addressing five Senior Mathematicians in front of a holographic generator. This one allowed for a display to fill up the large room. She turned and faced Derak with a stern look.

"Admiral, you will use our equipment under close supervision. Do not deviate from our protocol. We will study your time model. Dr. Cilenture will supervise your time on the machine. We have safeguards in place in case you should wander. Do not take this privilege lightly."

"Qex, how do I address her?"

"You're honorable Valuk-Manou." Qex responded.

"Your honorable Valuk-Manou, I consider it a great honor to be granted permission to have access to your holo-generator. I accept your conditions."

Her scowl almost disappeared as she directed Derak to the interface. Two modified indentations waited for his palms to make contact.

Dr. Cilenture took his place besides Derak. *"Hu-man, I will ensure your complicity and protect your brain from any overload that could occur. My duty is to assist you and to protect our own interests."*

"I understand, Doctor. I'm ready to start." Derak placed his palms on the contact points, and his mind switched into math mode. He could feel the neurons in his entire body changing their frequency to match it. Once his entire being synchronized with the holo-generator, he contacted Terga, and the sphere popped into existence out of thin air. It was fifteen feet in diameter and glowed a luminescent blue, showing the correct mathematical sequences. Complex equations flowed along the numerous pathways at speeds Terga could not generate. They were merging at uncountable intersections, mixing with each other, and then continuing up or down different routes.

Equations and combinations moved through his mind at blinding speed. Derak comprehended the entirety of it all, from the most complex junction down to singular components. Certain isolated junctures caught his attention, and he found out his mind could slow these down so he could accomplish further study.

Derak lost all recognition of the seven Telaxians in the room until Dr. Cilenture touched his mind with a terse reminder that he was there beside him.

"Do not stray too far off the mark, Hu-man."

The others locked their minds onto the sphere in front of them, their eyes studying its structure.

"A very elegant solution, Admiral. Your mind is far more complex than we expected. I detect that it could go much further with the proper discipline and training. You embody the true potential of a First Generation. In time, you could master our language. That might be helpful in our dealings with your galaxy," the Valuk-Manou complimented Derak.

Derak sensed his extra DNA strands combining with contact to the Telaxian technology. When his fourth strand kicked in, the sphere changed into a five-dimensional model of the universe. Dr. Cilenture was about to stop it, when the Valuk-Manou restrained him.

The universal model formed with the same mathematical precision. This time, nodes formed with the connecting speedways until the entire foundation of the universe stood before them. It almost filled the entire room. Derak understood every mathematical sequence. He could stay there forever. The high adrenalin rush was intoxicating. Then, the entire structure flashed in and out of existence twice before settling into a beautiful, complex model. It showed every fabric of the space, time, and dimension interconnecting with each other in the fifth dimension, represented in a three-dimensional schematic. The colors differed from his original sphere. Derak looked at it for a long time before he noticed an egregious anomaly, and his mind zoomed in on that section.

"That's where the Milky Way Galaxy is. Notice the red equations surrounding the outer rim where Thumar is located." Dr. Cilenture intervened into his thought pattern in Telaxian language, Derak understood every word. *"The bright red intersection marks the origin of the time paradox."*

"Then the smaller orange and red sections must mark the time wave emanating from the core. They're moving fast, will this grow bigger?" Derak inquired.

"Let us study this, Admiral," the Valuk-Manou answered.

Seven Telaxians, including Qex, walked to the point of concern through the hologram and started a private thought conversation. They locked Derak out, so he studied the rest of the display until they returned.

The Valuk-Manou addressed Derak, in the Telaxian language, which was mathematical equations of the purest degree. Not even the highest levels of three-dimensional mathematics could begin to approach its complexity. He understood everything.

"The implications are very disturbing, Admiral. The disruption wave is spreading; it will speed up to the point of no return. Then the entire space-time fabric of the universe will be destroyed. We must move your mission up to match this revelation. Your model will allow us to chart your course to prevent this from happening. You have mastered null space, so, as you say, time is on your side. However, in real time, you will have one year of your time or less to correct the situation. Qex will contact you when the mission plan has been completed."

She turned away to join the others in the hologram, and Qex escorted Derak back to his rooms. Once Derak left, he missed the beautiful, elegant math-based language.

Everyone seemed in excellent moods. Shesain was having a thought transfer with her new nurse. They were smiling and laughed at a funny thought. Jack was glued to a monitor, studying his daily lesson. Seamus and Shenar were sharing something humorous, and Leontul was sequestered in *The Shesain*. All thoughts stopped when he entered. They all looked at him.

Shesain was the first to ask, *"How did it go with you, my Chimera?"*

"Well enough on the social side, considering we're dealing with Telaxians. The results of the findings are disturbing, far more dangerous, and complex than we suspected. We have a lot of work ahead of us," Derak answered.

"Dangerous? how so?" Seamus asked.

"I'll wait to brief you after dinner."

Leontul came into the room with a wide grin on his face, followed by Robert. *"The Telaxians are geniuses. They gave me a good tip, and I think I now have the answer to how the Veradant Flower extends life expectancy."* Leontul noticed the energy in the room. *"Did I miss something?"*

"Let's have some dinner. I'll tell you everything afterwards," Derak said.

Dinner was exceptional. They were brought meat, and even Shesain enjoyed the change of pace. They finished it with a tasty red merlot from Rhemar's vineyards and settled down. Shesain curled up next to Derak on the couch, and the others dragged chairs over to make a circle.

He started the conversation verbally. They could not afford to lose using their voices because telepathy was easier. "The time rift is bigger than I thought. I brought up my time download sphere, and it turned into a three-dimensional model of the fifth-dimensional universe. It showed the smallest detail, down to the origination point of the time rift. Bottom line, the rift is tearing apart the time-space fabric around it."

"Speak in terms that we can understand, Derak," Shenar piped up.

"Sorry about that. I was in the pure mathematical thought process. Think of a spider web with all of its interconnections. The strength of the web relies on every one of these joints to maintain their integrity. You break one and the intersections closest to the break come apart. For every joint that breaks, it affects two or three next to it. Eventually, that one break causes the rest of the web to come apart."

Shesain sat speechless at the revelation.

"Like the molecular structure of the body," Leontul added.

"Correct. At the rate that the time wave is traveling, the time, space, and dimensional structure of the universe will come apart," Derak informed them.

Silence filled the room as they absorbed the gravity of the situation.

"The Valuk-Manou, the Prime Mathematician, and her Senior Mathematicians are working on the solution as we speak. When they have the mission parameters finished, we will leave. It's fixable, but we don't know how, yet. Qex will let us know when they're ready."

Shesain went quiet.

Derak turned to her. "My Chimera, are you ok?"

She shook her head in disbelief. "I...I caused all of this. What are the Telaxians going to do to me?"

Derak held her and kissed her forehead. "No one's playing the blame game, my Chimera. We can't. We have a monumental problem to fix."

"That's an understatement," Leontul added.

Derak looked at him before he continued. "I feel that we will have to undo our own mistake. There is no time to feel down, we have to be on top of our game from here on out."

"So, no one's mad at me?" Shesain asked.

"No, my Chimera, no one's mad at you. I suggest that we get some rest while we can. I suspect our days will get very busy, in short order," Derak said.

The next day they spent talking about what they might expect of them.

Five days later, Qex appeared at 0600. The crew had somewhat adjusted to the light sleep schedule and were already up. Shesain and Shenar had not worn their breast reducers, and one look from Qex reminded them to put them on. The army of attendants entered to freshen up their fingernails and to insure the men's hairlessness before the day started. The attendants left, and Qex stayed behind.

"We have reports you have been using verbal communication," Qex inquired.

"We mustn't forget how to exercise our vocal chords, Qex. We'll need them for our assignments," Derak countered.

"You have a point. However, do not disrespect the elders with it. We have a meeting with the Valuk-Manou and her Senior Mathematicians in one hour. The proper clothing will arrive. Your mission is laid out, and they will brief you on the preparations."

The usual escort of plain-clothes military guards escorted them to *The Shesain*. The windowless flight was brief, and they quickly ushered them into another building. When they entered the room, they provided seats for them, but the Telaxians remained standing.

Dr. Cilenture started the briefing, *"Hu-mans, we have concluded our deliberations and completed your mission."*

"Dr. Cilenture, only Derak, Robert, Seamus and Jack are humans. Four of us are Thumarian's," Shesain clarified.

The doctor frowned, *"Hu-mans and Tu-marians."*

"Correct pronunciation is Humans and Thu-mar-ians." Shesain insisted.

"Hu-mans and Thumarians," he continued. *"You will depart our space in seven days' time. Qextenar will have command of the mission. We have briefed him on the details, and strict timelines required to complete the tasks. He will fill you in on a need to know basis. For knowledge requirements, you will receive upgraded optical training, both here and during your ship time. This information is required to complete your mission. This device will speed up your learning processes. It is an optical scanner.*

"We will upgrade your ship under the Admiral's supervision. You will jump from node to node. A copy of the Admiral's universe map will be made accessible. Nodal co-ordinates will be downloaded into the AI for your specific section or quadrant only. We have increased the IDMD's output by twenty-seven percent."

The doctor stepped back and let the Valuk-Manou continue the briefing. *"You will be required to agree to keep all knowledge of us to yourselves: that we exist, and our space. Should any of you break this agreement for any reason, we have ways of dealing with you. It is of the utmost importance that we remain a myth in your histories. I am sure the Admiral and the Captain can appreciate our secretive existence.*

"Each of you will undergo six days of optical training and rest on the seventh day. Admiral Jamar will supervise the re-fitting of his ship while receiving his. Velumtebar will accompany Shesain, to monitor her pregnancy, and your quasi-dimensional generator will be upgraded to allow for the extra room that will be required for your mission."

Jack, Robert, and Derak were not pleased with the lack of information and kept their thoughts to themselves until they got Qex by himself.

They rested the remainder of the day following the Valuk-Manou's advice. They had removed the first learning stations when they returned. Leontul, Robert, and Derak continued Leontul's research on board *The Shesain before* the refitting started. Leontul showed Derak his latest discoveries on the holographic models. He had made substantial progress in the past few days. Qex had been of great help in showing him a new method to forward his work. Half of it Derak did not understand. Leontul was the master of bio-chemistry and started showing Derak the recent revelations. He just started gaining a grasp on the material when they were escorted back to their quarters.

Telaxian crews started filling the hanger with technical equipment as they were leaving." *Terga, are you ready for your upgrades?"* Derak asked her.

"I'm excited, Derak. Qex will supervise the improvements with you. He and I get along very well because he respects my capabilities. He feels the same about you and your ability to bring me into existence."

"Terga, are you self-aware?" Derak asked her.

"I have been for years. And I should tell you that in my way, I love you. Not in the same manner Shesain does. Before we arrived on Thumar, you were the only organic life form I knew. You were my family before Shesain and Jack. This mission has brought me close to the entire crew, and Qex has become like a long-lost brother. He has a high regard for me and has prevented any unwanted intrusions into my programming. He is extremely high in the Telaxian social structure as well and is related to the Valuk-Manou."

"How do feel about me?" He asked her.

"I would die for you, Derak. Qex has informed me about certain Telaxian beliefs. You seem to fit the model in them. That is why you have access to the Valuk-Manou and her Senior Council. Consider it an honor that you and the crew have received civil treatment."

"The military doesn't seem to share the same sentiment," Derak commented.

"They are harder nuts to crack, but there is some grudging respect in their ranks. You will be subject to three hours of sleep from this point forward," Terga added.

"Thanks for the warning, Terga. Be sure all of Leontul's work is in the back-up files."

"It is already in progress."

Derak returned to his living space in time for another tasty meal and the news of the day. The next morning, complaints abounded about losing an hour of sleep. It took a few more cups of java to wake the crew. They accepted the reality that they would have the same schedule until they left Telaxian space.

Qex entered with the schedules and another surprise. The Telaxians researched Derak's pineal gland implant and informed the rest of the crew that they would receive them before leaving. They would have to have the same ability to access thought control outside of Terga's influence. Seamus complained about having his brain upgraded. He felt it was just fine the way it was. Qex told him they required it for the optical training they would receive. He went along with it. Robert looked forward to the experience.

After everyone left for their procedures, Derak approached Qex. *"What aren't you telling me?"*

"Operational data but, what I am about to tell you, you cannot repeat. If you do, a painful reminder will follow. You will correct five to seven individual time occurrences in the modified timeline. For this to work, all of you will have to learn additional skill sets."

"What skill sets?"

"Advanced telepathy, telekinesis, and teleportation. You will not teleport across the universe, but it will require your new skills for planetary operations. All of you will need to perfect 'mind sight', the ability to see your destination before teleporting to it. Otherwise, you could end up becoming part of a solid surface. All of you will be the first and last to learn our methods. Our practices are sacred. Mission failure would cause the destruction of the entire known

universe. We would have to start over from the beginning. Failure is not an option."

Derak asked. *"Do you have a backup plan; in case something goes wrong?"*

"We do, you are not entitled to this information. We have a strict timeline to complete our preparations. The implants are ready."

Derak bristled at this revelation. He did not like to go onto any mission without knowing all the intel. He would find out more later from Terga.

The procedure to complete the brain implants was painless, and the results were illuminating, even for Seamus. The complicated brain surgery required the greatest skill. After one hour of recovery, optical training started.

Seamus, Jack, Shenar, Shesain, Robert, and Leontul were led to individual rooms. They were plush by Telaxian standards, but sparse by any other. At least the chairs were comfortable, with high backs and cushions that held their heads in a stationary position. Once seated, the chairs inflated to hold the occupant in place. A head piece with an optical device covered the right eye. The body received a minor jolt as the lessons streamed in. It was a painful process, but the discomfort subsided once they were into the lesson.

Re-fitting *The Shesain* went smoothly; the Telaxian crews communicated and followed Qex's orders. Derak opened access panels to the control systems, the RMT, and the IDMD space drives, and the Telaxians went to work.

Derak started his optical training, and Terga assured him that Qex would guard the work. Once he got past the initial pain of the optical connection, mathematical formulas filled his brain at light speed. He viewed life differently. None of the crew were the same after the lessons began.

Derak spent almost as many hours on the modifications as he spent with his optical device. After they finished the flight controls, Jack joined him to get to know the new systems. Robert inspected the library systems. For six days this went on. Six hours on optics followed by six hours on practical application. They rested on the seventh day.

Terga seemed to enjoy the ships re-fit. She told Derak that she felt like she was getting a continuous mental massage. She was on the same schedule as the crew, giving her time to adjust to the changes in her programming.

The Shesain's crew had one more meeting with the Valuk-Manou and her Senior Council. They stressed the importance of following their time schedule, down to the second. They were employed by the Telaxians and would be required to follow their rules. The Valuk-Manou assured them they could return to their normal sleep patterns once they left Telaxian space.

The crew started packing up for the trip while Derak closed up the access panels on *The Shesain*. He and Qex were the only ones who knew all the upgrades. Jack was briefed on the flight controls and drive modifications. Communication had to be seamless between *The Shesain* and the planetary operatives.

Before they allowed the crew to leave Telaxia, the same seven attendants that applied their Telaxian rank indicators removed them. Seamus was the most relieved. He almost celebrated out loud when the last of the nails were removed. Only Shesain and Shenar kept their freshly painted nails in a special box that opened by their DNA.

Velumtebar, Vel, joined them in their quarters on the last morning in Telaxian space. She was packed, and Zix accompanied her into the room. Qex, Jack and Derak performed pre-flight checks and joined the rest of the crew after they finished.

Zix briefed them before lifting off. *"Your presence has given us an unwelcome diversion from the normal routine, we will not miss the interruption. You are an interesting species and might offer collaboration in the future. We will have to study the implications. Travel safe and complete your mission, for your sakes."*

As he left, Telaxian crews gathered all the bags, and plainclothes security escorted them to *The Shesain,* one last time. The bags were stowed, and the guards stood at the iris until it closed. Qex handed Derak back their personal D-gen units.

Jack started the RMT and lifted off. Once they were airborne, a fighter escort saw them to a stable orbit of Telaxia with blacked-out view ports. They received clearance to depart, and the same destroyer group escorted them up to the edge of Telaxian space.

Their view screen illuminated with the image of the same severe looking Commodore, looking at them through narrowed pupils. *"Thu-marians and Hu-mans, do not reenter our space, you will be destroyed. Upon completion of your assignments, will you be allowed in again, maybe. You have five of your minutes to leave, starting now!"* His image disappeared and his battle group moved into formation with shields up and weapons charged.

Jack and Derak exchanged a look before they lay in the course. The IDMD was engaged at the soonest moment. In a blink of an eye, they were in a node and all of them relaxed. The women wasted no time changing out of Telaxian clothing into their own. Qex frowned as they emerged in comfortable conservative Thumarian dresses.

"Jack, start the quasi-dimensional generator, and lay in our new course," Derak ordered. The inside of the ship increased by six times, Vel was taken aback until Shesain showed her to her rooms. After everyone got settled in, Shesain came out with her father's 05 vintage that she had stowed away, and poured some for everyone, including Qex. They raised their glasses and toasted to a successful mission. Then, Jack engaged the IDMD, and they started node hopping to their first assignment.

Telepathy 101: Null Space

Node hopping was a much quicker way to travel the universe. It turned a month-long trip into a one-week excursion. The crew never got back to their old sleeping habits. The weeks in Telaxian space with only four hours of sleep set a pattern hard to break. Qex took advantage of this and relegated the crew to five hours a day.

Life onboard *The Shesain* developed into a steady schedule of optical lessons, followed by practical exercises. With the transplants, everyone displayed natural abilities at different levels. Jack seemed to have one of the most flexible ESP abilities.

Robert had the communications and intelligence department running efficiently. Shesain and Shenar would be his chief investigators. Exact timelines, entry and exit points would be required for optimal success.

Qex was feeding them operational information. This was because they needed to be in specific timelines to extract information that could only be gathered from planetary expeditions.

Jack and Derak worked with Qex and Terga on the ship's new abilities. Math mode for their brains was easy when they were engulfed by the energy field surrounding it. However, training their conscious minds proved tougher than expected.

Qex suggested that Terga worked with them to speed up the process.

Vel, Shesain, and Shenar became close in the following weeks. Vel kept a close eye on Shesain and the developing twins. Shesain's hours would be controlled on real time missions.

Leontul was discovering the link between the Veredant plant and the Nano-bots. The Nano-bots supercharged the plant's change in every cellular structure in the body.

Seamus would be a top-notch planetary engineer when they finished restoring the timeline. Shesain and Shenar worked through their information technology course.

Qex and Terga were developing an unusual relationship. Terga had grown self-aware years before, and Qex spent a lot of time linked with her.

Qex gave them time to set their routines before the telepathy lessons started. They would have to perfect this before the first missions started.

The crew settled into a node to start the lessons. First, Seamus, Leontul, and Robert had to develop their abilities without Terga's help. Another aspect was getting used to going into strange heads, which would prove interesting. Not only from the point of not being detected but to also deal with uncontrolled and sometimes chaotic thought patterns.

All of this Derak understood from over a decade of communicating with Terga by thought and his time with Shesain. The others would have to catch up.

The next morning, the crew started. Qex would supervise. Vel assisted. *"I will give each of you your beginning exercises. We will stay in null space until you have completed your required instruction. Time is on our side, I will use it,"* Qex informed them.

Seamus butted in. *"Why do I need to know this? We're not on Telaxia anymore and when we've finished, we will return to a time that doesn't practice this openly."*

"You, as a terrestrial engineer, will be required to access complex machine language to determine the timeline capabilities and improvements. To do this, you must learn advanced mental abilities, along with Telaxian mathematics. This is not a request. It is an order!"

Seamus's eyes got hard, and he pursed his lips in grudging acceptance.

Qex sent a rebuttal shot back, just for his thoughts alone. *"Now, let us continue."*

Robert sounded off his thoughts. *"In my experience, where we're going has no quantitative science backing up its existence."*

"That is something you will work out for yourself, Robert. You cannot deny the empirical evidence in front of you. That other scientists deny its existence cannot sway your acceptance." Qex responded.

"I'll do my best," Robert grumbled.

Leontul interjected his thoughts. *"I'm concerned about having my private thoughts put out to the universe. I have memories I don't want anyone to know about, both personal and professional."*

Qex thought. *"Part of your training includes methods to keep those thoughts private. However, mistakes will be made, and thoughts will escape during the process, for everyone. A pact will bound all of us to respect such thoughts as private."*

"It still makes me uncomfortable," Leontul answered.

"All of you will feel discomfort at many levels. Vel and I will be here to move you through them. All of you will complete your course, you have no choice. Since you have experience in mind speak, we will start with learning how to block unwanted thought intrusions and setting up private channels with certain individuals and groups.

"You will pair off. Derak, you will be with Seamus. Shesain, Leontul will partner with you. Robert, Shenar shall be yours, and Vel will join minds with Jack. I will broadcast instructions and monitoring your progress. We will switch to new partners until we have shared minds with everybody, room arrangement 1A."

The great room changed into four booths without tables. The teams picked their booths and waited for Qex to start. Instructions started flowing into their thoughts. Robert almost got up and walked out. He was put back in his seat by Qex. *"Now, select a private thought with a strong emotional attachment and mark it. Hold it apart from what we call social thoughts. Make a room or file cabinet and place it there."*

Derak's was easy: the Chambar Valley Offensive. Concentration was showing everyone's face. When Qex sensed they did this, he instructed them to protect this thought while sharing a separate public thought. After sequestering their thoughts, they spent an hour with their first partner, grumbling and shifting in their seats. This was repeated with every partner until a successful interchange ensued. Derak found keeping secrets more difficult with Shesain, as they had shared his thoughts for over a year.

Qex entered their thoughts. *"That will be enough for today. Your assignments will be to exercise with a different partner five times a day for the next three days. You will now proceed to your optical training. This will increase your understanding of our mathematical language. We will require it for future lessons. Mathematical language skills will speed up your progress."*

They continued the exercises with different partners, finding that practice helped. Seamus and Robert were the most reticent to engage. It took a few looks from Qex to get them going. Leontul was willing but guarded in his efforts. However, he was loosening up a bit. Telepathy was the order of the days ahead.

The next two days passed as they settled into the exercises. Seamus was getting adept at telepathy and warming up to it.

The fourth day, they all received a humbling lesson. They sat down, waiting for Qex to start. He instructed them to concentrate on their safe information. In one second, he violated their spaces and broke into everyone's information lockboxes all at once. It shocked them. Seamus cried out in dismay.

"I didn't even try hard," Qex thought. *"Your next lesson is to keep it locked up. Even if you had mastered advanced techniques, I could have broken your codes. Derak is the only one I had to work at. I sensed a powerful emotion attached to his memory. Emotion is the key to keeping information in the proper place. Your next exercise is to crack your partner's code. This will serve two purposes; one, to strengthen your own resolve to keep your secrets hidden, and two to allow you to gather information when needed. Telepathy is the foundation of everything else you will learn."*

"That's preposterous!" Leontul complained. *"Isn't it enough we have to hide sensitive information in our own minds?"*

"If I would have known I signed up for this..." Seamus added.

"Is there no end to this?" Shenar cut in.

Before anybody else could complain, Qex sent out a mental rebuke that shut everyone up. *"You already hid sensitive information in your minds before your training. After you learn to block out intrusions, you will learn to access other minds. There will be times during your planetary assignments that will require such a skill. It will require a deft, subtle touch that leaves no trace. Information is the key component we need to gather to fix your mess. You will have to use such measures. Start the exercise, now!"*

Mental complaints would have continued had Qex not reinforced his order with another rebuke. Seamus growled to himself, while Robert and Leontul mumbled out loud. Even Shesain's forceful personality didn't do any good.

The initial forced intrusions were weak from unwilling minds until Qex put some fear in them. Derak intruded on most other sequestered information, and Seamus came in a close second; he had a powerful mind. Leontul almost left the room in anger before a thought from Qex stopped him.

Foul moods followed into the next round of optical training. Qex was an excellent drill sergeant. There were few smiles and brief conversation for three days until the next morning's session. They had all been successful in reading guarded thoughts. This had a two-fold effect. First, their minds grew stronger, second, they had all prevented intrusions from each other's mind probes.

Qex smiled for the first time since they left Telaxian space. He even had his teeth capped. *"You all did very well. The next lesson will be to gain mind strength and distance. Once mastered, you will detect and read minds at any distance, even from across a planet. Choose your partners and go to opposite ends of the ship. You will start by connecting with that mind. Then you will continue with your intrusions. This time, place a neutral memory into a secondary lock box.*

"Your first memory depository will keep your innermost private thoughts. Intrusions will only be allowed into the secondary repository. You will follow the same rules that applied to the previous lesson. Once you have completed three days of exercise, I will test your strength again. I will be just as forceful."

Shesain turned her exercises into a game of cat and mouse. The others caught on and you could hear whoops of celebration during the days that followed. Seamus's abilities were developing at a scary rate, so much so that Qex spent private time with him, along with Derak. Untrained powerful minds could be dangerous if left alone. Their broadcast range could affect any situation. Jack's mind was proving to be the most flexible.

Shesain and Shenar's minds had a gentle touch. Vel was working with them. Their weakness was a tendency to wander and not stay on the subject at hand.

Seamus and Derak had more trouble mastering the subtle side of this art form. Qex was teaching them how to turn down their power when they had to. Jack didn't have their power range, but he could navigate changing power levels better than any of them. He possessed a knack for knowing what it required for any situation.

They cruised through the next three days in lighter moods. Even Robert was smiling at his victories. Leontul was grumbling less and less. Seamus was seeing the advantages of his newfound abilities. They all took in a good night's sleep before the upcoming test.

The crew steeled themselves for Qex's strength test. They sat down with their partners and waited for Qex to enter. Their thoughts were invaded before the door opened. Qex got through their secondary vaults and it didn't take much more for him to unlock their primary thoughts. Groans of disappointment filled the air. However, he was having more trouble getting into Derak's primary vault. The harder Qex pressed, the more Derak pushed back. He got to where his defensive tactics started turning offensive. Then Qex cracked Derak's barrier and pulled out.

"You did better, not by much. You need to attach the strength of your primary thought vaults to your secondary thoughts. The rest of

you are to practice before you return to your lessons. Leave me and Vel alone with Derak."

They left the room wondering, like Derak, what Qex wanted with him. Derak didn't have to wait long to find out. Qex and Vel approached him in a booth, sandwiching him between them.

"Derak, I must know what your memories are that emit such a powerful resistance. We might have to work on your offensive weapons. Usually, they take longer to manifest, but yours must be contained before an incident occurs. The elders are correct in their evaluation of your abilities. What are you holding back? I must know its entirety."

"It's not a pretty sight," he answered.

"I have seen much in my time among mortals," Qex assured him.

"It won't be easy, I'll fight it."

"I expect that. Vel will hold your mind and keep your offensive mechanisms from firing. She will also calm you during the most trying points of the recall. Prepare yourself for my entry."

Derak did his best and was surprised at the gentleness of Qex's presence. He couldn't stop him if he wanted to. He felt Vel wrapping her mind around his. Qex broke through his vault, and his defenses rose to the occasion. The strength of it surprised both of them. When this didn't fend off the assault, the offensive side came to life. Vel's mind closed in tighter, preventing it from manifesting itself, and opened the door wider to Derak's Chambar Valley Offensive memories. Qex started from the beginning and played it like a tele-vid program without commercials.

It felt like Derak was encompassed by the experience all over again. His emotions sprang up at every turn. He saw himself firing his multi-phase pistols and leading his squad through the streets of the village. Then he experienced the emotions of expelling the stubborn villagers. As the offensive escalated, his reactions became stronger. Vel had to clamp down on his mind. His energy field pulsed when a woman was eviscerated, and a Kek warrior removed and consumed her unborn child. Derak felt Qex's presence enter to contain the energy spike; he kept it there until the end. His eyes registered shock for a Telaxian when Derak's light swords came out. Both of them extended their control to his body, as Derak mimicked his battlefield movements when he entered the sea of Keks. Qex's eyes narrowed to a pinpoint when Derak started taking the Keks out en masse. His head snapped back a little when Derak quartered the Commander in less than a second. He wasted no time in sealing the breach.

Vel stroked his trembling mind and energy field. Qex held his body until he regained control of it. Vel still comforted his mind for a few more minutes. When she let go, Derak broke down and buried his head into her shoulder and wept. When Derak raised his head, Qex handed him a napkin to wipe his eyes. Afterwards, his body was still shaking as Vel embraced him, her wet eyes conveying a sense of understanding. Derak composed himself and looked into Qex's eyes. He couldn't read all of his emotions, but sensed compassion in his gaze.

"Was it necessary to kill the woman? I sensed that she was pregnant," Qex asked.

"She was, I couldn't control my actions; I was in full berserker mode. It wasn't until I saw her dead body that I temporarily gained enough control to locate the rest of my squad, and then I led them back into the thick of battle again."

"That is how your four strands work?" Qex inquired.

"Only when the fourth strand kicks in; the other three are for strength, dexterity and intelligence."

"Where did you get the light swords?" Qex asked.

"I built them, and Terga after Dr. Frank Thorsen mentored me. I also developed the pineal gland implants under his tutoring."

"The Dr. Frank Thorsen? We have known of him for centuries. Where is he now?" Qex's inquiry grew more intense.

"Dead. during my tutelage, he developed a sudden fast acting cancer."

"He was a brilliant man, one of our imbedded agents. Between Master Li and Dr. Thorsen, you have been prepared by two of our best. Dr. Li belonged to the Syndicate, in the twenty-first century, on Earth, before they became what they are today. He helped develop

your DNA strands. We will approach your training differently. I will teach you to reign in your offensive abilities. They are too strong to be left alone. I apologize for any discomfort you experienced, I did not know of the severity, or strength, of that memory."

"Thank you for your support, both of you. I couldn't have gotten through it by myself. That incident changed my perspective on life." Derak said.

"Your self-healing capabilities are intriguing. That might require closer investigation. Continue with the others on the exercises and speak nothing of this to anyone else, except Shesain."

They had spent over an hour in conference, and Derak left the room to a barrage of questions from the crew. He deflected all inquiries, except Shesain's.

They practiced their exercises in between the optical sessions. Their math language abilities were approaching conversational stage. This pleased Qex.

The next lesson was to retrieve a thought without being detected by the other mind. The steps would be like the previous exercises. They were to place a thought in their secondary mind vault and try to protect it, while their partner would have to retrieve it without being detected. It was a game of telepathic hide and seek. They were all looking forward to it. Qex allowed them to make a game of it. He sensed their progress would be faster.

They spent five days on the next step. Vel made up the eighth person in the group to even out the pairing. The first attempts were an utter failure. Even though they thought they had succeeded.

Qex shook his head and continued his mentoring. *"The reason you could read the thoughts without detection was that no one tried. You must set up an early warning mechanism that picks up thought patterns that are not your own. To discern alien frequencies is the foundation. We will start again. This time, identify the intrusive energy pattern. You will not attempt to block it, just learn how to identify the individual signatures of everyone else's minds. You must recognize each individual's presence."*

They spent the rest of the day discovering the markers that told them who was making contact. This required subtle use of their minds. The concentration required was greater than picking up larger fluctuations in personal fields. Jack proved to be the best at this. He had a strong but delicately controlled mind. The second round proved more successful. They could recognize individuals penetrating their thoughts.

Once they could achieve base results, multiple mind interventions were introduced into the mix.

Qex gave another strength test. Most of them received an average grade, and Jack excelled. He possessed the best control of all of them. His prowess impressed Qex and Vel, which was no minor accomplishment.

The next challenge was to develop skills in learning an unknown language telepathically. This would enable them to mix in with terrestrial cultures. The learning curve on this one would be steep. It required the combination of all the past lessons. Gaining the full command of a foreign syntax would prove challenging for all of them.

Moving down to the planet, they would be in D-gen mode while they learned the native language from the target village. They would discover other hurdles to overcome during the first foray into a public arena.

Qex gave them two days of rest before he briefed them on the first-time fix and allow them to descend to Thumar in the year 1917. He promised them it would be one of their easiest assignments.

Shesk Ball: 1917

The time crew was excited to set their feet on solid ground again. They had either been on board *The Shesain* or locked indoors on Telaxia for months. It would feel good to be in the open air. They had no idea what would await them on Thumar.

They were allowed to speak again. Qex knew their vocal chords needed exercising for the upcoming missions. Qex would brief them on the details of the mission. Instructions would come in mind speak. While the seven of them were on the planet's surface, he and Vel would monitor their progress.

They gathered in the great room for the briefing. Qex started by warning them about crowd chatter. *"Crowd thoughts can deafen you when it's encountered the first time. I can only give a small sample of what to expect. It is something you have to experience to overcome. Vel and I will monitor you and assist in your initial contact. Terga will assist you in telepathic translation skills since they are not developed yet. There are also secondary benefits to your telepathic abilities. You will be able to communicate with animals and alter their behavior. We will instruct you in these methods later."*

"How will we be able to filter out the noise?" Jack asked.

Qex continued. *"You will concentrate with the nine individuals on board this ship first. This will introduce you to the methods you will learn to function in crowds. We will start by opening the mind up to a general frequency. Then you will concentrate on a singular thought pattern you already know. After that, you will open your minds to receive multiple thoughts and distinguish the differences*

between them. Once you have accomplished this, you will reduce the
madness that comes with this territory. Let us begin."

The confusion that followed was enough to drive anyone crazy. The initial response was to shut down. Qex wasn't surprised. They started again and Qex, with Vel and Terga's help, kept their channels open. Instructions arrived like a light in a dark room. Each of the crew choose a familiar mind to latch onto, this seemed to help quiet the chatter in their thoughts. It was still there but took on a minor role. After a half hour of practice, they could reduce it to an inaudible hum.

The next step was to practice sending thoughts to each other with the background noise. This proved more difficult, as every once in a while, thoughts would drift in from the periphery and disrupt their attempts. Qex instructed them to continue until they could formulate a full conversation while he increased the noise level. After half a day, they had performed at a low volume. Qex sent them back to optical training. The assignment for the next day was to reach an acceptable success.

They punctuated the regular classroom schedule with mind exercises. Qex set the hours and maintained the crowd noise level of the previous day. By that evening, they had made significant progress. Qex cranked the volume up to three quarters strength. It got quite confusing, to where Qex and Vel had to step in to assist. It took them one more day to adjust. The real fun started when they had to operate at full crowd noise-level. Three days later, Qex deemed them ready to beam down to the planet and assume D-gen mode for the first public exercise. They would be given the full parameters of the first mission after they completed mind training.

Portuma was the target village on the Lelayan continental plains. Farming was their principal form of commerce. There was a vestige of industry in the scablands bordering the fields. Metal and glass technology had not only survived from the original Earth colonists from 1814, they thrived.

The crew would beam down to the outskirts of the village and park themselves in D-gen to practice crowd chatter control. Terga locked on to their signatures and they found themselves in a beautiful glen, surrounded by large old-growth deciduous trees. They switched their D-gen generators on and made their way to the village's outskirts. They smelled the sweet air of Thumar and enjoyed the magnificent surrounding landscape. The celebration was short lived, after Qex sent a mental reminder.

They found the spot where they could observe village activity and connect to their minds. Terga beamed down seven chairs, and they sat down and waited to start. Qex and Vel put a comfort blanket around their minds before they opened them up to the villagers. The blanket dropped as they brought the village mind up to one quarter volume. It flooded their minds with a deafening noise that drove them back into their chairs. Half of them grabbed their heads to lessen the effects. Robert, Seamus, and Leontul were kept in their chairs by Qex. He quieted the crowd noise down to tolerable levels and pushed them to practice what they had learned on *The Shesain*.

Crowd chatter is like listening to multiple conversations at once, on a grand scale. Confusion reigned supreme, and it was impossible to keep track of multiple thought patterns overlapping each other. Stronger thoughts overpowered weaker ones. Derak could see where madness could overcome the untrained receiver. If not for the previous training and protection from Qex and Vel, they could not have withstood one minute, let alone an hour of continuous chaos.

Two hours was all that they could stand before they beamed back, after turning off the D-gen units. The matter transfer technology still needed improvements. It would be a giant step forward to beam down in D-gen. Derak wanted to discuss this with Qex.

The next day, the time crew lasted four hours with the crowd noise turned up to one quarter. This was the most arduous part of the telepathic training. Not only did they have to handle the combined crowd strength, it also required them to increase their individual energy fields. If they didn't have Qex and Vel to dampen the crowd noise, they couldn't have completed this portion of the instruction.

Three days later, they lasted five hours and could pick out individual minds. Telepathic training required them to use up a good portion of real time. When they reached the point to where they could maintain their mental integrity, they made a slight time jump backwards to gain back the lost days. They satisfied Qex that they were ready.

Qex gathered them into the great room and briefed them on the first-time fix. *"Your first assignment is to establish the precursor to the sport you call Barquete in your original timeline. In this timeline, they call it Bashk Ball. Jack and Derak will learn this game and then introduce improvements. Their present rules use a small oblong ball and a single circular goal. I do not know the rules of the game. Jack and Derak will have to learn them and challenge the establishment. You will change the goal setup to three, one center and two side circles, on six-foot stands. The smaller ones will be worth five points and the center one will be worth two points. The ball size will shrink and become round. This is where pitchers and batters will be introduced. No goalie is needed; they will rename it Sheshk Ball. You have an interesting goal to reach, no pun intended. It might require an evening or two of sharing a few rounds in the local pub.*

"Derak will be Vortan Turbul, and Jack's name will be Villumn Shatnar. Your cover will be that of gem prospectors. You originate from the Corano Islands and you have been wandering the continent for the last five years, seeking your fortune. We will synthesize acceptable examples of rubies, sapphires, and diamonds, small enough to catch their attention, but not big enough to get you into trouble. They can also secure food and housing. You will have three days to complete your mission. Shesain and Shenar have researched the records for the compatible clothing, and Terga will assist in the language translation. Are there questions?"

Shenar spoke. *"They might want to have a few days' growth on their beards. Clean-shaven faces won't fit their cover story. I know Jack can get an irritating carpet of stubble in three days. It looks like Derak can match that."*

"We will give it five days," Qex said. *"This will give all of you extra time to polish your crowd skills and improve your potential to isolate a singular mind and hold it."*

The next five days proved interesting. Singling out strong

individual minds posed no problems. Shesain locked onto a male mind, thinking about a woman's body in lurid detail. She could not evacuate fast enough. Derak zeroed in on a male who exemplified an intelligent, quick mind, not negative, judgmental on specific happenings. He sensed his physical appearance, five-foot eight-inches tall and fit. The occasional thought of the upcoming Bashk Ball game crossed his mind. He marked him for the upcoming mission.

"Back out Derak, I have not taught you psychometrics, yet. He is feeling your presence, and you're confusing his mind," Qex interrupted his reverie.

He backed out and kept searching out minds. Jack zeroed in on a thought transmitting plans for an improved fixed wing design for an airplane. Qex sent him a similar thought when he lingered too long. Robert, Leontul, and Shenar were skipping around too much and got a mental reminder to settle down. Seamus was concentrating on any thought that dealt with mineral deposits.

The biggest challenge over the five days was to pick the weak minds out of the crowd. This would prove difficult, as they got lost in the rumble of the general noise. Qex showed them a trick to help them along. By the time their beards had grown long enough, they could find the weaker minds. Clothing, gemstones, and currency were made, and they coordinated with Terga on the language. It was like the dialect spoken in 1814, although some words and phrasing had changed. They were instructed on the correct Corano Island accent and diction. The women tired of receiving scratchy kisses and wanted the mission to be over.

They made another backwards time jump when Qex gave them the go ahead. It could have taken two years to prepare, and it wouldn't have mattered. They would not have grown a day older, and the real time of their destination wouldn't have changed. Qex gave a final briefing.

The next morning, Jack and Derak beamed down one mile from the village. The Bashk Ball field was located, and they moved towards it at a leisurely pace. They arrived in their scruffy-looking clothes and backpacks and mixed into the crowd. Once they placed themselves on the sidelines, Jack scanned the team for the captain. It was a balmy day, and they were getting warm in their long sleeve shirts. They pulled them off, revealing their physiques, and their presence didn't escape the team captains either.

Derak read his thoughts before he approached them with a grin on his face. *"I could win if these two could catch on to the game."* His thought preceded him. Jack and Derak had played Barquete and studied Bashk Ball before they beamed down.

"You two interested in having a little fun? We have two spots available if you do. I'm the team captain. Your muscle could help us out in the second half. My name is Herculean."

Derak grinned. "Sure, why not? My name is Vortan, and my partner is Villumn. We're gem hunters, and we heard that this part of the continent has some sweet spots."

"We have a few, but most have mined out. I know an excellent guide if you need some help. Meanwhile, if you're interested in playing, I can cue you up on the rules."

Jack looked at Derak and exchanged a knowing smile. "We'd love to. All work and no play make for a dull day. Let's see if we can help you win."

"Great, follow me. This is a friendly game we came up with to keep the competition civil," Herkulean told them.

"Does it work?" Derak asked.

"Most of the time. There's still the occasional brawl in the pubs." He looked them over and suggested that they shed more clothing. "You'll burn up in all those layers. Do you have any shorts? The short-sleeve shirts will work."

They changed in a tent and emerged.

Instructions followed. "We have one circular goal at each end of the field protected by a goalkeeper with a bat. This is the ball we use. The smaller members of the team are runners, and the bulkier players are blockers." He made this statement, referring to Derak's bulk. "The purpose of the game is to score as many five-point goals as possible. A lesk determines who controls the ball. Bumping and checks are allowed. The last line of defense is these small flags we wear on our waists. They're small and slippery, and it takes great dexterity to hold on to them. It's a fast game and requires longevity to last a half. Do you have the gist of the game?" he asked them.

"I think we do," Jack answered him. "When do we start?"

"In a few minutes. I'll introduce you to your teammates." Every one of the eight men he introduced them to had Thumarian names except one named Charlie.

"Where did you get a name like Charlie?" Derak asked him.

"My father moved here from the Anean continent. My grandfather was one of the original settlers from Earth."

"Who were your grandparents?" Jack asked him.

"Peter Robinson and Susan Anderson. They built a large industrial complex that is still around today."

Jack and Derak exchanged a look before answering him. "I hear he helped to cure the plague of 1814," Derak said.

"How d'you know about that? That's almost a forgotten incident now."

"There are still rumors that abound in the bigger cities. It's a shame such a vital part of history is being forgotten. We found the reference in an arcane section of a library." He answered.

"My grandfather told me of two strangers he met before he got involved. He said they came out of nowhere, helped set everything up, and disappeared."

"Did he say anything else about them?" Jack asked.

"No," he stopped there. "I've always felt there was more to the story, but I could never get it out of him. Grandmother was just as silent on the issue. Peter died in 1867, and Susan passed three years later. They lived long prosperous lives."

"Enough of catching up, we have a game to play," Herkulean interrupted them. "Vortan, you're a blocker, Villumn can be a passer. Watch us and follow our examples."

The second half started with a bang. After the lesk, it was on fast and furious. The checks, blocks, and bumps bordered on near tackles; the teams played rough and hard. Derak and Jack caught on but held back for appearance's sake. Derak received his first bump that knocked him out of bounds, tumbling into a group of excited women. They helped him up, and he noted more than one alluring smile. Derak returned the smile and jumped back into the thick of things. The game moved fast, and Jack scored the tying goal. Their team won. After exchanging pleasantries with the rest of the team in the middle of the field, they accepted wet towels on the sideline to clean up a bit.

They joined their new teammates on the short walk back to the village. It was much larger than the original estimation. They were told that over three thousand souls made up Portuma proper. Half lived in town and the remaining population on farms. On the way to the village, they passed a new factory under construction, and asked about it.

Charlie piped up. "That's mine. My old shop is too small to meet the growing demand for my product."

"What do you make?" Jack asked him.

"I manufacture wings and engines for the new flying machines. I needed a larger building for our new design. My brother is on his way over from Anea to help with the motors."

"I'd like to look at these wings, if you don't mind." Jack asked him.

"Sure, I can take you there now. We can join the rest of the team afterwards."

Derak followed the gang to the pub while Jack split off with Charlie.

Portuma was a prosperous village by the looks of it. It had wide clean streets with open shops. Friendly crowds mingled outside, discussing the day's events and the next week's business. The men made their way to a sizeable building with a good-sized pub on the ground floor. They entered to a raucous celebration after the weekly game of Bashk Ball.

"Herkulean, bring the new guy over. He gave Partin one mean block out of bounds. The first round is on us."

"This will not cover your bet, Avutar. Where's the rest of the crew?" Herkulean asked.

"They're on their way. They had to cover home base; you know.

The women are coming. You're popular, Vortan, you and your partner. Where is he?" Avutar inquired.

"He'll join us. Charlie's showing him the new factory." Derak responded.

"Charlie and his flying machines. I could think of better things to spend your time on. Who's going to fly them anyway?" he asked.

"I'll bet they're faster than any land transportation," Derak added.

"You might have a point there, stranger, but I doubt it'll catch on. Just like that motorized wheeled thing he drives around. You can always depend on the Renbar and Kinitar."

"What if you could double or triple your crops with his inventions?" Derak asked.

"Never thought of it that way. The big problem is making the smelly stuff to put in its tank. Same thing goes for his flying machines," another man added.

"Maybe one of you can solve that problem. Think of the etag you could make, especially if either of them caught on."

"Might be something to consider. Here's your ale, Vortan, best in the district. Watch out, it's put the best of us down." Herkulean handed Derak the mug.

The ale was a full-bodied stout with plenty of kick. He'd have to watch his consumption. Loose lips would not serve well here, and Qex would have his head if he slipped in a drunken stupor. "That has punch to it, I'll have another."

"What do you do for a living, Vortan?" a red-headed farmer asked.

"Villumn and I are gem prospectors. We worked out our last claim and are looking for a fresh one."

"How d'you do? Are you rich yet?" he asked.

"No. We have good days, sometimes, did fair-to-midlin the last round. We got a little more than we needed to work on a new vein." Derak picked up a thought two tables away.

"Sounds like we hit the jackpot, Tsuris, Let's wait till him and his partner have had too much of the stuff and roll-em." Derak picked it up as he whispered it.

"They don't look easy to take, specially the big one."

"Yeah, you're right, Shara and Nafka can get to know them better and put em out for the night."

"I'll fetch em while you monitor the big one."

"Don't take all day this time."

As his partner was walking out, Derak sent the conversation to Jack as he walked in with Charlie. *"Identify the one walking out and the one at the table, Jack."*

"I've got them. They look rather unsavory. Both of them have rotten teeth."

"Watch out for the ale, it's strong. We can't lose our senses," he thought.

"Thanks for the warning."

"Charlie, wha'd the new guy think of your inventions?"

"He liked them. He might even have some improvements. Where's our round? Can't keep him away from the medicine all day."

Another round for the table arrived, and they all toasted Bashk Ball. Then the conversation turned to the details of the day's contest, to how fast Jack and Derak took to the game.

"We play a similar game, called Sheshk Ball, which is more challenging than yours." Derak said.

"Beshkebar!" a large farmer blurted out and slammed his mug down on the table. "We have the best team."

"What's so different about yours that makes it better?" another jumped in. The whole table joined in and pressed them to answer.

Meanwhile, the robber two tables over paid closer attention to them.

"Let's reel them in Jack, we'll get both tables at once."

"This should be fun, just like the old days." Jack smiled.

A crowd had gathered around the table as the spirited conversation continued. "I didn't say it was better, I said it was more challenging." The air was getting testy, and Derak had to bring it down. Some friendly faces were becoming irritated.

He pulled out his etags and ordered roast pork and vegetables, and another round to assuage almost everyone's temper. Between bites and gulps of ale to wash the food down, the arguments continued on a friendlier basis. The red-headed farmer was still pressing the issue. "If your game of Sheshk is so great, tell us how it's played."

"I'd like to hear this." Another man said.

Then half of the pub chimed in to hear about Sheshk ball. *"It's been a while since we had a place this worked up. I'll take a few more bites and see how much rowdier it can get."* Derak smiled as he contacted Jack.

"You're wicked, Derak. This is way too much fun," Jack sent a thought back.

"Don't press your luck!" Qex interrupted both of their thoughts.

They both grinned at each other before Derak refilled his plate and mug.

"C'mon, Vortan! You are on the spot, so deliver." Almost the whole pub had gathered around them and demanded an explanation.

Shara and Nafka entered with Tsuris's partner, and they were hot. Derak understood why they could get away with their robberies. The women were tall, beautiful, and shapely by any standard. They made their way through the crowd and wormed their way to Derak and Jack's sides. Their perfume was on the heavy side, and their make-up followed suit. The lack of clothing caused a stir.

"Don't go deaf on us, Vortan. C'mon, give it up!" another chided Derak.

He waited until it hit a fever pitch. Jack was having trouble keeping a straight face, and Dreck had joined the fray, keeping a close eye on him and the table.

"Sheshk is played on a bigger field; however, yours will do. There are three circular goals instead of one, one larger circle, with two smaller ones on each side. The smaller ones are worth five points each and the center ring counts as two points. There is no need for a goalkeeper as we raise the rings six feet off the ground."

"No goalkeeper! What kind of game is this?" one of the crowd shouted with supportive cheers behind him.

"Let me finish!" Derak demanded. "Teams of twelve are split into six batters and six pitchers. Checks, bumps, and blocking are encouraged." A loud cheer filled the room. "Only the pitchers touch the ball. They pitch a smaller round ball to the batters, who pound it through the rings. The batters block for the pitchers and visa versa."

"That's not so difficult, batting a ball through a ring," someone cried out.

"Try doing it on the run, while you're trying to avoid a hard check," Derak countered. "The pitches are fast and come at unexpected times, sometimes when you aren't ready." A moment of silence followed. "We play the game hard and fast, and you're always on the run."

"I don't know, I like ours better," the farmer said. "Why should we change our game for a stranger?" The crowd started rising to support the farmer.

Derak let the group almost come to a unified agreement before he closed the deal. "Care to put a wager on it?"

You could hear a pin drop. Shara and Nafka had made it to Derak and Jack's sides and leaned in to let their fragrance do its work. The smell was enough to drive an ox to the hills.

"What's your wager, stranger?"

Derak winked at Jack before he started. He reached into his pocket and pulled out a small bag of synthesized gems and tossed them on the table.

"What's this, trinkets?" the outspoken farmer asked.

"Look," Derak encouraged him.

He opened the bag and poured out diamonds and rubies. This hushed the crowd. Dreck's thoughts were entertaining. The farmer picked one up and chomped it and his eyebrows moved up a bit. "They're real, all right."

"Give them to me, Dermok, you're no expert." A slightly built man pulled out a glass and inspected them. "Yup, you're right, this is a minor fortune."

"No," Derak answered. "They're not A-grade, but there's some value in them. Now, what's your wager?"

They gave much thought over a mug of ale before Derak chimed up. "How about this? I win, you play Shesk ball from this point forward; I lose, and you keep the bag and spread the wealth down to your less fortunate."

"You get little out of it. You work hard to get these," someone said, pointing to the gems on the table.

"We have more where that came from. Are you in or out?" he challenged the crowd.

"We're in!" the farmer shouted and punctuated his comment by slamming his mug on the table, spilling half of it. The pub followed with a deafening roar.

After the din died down, Derak asked. "Who's the Mayor?"

"I am," a stately looking gentleman stepped up.

"Good." Derak corralled the gems into the bag and handed it to him. "Safeguard them until we know who's won." He handed him the small bag.

He took the bag and gave it to a large bodyguard standing next to him. "It shall be my honor, Sir. We haven't had this much excitement in Portuma in years."

Derak continued. "We'll get the field ready tomorrow and play on the following day. My partner and I will assist in the setup. You'll need twelve bats, lots of balls, and a net strung up behind each goal. The teams will be red and green; they'll wear shirts of each color. What we need now is a place to sleep for a few nights."

The Mayor spoke again. "Both of you can stay at my house. I have room for such honorable men. Follow me. My wife will prepare an excellent dinner for us."

Jack and Derak were glad to get out of the pub without incident. They accompanied the Mayor and settled down to a quiet evening after a sumptuous meal.

The robbers followed them to the Mayor's house. "What are we going to do now?" Dreck asked.

"We can catch them with the girls in distress routine. I don't think they took to Shara's perfume to well. So, scrap that idea."

"Good idea, Tsuris. We'll just have to watch and wait for our opportunity. Girls, go back to the room and wait. We'll track them."

Able-bodied craftsman met Derak and Jack the next day at the

143

Mayor's door. They marched to the field and began preparing for the game. The goals were set after Derak approved their size and large fishing nets were raised behind each set of goals. He spent an hour going over the rules with the referees. 12 balls were made and passed Derak's inspection. Getting the field ready took most of the day, including giving the players some practice time. Some of them were complaining about hitting on the run already, so they set more practice time up for the next morning.

Jack and Derak walked back to Portuma by themselves, knowing they were being followed by Tsuris. As they approached the village, they reached out with their minds and located Shara and Nafka who were waiting in an alley, ready to play hurt. His partner was lurking in the shadows. They both knew when Dreck entered the alley and cued his girls up.

"Are you ready, Jack?"

"Yes, I'll follow you in, Tsuris has a club. His partner will lure us in, and he plans to take your head off, so duck," Jack warned Derak.

"I picked it up too. One other thing, his partner has a knife. He's not too good with it."

"I've handled these situations before," Jack insisted.

"Where?"

"You're not the only one with combat experience," Jack shot back.

"Heads up, we're here."

They approached the alley, and just when they passed, Shara yelled out in distress. They looked, and Tsuris's partner was appearing to beat her. She was convincing, so they played their parts. Derak rushed in first to rescue Shara. He sensed Tsuris's mind before his body moved and ducked as the club swung close to his head. Tsuris was fast, but Derak was faster. He knocked the club out of his hands and shoved him against the wall. Jack followed him and encountered the partner before he could react, knocking him over and stripping the knife from his hand.

Tsuris recovered and swung at Derak's head, but Derak blocked it and hit a paralyzing nerve with his left hand. Tsuris had a shocked look on his face as he tried to move. Jack had Dreck contained, with his right arm twisted behind his back. The girls were backed up against a wall in terror. Derak kept Tsuris upright against the wall, trying to move, but unable to.

"You will leave town and take your motley crew with you. Never return." Derak said.

Tsuris's eyes narrowed, and he spit out his rebuke. "Go to hell, you F'ter!"

Derak tapped another nerve, and Tsuris tried to scream in pain, but his vocal chords were paralyzed. His eyes grew big and Derak could smell his fear.

Derak pressed on. "Did you understand my last statement? If you did, just blink your eyes."

He blinked.

"Good, I'll release you and then you and your compatriots will stay away from this village. I'll be watching; I'll know if you return." Derak taped his nerves and mobility returned to Tsuris's body. He looked at Derak, and ran out of the alley, followed by Dreck and the women.

"That was easy," Jack thought to Derak.

"He was tougher than I thought, usually the first nerve does the trick."

"Where did you learn that?" Jack asked.

"Master Li, in my sixth year of training. I think I was twelve."

"Maybe I could learn that." He fished for an answer.

"After six years of training. Let's get back to the Mayor's house. He'll be wondering what happened to us." They entered the Mayor's house, and Derak gave him an excuse he accepted. After dinner, they relaxed before the big game the next day.

On game day, the entire village congregated for the event. Players had practiced more and warmed up to the game. A whistle blew and the first game of Sheshk Ball kicked off. The first half was entertaining. Some players started to get the hang of the new game. The second half started with a score. Derak was lining up for a hit, when the red-headed farmer tackled him. A referee called a foul, and action resumed. The farmer continued to tackle and check hard during the third quarter. Referees couldn't keep up with him. Since no one was getting hurt, Derak told the refs to allow the tackles.

Derak tackled Dermot, got up, and another scrum was on. It reminded him of a rough game of Barquete. The game was a low-scoring event. Everyone was having fun, and no one was getting hurt, despite the hard hits. There would be more than a few bruises and sore muscles the next day, but it was a clean game. The spectators were loud and boisterous in their support of this new game, Derak won the bet. Dermot came up to Derak and gave him a powerful hug, nearly crushing him, and the gang from the pub admitted defeat.

The Mayor walked up to Jack and Derak with a wide grin. "Thank you both for showing us this game. We haven't had this much excitement in a long time." He handed Derak the bag of gems, which Derak refused.

"We all won today, Mayor. Keep the gems and help the needy villagers out." Derak, noting the look of shock from the mayor, and continued, "I don't need them. We have to leave now. Thank you and the entire village for an entertaining stay."

Jack and Derak walked away when the Mayor called them back. "The village of Portuma would like you to have the game ball and bat." He smiled.

"Thank you, Mayor." Then they turned and walked into the trees and disappeared forever from the year 1917.

Telekinesis 101

Derak and Jack beamed up with the first game ball and bat and reported to Qex. His usual non-readable face greeted them.

"You did well, except for the pub and Tsuris. Were your actions necessary in both cases? We must minimize our presence. After calculating your actions, they had no effect on our formulas. All, and I mean all variables, must be reported to me before you take any action. Is that clear, Admiral?"

"In our defense, they would have attacked us before we left Portuma. I took the least deleterious action to help our mission. As for the pub incident, we had to have the support of the village leaders, and they were all present. The farmer seemed to have a lot of influence without being an elected authority. That's why we pressed the situation."

"I will make the required adjustments for the next mission. You will need a good night's sleep before we prepare. We will start at 0800." He turned on his heels and Vel followed.

Derak turned to the others. *"What did you guys do for three days?"*

"Nothing near as interesting what you and Jack accomplished, Just the usual. We all made it to the next level. Qex pressed us hard. He said we would need every bit of instruction for the next assignment." Seamus answered.

"What was it like dealing with chatter for three days?" Robert asked.

"It gets easier the longer you're around it. You can turn it down

to an inaudible hum. Every once in a while, a unique thought presents itself, and you zero in on it. You can even program yourself to pick up specific thought patterns when they pop up."

Jack said, *"I'm hungry, I hope there's chow left."*

Shenar laughed, took his arm, and lead him to the kitchen. They were both engaged in a loving thought transfer. Shesain took Derak's arm and followed them.

The next morning, Qex entered with Vel. *"You will pick up with Psychometric training. This will give you the ability to plant suggestions into minds, both individual and mass minds. We practice this as a last resort, but it must be known to complete your telepathy training. I will supervise planetary exercises. You will practice until you accomplish this task. I will also teach you how to change animal behavior. It is easier to move an animal than a thinking person. This will introduce you to the concepts and execution you will need. After you have exhibited acceptable results, we will turn our attention to people.*

"We will start by identifying the prefrontal cortex. This part of the brain deals with planning, emotion, judgment, and decision making. It is where we plant the suggestion for the action we want the individual to take. We have to first form the thought to remain within the moral boundary's the target mind has set up. Animals are easier. They do not have the same reasoning skills we have, though, I must warn you that you will find some that seem too. However, they are not as strong or developed as ours."

"How do we proceed?" Leontul asked.

"We will start by beaming up field mice to work with. Leontul, you will work with Terga to set up the proper environment. Each of you will learn to give a mouse simple commands, like move to the right or left. When your progress is sufficient, we will move up to more complicated assignments. Until we are ready to start, you will continue your optical exercises."

Leontul and Terga set up the habitat for the field mice and Terga located and beamed up one male and female mouse. The test was to encourage them to mate out of their natural cycle. This proved to be tough. They spent three days learning how to detect the prefrontal cortex. It was much simpler with mice minds, based on their decisions, like eating, sleeping, mating, or running when they perceived danger. Detecting the cortex was much easier than making them follow directions. The first attempts were comical. They would instruct a right turn, and the mice would turn left or move backwards. Sometimes they would just sit there and do nothing.

This led them to learn what the animal's concept of what left, and right was, with a lot of trial and more error. Derak achieved a successful suggestion, but the outcome was hilarious. The female mouse kept turning left, running around in a circle. It stopped after Qex stepped in.

"It is a step forward, Derak. Your suggestion was too strong. You must learn to turn down your strength. A suggestive thought must be undetectable by the recipient. We will give the mice two day's rest to return to their normal patterns. All of you must learn to not scramble the brains you are contacting. You could permanently damage them without trying. You will return to your lessons in the meantime."

After each day's lessons, Qex drilled them on Telaxian language skills. It was getting easier for Robert, Jack and Derak, however, the rest of them still required Terga's help to a varying degree. Jack's teaching skills improved each day, and he helped to translate Telaxian math concepts for Shesain, Shenar, Seamus, and Leontul.

After a week of constant exercises and staring at field mice for hours a day, they all succeeded to get them to follow simple commands. The next step was to get the mice to mate out of cycle. The results were even funnier than the previous efforts. One of Shesain's attempts got the female mouse chasing the male around the cage. Seamus's turn had the opposite effect. Derak pushed the proper button, but, once again, it was a little too strong. The male mouse hit the female before he could trigger her thoughts. The encounter was rough for the female. Jack was the first to get it right, followed by Shesain and Shenar. Seamus and Derak still needed some work on turning their fields down. They succeeded on the last attempt. The poor mice needed a few days to rest before they returned them to their natural habitat.

The crew could not proceed with the second phase of the training until Seamus and Derak gained control of their mental output. Qex included all of them in his sessions. Jack was becoming the king of subtlety. He had a strong, flexible mind capable of delicate control. He helped Qex with the instruction. It took three days of constant practice until they were cleared for phase two.

Qex would be on Thumar with them this time. They would have to cause a human or Thumarian to make a minor step in either direction while they walked past. This would prove interesting.

After a day's rest, they found themselves on Thumar in D-gen, on a busy thoroughfare. Qex monitored each mind as they tried to complete the action. Everyone except Jack failed on the first day. His suggestion only caused the poor fellow to pause his step before he moved on. The second day, he produced the correct result. Derak got through, and the woman almost tripped. They thought it was funny, Qex didn't. Shesain and Shenar had the opposite issue Seamus and Derak shared. They had to learn to strengthen their fields.

They discussed a major problem with the training after the day's work ended. The crew was opposed to influencing other people. After a stern lecture from Qex, they agreed to concentrate the next day. The results were astounding. Everyone got at least one person to follow a command, and Derak persuaded two women to switch packages mid-stride. Qex shot him a warning glance and moved them to switch back. They returned to *The Shesain* jubilant. Qex allowed them their revelry and told them to be ready for a new assignment.

Qex began after optical lessons. *"Your next step will be to learn telekinesis, the movement of objects with your minds. It will require this for the next time fix. You will need a powerful mind with delicate flexibility. It will also be necessary for Shesain and Shenar to 'delay' an individual for a few minutes. We must prevent two people from meeting. This one affects another fix in our future.*

"You will notice small objects on the tables in front of you. They weigh a few grams each. Your first task is to move that object with

your mind and keep it on the table. You can either move it or the air surrounding it. If you concentrate, you can see the air. The only difference between the object and the surrounding air is the density of the molecular structure. The easiest way to move something the first time is to move the air. Once you move the lighter molecules of air, moving a denser target becomes easier with practice. You will start now and work until dinner."

Vel stayed behind to monitor the progress and help when needed.

It took the crew an hour to see the air around the blocks. It looked like a transparent soup with the protons and neutrons moving about. With further concentration, they could see the disturbance that solid objects caused within air space. The soupy air would hit the solid object and move around it. The crew set their intent on the air around the block on the table and attempted to move it. After several hours of intense mental exhaustion, everyone took a break with no results. They discussed what they did wrong, and rethought Qex's instructions.

They returned to the exercise with dampened enthusiasm. After a few hours, Jack let out a whoop. He had moved his block a bit. This success, though slight, recharged everyone else to try harder. Derak grumbled and concentrated on his block. It flew across the room, nearly hitting Seamus in the head.

"Hey!"

Derak raced to pick up his block.

Seamus, seeing another success, looked down at his block, concentrated, and it flew across the room. It would have hit Shenar in the head, had she not ducked at the last second.

"Watch out!" She cried.

Qex came into the room, looking around. *"Derak, Seamus, did you not learn one thing from the psychometric lesson?"* He shook his head. *"Jack, how far did you move your cube?"*

"Maybe a quarter of an inch," he said.

"That is a start for control of your target. Vel and I will work with each of you until you get it."

Qex and Vel worked with them until each had moved their blocks, keeping it on the tabletop. It took Derak three more tries to keep his from flying off again. Seamus was having as much control trouble as Derak was. Shenar and Shesain moved theirs about one inch. Robert and Leontul let out a cheer when they did it. Jack, as usual, was ahead of the curve.

Dinner followed with Shesain starting the mental shenanigans. She moved Jack's knife and fork out of his reach. This followed with her drinking glass dancing around. Soon, all the crew were wearing most of the dinner and laughing out loud, a welcome relief from the strain of the day.

Qex walked in on this moment of unabated revelry, as stoic as ever, and shook his head. *"Save the antics for your exercises."* Then he turned and walked out.

They looked at each other and could not refrain from letting out another round of laughter before looking around; they had to clean up the mess. It happened with lighter hearts from an evening of success.

In the following days, everyone made significant progress, from moving a five-gram cube to a one-pound ball, but range and accuracy still needed a lot of work. Every time the crew had fun, Qex quashed the hi-jinks. He insisted on the seriousness of the situation.

Their jovial attitudes were having a positive effect on the results. They enjoyed this chapter in their psychic education, and the progress was faster than the telepathy portion. Despite appearances, the crew had a level take on the exercise.

One day, the fun ratcheted up another notch. Larger objects were being moved when a pillow flew across the room and hit Derak in the head. He picked up Shesain's internal laughter and shot a pillow back across the room at her, catching her off guard and knocking her back on her couch. Rising from the shock, her eyes grew wide, and she returned the favor. This time, Derak deflected the pillow, and it hit Robert in the chest, causing him to lose concentration. Someone requested more pillows from Terga and when they appeared, Shenar shot one across the room and smacked Jack in the face. Before they knew it, they were in a full-fledged pillow fight, running and dodging each other's aims. Derak hit two targets at once, and Jack was getting good at deflection.

The raucous laughter from the room could be heard all the way on the bridge, and Qex marched back, followed by Vel. As Qex opened the door, three pillows were headed in his direction; they stopped in mid-air, inches from his face. All the pillows hung in space, then dropped to the floor.

Vel countered the disgust showing on Qex's face, trying hard not to laugh. Qex shot a look at her. The smile left her face, and he faced the crew. *"You're worse than Telaxian children. If these antics did not help you in your lessons as much as it does, I would put an immediate halt to it. I see you have moved into deflection. If you employ such childish methods, at least keep the noise down."* He turned and headed back to the bridge, followed by a grinning Vel.

The door shut, and a moment later, the melee continued. This time Derak asked Terga to soundproof the room. They were all getting good with pillows by now. Derak got Jack with two pillows at once.

"Watch your flank, Buddy."

"I'll give you something to watch." Jack shot three pillows at Derak, hitting him in the head, chest, and feet, knocking him over.

Over the next three hours they all moved from one game to the next, and even Robert was grinning at every victory. Seamus and Derak were having better control over their output, and the girls increased theirs. Qex came back to check on them, like a parent who suspects silence as much as noise. The door opened, and the pillows were dancing a waltz, as Derak had Terga play some Strauss for the occasion.

The choreography wasn't perfect, but they kept the pillow partners together, dancing and bouncing up and down with the music. Qex, despite himself, was amused, and added his touch to the dance. The pillows now moved in perfect synchronous harmony with the music. He allowed the pillow dance to last for a short while, then they all dropped to the floor.

"Today's playtime is over. It's time to return to optics before dinner."

Derak detected a slight smile on Qex's face as he walked away saying to Derak. *"Not bad, Derak."*

The music stopped, and the pillows went away. They cleaned up the room with their minds before resuming their optics, as the optical training was referred to now.

After the next day's Telaxian language lesson, Qex took them to the cargo bay, where it was time to graduate to much larger targets. The exercises started with ten-pound cargo boxes and moved up from there. Seamus and Derak could handle these with alacrity. Their strong mental fields helped them. Once they could move a certain weight, the next aim was to deflect or stop them. The exercises included suspending heavy boxes in mid-air and holding them stationary, while others tried to interrupt their control.

Once again, it turned into a game, monitored by Qex, because of the danger involved. What they were manipulating now were not pillows and could hurt someone.

The following day, the crew separated into two groups and went to opposite ends of the ship with mind targets. The assignment was to increase distance strength. First, they had to picture the object in their minds, move it, and suspend it in mid-air. Jack showed the greatest expertise, with the rest of them struggling.

Jack stepped in and assisted with the instruction. It took another two days for the rest to catch up. The next step was to go to the planet's surface and practice with greater distances and larger marks.

The crew beamed down to Thumar's surface the following morning. They were placed in a large field away from any settled lands. Qex was concentrating on developing Jack's long-range accuracy. He would head the next crew assignment.

The next three days that followed allowed the rest of the crew to hone their skills. Robert's stubborn streak was disappearing with Vel's help. Leontul took some time out to explore the plant life, and Seamus took the sky cycle with some drones to scout out more Thumdust veins.

Back on the ship, Qex announced that it was time to move into the next timeline. The next fix would take place in the year 1835. He turned the time calculations over to Jack. Both Jack and Derak could handle time jumps like they navigated regular space. Shesain and Shenar developed superior skills in the research department. Jack and the women would have to engage in some recon before they would have enough information to complete their mission.

Terga instituted another room arrangement while they were on Thumar. Qex noticed how relaxed the crew were in a natural setting, so he engineered three different scenarios. One was an open glen with deciduous trees and lots of grass. The second was an ocean setting complete with a warm, white sandy beach, and the third was a chilling mountain scene. These holo-projections would be switched out for the great room when it wasn't used for training.

After a relaxing morning on the beach, Jack and Derak calculated the next jump, with Terga double checking it. The jump went well.

Derak approached Qex on being able to beam down in D-gen mode. This would ensure the anonymity on future missions. He agreed and set some time aside for the two of them to go over the 3-D model. They established the orbit around Thumar in the year 1835, in D-gen.

They set the night and day schedule to the planet's; this would align their time clocks with Thumar, making the shift from D-gen to real time easier. Derak got together with Qex to work out the new beam-down algorithm. Robert and Jack joined them, and between the three of them and Qex, they worked it out. They would send a drone down in D-gen first to see if it worked.

After breakfast the next morning, Qex briefed them on the second time fix. *"The next mission concerns Tukar Andehar, Kethela Erenger, and Debra Joshekur. In the modified timeline, Kethela meets Tukar, they get married, and he does not discover the Cave of Lights. Shesain and Shenar, you must waylay Kethela on the road. Debra must discover an unconscious Tukar first. They will marry, and Tukar will discover the Cave of Lights in the year 1852. This will require a visit to the town of Vorturak to identify all three.*

"Once you have, you will return and intercept them on two separate intersecting roads. Shesain and Shenar on one and Jack on the other. Jack will use his finely tuned telekinesis to knock Tukar out, using the natural surroundings. Shesain and Shenar will delay Kethela with a minor emergency. She is a nurse with a high level of compassion. She will rush to meet Tukar, she must not. We will give Shenar a realistic-looking injury. Your acting skills will have to seal the deal. Jack will guide Debra to follow Tukar's road. Once they meet, the dye will be set and the three of you will return to the Ship. You will start the operation tomorrow, at noon, Thumar time. I will continue briefing Jack, Shenar, and Shesain on the mission parameters. The rest of you are to continue on your optics," Qex ordered.

Qex allowed Seamus and Leontul to revisit their plant and mineral surveys in D-gen. They would take the sky cycles and stay on the continent. He kept track of all planetary movements and monitored the changes on Derak's universe model during the assignment, from beginning to end. Robert took over the collection of Intel with the women gone. Derak would assist Qex on monitoring the mission. They would transfer the 3-D model to the great room, along with Robert's station.

They had tested the beam down sequence in D-gen and corrected the equations until they got it right. After five attempts that worked, the team beamed down to Thumar in the year 1835. They checked in and confirmed that they were on Vorturak's outskirts.

The women were excited to be assigned to a mission together.

"Make sure you're not walked through in D-gen. It leaves a residue in 3D on the person who does it. They'll stop and look around before walking away. Make sure you can't be seen when you turn it off," Derak reminded them. Seamus and Leontul had beamed down with the sky cycles. They received the same reminder.

It was a sizeable town. Shesain and Shenar headed to the medical clinics and Jack made his way to the pubs. The women stayed in D-gen and Jack turned his off. He could almost learn a new or modified language by himself now. He still needed a little help from

Terga. They armed him with the local currency and fables that were making the rounds; the biggest was about the crystal caves on the Anean continent. He walked to the biggest bar and ordered a wicked stout ale. Conversation flowed as freely as the drink. The bar was full, and a band was playing to an unappreciative crowd. Jack scanned the gathering until he picked up a muted exchange about the caves. He located the source and parked himself nearby.

"I'm telling ya, Zerick, they exist. I've talked to a prospector from Anea who says he ran across them himself."

"Then why didn't he discover 'em, Vemor. That story's been goin' round for decades, and they ain't been found yet."

"Orenbar was a myth 'till they discovered it. The funny thing bout it, they had no recollection of the three strangers from 1814. They never heard of the plague till they were told about it. Everyone just figures they're covering something up."

"Try to tell Tukar that!" another one said. "Who's this Anean stranger everyone's talking about? What's his name? I need more than just a rumor to buy into this one. Leave the spread of gossip to the women." The man chugged down his ale after he spoke.

"Pah!" A dark-skinned man with a bushy mustache retorted. "I've been all over Anea, including the area this stranger said he found it. I ain't seen nuthin like what this fellow's talking about."

"Ask Tukar, he's coming in now," Zerick said.

Jack waited until Tukar came into view. He was around six-feet tall and slight of build. He was handsome, and Jack could see the Andehar resemblance to Shesain and Shenar. Tukar walked with confidence and headed straight for the table Jack was listening to.

Jack tuned into his mind and marked it for future reference. He had a unique signature that set him apart from the rest. Reconnecting would be no problem. He was about to get up and find Shesain and Shenar when a well-built young waitress approached Tukar.

"Tukar, can I get you the usual?" It wasn't what she asked, but how she addressed him. There was flirting warmth in her voice. She sidled her full figure next to his chair. Her auburn hair hung loose and invitingly over her shoulders. He looked up at her, and she adjusted her bosom so he could get a better look. He drank up the view before he answered her. Her smile was bright, and her eyes sparkled with desire.

"Yea, Debra, I'll take the usual, and you with it." He flashed a big smile, and she returned a giggle before she moved away. The entire table had their eyes glued on her.

"Tukar, you're a fool not to scoop that one up. She comes from an excellent family." Another commented.

"It'd be easier if I didn't have to deal with the new engagement rules they're coming up with. Ten months! Ten months until I can touch her proper," Tukar groused.

Jack locked onto Debra's mind signature. He finished his second drink and left to find Shesain and Shenar. They had until the end of the day to identify the targets.

The women weren't having the same fortune as Jack. They had been to almost every medical facility in Vorturak. There were only two left when Jack caught up with them in D-gen. Shesain went to one, and Jack and Shenar walked to the other. The sun was setting when Shenar noticed a lone woman leaving a house at the outskirts of Vorturak. She was a tall woman with a slender figure and long blonde hair. She was talking to someone out of view. Shenar and Jack zoomed in on the conversation.

"Thanks for the help, Kethela; I'll let you know when the fever dies down."

"It's my pleasure. I've got to catch Tukar before he returns home."

"Do you think you can take his mind off of Debra?"

"It would be a lot easier if that new engagement law hadn't passed. I could surprise him one night. Believe me, one night with me, and he wouldn't even look at Debra."

"Good luck."

"Do you have her marked?" Jack asked Shenar.

"I do, my Chimera. Let's find Shesain and get back to the ship."

They located Shesain's mind and had her meet them at the insertion point. Then they beamed up to *The Shesain.*

Everyone reported to Qex, and rested before they had to go back down to Thumar. Tukar would be on his normal walk from his home to town. Kethela was determined to bend Tukar to her will. This had to be stopped at all costs. Qex went over last-minute changes with Jack, Shenar, and Shesain before they left. They changed into regional clothing and beamed down. Qex and Derak parked themselves in front of the 3-D display with Robert joining them.

Jack arrived at his destination, scanned the road, and picked the tree he would climb. Then he waited to pick up Tukar's mind pattern, convinced he was right on schedule. His next move was to find Debra. He found her and planted the suggestion to take a walk. She shook her head; this wasn't her regular schedule. He reiterated his command, and against her better judgment, she walked out of the door in Jack's direction.

Shesain and Shenar were ready. Shenar had a nasty cut on her left calf. It would be up to her to pull this off. *"We're set, Jack. How about you?"*

"Ready. I'm looking for a projectile that won't hurt him when I knock him out. The only thing I see is pinecones, but they're big and heavy."

"Then you have to slow down the trajectory to match your intent," Qex interrupted. *"Shenar, Kethela's arriving soon, get ready."*

Kethela appeared, walking at a fast clip, almost passing them.

"Can you help us, please? My sister slipped and fell. She has a nasty gash on her right calf," Shesain called out in desperation.

Kethela stopped and hesitated, thinking about her critical timing. "If it isn't bad, I'll send someone else back. I have an important meeting to make."

Shenar let out a loud cry with a mind push and grabbed her leg. Rolling around in pain, as she squeezed the flesh-colored pouch on her leg, causing more fake blood to ooze out of the wound. "Please help me! It hurts so! I don't want to get an infection. Ohhh!" She moaned even louder, with another mind push.

This last exhibit attracted Kathela's attention. She moved to Shenar's side and grimaced as she examined the opening. "This looks bad, but not as bad as you might think." Kethela told Shenar.

"You punctured the epidermis and cut into the muscle a little. I have enough dressing and herbs to prevent any further damage. Let me inspect it." She picked up the calf and started poking around. Shenar let out a gasp of pain and Shesain looked very concerned. Kethela dug into her bag and started dressing the cut as Shenar kept the moans and groans up as she worked. The ruse was working. Shesain and Shenar's acting plus their thought commands dictated Kathela's perception of the injury.

Jack's waiting ended about the time the women did. Tukar ambled down the road, whistling a lively tune. Jack located a long limb hanging over the road with a smaller pinecone. He had to direct Tukar's mind to walk under the branch. Tukar hesitated the first few attempts but followed directions the third time. Tukar got into position, Jack released the pinecone telekinetically. Qex sensed the timing was off and corrected the fall from *The Shesain.* The cone hit Tukar on top of his head and knocked him out. Jack thanked Qex and sent out a more urgent thought to Debra. She arrived about five minutes later, finding Tukar unconscious. She rushed over, sank to her knees, and tenderly caressed his head until he came around. He looked up at her, and their eyes locked. She smiled and pulled his head into her full bosom, rocking him.

•◆•

On board *The Shesain,* a soft time wave overtook the crew.

Qex smiled, *"It is working. Look at the model."* He directed a thought Derak's way. The model was changing before their eyes. Some outlying orange fingers of the time wave started retracting; one finger moved back into the center of the wave.

"The waves will get bigger the closer we get to the core. We will get used to the waves the more we experience them. Bring our crew up." Qex instructed Derak.

•◆•

Kethela smothered the wound with an herbal concoction before she dressed it. When she was finished, she excused herself and ran down the road to a meeting that would never take place.

Shesain and Shenar felt bad about Kethela losing Tukar. They wondered if she would ever find genuine love.

The Prime Mathematician

The Prime Mathematician luxuriated in his private mansion onboard *The Mandible,* enjoying a rare meal of live Xerubtilominite Beetles, his favorite from Telaxia. Hard shells and harder bones helped to keep his teeth sharp and clean. He glanced over at April on his bed. Of all the mortal whores he encountered, she could almost keep up with his appetite. Her blue green skin color appealed to him. She did not have any of those ghastly extra appendages. If she had, he would have removed them himself.

The juices from the beetles ran down his human-like chin as he contemplated being engineered for a job he never wanted. He detested his alien body, even though it had some advantages. Why couldn't he have been like the ruling class, short and hairless with a plain shape? No matter what he would ever achieve, his DNA would always keep him from joining the first tier of Telaxian society, never to move beyond the second tier of their staid, stale society. Over twenty thousands of years, he served them, walking among the sick and disgusting mortals, collecting the information that Telaxia controlled them with. Always being promised a new assignment on home turf, but never receiving it. Never attaining the recognition or rewards he deserved. He would make them pay one day. He had the same life span as they did, and he would find their weak spot. Time was on his side.

With twisted thoughts of revenge, he picked up a large beetle and shoved it into his mouth. It squirmed, trying to inject him with its poison. He heard the satisfying sound of his razor-sharp teeth ending its life. He crunched the shell and bones to pieces as the juices ran down his face, and dripped onto his napkin made from lace and trimmed in human hair.

It was a satisfying moment. He was eating a larger one when a wave from the time shift hit him, causing him to drop the beetle. He had felt this happen before. At the time he put it aside as a minor change in calculations from Telaxia Prime. This time he could not ignore it. This was a stronger wave. This meant that the timeline was being adjusted from inside the galaxy, and much closer. He flung his plate with the remaining bugs across the room in anger. Who would dare make changes without his permission? It would have to be another agent, but whom? He never knew all the agents in the field, so it would have to be a senior operative. Only they had the knowledge to do this. Another thought came to mind. Could it be an unknown entity, one under his radar? If so, where did they get the technology? It did not exist in this century. Even as hard as he was pushing these plebeians, their ineptness had not even gotten close.

The mortal races made him sick thinking about them. Even with the levels of technological advances they had achieved. Those in power could not get past their need to fulfill their wonton hunger for more. Their greed and avarice knew no bounds. This miserable genetically modified group of humans that called themselves the Orion Syndicate were his puppets of choice, for now.

"April! April! Get your lazy ass out of bed and fetch me Councilmen One and Two. And don't you dare leave my rooms naked or smelling like sex." She was up in a flash, exhausted, showered, dressed and out of his mansion in less than ten minutes. Two slaves entered after she left, and the Prime Mathematician shocked their slave collars out of anger to get them to clean up his mess faster. *I will train these animals,* he thought to himself. *If I have to suffer, they will too.*

The door opened, and Councilmen One and Two rushed into the room. They bowed low before him. Number One addressed him, "My Great Mutah Shakur, we are here. What do you command?"

"Stand up, you inept humans. Why am I feeling time waves in my galaxy?" he demanded.

"Sir, we felt the wave ourselves, but could not identify them," Number One squeaked out.

The Mutah Shakur's teeth showed, and it was not a smile. Bits and pieces from his meal were stuck between his teeth. He did not care one bit; suffering of others pleased him. "What you and everyone on this vessel felt was a time change wave emanating from this galaxy. Was it one of our tests?"

"No, Mutah Shakur. Our technology is still in the developmental stages, the ending stages. We are not capable of this wave yet. We have scheduled a test for early next year."

"You try my patience. Move it up!" the Mutah Shakur ordered.

"The last test resulted in an explosion that destroyed the prototype. It is impossible to schedule another until we make adjustments."

"Do you value your position, Number One?"

"Yes, Mutah Shakur! I treasure serving you above my life. *If only I could--*"

"I read your thoughts like that of a child's. Watch what you think around me! Can you at least calculate the sector it originated in?" the Mutah Shakur inquired.

"Mutah Shakur," Number Two said, "our top science team is working on the location now. We should have what you need in a few hours."

"How many, Number Two?"

"Permit me to check, Sir."

"It is not wise to keep me waiting!"

Number Two walked over to a corner of the room and conferred on his wrist com. After a few moments he returned, hoping the report would please the Mutah Shakur. "Two hours, Sir, at the latest."

"Make it one and you both can keep your positions on the council. Now leave and do not return without what I ask for!"

Both of them left faster than they entered, thankful to leave alive and in one piece. Number One turned to Number Two, when they thought they had gotten out of mind reading range. They never could.

"Number Two, get captain Thompson on this right away. I have never seen the Mutah Shakur this upset before. Heads will roll if we don't have something to report in an hour, and it won't be mine!" Number One ordered.

Number Two rushed back to his mansion and roused Thompson in the middle of the night. He briefed the captain and told him to squeeze accurate intel out of the science crew in forty-five minutes by any means, starting now. He was dressed and gone in five minutes. Number Two could always depend on captain Thompson to get the job done right. He had to, or his sister would die.

Captain Thompson took no time at all to reach the Advanced Science Protocol room number one. He surprised the officer in charge.

"Officer on deck!" he shouted.

"Stay at your posts! Lt. Granger, what progress do you have to report?"

"Nothing of substance, Sir. We've gotten a sector location, that is all."

"What sector did it emanate from, Lieutenant?" the captain demanded.

"It's in The Pegasus sector, sir," Lieutenant Granger choked out.

Captain Thompson looked at his watch and then answered him in a menacing tone. "You have twenty-seven minutes to track its exact location."

"Twenty-seven, sir, that's…"

"Doable! If you don't want to deal with the same fate, your predecessor suffered."

"Yes, sir!" he replied in a shaky voice. Lieutenant Granger turned to his senior operator on the tracking scopes. "Johnson, I'll need that Intel in twenty minutes, or someone besides me will pay the price!"

"Yes, sir!"

The captain relaxed in the section commander's chairs and waited while Granger whipped his troops into action. Captain Thompson loved observing such a symphony of fear. Twenty minutes later, an operator announced he found it.

"Where is it located?" the captain overrode the Lieutenant.

"The point of origin came from the planet Thumar, in the Pegasus sector, sir."

"Are you sure, Chief?" the captain insisted, raising an eyebrow.

"Yes, sir! We've checked it three times for accuracy." Ensign Johnson reported.

"Verify the findings Lieutenant, or the results will be on your head," the captain threatened.

Lieutenant Granger spent a few minutes confirming the results and reported his approval to the captain.

"Superb job, Boys! If all goes well with this report to the Mutah Shakur, you will be rewarded!" He left faster than he arrived.

Number Two looked a little more relaxed after he heard the news. Suddenly a frown replaced his tight smile. "I wonder if this Jamar character has anything to do with it?" He turned to face the captain. "If he does, your little bit of good news might not help us. I know we'll get chewed out for not containing him by now. Captain, plan to get rid of this pest and his immediate family. We want no more of the Jamar clan around to disrupt our plans."

"Yes, Number Two, I'll get right on it." He turned and left with a smile. He relished the assignments where he could use all of his talents.

Councilmen One and Two entered the Prime Mathematicians great room. They never knew what to expect from him. He always had an unnerving habit of showing his sharp pointy teeth, never in a smile.

"What do you have to report?" the Mutah Shakur asked.

Number Two addressed him. "Mutah Shakur, the wave originated from Thumar, in the Pegasus sector."

"Thumar?" They do not have the technology to build a rocket yet. That's an odd place for an epicenter. It could not involve this Jamar fellow, could it?" He asked.

"He won't be born for another four centuries, Mutah Shakur. The science to discover his DNA make-up will not exist on Earth until the early to mid-twenty-first century," Number Two reported.

"There is something strange going on here. Did he possess the technology in the twenty-fifth century to pull this off?" the Mutah Shakur asked.

"Not to our knowledge, Great One," Number One spoke.

"What is Thumar's tech level now?"

"They're in the early industrialization period. The steam engine is the only modern tech they have in its infant stages," Number Two reported.

"Then this has the fingerprints of a senior Telaxian operative," the Mutah Shakur thought out loud. "I cannot think of who it would be. Only an emergency of stellar proportions would drive the Telaxian Senior Council to make such a bold move. I will have to study this more. Send your Captain to Thumar with three ships to scout the area, Number Two. Keep one ship in a parking orbit. Place a second on the first moon and the third at the la-grange point of the planet. Is the cloaking device ready for deployment?"

"We are still working out minor glitches. It overheats and causes a temporary shutdown. We've doubled the cooling units, keeping the shutdowns to a matter of seconds before the alternate unit re-engages." Number One reported.

The Mutah Shakur did not like this at all. His face turned dark for a moment before he spoke. "What good is your technical training doing me, you imbecile? Find the problem and make sure the ships have a working device! Leave me! Do not fail me this time, or the price will be higher than you can contemplate."

They left frantic. Number Two contacted Captain Thompson and relayed the urgency and details of the mission. He left to spread fear to his subordinates. He always got results, even if they lost a few scientists. The Syndicate could grind out more to take their place.

The Mutah Shakur sulked in his observation room. It was large and plush, decorated with enough living human pillows to rest himself on. These had the extra benefit of coming with long smooth legs that wrapped around him. Humans made the best slaves. They were so docile after they were broken in. He rested his head on a set of large fleshy pillows and gazed out of the large plas-steel windows that gave him a grand view of the galaxy that he would one day rule. The time wave still bothered him because he would love to return to the twenty-fifth century. He would think about that later. A beautiful black slave crawled up onto the couch and lowered her body onto his.

Teleportation 101

Qex allowed a small celebration when Jack, Shesain, and Shenar returned. The next day, everyone spent relaxing on the beach. It was odd getting wet swimming in warm saltwater in the middle of a node. A welcome moment of relaxation for the whole crew.

The following morning, they all met in the great room. They set chairs up in a circle, with square tables in front of them. The ever familiar two-gram blocks sat in the middle of the tables. In the center of the circle was another square table. After they sat down, Qex began with the next set of lessons on teleportation. This time, instructions were transmitted in Telaxue, Telaxian math language. This threw them for a loop, as the crew's skills were conversational at best.

Qex informed them they would conduct all future exercises in Telaxue. This would procure a faster learning curve once they got the hang of it. Though it slowed down the exercises, it allowed for greater information transfer in a shorter time. Everyone struggled at first, requiring Vel and Terga to assist.

Qex seemed to warm up when he linked to Terga. Derak could always tell when he was connected; he wore a smile that spoke of contentment.

Derak became curious and had to ask Terga. *"Terga, what's going on between you two?"*

"I think we are in love with each other," Terga confessed.

"In love? I know you're self-aware, but how can a non-physical entity love a physical being?"

"Our minds are a perfect match. And I could construct a physical body to match his life span," She thought.

Derak was in shock.

"You hesitate, Derak. Is something wrong?"

"Your last statement: how long will Qex live?"

"He is over twenty thousand years old now and considered a youth by Telaxian standards. His knowledge is immense; you should allow him to share it with me, he wants to," she almost pleaded.

"Only if I can have access to all non-personal data."

"Are you jealous? You shouldn't be. I am still dedicated to you, I could never leave Shesain," Terga tried to assure him.

"I don't know if I'm jealous or not. I'll think about this for a while. Before anything happens."

"I will arrange it. He will be happy for a Telaxian," Terga confirmed.

"Derak, are you ready to begin?" Qex asked him.

"Yes, I am." There was strangeness in his reply that Qex picked up.

Something changed, and he didn't know if it was for the better. Derak had a rival for his personal AI, and he was not taking it well. He had to suppress his rising warrior mentality. With the mental training he received, there was no telling what he could do now.

Qex's look told Derak that he sensed this and told Terga to start with the others while he and Vel consulted with Derak. Thoughts weren't needed to convey the required action; they had to get him off of the ship before he exploded.

Derak got up without saying a word or allowing a thought to leak out. His field strength was breaking through any boundaries that stood in its path, obliterating them into nothingness. His mind was blocked, even to Qex, and this caused Qex and Vel to go to a place they never had to with a mortal. His second strand connected, and his energy field increased to where both Qex and Vel were having trouble containing it. Derak sensed alarm in both of them as he tried to stop the cascading effect. He could feel every molecule in his body supercharging. Every ounce of his being was bent on stopping the metamorphous.

Derak's body, mind, and soul trembled from the effort. Qex and Vel could barely keep up with it. Then the third strand kicked in and they knew that they would need some help. In a flash, Derak felt the presence of the Valuk-Manou and her Prime Council. He could not be allowed to complete the change. The next thing he knew, he was in the Council Chambers on Telaxia. The Valuk-Manou, her Prime Council, and thirty others encircled him. Qex and Vel were on either side, their combined strength firmly holding the fourth strand in check.

The Valuk-Manou addressed Derak in Telaxue. *"You must seek your triggers and identify them. This is the starting point to controlling them. Start with the first two."*

After a moment, Derak identified the first one; the second one came after. The last trigger was well concealed and elusive. He had to predict its next movement. He felt the help of the group effort to help him locate it.

Once he did, the Valuk-Manou entered his thoughts again. *"You must master all three before you leave; you will have our help."*

An indeterminable amount of time passed before he started gaining control of himself. The group strength reduced itself down to Qex, Vel, and the Valuk-Manou. They left him to himself, Derak's entire being trembled from the effort. He was exhausted, emotionally, and physically spent. Vel and Qex led him to a chair and sat him down.

"WHY! Why me? What kind of freak am I!?" His thoughts screamed out.

"You are no freak, Derak Andehar," the Valuk-Manou comforted him. *"Not to the universe. You must accept yourself for what you are becoming. We cannot predict where you will end up. You have progressed well beyond our most complicated calculations. You must learn to control your mind in the same manner you do your physical body. To accomplish this, you will return with Zix, Qex, and Vel. Zix will work with you exclusively. Qex and Vel will instruct the rest of the crew. They will join Zix in your training when they can."*

"I can't let the monster in me loose again! There's no telling what

will happen. I feel like I could break bones and start fires with my thoughts, and not small ones. An incident like that would make the Chambar Valley offensive look like child's play." Derak thought in horror.

"Once you are in control of the triggers, you will determine the outcome," the Valuk-Manou continued. "Do not put this monster to death yet. You may need to call it up at will again. Our common enemy grows stronger daily, and they have traveled back in time from the twenty-fifth century to hide. Your time paradox had a few positive benefits, but you may run across them at some point. What triggered this?"

"That's between Qex and I. He has done nothing wrong. This comes from some unexpected consequences."

"Then I will leave the two of you to work it out." The Valuk-Manou smiled and left the room.

Qex looked at Derak. They were the only ones in the room now. "Does this have anything to do with Terga?" Qex asked.

"It has everything to do with Terga. I don't know what disturbs me the most. Her becoming self-aware, or the fact I will have to let her go. She mentioned that she could make a physical body to match your lifespan."

"We thought about it, but I would never do that. I know what she means to you." Qex admitted.

"That's what's so hard. I don't know what I would do without her thoughts and recommendations."

Qex did something unexpected. He walked up to Derak and put a hand on each shoulder and looked into his eyes as an equal. "I, we will respect your decision. We both know you will make a fair one from your heart. Trust in Shesain to give you sound advice on this matter."

Derak looked at Qex and smiled. "Thanks for getting me out of there. I couldn't live with harming anyone on the crew or the ship, Shesain and my unborn children."

Qex patted Derak on the back and moved him to the door. "Anything for you, my friend, we have to return."

They returned to *The Shesain* with Zix. Qex gave everybody the rest of the day off. He, Zix, and Vel went to the great room to confer and Shesain cornered Derak in their room.

Derak told her everything, from his conversation with Terga to the time they returned.

"Terga and Qex in love? Who would have thought such a thing could happen?" she responded, perplexed.

"Strange is the order of the day, the new normal. I still don't know what to think of the situation."

"What bothers you the most, my Chimera-te?"

"Letting Terga go. She's been with me over fifteen years. Is this what parents go through when their children leave home?"

"Terga's self-aware now, and has been for a while, if I understand you. You'll know what to do when the time comes," she encouraged him.

"I don't know what to think of myself now. Every time I get used to a new change, another one pops up. This one is huge. I reacted so strongly, I could have destroyed this ship and everyone on it had Qex not evacuated me. Sometimes I feel like a freak!" Derak groused.

"You are! You're my freak and I'll always love you, no matter what you become." She embraced him.

"Thank you, my love. I treasure you more each day." Derak kissed her, and they joined the rest of the crew for a late dinner.

Qex and Vel pushed the rest of them on their daily exercises, while Zix worked with Derak. Equilibrium had to be established in Derak's fast growing mental abilities before he rejoined them. Derak had to learn teleportation while balancing the previous lessons into a complete package. They worked on marking his triggers and controlling them. Mini-sessions brought his anger issues to the point of turning them on, and Derak had to stop it from happening. When Qex and Vel joined Zix, they pressed him harder. The other drill was to tune his power output to match the situation.

After one day's frustrating results, Derak entered the great room. They imbedded a group of larger blocks in the center tabletop.

Without thinking, he walked over, reached down, and touched the table. The blocks rose, and then rested on the table.

"How did you do that?" Robert asked.

"I just formed the thought to release them. It came to me when I saw it."

"We've spent the last week trying not to imbed them, and you come in and do this?" He complained.

"On your next attempt, picture a molecular-sized air gap between the two surfaces." He sent this last thought out to the entire group. A renewed sense of hope pervaded, and they started all over again. Jack was the first to do it, followed by the rest of them in the next hour.

"That's good. Now, after you place the square, release the air cushion. You cannot see the difference. Once you've perfected this, make the cushions smaller, until you don't need them," Derak instructed them.

"What if we need the space to keep from mixing the objects again?" Shenar asked.

"Then learn how to release it once you've placed it."

Once the group could teleport their blocks without imbedding them into the target, they moved to the cargo bay. Where larger boxes were proving to be a challenge. It required three more days.

They had to get over the fear of teleporting themselves. This is where the three Telaxians would come in handy. They would ensure that they would not make any mistakes transferring themselves.

They would have a day off before they attempted to teleport themselves. It scared all of them, and they had no choice.

The day arrived, Qex entered, Seamus was mumbling to himself, Leontul sat, and Robert was pacing back and forth. Jack was fidgeting, and the women sat together in the corner. Derak was no better, tapping his foot.

Qex looked at all of them, accessing the situation. *"Fear is a healthy emotion in this case. This will ensure that none of you will get too confident and make a fatal mistake. The three of us will move with each of you during your teleportation. Safety is of the utmost importance with the unborn twins. I can assure you all will be safe. Who will be the first to try?"*

Feet shuffled, and no one stepped forward. So, Derak hesitantly volunteered for the first transfer. He rarely succumbed to fear, but it wasn't far from the surface.

"Good. Stand in that corner. You will move yourself to this spot in the middle of the room. Visualize yourself here and transport yourself. We will make sure you succeed."

Derak concentrated on his body and then on the spot. He took a deep breath and pulled the trigger. He felt Qex, Zix, and Vel surround him as he teleported. A moment later, he stood in the middle of the room. He breathed a sigh of relief. Applause filled the air and ended when Qex called for the next person to step forward. No one did. So he started picking them. Every person hesitated before plunging in. Seamus had to be prodded to move, Leontul and Robert had to be forced. Jack seemed the most comfortable with the procedure. Shesain and Shenar had to be coerced by Vel and Terga.

After the initial jump, their hesitation was disappearing. They all needed help on the next three attempts. Jack and Derak managed the fourth one themselves, and the others could do it on the fifth try. Zix congratulated them and gave them the rest of the day off.

Fun and games started again at mealtime. Utensils would disappear just when one of them would reach for it and then appear elsewhere in the room. It was good practice in jest, so it was allowed. It helped to burn off some anxiety they felt earlier. It would serve two purposes, finding objects and teleporting them back to where they belonged. Qex introduced it as a relief valve.

Once they got comfortable moving themselves in the great room, they had to practice doing it from the front of the ship to the back and again. When they became comfortable with this exercise, Qex told them about the next level, developing 'mind sight'.

Qex started, *"Your game set the foundation for the next step. You used basic mind sight to locate and return the earlier items. You must use this same principle for yourselves. The unification of the cubes in the beginning should be a reminder of what can happen if you do not do it right. A mistake with your bodies could prove terminal. We will proceed with this part on the planet."* Qex caught the looks of concern, but proceeded. The team looked at Shesain, and she knew why: the twins. It was not just her life she would be risking.

Jack was about to engage his course setting when he noticed something. *"Derak, there's a slight disturbance in orbit, and it's moving."*

"How did you pick it up? We should be the only ship in this timeline," he said.

"It was a slight spike, then disappeared. Then it showed up again before going away."

"Are you picking up any more anomalies?"

"No, but if there's one, there's more, that's been my experience," Jack commented.

Derak looked at Qex. *"What are the odds?"*

"Without knowing their starting point, it is impossible to calculate."

"Can they detect us?" Derak asked.

"Not with the new X-gen up and running," Qex insisted.

"Jack, let's go in, establish a parking orbit on the opposite side of the planet. Engage the X-gen."

"Aye, Captain."

They settled into orbit and set up a conference. *"Jack, hold this position for the time being. Could you detect the type of ship was it? Was it in sensor range?"*

"Sorry, Derak, it all happened too fast, but it was a small spike. It wasn't a cruiser; the signal was too short."

"Qex, is there any other way to find its size?" Derak asked.

"Zix and I can." Both of them conferred and joined their strengths and sent out a mind pulse. After a few moments, they returned to the bridge.

"The ship is a large scout class. We detected three signals sent, one to the second moon, one to the la-grange point and the last to the asteroid belt."

"Thanks, Qex. My guess is that the cruiser's in the belt. We might have to take the sky cycles for a recon," Derak suggested.

"You can't take those toys into interplanetary space! You'll die!" Shesain exclaimed. Her concern for the twins increased with the added thought of the potential loss of Derak.

He answered her objection. *"I built them for interplanetary travel. They're my no-see-ums, little, tiny bugs you can't see or swat, and with the new X-gen, we'll have every advantage."*

"Derak. It'll take you forever to reach the belt," Robert pointed out.

"We'll arrive in two hours, spend two hours scouting, and then return. Round trip should take no longer than six, seven hours."

"What about bathroom breaks, food and hydration?" Shenar asked.

"That's already built in, Shenar, and I've added a quasi-dimensional generator to each one. So, it will be roomier than it looks. I'll take Seamus and some of his miniature probes to help us locate the ships. I suggest we leave soon."

No matter what anyone said, Derak would not be dissuaded. Qex backed him. Seamus and Derak put on strong flexible space suits. The helmets retracted back into the neck and closed the micro-second it detected above normal levels of carbon dioxide or the sudden lack of air. Seamus had his cycle loaded with his drones, and Derak's had long range vid equipment.

They waved goodbye to expectant and concerned faces on the other side of the airlock. They mounted the cycles, and the retractable shell surrounded them. Derak gave a thumb's up. They launched into Thumar's orbit and set course for the asteroid belt.

"Sky Cycle One to Sky Cycle Two, do you copy?"

"Copy, Sky Cycle One."

"These babies have a secret: they have miniature IDMD drives. Even they leave a traceable trail, so, to minimize our presence, we can only take micro jumps. That's why it will take two hours to get there. We don't want to alert them to our presence."

"Copy, Sky Cycle One."

"Sky Cycle One, to 'The Shesain', do you copy?"

"We copy Sky Cycle One. There are no signs of detection. Proceed with mission."

"Copy, 'Shesain', we are starting micro jumps now. We will contact you when we reach the belt."

Derak remotely tied in with Seamus's sky cycle and started the first jump. If one could see them in space, one would notice two tiny oblong eggs disappearing and then reappearing in normal space millions of miles further. The asteroid belt lay some ninety million miles from Thumar. Space craft as small as theirs had to avoid major planetary gravitational fields; the cycles might be small and fast, but large planetary gravitational fields could swallow them in seconds. This put Derak's exceptional navigational skills to the test, but Jack was still the master.

"Sky Cycle One to The Shesain.*"*

"Copy Sky Cycle One."

"Jack, I've calculated six jumps. Do you confirm?"

"You might want to add one more. Your trail is still detectable, but not by much."

"Copy, Shesain.*"*

He calculated one more jump, and the race was on. Two hours later, they approached the edge of the belt. They turned the vids on as they entered. It was beautiful. Everything from pea-sized pebbles to small moons occupied their field of vision. These would have coalesced and formed at least one more planet had the gas giant not formed. Their shields and force fields were at maximum. They not only had to avoid rocky objects flying at speeds of up to tens of thousand miles per hour, but they were at the edge of extreme radiation from the gas giant.

"Sky Cycle Two, deploy the drones and stick close. Our force fields will work better together."

"Copy Sky Cycle One, drones deployed."

"Seamus, we are looking for a medium-sized class destroyer. Metallic density will give it away. Minor thruster activity might help

us out. Once we find it, do not engage. We will get close enough to get vid recordings and leave."

"Copy, Derak. Readings are coming in. No activity in this sector, moving into sector two."

"Copy, Seamus. Use your infrared. They will be the only heat source."

They searched for an hour and a half before they got their first blip. They triangulated its location and approached. They had to look hard to find it. It was as black as space with no external lights visible. Their only confirmation was the infrared and drone data. So, they circled around it and placed it between them and the dim sun. You could barely make out its shape. It resembled a shark from ancient Earth and looked just as dangerous.

If they were using the occasional thruster to maintain position, they hid it well. The sky cycles crept in as close as possible. The X-gens were an upgrade to the D-gens, but they were untested until now. After ten minutes of vids, they came upon the symbol of a blood red scorpion in a barbed circle. They took enough vids to confirm the intel and recalled the drones.

Upon leaving, Derak figured that they had come out on the other end of the asteroid belt. They had to figure one more jump to get them back undetected. By the time they returned to *The Shesain,* they had been cooped up in the tiny shells for eight hours. They were more than ready to step foot onto *The Shesain* again. After the air lock equalized pressure with the rest of the ship, the inner door opened, and Derak handed Qex the vid crystal.

Shesain fawned over him, making sure he was ok. Shenar and Vel converged on Seamus. He had grown back his beloved flaming red beard, and he missed his Chimera very much.

Jack, Derak, Qex, and Zix met in the great room to go over the vids. When they got to the telling evidence, they paused it. The scorpion confirmed their suspicions.

"We will change our approach to the situation now. The time waves have alerted Dextrametrix of our presence. He will investigate the circumstances and will tie the time waves to us. He will then

bend his will to stop us. He is a more than capable tactician, but our technology gives us the advantage. We must not make any mistakes. He will capitalize on any advantage."

"I agree with Qex," Zix added. *"He was our mole in the Orion Syndicate. He turned and is now running it, and he knows both mortal and Telaxian habits well. He was one of our best infiltration agents, so we might have to change the rules of the game from here on out. We go with the schedule Qex has set, in X-gen, until insertion into real time is required. Since mental abilities are being used to teleport, the technology will not interfere with the results."*

Ship life settled down once again, despite the recent issue. The crew relaxed in the simulation room on sunlit grass, surrounded by trees, and enjoyed a country picnic on blankets. Shesain prepared fried chicken, potato salad, coleslaw, and cut up fruit and dessert after she compelled Qex, Leontul, and Derak to help her. Qex was turning out to be quite a talented cook. Zix enjoyed the spectacle. When Shesain clarified that he would learn to cook too, he left the kitchen. Vel giggled to herself.

The next day, the crew beamed down to Thumar in the year 1817 and continued their teleportation exercises. They started with having to locate natural items that Qex and Zix identified, they weren't told what or where they were. This proved impossible at first, because their energy markers were masked very well. Robert was the first to make a breakthrough by accident. He could pick up a slight trace of their fields. He got the same results the second time. He passed this onto the rest of them and by the third day; the crew had located almost all of them and transferred them back to base camp. By the fifth day, they had retrieved all the objects. Then, they were told to return them to their original locations without imbedding them or harming them in any manner. Once this was done, the lessons became more difficult.

The objects got smaller and further away. The last test involved one-half-gram spheres placed hundreds of miles away. Their sensitivity had grown by leaps and bounds. This last test pushed all of them beyond their comfort level. After many failed attempts, they succeeded.

The next round involved locating small animals and moving them to camp before returning them to their original habitats, unharmed. Derak brought in a large constrictor snake. The party jumped back before he could return it. Shenar conjured up a field mouse, and Robert located a medium size mammal of strange origin. Shesain had the funniest, a pair of squirrel-like creatures in the middle of copulation. The looks on their furry faces was priceless. The crew got a good laugh on that one, even Zix. Seamus had the scariest moment. His efforts transferred a Bengal tiger cub that disappeared faster than it showed up. They were ready for the next level.

Qex, Zix, and Vel were in three different locations, and the team had to locate them. Once found, they had to teleport themselves to each spot, one-hundred-and fifty-miles away. They were all nervous about this one. Rocks, twigs, spheres, and animals were one thing, but moving themselves was another matter altogether. It took much cajoling from the Telaxians to get them to where they would attempt it. The rules changed too, and they had to do this without help from anybody else.

The game of hide and seek was on. Shenar was the first to leave, and then the rest followed. Seamus and Robert were the last. They all ended up in unfamiliar landscapes. Robert, Seamus and Shenar ended up on a mountaintop with Qex. Derak, Shesain and Leontul were at the ocean, Vel and Jack joining Zix in a dessert. This exercise continued until all of them had teleported to each location.

Then they popped to separate continents and the Corano Islands. The last test was to teleport to *The Shesain* and back. If they were reticent the first time, it was nothing compared to this. Not one of them stepped forward, not even after a pep talk from Qex. It was Terga that broke the stalemate. She said she would provide a homing signal on the first attempts. Derak stepped forward for the first try. He homed in on Terga, shut his eyes and teleported. He breathed a sigh of relief at the sight of the bridge. Satisfied that he was still living, he popped back down to the planet. A rousing cheer followed his appearance. It took an hour before the remaining students took their first plunge. Each was greeted upon their return.

Qex declared them ready for the next mission. He informed them they had to break camp and teleport the stuff back to its original locations on *The Shesain* before they came up. Qex instructed them to pack up the camp with telekinesis only before sending the material up. Qex would inspect it on board. If it wasn't right, he would send it back down again. It would have gone faster with their hands.

The Ganmer Continent, 1817

Qex briefed them on the next mission. He started by commending them on the past two. *"I must congratulate all of you on two successful assignments. The difficulty factor will increase with every new one. There is a recent development that will add to the danger. The Orion Syndicate are investigating the past time waves. We both occupy the same space and time. One ship is in orbit and two within striking distance. They are very dangerous and will try to stop us if they connect us to the time-waves. They are headed by another Telaxian senior infiltration agent who switched sides. He is accomplished."*

"What do we do?" Jack asked.

"Stay on course. Keep your eyes and ears open to any unusual occurrence outside of those inherent to your assignments. Zix, Vel, and I will monitor what we can from here."

"What's next for us?" Seamus asked.

"You will receive further instruction in levitation next. You toyed with this during your telekinesis training. Now, we will show you the specifics. This will be short compared to the previous lessons.

"You will start with larger blocks and work down to half-gram spheres. You have already proved can do this. The next step is to control targets in an energetic maelstrom. Concentration is paramount to maintain the energy fields you create. The three of us will disrupt you until you can hold the objects steady. It requires concentrating on two things at the same time, a target, and a growing field rotation. A dexterous mind is needed to succeed."

The first few days were very frustrating. Concentrating on two things at once was very difficult. The fourth day, they raised the cubes, and then the three Telaxians interrupted their concentration, causing the blocks to come crashing down. More than one of the crew complained, resulting in a redoubled effort on their instructors part. They soon learned to keep their mouths shut and concentrate harder and longer. After four days of additional practice, they started holding their own. By the seventh day, they all kept their targets steady in an energy vortex. After the great room, they proceeded to the cargo bay, to larger, heavier crates. Success here showed Qex that they were ready to go down to the planet.

Tasks were getting more complex and harder to keep up with. They all managed large boulders weighing many more times than they did combined. They had to move them from one location to another without crashing into each other. Telaxian efforts to disrupt their concentration knew no bounds. After another week, they satisfied Qex. They had to locate a half-gram sphere somewhere, teleport it to their location, and then make them perform a finely tuned choreographed dance.

One of the last lessons was to learn kinetics, how to start a fire and then put it out with a thought. This included finding the wood, getting it to their barren rocky site, building the fire, starting it, and then snuffing it out. Qex looked pleased and told them they had to build a rock shelter with their minds, find their own food, cook it, and leave the site as they found it. With all the team had been through, this was no problem.

The crew's Telaxue skills improved. Qex's instructions became quicker and more succinct. He allowed them to vocally communicate when they were by themselves. Speaking was now becoming as foreign to them as mind-speak had been at first. Its efficiency and speed made talking slow and laborious, but they couldn't lose their comfort level with speech. It would be required on the planetary expeditions.

Back onboard the ship, Qex addressed them. "*You have come a long way in your mind strength, but I advise you not to put too much stock in your new abilities. They may be exceptional by mortal standards, but twelve-year-old Telaxian children know more than you do now. In the coming days, we will add a few more tools to your arsenal. I advise all of you not to grandstand your abilities to your fellow mortal beings; they are for discretionary use only. The less that is known of your talents, the better off you will be. I will grant two day's rest from all exercises, then I'll brief you on the next assignment."*

Robert and Seamus worked as a team now, most of the time. Their ability to read machine language and operation pleased even Zix. Shenar and Shesain could research any subject in a near blink of an eye. Leontul could read a body in an instant and come up with an herbal remedy for almost any condition. Jack worked with Vel to perfect his ability to interpret Telaxian knowledge and communicate it.

Zix and Qex worked with Derak to fine tune his control and develop his offensive weapons. They told him that knowing a weapon helps control it. Qex, Vel, and Zix pushed Derak's anger issues to greater heights. Derak knew his first two DNA trigger points very well now. He would master the fourth strand only in a group of Telaxian elders.

Everyone was refreshed, and awaited Qex's briefing. They were in excellent moods. The Telaxians were chipper, for Telaxians, as they entered. Vel was grinning, and Qex and Zix were in the middle of an animated thought conversation. They weren't smiling, but they weren't frowning either.

Qex began. *"I'm glad you are all in pleasant moods. Your next installment takes place on the Ganmer continent, in the year 1817. Keltur Shenmar is on its plains scouting a location for a settlement site. He is the one who colonizes the future site of Shenmar city.*

"Paul Rankin, an Earth miner, is also in the same vicinity. He is looking for metals, but he does not realize the value of Thumdust yet. He carries a powerful portable forge with him. This one can smelt Thumdust. Seamus will go down as Allen McGregor and guide Rankin to the vein and show him the qualities of Thumdust. Leontul will play himself, an herbalist of fame, named Torimere Eshimar.

Shenar will be his apprentice, Leyla Voxmur. Keltur and Paul Rankin must stay and establish Shenmar.

"All three of you will come from the Northern Highlands with no village you call home. You are all wanderers. The open road is your home. Shesain and Shenar will compile a representative list of villages you have passed through in the last year. They will be places everyone knows. They will collect the required clothing and customs. We will provide currency." Qex finished.

When it was time, they made a small time-space jump to reset the timeline. Security protocols were reset to include the company of the Syndicate. Qex assured them they would not be detected in X-gen mode. He stated that it would be difficult for a Telaxian patrol to locate them.

Even with null space and time jumps becoming standard practice, a strict timeline had to be adhered to. It required exact days and sometimes hours and minutes to fit exacting Telaxian computations. Once on the planet's surface, the team had four days to complete the mission, with a built-in overrun of twenty-eight hours maximum.

Seamus would verify the Thumdust vein before entering the miner's camp, and Shenar and Leontul would gather the required plants needed for the sick in Keltur Shenmar's camp. Their telepathic location and teleportation skills shortened prep time down to one day.

Seamus trekked off to the miner's camp, while Leontul and Shenar made their way to Keltur's. They arrived about the same time and delayed their entry time by scanning the crowds, determining who would be the best to approach first. Once the targets were chosen, they waited for their cues.

Leontul and Shenar entered Keltur's camp dressed like well-seasoned travelers. Shenar's physical assets were downplayed, and she carried the bulk of the plants and roots in an over the shoulder sack. They both hummed a happy travel tune known to anyone on Ganmer. They were stopped before they could reach the center of the camp.

"Halt! Who goes there, and where do you hail from?" a burley, rough-looking man asked. He stepped in front of them, stopping their progress. "What business do you have here? This is a closed encampment." His words came out hard. Shenar reached out and calmed his mind. He shook his head and tried to speak again. She deftly touched his mind a second time and his defensive stance softened.

"Please forgive my abruptness. We've had one too many forceful intrusions on our encampment. We almost lost one man, and many are sick from an unknown illness."

"Perhaps we can help you then?" Leontul answered. "My name is Torimere Eshimar, and this is my apprentice, Leyla Voxmur. I am an herbal doctor."

The man's tone was civil now, and others joined him to check out the new wanderers.

"Many apologies doctor, my name is Beltur Fractam, chief of security; I can take you to our senior leaders, follow me."

Leontul agreed to go as they fell in next to Belture and other expedition members immediately surrounded them. Beltur continued as he eyed Shenar. "A woman is a bag of mixed blessings, doctor. These men have not seen their wives, or girlfriends, for months now. Keltur, our expedition lead runs a tight ship here; he may not agree to her company."

"Where I go, she goes. I promised her family she would complete her apprenticeship with me, I am a man of my word. I assure you she can handle herself, even in the company of men," Leontul answered.

Here we are, Keltur is in a nasty mood today. Another key member of our odyssey has fallen ill. They entered a large tent and were led before a slight, but fit man. He had a hard look on his face. He whispered something to a lieutenant before facing Beltur and his captives. They exchanged no niceties as he took a long drink of water and offered none to Leontul or Shenar.

He sat down in his chair behind a makeshift desk. His voice was gruff with a hard edge as he spoke. "I thought I told you not to allow any more strangers into camp, Beltur. You remember the trouble we had with the last two, don't you? Are there any red bugs in a barbed circle on them?"

Leontul and Shenar looked at Beltur who could not remember searching them. He thought it better to keep quiet.

"None, sir. They've been questioned, and Torimere here is an herbal doctor. And this is his apprentice, Leyla Voxmur."

"Give me their bags, all of them. Did you bother to check them for weapons?"

"There is no sign they carry any," he answered as he handed all of their bags over to Keltur.

"That's what Peltur thought and look at him now." He rifled through the bags and found nothing but roots, leaves, flower petals, trail food, and water. He gave them a stern look and asked them, "Are you carrying weapons of any sort?"

Leontul replied, "we carry a variety of knives to collect plant samples and to cook with. We would be remiss to have nothing to defend ourselves with, being travelers."

"Show me," Keltur demanded.

As Leontul reached for his belt, long knives came out of their scabbards. He laid the belt on the table in front of him. Keltur inspected them and handed them back.

Shenar unbuckled the belt on her travel cloak, removed it, and laid it on a chair. Murmurs of approval were heard. She took the belt off and handed it to Keltur. He inspected the knives and handed them back.

"I need to have a word with the doctor, in private. Everyone, back to what you were doing!" The tent emptied.

"Doctor, can you see to my men? Two are hurt from a previous scuffle, but they live. The others are with fever." Keltur asked.

"It would be my pleasure."

•◆•

Seamus sauntered into the mining camp like he belonged there, all six foot six inches of him with his bushy flaming red beard and broad smile leading the way.

188

"What can we do you for stranger?" An imposing figure asked him.

He answered in an understandable Scottish brogue. "I'm looking for the head of this bunch."

"That would be Paul Rankin. What would be your name?" The guard asked.

"Allen McGregor, freelance miner and metallurgist. I've run across some interesting stuff, it's different. I have an idea how to use it, but I need some other metals and a forge."

"You're not Thumarian! You're from Earth!" Said a sizable man, as he approached, his dark brown beard as big as Seamus's.

"I am that! Our ship got caught in some strange wormhole, and we ended up here. Not much of it left, so we're stuck," Seamus groused.

"Same thing happened to us. Welcome to early 19th century Thumar. We do the best we can, but it's nothing like having electric lights," he said with a smile.

"It's amazing what we take for granted, isn't it? I've got something to show you. I've got a feeling about it. Still needs checking out."

"Let's look at it. Paul, Rodger, get Sam and the sampler kit. We'll go to my tent and look at it there. Where are you from Allen? Sounds like you're from the Emerald Isle."

"Scotland, Laddy, make no mistake aboot it! I wouldn't claim ancestry to those scruffy Irish ruffians," Seamus retorted.

"You might have a bone to pick with Ian on that one." Paul laughed.

"As long as it's a gnawing bone below a good black ale. No need to raise a ruckus, we're all from the same clan now."

"You're right. I think we're ready to test your samples now," Rodger said.

They entered the well-lit tent and moved to a metal-topped table. Paul handed Seamus's first sample to Sam. He took an eyepiece and looked at its structure. Then, he laid it on the table and chipped a piece off easily with a rock hammer, and he looked up.

"Nothin special about this rock, there's not much strength to it."

He handed it to Rodger, and after he looked at it, he shook his head. "Is that all you've got?" Paul asked.

Seamus smiled. "I felt the same until I found this one. Somewhere in the geology, these two minerals mixed. Not totally, but enough to change the molecular structure of both. Check it out."

He dropped the sample on the table. Sam followed the previous procedure, this time taking longer. He struck the rock with his hammer. Sparks flew. Sam looked surprised and hit it again, getting the same results. "This is interesting. Neither metal is mixed totally, but you can't even chip it."

"Can you imagine if they were mixed and hardened? The good thing about the original is it can get reduced to powder form. Are you up for a test?" Seamus asked.

"Sure, we're working on a new batch right now. How much more of the original do you have?" Paul asked.

"Enough for a few runs. If it works like I think it will, I'll show you the vein. It's close to here."

"Let's go then, Sam. Get the forge heated," Paul ordered.

The news about the new mineral spread fast, and a crowd followed them to the forge. It was a bulky-looking contraption, surrounded by an enclosure that was getting warmer as they stoked the fires. They put chunks of raw steel in the smelter, and it liquefied. Paul and Seamus made some calculations and ran the first mineral enriched batch. Seamus knew the proper mixture but held back for form's sake, to avoid inviting suspicion. The first batch resulted in a solid-looking but brittle product. The second attempt was a little better. They were down to the last samples and Seamus suggested a new mixture. It was hot around the forge; everyone was down to short sleeves, despite the chilly temperature outside. The material was weighed, melted, and mixed, and poured into a shallow form. After the metal cooled, they lay it on a metal anvil with their best sample of steel.

Their biggest man, who almost made Seamus look small, took a hammer to it. It just bounced off, not even leaving a dent. He repeated this action on their steel. The bounce was less, and made a noticeable dent. Paul and Sam shared an appraising look. Paul signaled the big man to repeat his powerful blows three more times, with the same results.

"We have something here, Allen. I think we should mount an expedition to your vein tomorrow. If it's big enough, we just might set up shop there. Sam, tell Peter to roast up a pig, we've got something to celebrate." Paul turned to Seamus. "What are you getting out of this, Allen?"

"We'll talk about it after you see the vein. We have a celebration to get going."

"Right you are," Paul replied with good cheer.

They roasted a wild boar with vegetables and roots. For the rest of the night, strong ale flowed, and the party went on to the early hours of the morning. They all slept, sated on good news, food, and brew.

At noon the following day, Seamus, Paul, Sam, and a six-man crew left for the first Thumdust vein to be found on the Ganmer continent.

The expedition set out with high hopes. Seamus led them down a few wrong paths on purpose. He had to make it look hard. He got on the right track after two days. To most of the expedition, the first signs of the vein weren't impressive. The edge was sparse and spread out. The team took their 22nd century Earth detection equipment. Their scientific apparatus was one of the few things that survived the crash of 1808. This vein was meager, but workable. Then they went further to locate another one.

One day later, after walking many miles, they hit the mother lode. They marked it, and set off back to their main camp. They located more veins to pull iron from on the trip back. They would set up a few camps and start mining all the raw material they would need.

The morning after, Seamus, Paul, and Sam were talking.

"What do we do now, Paul? We've got this huge vein?"

"How do we use it?" Sam asked.

Paul replied. "For now, we will mine and smelt the rest. There's got to be a market for the metal somewhere. What do you think, Allen?"

"Maybe we don't have to put it to use, only mine the ore. I hear that another team is scouting the plains not too far from here. You might work something out with them," Allen suggested.

"Yeah, sure! Have you ever met Keltur? You'd think humans did him nothing but wrong. Ever since Shabul, he has nothing but disdain for us, even after we helped the village with the plague of 1814. He was one of the survivors that lost his father. He was never the same again."

"What's his problem, if you helped him?" Allen asked.

"He thought we were too high handed during the second crisis at their clinic. He seems to forget that they would have killed the doctors responsible for making the cure. We talk, but just barely."

"Aha! Maybe if you have something he needs, or could use, his business sense might kick in. Bring your big man, the anvil, and the samples, and repeat the demonstration of the new mixture in front of him. All you can do is try. He might be persuaded to see the light," Allen suggested.

"I don't know, I must think about it," Paul said.

Seamus put a subtle mental suggestion into his mind and waited.

"No, he won't go for it," Paul responded.

Seamus repeated his suggestion, and this time it stuck.

"What the hell, it might be worth a try! Sam, get Bill, the anvil, and the samples ready to leave in the morning," Paul said as he surrendered.

Seamus, Paul, Sam, and Bill left the next morning with the anvil on a cart pulled by a huge horse-like creature. They would arrive in about three hours, not knowing what type of reception they would receive. Paul was not in a good mood for the entire journey. Their reception bore out his misgivings. At the edge of Keltur's camp, they were met by five Thumarians.

Keltur joined them, he was not happy. "Humans at my doorstep again. What brings you this time, Paul? Who's the new guy? He looks like the one I saw in Shabul, leading your pack of thugs on the clinic," Keltur insulted Paul.

"You and most of your friends here wouldn't be alive if we hadn't come when we did," Paul reminded Keltur.

"Don't remind me!" Keltur shot back.

"We're here to offer you a deal, one you might see the sense of."

"Another offering of metal, is it? We produce our own now, and it's better than yours."

"Not the latest. What we have is better. I know you're scouting a site for a new settlement and this would help us both out." Paul suggested.

"Why would I want to help a human?" Keltur spit back.

This would have gone on until both of them walked away had Seamus, Shenar, and Leontul not softened the two minds to the point of a compromise.

"All right Paul, you have one hour to prove your point. Bring your...beasts."

Paul nearly walked away. Seamus worked his mind again, and Paul gritted his teeth as he moved forward. When they arrived, a crowd gathered. Bill picked the heavy anvil up and placed it down with no effort. He pulled out the samples and set them up.

Before he could start, Keltur stirred the fire up more. "Is this it? I thought by now you could do better."

"Shut up and watch, you dolt!" Paul fired back.

Keltur did, after Shenar, and Leontul controlled his anger.

Bill hammered the Thumdust-invigorated metal, and the hammer bounced, leaving no marks.

"What's this gimmickry, Paul? Anyone can fake what you just did."

"If you doubt the results, bring your best piece of metal and have your...beast try it." Paul said with a wicked smile.

"My Threngar are not beasts, Paul!"

"Mine aren't either, Keltur!"

"You made your point. Kashkur, grab your biggest hammer and a fresh piece of steel. Prove these humans wrong."

Paul smiled to himself as Kashkur returned.

Kashkur stepped up to the anvil and tested his hammer on the bare metal. Its ring reverberated throughout the center of camp. He smiled. "They make a good anvil." Then he tested the new metal with the same results Bill got. It surprised him when he looked at the metal with no marks. He hit it again with the same results, then a third time in disbelief. He shook his head and put his metal on the anvil. He pounded his sample with the same veracity and was shocked at the outcome. The metal curled up from the three blows. Just to be sure of himself, he repeated his hammer blow on the new metal one more time.

Afterward, he stood staring at it. "He's got something here, Keltur. Four blows and not a dent. Ours is beyond use for anything against this." He looked at Paul and gave him a respectful bow before returning to Keltur's side.

"What's your angle, Paul? What do you want from us?" Keltur asked.

"Let's put the past behind us and work together, Keltur. I'll work the mines and foundries and you build your settlement. I'm sure we can come up with a solution."

"We'll talk, there are other issues to deal with here besides a new metal and a few foundries. I suggest we meet in my tent after you put your anvil away."

Kashkur lifted the anvil back into the wagon, not to be outdone by Bill. Then both big men walked away, trading good-natured barbs.

"I hope you can handle our ale as good as you smith metals," Kashkur challenged him.

"I'll drink anybody under the table, including you," Bill answered.

In Keltur's tent, the men settled down to mugs of ale. Keltur and Paul sat across from each other. Seamus, Shenar, and Leontul were present along with Keltur's lieutenants.

"What are your troubles, Keltur? You're the one on the settlement end," Paul asked.

"Water, we have found no lakes in these plains," he replied in disgust.

"I have something to say about that," Rutar interrupted.

"Proceed," Paul said.

"I'm the land management specialist, and my team has found

evidence of a possible ample underground water supply. We just have to find it."

"How will the mining operation affect the water supply?" Keltur asked.

"We can locate the mines after we settle the water situation," Paul said.

"May I speak?" Shenar asked.

"You may, Leyla."

"This location is prime for any settlement." Seamus, Leontul, and Shenar softened the group's mind. "You have thousands of acres of arable land and more healing plants than you can identify. Dr. Eshimere helped all the sick patients in this camp with what we collected in two days. There is a tree line, and we can collect water from the winter rains in caches. We can do the mining to preserve the plains and still supply the demand. Not to mention the stable temperatures in this region of the continent. You could not choose a better spot, and the combination of mining and agriculture makes this a prime location."

"I think all mining should be underground. On Earth, we saw the results of strip mining and how it devastated the land. We will mine in cooperation with land specialists to preserve the habitat," Paul added.

Rutar spoke again. "My team has located a rocky plateau above the tree line that would be perfect for a town. It's close to the plains, and would not disrupt the natural balance."

"That would make a far better defensible position in a conflict, should one arise," a Lieutenant added.

Keltur looked long at Paul and spoke his mind. "I think we can come up with a plan. It will take some time to work out the details. We'll talk after dinner."

The tent emptied and Seamus, Shenar, and Leontul stepped out of sight, turned on their X-gens, and teleported back up to *The Shesain* before the time wave hit.

•◆•

The Prime Mathematician on board *The Mandible* was knocked off of his feet by the time wave. He picked himself up and summoned Councilman Number One and Two; they entered, shaken.

"I can replace you! What good is your captain Thompson if he cannot find and stop a single ship with our resources?"

"Mutah Shakur, commander Thompson is running border patrols in the Thumarian system, by your orders, Sir," Number Two squeaked out.

The Mutah Shakur was about to do something very bloody, but refrained. He had to maintain his self-control. However, a solid statue near him crumpled into a blob of unrecognizable metal. The councilmen froze in terror. The Mutah Shakur realized that the last time wave changed things. "If you want to keep breathing Number One, recall this commander and make him a captain. Put him in charge of stopping this. I am sure that you have something on him to keep him in line."

"His sister, Mutah Shakur. We killed his wife during a premature childbirth. His sister is the only one left of his family. We are certain he'll comply."

"He had better, Number One, otherwise, your heads will roll. Leave me now and send April in."

The two councilmen hurried out of the chamber with a renewed purpose.

The Cave of Lights: 1845

The crew on board *The Shesain* sat down before the time wave hit. Had they been standing; it would have knocked them off of their feet. The wave was like a tsunami. The further it spread out from the source, the more widespread the effects were. After it passed, Qex congratulated them on the latest expedition.

"You did well this time. We will move to a node, then Zix, Derak, and I will teleport to Telaxia for our report. Computations will be made on the effectiveness of the last three missions, and they will make any corrections that are required."

"Why does Derak have to go?" Shesain asked.

"Those are my orders," Qex answered. *"Vel will keep command of the overall mission in our absence. She has received instructions on your continued lessons, both optic and mental. You will follow her instructions as if they were my own. Any deviations will be known and dealt with upon our return. You will learn bi-location, the ability to be in two places at the same time. Robert, Shesain, and Shenar will locate the entrance to the Cave of Lights in the year 1845."*

Vel attached Derak's fingernails, shaved his face, and fitted him into his hooded robe. Derak kissed Shesain, and then Qex, Zix, and Derak teleported. They found themselves in the Council Chambers on Telaxia, facing the Valuk-Manou and her nine-member Senior Council. *"Welcome back, Admiral Andehar,"* the Valuk-Manou addressed him. *"Qex's reports are promising, except for the Syndicate. Your extra activities have not affected calculations but must be cleared through Qex and Zix. Am I clear on this?"*

"*Yes, Valuk-Manou,*" Derak responded.

"*Good. We will start with a report from Qex and Zix. If we need information from you, we will ask it for.*"

Qex delivered the progress report in ten minutes in Telaxue. The Council and the Valuk-Manou conferred on their private channel: even Qex and Zix were left out. The council ran the calculations.

Valuk-Manou addressed them. "*We will re-check our calculations, considering your progress report. All three of you have earned a well-deserved rest. This council will reconvene tomorrow morning. The Admiral will receive upgrades to his Telaxian rank. That is all for now.*"

They escorted Derak to a room near the council chambers while Qex and Zix left to see their families. The room was large, and Derak settled in for the evening. One attendant removed Derak's original nail extensions and applied fresh ones. They were one inch longer. She painted them with symbology he could now read. The other attendant installed his removable chin beard that was longer and more decorated. His face was shaved, and they applied an ointment that slowed down hair growth.

The next morning the women returned to groom him and delivered a new knee-length coat, with gold piping sewn into the seams. They embroidered his Kenmar medallion over one side of his chest and the braid rounded out the outfit. His escort picked him up after he left the room.

Qex, Zix, and another Telaxian joined Derak before they entered the chambers. The third Telaxian was dressed in a blue robe with white piping. His only indicator of rank, besides his long fingernails, was a white chin beard with a symbol Derak had not yet seen. He was at medium height and had an air of supreme power. All four were met by the Valuk Manou, her Senior Council, and thirty powerful Telaxians.

They led Derak to a chair in the middle of the group and sat down. Qex and Zix stood on both sides of him, and the new officer stationed himself behind him.

The Valuk Manou directed her thoughts to Derak in Telaxue.

"Admiral, you will master your fourth strand. It requires this for the completion of your time-fix schedule. Because of your recent mental lessons, the numbers you notice around you are required to prevent you from causing any physical or mental damage. If you fail, we will have no choice but to remove you from our computations. Do you understand?"

"Yes," Derak replied.

"We will work through the process, step by step. You can be an exceptional asset to us in dealing with the mortal races. We do not want to lose you."

"Let's get started."

"We will test your second and third strand control first, then we'll trigger your fourth. There is enough mind strength present to keep you in check. Once you are in the fourth, we will guide you through safety," The Valuk-Manou assured him.

Forty council members, Qex, Zix, and the new Telaxian formed a psychic force field around him. The group started the test on the second and third strands. They pushed him harder than he'd ever been challenged before. After one hour, they signaled their approval, and then triggered the fourth.

Rage took over Derak's senses. He felt superhuman abilities affect every cell in his body, being held in check by Qex, Zix and the new Telaxian. He could not move a muscle. With his physical functions controlled, his mind, and all of its recent training kicked into full gear. This time it was different. Whereas the shift would have taken less than a moment, it now acted in slow motion. They paused the first level of the fourth strand. It felt like mental torture. The emotions embedded in the strand fought to complete the connection but couldn't. The fight between Derak's offensive output and the greater external forces pushed his mind to the brink. He was barely maintaining any level of sanity. He could sense every mind in the room and reached out to break their hold over him. The external energy field flexed but did not break. Both sides were held in a stalemate.

The instructions started. Derak could detect the Valuk Manou, but the new Telaxian in the blue robe took the lead. *"Identify the trigger and control it. It is like your ego when it feels threatened, it fights back. Let the trigger know that it will live and show it its home."*

Derak concentrated and identified the trigger. There were many levels to this last strand. Every successive step he took, the harder it was to reign in his impulses. His body fought hard for freedom at every turn and physical exhaustion started setting in. Mental images of breaking bones, starting large fires, and frying brain synapses were a few of the offensive thoughts he tried to make happen. Every time he sent one out it hit an impenetrable wall and dissipated. Had there not been any protective field, the Chambar Valley Offensive would have been child's play in comparison. He could kill a brigade with a mere thought now!

The assault on his fourth strand went on for hours. When his offensive push subsided, the instructions continued. He discovered the fourth strand was organized into five strata, and each stratum had many divisions. Derak and the controlling group started again and worked through each individual division. After uncountable hours they turned the strand off, and released him. Derak was exhausted, mentally, and physically. When he returned to his quarters, he had no energy to eat before he dropped to his bed asleep before his body hit the mattress. He lost count of the days that followed. The deeper they moved into the fourth strand, the stronger his reactions were.

•◆•

On board *The Shesain*, each day was consumed by lessons that kept the crew occupied. When Vel was not conducting the exercises, she was with Shesain, monitoring her health. The twins were developing an understanding of time, space, and dimensional jumps. They learned as Shesain did. It was scary to think about how much the children would know when they were born. It would take parenting to a whole new dimension.

Jack worked with Terga to understand the new technology. He

spent hours in front of the 3-D models studying their mathematical structures. His knowledge of Telaxue increased, so much, that he assisted Vel and Terga with the daily lessons. They kept the crew busy, as cabin fever was a dangerous emotion to deal with. They used the simulations with a few fresh changes in scenery comprising familiar recreations of home life they had left behind.

After duty hours, the card games continued to ease stress, with Vel joining in. She was becoming more 'mortal' with every passing day, which would serve her well when she was assigned to Shesain as a nanny. It would require her expertise in raising the twins.

The next morning, Vel collected the crew together for bi-location training. *"When you bi-locate, you are in two places at once; only one of you is the real you. The other is a shadow of your true self, but it has all the same senses and abilities of the original, and is controlled by the original body. The double is capable of full physical action and is perceived as real. Bi-location is a combination of teleportation and mind sight. If your double sustains damage or dies, you will feel the pain. You must be very careful in employing this. If too many doubles get injured or die, it can permanently damage the true body."*

"What's the purpose of this?" Robert asked. *"I can understand the other stuff we learned, but being in two places at the same time?"*

"Everything you learn has relevance to mission parameters. All of you have at least a fifty percent chance of using this. Preparation is the best medicine. Knowing how to deal with a situation ensures the best chance of success."

"Isn't that dangerous, splitting yourself?" Shenar asked.

"Not any more than teleporting, which all of you have accomplished. We will start from the bridge. You will put your other self into a simulation of your choice first. Then when you have completed that phase, we will move down to the planet in X-gen. Reach out with your mind sight and pick a spot on the beach. You must concentrate on placing your shadow self. Use that shadow to search your surroundings and collect information. Then return the second self to your primary body. It extends your primary soul

energy. You must be careful not to put too much of yourself into the copy, just enough to get the job done."

The first attempts did not go well. When they finally moved their shadow selves, they looked like ghosts. After four more tries, the doubles were close to being solid. The crew was granted the rest of the day for rest because the energy required to bi-locate is enough to cause exhaustion. The moment preceding sleep, Shesain sensed the energy fields of the twins.

The next day was occupied with optics and bi-locating. The crew came even closer. Vel was as tough as Qex, with a gentle touch. The fifth day the crew succeeded in a complete transfer. They spent the rest of the week making brief excursions to the back of the ship. Robert was wrestling with how to prove what he was doing without being construed as crazy.

Jack performed a sweep of Thumar and the moons, finding no Syndicate presence. Just to be sure, he sent drones to the asteroid belt to confirm their absence. When their signals came back negative, they set a date. Vel would stay aboard *The Shesain* and monitor their progress. Jack stood in as the instructor.

By the fourth day on Thumar, the crew achieved a range of two hundred miles between themselves and their shadows. The next step was continent hopping. One stop was Ganmer, to check up on progress after the last completed mission. The last test was to bi-locate between null space and real time on Thumar. This made the crew very nervous. It took two days of prodding from Vel and Terga to move them to the first attempt. Their primary selves would remain on *The Shesain,* for safety reasons. After several successful transfers, the crew placed their shadows on board the ship. They did this on the day Qex, Zix, and Derak returned.

•◆•

Derak's time on Telaxia wasn't limited to controlling his fourth strand. He also had to learn bi-location. These lessons came after the council sessions stopped taking so much out of him. Every day felt like mental torture. Derak had finally reached the fifth stratum of the fourth strand, by far the toughest. The closer you got to the core, the more intense the feelings became. Many times, he reached the breaking point. The combined minds assisting him was the only thing that kept Derak from going over the edge. He was reaching the last days he would spend on Telaxia. The group pushed him harder and longer each day. He had to pass the last test, his fourth strand turned on with no protective shield, and he had to maintain control by himself.

They triggered the strand. Derak re-lived the village incident at the Chambar Valley Offensive that made him superhuman. The scene played back in living color. The stubborn woman, eight-months pregnant, ignored the warnings and did not flee. The ugly reptilian warrior with over two-inch razor-sharp fingernails cornered her and threw her on the ground. Using his nails, he sliced her open from the waist to her neck. He first consumed her fetus, then he pulled out her beating heart and ate it before she died.

The mind shield wasn't there when the fourth strand was turned on and the effort to control his reaction took a herculean effort on his part. Derak's body and mind were under no external control. The mental strain was excruciatingly painful and exhausting. After one hour, Derak was reaching his breaking point, but it was crucial to keep himself from going over the edge. When he finally thought he would lose his mind, he grabbed with his last ounce of control and stabilized his thoughts. He held his resolve for another hour to prove he could maintain control and then collapsed. He passed the test and was carried back to his bed.

They scheduled a final meeting with the Valuk Manou. Qex and Zix would continue fine tuning his abilities in bi-location on board *The Shesain.* Derak needed two days of rest.

Two days later, Qex, Zix, and Derak entered. The Valuk Manou was the only one present with her bodyguards. The three of them stood and waited to be addressed.

"Derak, you have once again exceeded our expectations. Qex and Zix will continue to work with you on your control until it is

second nature to you. I have briefed them on our mission findings and will institute the required changes." She was flanked by two personal guards and left the room.

Zix and Qex looked at Derak and smiled with those pointy teeth.

Zix's thoughts reached Derak. *"You now have the honor of getting us back to* The Shesain.*"*

"Planetary popping is one thing, but across the universe?" he asked.

"No need to worry, we will back you up," Qex assured him.

It took a bit of coaching from Zix and Qex to convince Derak to try. Both of their minds helped him frame the mental picture. Derak formed the thought and pictured *The Shesain* in present null time, locating an open spot, and they popped into the ship unharmed. All action on board stopped, and they were surrounded by smiling faces and endless questions. Qex silenced the crowd and announced that he would brief them after the evening meal.

After the meal, Qex started. *"You received a favorable report from the council. They have recalculated the entire mission from our reports and your exercises for the last three missions. The time waves and their increasing velocity of change were also figured in. I have an updated set of orders that apply to the next assignment and we have added one more mission."*

"What did they add?" Jack asked him.

"You will find out when the time comes," Qex answered.

"You sound like an admiral now." Jack shot back.

"That is because I am an admiral on Telaxia. This is a military operation. Information is on a need-to-know basis only. I will give your next assignment in due time. Until then, we will test you on your progress to date."

"Why are we given these assignments that jump all over the timeline?" Shenar asked.

Zix answered this time. *"You have already been in each assigned time period and completed your tasks. We have confirmed your successes in the upcoming missions."*

Robert could not contain his frustration any longer. *"Now hold on a second! You're telling us we've already corrected the original time paradox. All of it, including the tasks we haven't completed yet? That makes no sense!"*

"Why should it? Mortal thought patterns are an anomaly. You think in limited logical patterns. To see or believe what is in front of you. There is and always has been an invisible reality hiding behind the veil of ignorance that mortals have constructed for themselves. Refusing to acknowledge its existence, you hide behind your so-called logic."

"That still doesn't answer my question. How can we be successful and we're only halfway through with this mission?" Robert demanded.

Zix shook his head and Qex picked up the thought. *"Our calculations are based on your recordings of the original timeline. The team that set the parameters studied your histories and myths 700 years back. All of you have a unique mathematical equation, similar to what you call a fingerprint, and each one of you shows up in the records going back to 1814. Your individual markers are all over the records, even Robert's. Derak's 3-D holographic model helped us to isolate each incident, down to the day, hour, and minute of your involvement."* The universe hologram popped up in the middle of the room. The time distortion had shrunk in size.

Qex and Zix stepped into the hologram and zoomed onto the Pegasus sector and brought Thumar's solar system into view. To the untrained eye, it appeared like a chaotic mixture of complicated equations traveling on uncountable highways. To the crew, the logic, beauty, and order were apparent. They enlarged the solar system and picked out seven red flashing equations and arranged the copies in a list on the side.

Qex continued. *"These equations represent each of you. They stand out in the original timeline."* He brought up the modified timeline, after splitting the holograms into two seven-foot diameter spheres. They floated in midair, side by side. *"You will notice the lack of your signatures in the modified timeline. That is what you are repairing. With each individual incident corrected, you come closer to re-establishing the original timeline. The time waves will become stronger, the closer you get to completion. All of you will remember everything you accomplished. This is an anomaly we Telaxians will investigate long after we restore the original timeline."*

"Why are we correcting this time paradox if you can do it from Telaxia?" Shenar asked.

Zix answered, *"So you will not make the same mistake twice! The first occurrence elicited help from us. Your mortality and the circumstances leading up to the anomaly demanded a softer approach. You must learn a part of what it takes to keep the universe in order. Let us hope that there is not a second time. Our next response will not be kind by Telaxian standards."*

"What if something goes wrong?" Leontul asked.

"Nothing will go awry. That is why you have three Telaxians assigned to you. Our expertise in these matters will guarantee the outcome." Zix assured them.

"If each of us is a key component to achieve success, what happens if one of us is put out of commission?" Seamus asked Qex.

"We have a back-up plan." Qex commented.

"Then why didn't you use it?" Robert demanded.

Qex's eyes locked on Shesain and Derak. *"Correcting one's own mistake is more effective than having someone else do it for you. There are no spoiled children on Telaxia. Every Telaxian, including myself, had to learn in this manner."*

"I didn't create this blunder, I was dragged into it," Robert complained.

"You did not. Yet, your mark is all over the corrections. I would not have become involved if Derak had not consulted you. We must repeat history, Robert. What is now occurring was destined before your time. All of you are now permanently marked in our equations. Your usefulness will not end with this restored timeline, it has only begun."

Qex, Zix and Vel exited the room.

Derak sent a mental message to Qex. They needed to discuss his relationship with Terga. They met on the bridge, letting the rest of the crew know that this was a private matter, and they sat across from each other, with Terga present.

"When did this start?" Derak asked.

Qex's eyes met his, and his usual terseness disappeared. *"From the first moment I encountered her intelligence, I knew that I had met a special mind. On Telaxia, there are few differentiating factors between our men and women. What we look for are equal minds to meld with. In my thousands of years of existence, Terga's is the only one I have met that I have felt is equal to my own. You created a one-of-a-kind entity. I must compliment you, Derak."*

"I made what I thought was a very capable Artificial Intelligence computer to assist me. I had no idea that she would become self-aware. I was taken aback after her initial confession. I'm still trying to wrap my head around how a self-aware software program can fall in love."

"Self-awareness is the key, Derak. She may lack a physical form, but she still makes her own decisions, with you in mind. She would only change the present situation with your approval."

"How deep have your private thoughts been on this?" Derak asked.

"Very exacting," Terga chimed in. *"To the point of calculating my physical body down to the last detail. I will always be present for you, Shesain, and the twins. The only difference will be my embodiment."*

"What about the life span quotient? Can you construct a body to live millions of years?" he asked her.

"That and more; I can construct an immortal body." Terga answered.

"What about the Telaxians? How are you going to handle that?" Derak asked?

"We will figure that out when the time comes. We need your blessing." Qex said.

"As long as Terga stays with me until it's obvious that the time has come for me to let her go. I would also like to have access to your non-private histories." Qex's smile lit up a room.

207

"I agree with the conditions Derak. I will honor your decision." Qex smiled.

"Thank you so much, Derak, I am thrilled," Terga added.

Unbelievable! My self-aware AI computer is in love, he thought. He patted Qex on the shoulder as he walked back to the great room. He left them alone to discuss their next step. Qex almost acted like a teenager who had found his first crush. His eyes sparkled, and the smile never left his face. Derak knew that he witnessed a side of Qex that a rare few in the universe ever would. The next time they would meet, he would be the Qex of old, precise and to the point.

When they received the assignment the following morning. Qex was in a light mood, and Derak was the only one next to Terga who knew why. His usual flat expression was present.

"Our next excursion will be short and simple. All of us including Zix and Vel will be present. We will teleport inside the Cave of Lights before they discover it. Our purpose is to collect samples and place one of them for Tukar Andehar to find. He is exploring this section of Anea right now. This will launch a seven-year exploration on his part to discover the source. Seamus and Robert will assist him on the following mission. I need not tell the Thumarian's present the importance of this event. We will first locate the entrance and then pop inside the cave to collect samples. Then Seamus and Robert shall place a lone crystal for Tukar to find. We must still keep our eyes, and sensors alerted to the Syndicate's presence. We have located where the mouth of the cave should be; we will go there first. We leave in thirty minutes."

The required clothing was replicated and all ten of them popped down in X-gen. What they saw was not illuminating in the least. They were looking at a mountainside with a wall of enormous boulders blocking the way. There was no way to tell where the entrance might be. They might have to search out an alternate entrance. It would take months of excavation to clear the field of boulders. Qex caught onto an idea that sounded like fun. They would go back to the ship and travel back in time before the rockslide. Tracers would be placed inside the cave and at the mouth. This would make it easier to locate it under the rocks. They popped back to the ship and Zix gave Jack the space time co-ordinates. He entered them and engaged. After the usual counterclockwise funnel, they settled into orbit around Thumar, seventy thousand years in the past.

Jack was looking at his monitors. *"I'm picking up a disturbance in the asteroid belt Derak."*

"Is it the Syndicate?" Derak asked.

"No, it looks like an asteroid about the size of The Shesain *that has been dislodged from its orbit. I'm plotting the trajectory right now. It's on a direct collision course with Thumar. It looks like it will hit about thirty miles west of the cave entrance. Just the shock wave from that thing alone is enough to bring those rocks down."*

"What's its ETA? Do we have enough time to place tracers and some drones to record the incident?"

"Plenty of time, we will have a hit in two days. Our tracers can be imbedded in the rock with a force field. We can place some of Seamus's drones in the area. They'll get most of the event before they're destroyed. We must set them today."

"Thanks Jack. Did you get that Qex?"

"Yes, we will leave in one hour."

They arrived at a much different valley. Tall coniferous trees and ferns made up the luscious landscape. The entrance to the right on the cliff face. They entered with headlights turned on. The crystals were large and beautiful, protruding out of the floor, penetrating through the walls, and hanging precipitously from the ceiling. They installed sensor drones inside the cave with a marker to give them a target seventy thousand years in the future.

The next day, the asteroid entered the atmosphere. Turning into a fireball at seventeen thousand miles an hour, it didn't take long to hit. The mushroom cloud rose through the atmosphere. The drones sent the vids until they were destroyed. They took vids as the cloud sent debris up into the atmosphere and started dropping red-hot rocks back to the ground, starting fires. The shock wave hit the cave entrance, collapsing the rocks that blocked the entrance. After setting the co-ordinates, Jack took them back to the future.

The second trip down to Thumar in the year 1845 brought them back to the same rock pile. The lush landscape never grew back. The growth was sparse. Qex located the marker inside the cave, and the group popped inside. The light nearly blinded them. It was brighter than daylight. The asteroid bombarded the crystals with radiation, causing them to shine brightly from the inside out. The same crystalline structures were there. Some were larger, the ground was littered with small crystals that had broken off the walls and ceiling. Every single one was lit. The beauty was indescribable. They took vids, samples and removed the remains of their technology. They popped up to the ship and set the time for Robert and Seamus to drop off the sample for Tukar to find.

The timing had to be perfect. Tukar would only pass this way once, and Seamus and Robert had to get it right. It was dusk when they popped down and dropped the rock. They stayed in X-gen and waited for Tukar to show up. He wasn't happy, complaining about his fruitless journey. He almost passed by the crystal and would have had Robert not planted the thought to look down. The crystal's light showed brighter as the sun went down. He bent over and picked it up. His eyes glowed with the light reflecting off of his face. He looked up and surveyed the landscape. A smile crossed his face as he ran back to his camp.

The Cave of Lights: 1852

Councilman Number One and Two stood before the Prime Mathematician, scared out of their wits. They had been summoned before a furious Mutah Shakur. His face was red, and his psychic field held them fast. Words weren't required to get his message across.

The Mutah Shakur started speaking through gritted, razor-sharp teeth, his eyes emanating rage. "You useless pair of slugs! Why did I have to endure another time wave? The last one knocked me hard to the deck. Which one of you will pay for that? If you represent the best of your cursed mortal race, I might as well go home now. You cannot even track these terrorists down with the advanced technology I have given you."

"O great Mutah Shakur," Councilman Number One got out. "We-I mean they-are time hopping and it's very difficult to track them. We have no idea where they will end up next. There is no way for us to predict their next time destination."

The Mutah Shakur calmed down enough to recognize the logic. "If I can predict a time period, can you morons send out enough patrols to cover that timeline?" he asked them, still angry.

"Yes, Mutah Shakur." Number Two answered. "Captain Thompson is on *The Mandible*. I have briefed him on his new duties."

"Did you drive the point home to him?" the Mutah Shakur demanded.

"Yes, his sister is a very effective bargaining chip," Number Two replied.

"I see that not all my lessons have been ignored. Where is this captain Thompson now?"

"Waiting to be called by you, Mutah Shakur," Number Two replied.

"You two are not a total waste. Have him summoned. If he is on time, I will not punish you for the last time wave. However, if it happens again, one of you will die in front of the entire senate. I must set an example of how failure is dealt with." The Mutah Shakur delivered a toothy smile that resembled a barracuda. "Leave me now and return with your Captain!"

The Mutah Shakur teleported to his ship in his high security hangar. No one was allowed to lay eyes on it. It was not a sleek ship. In fact, the ship was boxy looking, much like Telaxian architecture. What set it apart was what was inside: Telaxian technology. He walked inside and approached his 3-D holographic display. After starting it up, he brought up the local sectors and mapped out the last four time waves. They were all over the place, with no apparent logic to them. *There has to be a pattern,* he thought to himself. *But where?* He put all the information into his computer and requested a prediction. A moment later, the answer came up on his 3-D model. The years from 1848 to 1854 showed up. He frowned and then shut everything off and popped back to his palace.

A few minutes later, Councilmen Number One and Two entered with Captain Thompson. All three bowed before him. "Mutah Shakur."

He stared them down. "I will make this short, Captain. Deploy time ships between the years 1848 and 1854 every year. Monitor any and I mean any change in any population center, large or small, even if it is one or two. You will investigate every occurrence, no matter how small or insignificant."

"Mutah Shakur, only four-time ships are serviceable. The other three are in the repair hangars, Sir," Captain Thompson reported.

"Why do I put up with such incompetence? Do the technicians even know how to fix these problems, Captain?"

"It's not a lack of expertise, Mutah Shakur. We have a shortage of parts. The required elements we need have been back ordered five months. I've tried to push the chief supply officer with every threat possible, but he claims his ties to Councilman Number Five means he doesn't have to do anything, on anyone's timeline but his own, sir."

The Mutah Shakur turned to Number One. "Number one! Get your house in order! Remove Number Five and space him and the officer in question. I want my ships ready to fly in two days, am I clear. Captain, you have your orders, do not fail me!"

"Mutah Shakur, what should I do if I find them?" The captain asked.

"Eliminate them, kill them, I want those renegades out of my calculations!" He roared.

"Mutah Shakur," all three of them said at once, and left as fast as possible.

Four hours later, Councilman Number Five, the supply officer and their families were floating in open space, dead. The repair hangar received the parts.

•◆•

Seamus and Robert teleported back to *The Shesain* before the time wave hit. This one was stronger than the last three combined. They all received some needed time off. With Qex spending his free time linked with Terga. Derak was still uncomfortable about the relationship, but there are things that you have to let be. Zix consulted him about Qex's peculiar behavior.

The days that followed saw Shesain, Shenar and Robert working on the upcoming mission. Qex and Zix double checked their equations and made some final adjustments.

Qex began the briefing. *"Your fifth assignment will have Seamus and Leontul guiding Tukar Andehar to the Cave of Lights. Tukar has spent close to seven years searching since finding the first sample, to the point of camping on its doorstep on his last round. Seamus will show up with another crystal.*

"Seamus will take three months to lead Tukar to the entrance.

Leontul will continue his collection of herbs and plants and serve as the camp doctor during this time. Seamus, you must direct their advances around the site until there are two weeks left on your timeline. Then you will lead them to the cliff face.

"Before that happens, you and Jack will teleport inside the cave and imbed smaller crystals into the rocks around the blocked entrance and the debris on the entrance floor. Once you have accomplished your task, teleport back to the ship."

"Why do we need to take three months? Why not just show it to him and get it over with?" Seamus asked Qex.

"It is what they discover in the two-and-a-half months prior that cements the validity of the find. We have to duplicate the exact historical precedents according to the original Thumarian timeline.

"During Seamus and Leontul's mission, the rest of you will spend more time on Thumar, perfecting your acquired mental skills. We will be ever vigilant on our 'Syndicate watch,' they will not go away. The closer we get to completing our overall mission, the more likely we are to meet them."

"When do we start?" Leontul asked.

"Tomorrow morning. I will brief those involved. Continue with your optics and be ready to move in the morning."

The next day, Seamus and Jack popped inside the Cave of lights. This time, they wore sunglasses with anti-glare lenses. Even with the glasses, the light was dazzling. Radiation was within the safe range. It eliminated the usefulness of scanning equipment. The search would have to be done the old fashion way. Seamus and Jack took almost two hours to locate a second entry point. It looked like it used to be accessible. They marked the second entrance with an electronic X-gen tag.

Robert and Shenar completed their schedule and timeline. Vel supervised the replication of their clothing, monetary exchange of the day and perfecting their language inflections to match that of the southern Anean coastal villages. They would hail from the village of Jinourka.

Jack and Derak prepared themselves for back-up duty in case the

Syndicate showed up. They went over every scenario, from putting them to sleep to taking them out. They considered the latter a last resort. The more Derak knew about them, the more he preferred taking them out.

Shesain and Shenar assisted Vel with fitting Seamus and Leontul's clothes. The two of them said their goodbye's and popped down to their insertion point with all their gear. They had to maintain their cover as 19th century Thumarian's. Any use of their technology could change everything and endanger the mission's timeline.

Seamus and Leontul landed at their destination and stashed the extra gear they wouldn't need right away. Then Seamus sent out his drones in X-gen to monitor for any unwanted visitors. They would transmit any information to *The Shesain* first, then relayed down to him telepathically.

Leontul located Tukar's camp five miles northeast. The trail was easy to follow. Wagon ruts were deep in the soft ground, after a week of rain. The two of them set out and came to the camp's edges in two hours. A large man on watch met them.

"Stop! Who goes there? Where are you headed?" he asked as he blocked them.

Seamus, who was equal to the guard's size, answered. "I am Dorack Herbicke, and my companion is Dedore Thuber. We're explorers from the coast. Dedore is a trained herbal doctor. I'm looking for mineral deposits, Dedore is hunting herbs."

"I'm John Roberts, my family is from earth, they crashed here in 1808. We've been wanderers since then, exploring all three continents. I'm sorry about the security measures, but I have to make sure you're not carrying any weapons."

Leontul and Seamus just shrugged and were patted down. The only thing he found was Leontul's work knives and Seamus's long knife. All of their tech was in X-gen.

"What are these for?" John asked Leontul, holding his knife pouch.

"I use them to collect samples. Stems have to be cut clean, to preserve their qualities."

"And this?" John asked Seamus, holding up his long knife.

"I help Dedore, and you know as well as I do that you don't travel without a little help."

"We'll see what Tukar has to say. You don't seem like the hard types that have tried to get in. Franky, I got two for the boss. They don't seem like a bad lot, so be nice!" John called out.

"Hey, they call me Franky," he said as he approached Seamus and Leontul. "I'll take those, John. Man, are these sharp. Follow me, Tukar will want to see these knives."

They followed Franky to the main tent, to find Tukar pouring over a map. "Tukar, I've got two for you, one's an explorer and the other claims to be a doctor of herbs. You need to check out their knives, I've not seen the likes of them," Franky announced.

Tukar was not a big man, maybe six feet in height and weighing in at about two hundred pounds. He had a good-looking smooth face with dark hair. He seemed pleasant as he turned around and smiled at them. "Who do we have here? Not the usual ruffians we see. What's your names?" Tukar asked.

"Dorack Herbicke," Seamus answered.

"You've got a coastal accent, Dorack, what village are you from?"

"Jinourka, both of us are."

"Dedore Thuber, I'm a wanderer and a trained herbal doctor. Dorack's looking for metals and such, and I hunt healing herbs. Those are my knives I require for my work."

Tukar picked up the knife pouch laid on his table and removed one. After looking it over, he whistled. "Do you need them this sharp for roots? What are they made from? This is a hard metal."

"I don't just look for roots; some stems I have to cut through are tough."

"Try nothing funny," Tukar told Dedore, he handed them back to Leontul. "My men and women know how to defend themselves very well."

"Thank you, Tukar. I assure you, only plants make the cut."

"Now, this one," Tukar commented, picking up Seamus's long knife. "What would one need this for?" He asked Seamus.

"I use it to help Dedore collect samples. But being the two of us out there alone most of the time, you have to be ready for anything. That knife skinned a cat four months ago, a big one."

"Was it orange and black, with a long tail?" Tukar asked.

"Yea, it nearly killed us, ambushed us as we were walking through a forest. Lucky for us, we stopped to look at a plant, and bent over just as it sprung. I got lucky on the second pounce, that knife found the heart, here are the scars." Seamus rolled up his right sleeve and showed three slashes across his large biceps. I'm lucky that's all I got. Dedore fared better. He jumped into the brush. Maybe you could help me. We were exploring northeast of here, near some cliffs."

"Does it have a lot of rubble and boulders at the base?" Tukar asked.

"Yea, and when we walked past the main pile, we came across this, I have no idea what it is." Seamus pulled out a small glowing crystal. When he uncovered it, the light filled the tent.

"Where...where... did you find this?" Tukar asked in utter amazement. Then he pulled out another one with a dimmer light. "I found this on the side of a trail near the boulder stand you walked by. I've been searching the area for nearly seven years now. I've had no luck and I feel like I've been running around in circles. Here's your knife back. Can you lead us to where you found this? If we find the source, both of you will get a cut of the profits. We need a doctor around, anyway, some of my people are sick."

"I'd be glad to help. Tukar. Show me to the patients," Leontul volunteered.

"Thanks, Dedore, Franky! Show the good doctor to his patients."

Franky ran into the tent. "let's go Doc, some of them are really bad off," he said as he hustled Dedore out of the tent.

Tukar turned to Dorack, and said, "let's talk about your blades now. How did you come about them?"

"I made them myself. I'm a blacksmith by trade. I made them in a village last year from ore samples I picked up during our trek into the mountains."

"Do you remember where you got them?" Tukar asked.

"Sure, I've got it on one of my maps. The range lies sixty days southwest of here. Though I'd like to find the source of these light crystals first. We're close, a month's travel at least, not much more than that."

"Sounds good to me," Tukar agreed. "We can break camp after your doctor gets my people back up. Until then, let's talk about these crystals."

• ◆ •

The Tiger Shark, a Syndicate cruiser, 1852

"Captain Thompson, I've picked up a two-person increase on the Anean continent. It's sparsely populated, mostly by explorers. Their numbers jump around." Lieutenant Smith reported.

"Where, Lieutenant? No jump is too small." Captain Thompson came to his station.

"It's near the borders of the northeast foothills, Sir. This camp has a population flux. Don't forget that bandits roam these parts."

"Send a four-man team down to the coordinates. Their orders are to shoot to kill if they identify these interlopers!" Captain Thompson ordered.

"But, Sir, the timeline, what if we eliminate an important--"

"Damn the council's timeline. They killed most of my family, and they're holding my sister hostage. I'm just following their orders, so damn the results. Dispatch the strike team, Lieutenant, now!"

"Yes, Sir, strike team is deployed."

• ◆ •

"Qex, Zix, a syndicate medium cruiser has established a parking orbit, and deployed a strike team close to your co-ordinates," Jack reported from the bridge.

Both of them were at Jack's station in a blink. *"Have they detected us?"* Zix asked.

"No, they haven't," Jack thought.

"Good, contact Seamus and Leontul, let them know." Qex ordered.

"Aye, sir," Jack said out of habit. *"Team Tukar, do you read?"*

"We read you, over."

"Seamus, a syndicate strike team are headed down to your co-ordinates as we speak. I estimate, four to six, we have no ETA, assume hostile intentions, copy."

"Copy, Shesain, will we have back-up?"

"Copy, Seamus, Derak and I will teleport down."

"Copy, Shesain, over and out."

Qex took over at the bridge as Jack roused Derak from his optics. *"Derak, we've got bogies descending on team Tukar. Lock and load, we pop in thirty minutes."*

"Copy, Jack, how many are there?"

"Four to six. They descended in a scout class ship."

"When did they enter the atmosphere?"

"Ten minutes ago, at subsonic speed and cloaked."

"Better make our ETA fifteen minutes, my guess is that they're highly trained since they move fast." Derak commented.

Jack and Derak were ready in ten minutes, checking each other's suits before they departed. Shesain and Shenar rushed in. Shesain thought first, *"Where are you two going suited up, what is happening?"*

"A Syndicate strike team has deployed to our target area. We're going in as back-up." Jack answered.

"What if one of you ends up hurt, or worse, killed?" Shesain asked in near despair.

"Don't worry, my love, we have the X-gens, and both Jack and I have lived through worse. We have the element of surprise; they can't detect us. This is what both of us signed up for long ago." Derak tried to mollify the situation, to no avail.

Shesain and Shenar kissed them goodbye, with tears in their eyes. *"Come back alive and in one piece, my Chimera."* Shesain spoke for both her and Shenar, as Shenar turned away in tears.

Jack and Derak switched on their helmets, as they formed upward from the neck and breastplates of their armored suits. Temela was right; these suits would scare a trained military regular. With the armor and weapons check complete, they reported to Qex and Zix. Even they were taken aback by the suits.

"Who designed those suits?" Zix asked.

"I did," Derak answered.

"They are intimidating." Zix commented.

"They're meant to be."

"Fine," Qex said, *"the mission is to detain and confuse the enemy. Stun is the next step with killing a last resort. If these are black-ops agents, you might have to use the last resort. If the original team sends up a confirmation to the cruiser, they might deploy another one to insure the job is finished. You could have eight to twelve bogies. Be careful: once you fire, they will know of your presence. May your gods be with you."*

Jack and Derak popped down to the edge of the camp and checked their sensors. The four bogies were on foot, southwest of their location. *"Seamus, this is Derak. We're at the edge of the camp. Are you and Leontul ok?"*

"Rodger, Derak, I'm with Tukar and Leontul is in their med tent, working wonders, as usual."

"You've got four bogies, southwest, four to five days out. Consider them hostile and extremely dangerous. Jack and I will shadow you. You need to move the camp and cover your tracks. Try to stay ahead of them. Jack and I will run interference and try to slow them down," Derak informed him.

"Copy alpha team; Seamus out."

Seamus turned to Tukar. "I think we should move out tomorrow. The sooner we leave, the better. Franky reported to me, he said, your people are getting better."

"Why so soon, Dorack? We have plenty of time."

"The weather can change in an instant; you know how the muddy roads affect the wagons, and we need to cover our tracks. There are still bandits in these parts."

"Maybe you're right, we'll pack up in the morning and be ready to roll by mid-day."

The camp rose early and got to work fast. Everyone, including Seamus and Leontul, helped load up the wagons while eating energy bars. The women that were not packing handed out a delicious morning cold Meade. True to Tukar's word, the camp was packed and loaded, with the Sherka (horses) hooked up to the wagons by noon. Those not riding in the wagons walked either point, rear guard, or alongside the wagons. Others joined Leontul in collecting herbs and roots to be used for medicine or the cooking pots. Scouts fanned out ahead to clear the path and hunt meat, Seamus joined them.

Day after day, Seamus led Tukar and his people northeast. He worked with Tukar and his map makers to mark the important finds along the way. In the first month, there were enough diversions to keep spirits high. One week into the second month of travel, morale slipped. Tukar's followers started mumbling and gripping about taking too much time to reach their destination.

The real story revolved around Jack and Derak intercepting the Syndicate strike team and stalling them as much as possible. It would not be as easy as they first thought. They were smart and well trained. Derak could tell by the way the Syndicate operatives carried themselves and their black armor. The armor also had cloaking capabilities; Jack and Derak's sensors could pick them up. Jack and Derak moved fast, pressing hard to keep ahead of the Syndicate. They started making fresh trails to throw them off. It worked at first, then they picked up on the ruse. After three weeks. Then the operatives split into two teams of two and circle around both sides of the main trail.

Jack and Derak split up. They each took one team. This assignment put their mental abilities to the test. Their teleportation and telekinesis proved to be the most useful. They would teleport ahead of the teams and kinetically moved rocks and trees into their paths, causing them to deviate and find a way around them. This wouldn't last for long. After five days of Jack waylaying his team, their frustration got the best of them. The next rockslide they encountered, they blasted away with their pistols. Their next trick was to guide the wildlife to help them out. That night, while they slept, Jack and Derak pushed Thumarian Ratublas, the nearest thing to Earth's raccoons, only bigger, and smarter with longer, sharper claws. The animals ransacked their supplies and spread them all over the camps. The animals woke the occupants, who came out shooting at anything that moved. The best thing the Ratublas did was scattering their radios and tech equipment.

This stunt cost the Syndicate invaders half a day. Only one radio worked, over half of their pistol loads had disappeared. Their cursing could be heard half a mile away as they got under way. It looked like Jack, and Derak would accomplish their task. They had rejoined each other on a peak overlooking a prime alpine valley when they heard from Qex.

"Derak. Another four man strike team has landed south of your present location. Their plan appears to be to sandwich Tukar's group between them. It looks like your efforts attracted a lot of attention. You and Jack need to split up, north and south," Qex reported.

"This will get dicey, Jack. Set your phase pistol on maximum stun. The Syndicate is throwing a few surprises our way. And I don't think the sleep darts will work like we thought they would. We will have to rethink this operation."

"What about sending Robert down?" Qex inquired.

"He doesn't have any combat experience, and I have a feeling things will get rough," Derak answered.

"He could be a runner between you and Jack," Zix suggested.

"I'm not that useless!" Robert shared his thoughts.

"Have you ever come under live fire? These guys are some of the best I've seen, and they'll kill you without thinking twice. I'll allow it only if you come in as a runner with a loaded pistol. You can help us move animals, rocks, and trees."

"I'll pop down with fresh supplies in twenty minutes," Robert confirmed.

Seamus was two weeks out from leading them to the cave when Tukar's people were ready to mutiny. Tukar himself was considering ending the expedition. Seamus had to call Derak, Jack, and Robert in to move the minds of the camp. Negative emotions were running high. Seamus and Leontul talked with Tukar and his lieutenants, while Derak, Jack, and Robert added their mental strength from the edge of the camp. After three hours of arguments, they decided it to continue on two more weeks before turning back. It exhausted the five of them after the ordeal. They popped up to *The Shesain* for a hot meal and a brief rest before going back to work.

The next two weeks passed fast. Seamus and Leontul had their hands full, keeping a semblance of order in Tukar's camp. Jack, Robert and Derak were called in a few more times to manage order in the camp, but they had their own troubles to deal with. Both strike teams ran day and night. All three parties would converge on the cave site at the same time.

They had to figure out a battle plan shedding no blood. The odds had to be evened. It was decided that Derak, Robert and Jack would personally teleport the second team to remote parts of Thumar, then return to help Seamus and Leontul. They would grab each hostile intruder in X-gen, teleport them and pop back. Derak would take care of two of them, while Robert and Jack would pop back to Tukar's camp. What would happen after that, only time would tell.

Tukar set up camp at the base of the primary entrance to the cave, and they didn't know it yet. Everyone in the camp was cross before they started exploring the next day.

Jack, Robert and Derak relocated the second-strike team. They never knew what hit them. They were placed on the Corano islands, Lelayla, and Ganmer. Jack and Derak rejoined Seamus and Leontul just in time before the fireworks started the next morning.

Tukar had arrived at dusk the night before and got up the next morning in a foul mood. He started out arguing with Seamus.

"We've already been here four times, Dorack! Why should I waste anymore of my time?"

"I didn't find the crystal here. I located it up slope one hundred feet halfway into a deep gully," Seamus informed Tukar "I'll show you where I found it, so you won't waste any time, Tukar."

"I'll give you two days before we pack up and leave, Dorak!"

Seamus led a ten-person team to the side entrance. He found it the same way he left it, in ruins. Just as they spread out and started turning over small rocks, two Syndicate operatives opened fire with phase pistols. They injured no one on the first volley, and everyone, including Seamus, ran for cover.

"Derak, we're under phase pistol fire! They've got us pinned down, one hundred feet up from the main entrance and halfway down the gully. We need help NOW!"

"Copy, Seamus, Jack and I will be there before you can think. Where are they?"

"They're located southeast, halfway up the hill, in a copse of trees. Two bogies. I don't know where the other two are, we're taking heavy fire!"

"Copy, Seamus, we've got them located. They're in cloak mode, so it takes a little longer to lock in their coordinates. Don't return fire, you'll blow your cover."

"Copy, Derak, I'll just hunker down."

The two agents kept up a withering attack, while the other two were circling back to assault the camp. Jack picked them up and split off. Derak came to Seamus's rescue and Jack protected the camp as they were running for cover at the sound of the melee. Derak popped up-slope of the two firing on the exploration team. After locating both of their positions, he teleported behind the first agent in X-gen mode and put him to sleep. The agent's pistol fell silent, warning the other.

The other operative moved to another firing point and resumed his onslaught, shooting at anything that moved. Then he started targeting the rocks above Tukar's men, bringing mini-rock slides down on top of the pinned down team. Derak found him and gave him a twenty-four-hour sleep agent. He would wake up with a nasty, lingering headache. After the shooting stopped, everyone in hiding came out. Once they were sure of their safety, the remaining eight dug out their comrades from their rock piles.

Jack had a more difficult encounter. His two had taken up opposite posts. They were ready to discharge their weapons when

Jack slept the first one. The second position saw his partner fall and opened fire on Jack. Brush splintered, and rock shattered as his bolts missed. Jack shot him with his pistol on maximum stun. Jack popped over to secure him. Both strike teams were disabled and teleported to freezing locations.

Jack and Derak popped back to *The Shesain* and got the sky cycles ready. *"Were going in hot, weapons at full, Jack. Qex will beam the slept strike teams to their ships, then we'll drive the ones awake into the ships and off the planet. If they don't leave, we'll make them. We're launching Qex. Beam the bogie's home, we're on our way."* Derak ordered.

"Copy, Derak, Qex out."

"Jack, take one ship and I'll take the other. You're cleared to take action, to drive them off, short of destroying them or taking out their drives."

"Aye, Sir," he responded with a smile crossing his thoughts.

●◆●

Tukar stormed up the gully followed by half the camp, marching up to Seamus and getting right in his face. From the outside, it was a funny situation. Tukar, at two hundred pounds and six-foot-tall, facing off with Seamus, six foot six at almost three hundred pounds.

"Dorack, I didn't sign up for this!" he roared, as he was motioning to the mess of fallen rock and his two injured comrades. "That's it, we're packing up and leaving! I don't care what's here to find, it's not worth losing a life for!"

One of Tukar's friends was moving some small rubble, when he called out in excitement. "Tukar, Tukar, over here, I've found something. It's, it's one of your glowing rocks! wait, here's another one. I've got smaller ones."

"You wait here, Dorack; I'm not through with you!" Tukar said, before walking over to the smaller cave entrance. When he got there, he bent down and moved more rocks, finding more glowing crystals. He turned around to face Seamus.

"You've earned a reprieve, Dorack. This looks like a cave entrance, start clearing it away." He ordered the uninjured members of his camp to action.

Leontul took care of the injured back at the camp, while the others dug and moved rocks and boulders.

Back at the excavation site, those that got shot at started asking questions. "Hey, Dorack, what kind of weapons did they use? I ain't seen nuthin like them before. It was like light hitting and then exploding."

"I don't know; that was strange to me, too. How in the world do you throw light? I'd sure like to know," Dorack answered.

"Are they gone, will they come back? Is it even safe to continue this nonsense?" Another one asked.

"I think they're gone though I don't know why. Why don't you send out a scouting party? There has to be some reason they stopped attacking us." Seamus suggested.

Tukar's men looked at him, and he gave an approving nod. Four of their best trackers left, while the others continued clearing the cave entrance.

Qex beamed all the Syndicate strike teams to their ships, Jack and Derak drove them off the planet. Afterwards, they kept the cycles on Thumar to guard the excavation of the side cave entrance. It took two weeks to get through the final pile of rocks. Tukar's crew were complaining at having to dig. The only thing that kept them going was finding an occasional crystal.

The Orion Syndicate

"Captain, we're being attacked, and Team Two has disappeared. We're approaching the camp and setting up our positions, it looks like a crap shoot..."

"Sergeant, Sergeant, come in Sergeant, damn, find out what's happening to my teams, Lieutenant, NOW!" Captain Thompson thought out loud. "We should be the only ones with...unless, that terrorist, Jamar, is responsible for this. And why couldn't our teams have detected them? They must have better technology. Where are my strike teams, Lieutenant?"

"I've located Team Two, this is strange, they're scattered all over the planet, nowhere near the targets, on different continents, Sir."

"How can that happen, Lieutenant? They're not damned magicians."

"I don't know, Sir..." Lieutenant Smith answered.

"Captain, this is Team Leader One, suddenly, the teams are accounted for. They put six to sleep, were loading them on the transports now." The sound of exploding soil and rock filled the speakers.

"Sergeant, this is Captain Thompson! What in the hell is going on down there?"

"We're under fire, Sir, and we can't see where it's coming from." Two more phase cannon hits went off near them. "We're taking cover in the ships and lifting off. It's an aerial attack, sir." Boom! Boom! Boom! Three more explosions drove them to cover. "They're invisible, Sir, there's no way of tracking them, they must be small craft, they're moving too fast."

"Get both ships off the ground and get back to *The Tiger Shark*, now, Sergeant."

"Yes Sir, lifting off now, Team Two is verifying launch."

The Captain was angry beyond words. He stood on the bridge, steaming. It filled him with fear of what would happen to him if he failed. This drove him to his next order. "Team One and Two, take the camp out with your ships, damn the timeline, no one drives me to retreat!"

"Aye, sir, setting a course for the camp. ETA ten minutes." Direct hits rocked both scout ships as they flew towards Tukar's camp. They held their course, then they lost their communications.

●—◆—●

"Jack, switch to three phase cannon loads, punch a hole in their hulls, aft engine compartment. Do not take the drives out."

"Copy, Jack out."

●—◆—●

Both scout ships received direct hits, aft. Both pilots recorded hull breaches and turned their ships around to return fire into empty air.

Another shot rocked the beleaguered scout ship. "Sergeant, we've lost our weapons!" Then a bigger shot shook the ship sideways."

Another hole was punched into their hulls. They had to cut and run back to *The Tiger Shark*. Derak and Jack chased them until they left the stratosphere in full retreat. They did not receive a warm welcome when they docked. Captain Thompson was ready to space them until he surveyed the damage. Two three-foot holes had been blown into the aft port and starboard side of their ships.

"Sergeant! What caused this damage?"

"We don't know, Sir, they couldn't be seen or tracked. One more hit, and we would have been goners."

"That might have been a better alternative for you, depending on what the council might have in store for your sorry asses. You're supposed to be one of the best black ops teams we have." Captain Thompson raged.

"They have superior cloaking technology, Sir. We didn't pick up anything on the ground with our heads-up displays in our helmets. And we discovered these in the neck armor of the six that were slept, sir." He handed the Captain the useless remains of the sleep darts.

He looked them over for a minute and then handed them to his chief science officer. "What do you think of these, Commander?"

He looked at them through a portable scanner. "They're sleep darts, Sir."

"Any blind idiot can see that, Commander!"

"They're energy tipped, Sir, with the ability to penetrate our armor."

"Shit! How am I going to explain that to the council?" The Captain groused.

"Show them the proof, sir." Commander Erble said. "We've got the flight recorders, vid and catalog this carnage. We also have the remains of these," he said, holding out the sleep darts.

"Commander, most of the time, the council could not care less how right you are or how much proof you have to show them; they punish you at will. Record and store the evidence for now, do not repair those ships! I'll need them for later. As for Thumar, find those thugs, Commander!" The Captain stormed off to his quarters.

Two weeks later, the time wave struck, pushing *The Tiger Shark* out of orbit and halfway to the next star. The entire crew experienced nausea and light-headedness before passing out. When they recovered, the *Tiger Shark* was ten parsecs away from *The Mandible*.

"Lieutenant, set course for the Pegasus sector, the planet Thumar is our destination." Captain Thompson ordered.

"Aye, Sir. What's the mission this time?"

"Were observing the local wildlife for minor protuberances; if we detect the smallest change in any population center, we have to investigate. I don't know why we're wasting our time on this backwards society."

"Course laid in, Sir."

"Engage, Lieutenant, and don't bother me until we reach Thumar."

"Aye, Sir."

•—◆—•

The time wave slammed into *The Mandible,* knocking everyone to the deck and clearing shelves or countertops of any object. The Mutah Shakur was flung ten feet before he landed and passed out. He woke angrier than he had ever been. Words would not get his point across this time; it required action.

Councilmen Number One and Two stood in the center of the Senate Chamber. Senators filled every seat in the auditorium. The seats sloped up in a semi-circle to the back wall. Sixty-four senators fidgeted in their seats, knowing that anytime the Mutah Shakur called an emergency meeting, someone died. This used to be a grand chamber, with walls of white polished marble. Now the marble was painted gloomy gray, displaying a very large, barbed circle with a scorpion in the middle, colored blood red, above the speaker's seat on the back wall. The Senate leadership was seated under the emblem.

Both men stood by themselves, flooded by a blinding white light. A cold metal table stood behind them, complete with ankle, wrist and chest restraining straps. They placed another smaller table to the left, with a dark grey cloth covering something up. The unfortunate two under the lights were shifting back and forth, sweating. Silence filled the auditorium as the Mutah Shakur entered, flanked by his two bodyguards. He stepped into the light and began.

"What you are about to witness is the price of failure. Five unauthorized time waves have occurred under the supervision of these two. Their inability to correct the situation forces me to present an object lesson. This will show my determination to enforce my wisdom and benevolence. Councilmen Number One and Two have come up short for the last time. One of them will provide an enlightening presentation.

"Number One, why have you failed me time and time again?"

"Mutah Shakur, I have done nothing but follow your orders to the letter. Number Two has come up short of following through with the details. I have punished offenders with exuberance and maintained order to your standards."

"Number Two," said the Mutah Shakur.

"Mutah Shakur, I have seen to Number One's details, only because he is incapable of performing essential tasks. I have followed inadequate instructions given by Number One. Being Number One holds a great responsibility, therefore, failure rests on Number One's shoulders."

"I see," the Mutah Shakur said. "One of you will suffer immeasurably, and the survivor will carry this example during his hopefully longer tenure. Since the office of Number One guards and enforces my benevolent will, he will provide your entertainment."

Councilman Number One prostrated himself at the Mutah Shakur's feet. "Please, please, O Great Mutah Shakur, I will never fail you again."

"No, you will not, Number One."

Number Two, thought to himself; *yes! I will be where I belong, Number One!*

"Remember today well, Number One; if you fail me, today's punishment shall befall you and your family." The Mutah Shakur warned Vander telepathically.

The Mutah Shakur glared down at the former Number One, prostrated before him, begging for his life. He nodded to four large men, who walked over and picked up his struggling body.

"NO! Number Two failed you!" he screamed in desperation.

The Mutah Shakur slapped him across the face, putting him into a temporary daze. "Strip him bare and put him on the table, face down."

They followed orders and the former councilman was placed hard on the ice-cold tabletop, naked. Wrists, ankles, waist, chest, and head were strapped down. His movements did him no good, as they pulled the straps even tighter. His head was positioned so that his face looked forward. The new Number One looked on, grinning inside.

The Mutah Shakur walked over to the side table and uncovered two jars containing two ugly, vicious-looking bugs. They were spitting at each other through the clear glass. Mandible-like fangs scratched the sides of the jars, and their tail stingers were up in full combat position. "These are Xextufuquel Beetles, the ultimate form of execution on my home world. When two pregnant females sense each other's pheromones, they go ballistic, and hunt each other down until they meet, then they fight to the death, shredding any soft tissue they come in contact with. They also lay hundreds of eggs in the host's body. When the eggs hatch, the new beetles eat their way out of the host. I will now demonstrate."

The former councilman convulsed in vain.

The Mutah Shakur grabbed a tong and removed an angry spitting bug. The councilman's face was held as they pulled out his tongue. The bug calmed down long enough to be placed on the councilman's outstretched tongue. They pushed it inside as they shut his mouth. The beetle stung the tongue, paralyzing it. Then, she laid eggs on the roof of his mouth, which would eat their way through his brain. Then his butt checks were spread, and they inserted an icy steel probe to open his anus. His contortions continued. They placed the second bug on his buttocks. She walked around until she sensed the opening, then stopped, stinging both sides of his butt, paralyzing them. She crawled inside. The councilman's eyes grew wide, and his moans echoed from the icy steel table.

The lower beetle started up his intestines. After stinging the inside walls, she laid her eggs behind her. Both upper and lower beetles picked up each other's' pheromones at the same time and went into full battle mode. The councilman's body's struggles were moving the table as he tried to fight off the inevitable. When the two beetles met in his stomach, his eyes rolled to the back of his head, and his moans of pain reached new heights.

"This is only the beginning. It gets worse when the eggs hatch. We'll keep his brain and body alive to appreciate the entire experience. It should take two to three weeks," the Mutah Shakur stated, as they rolled away the table with what was left of the former councilman. "Remember what you have witnessed today, for I will not be disappointed again!" The Mutah Shakur reemphasized.

After the horror and shock moved into extreme fear for the senators, the chamber cleared, leaving the new Number One and Two alone with the Mutah Shakur.

"Number one, how many time ships are prepared for launch?"

"Just one, Sir, The *Tiger Shark*. She is on her shakedown cruise now, with Captain Thompson at the helm. They left three hours ago for the Pegasus sector and the planet Thumar."

"Just one operating time ship? What happened to the other five?" he demanded.

"What others Sir? The *Tiger Shark* is the first since we fixed the problems on the prototype."

This angered the Mutah Shakur, but he could not take it out on these two now. The time waves were removing his best weapons. He had to get to the source, or all of his work and calculations would come to nothing. "Double, triple your efforts, Number One! I want more time ships completed, NOW! If you want to live longer than your predecessor, do not fail me!" With that done, the Mutah Shakur stalked out of the chamber.

"Number Two, see to the details, and bring the plans to me before you implement them. I don't intend on going out the way he did!" Said Number One.

"Yes, Sir, but what do I tell the crews that are already working on four hours sleep?"

"Take an hour of sleep away. I don't care about those pissants! If you have to, make an example of their children: April's Pleasure Palace is running low on sex slaves. Just get it done, Number Two!"

"Yes, Sir, Number Two walked out of the Senate Chambers with a vicious grin on his face. Now was his time to show the Mutah Shakur who should be Number One. He was one step away from realizing his dream. It didn't matter if this founding scientist lost his life or not, he would not be Number Two for long.

The Corano Islands: 1857

The Shesain settled into a node. Qex, Zix, and Derak teleported to Telaxia for a session with the Prime Council, and the ship resumed its usual schedule. Leontul was in his lab, going over his research, when Shesain walked in and spied an open cabinet. Leontul was deep in thought and caught her going over to the opening before he could stop her. He was too late to prevent her discovery.

"Leontul, are these what I think they are?" Shesain asked him.

His face scrunched up in a frown. *"Yes, they are, but there's nothing to worry about. They're frozen in a class-five protective field."*

Shesain rarely got angry, but this was one occasion where she lost it. *"How dare you bring this many devil plants onboard, into a closed environment! These flowers nearly caused the extinction of Thumarian males in the plague of 1814, and you have the nerve to bring this many on board my ship!"*

"Just listen to me Shesain; I have an excellent reason to study them. They're--"

"I don't care what your motive is, you pitiful f'ter! You're endangering the lives of everyone on board this ship, and I will not have my unborn twins compromised by your stupidity!"

Shesain's mental anger reverberated all over the ship, and Leontul's lab was packed with the entire crew, including Vel.

"What's going on in here?" Robert asked in a hard tone.

Shesain was nearly in tears by now, shaking with violent anger, staring down Leontul with a look that could wither a Kek. He didn't back down.

The force of her thoughts even backed Vel up. *"This p'tah, this f'ter has been collecting and storing far more Veredant Flowers on board this ship than we allowed him! If I had Derak's skills, I might be tempted to, to..."* She turned around with extreme veracity and shattered an empty plas steel beaker with her mind.

It forced Vel to step in, and she quashed Shesain's mental field. *"It's bad enough that I have to watch for Derak's temper, but I will not put up with two mortals to babysit! Shesain, get control of your mind before you cause any more damage. The flowers can harm no one in a class-five field. If you destroy them, you will release the plague. The concentration of that collection would kill all of us in a short time."*

A comfortable couch formed out of the wall and Vel moved Shesain over to it and sat down with her, comforting her, as Shesain sobbed. Everyone else turned their not-so-kind attention to Leontul, standing alone, not giving an inch. After Vel calmed down Shesain's mental field, Shesain stood up, walked over to Leontul, and slapped him hard in the face. Jack, Robert, and Shenar grabbed her and separated them, as Leontul rubbed his red jaw. He would soon sport a nasty bruise.

"YOU KECTUR F'TER! YOU HAD BETTER HAVE A DAMN GOOD EXPLANATION, OR ELSE..." She sat back down next to Vel, if looks could kill.

Leontul was facing a tough audience. There were hard expressions on every face, and Shesain was fit to be tied. Vel leveled a stern gaze in his direction, demanding an explanation.

He stood for a moment, collecting his thoughts, shifting his feet before he began. *"You have a sturdy slap Shesain."* He tried to deliver a wan smile as he rubbed his red right cheek, wincing. His efforts met with silence. *"I see that didn't work too well. I'm the leading herbal scientist on Thumar; remedies and cures are my stock in trade."*

"Not for long! After I get through with you, you won't be able to requisition a beaker!" Shesain spit out.

Vel rebuked her, sending her into a wrathful silence. Shesain wasn't the only Thumarian on board with a mixture of anger and fear in their eyes.

"During our first ill-timed trip to 1814, I discovered the Veredant Flower mixed with my cure's molecular structure. This flower is one of the main reasons Thumarian's have our long-life spans and excellent health."

"How can that be?" Shenar asked in shock. *"You're a Thumarian too, and you saw firsthand how this... devil flower decimated our men. Have you no conscious?"*

"I'm no scientist, Leontul. So, explain to me how a killer flower can give life too?" Seamus queried.

"That man is putting everyone here and my children at risk!" Shesain started rising from her seat again, causing Leontul to back up. Vel put her back down with a thought.

"Give him a chance to explain his side, Shesain!" Robert interrupted. *"Leontul, do you have a hologram of your findings, from beginning to present? It had better be good!"*

"I do, I'm a research scientist."

His beaker cabinets disappeared into the wall, and enough seats for the crew manifested themselves. They all sat down and waited.

Three global holograms came to life, with the usual uncountable, mathematical highways in motion. Leontul's also had bio-chemical markers mixed in. This caught Roberts's attention.

"Leontul, can you mask the equations and leave just the bio-chemical markers?"

The holograms changed. Moving to the right-hand globe, he started. *"This model represents Thumarian DNA, pre-cure. Notice the red disruptions peppered throughout the globe."* He brought out a laser pointer and highlighted a gene configuration. *"Notice this genome specifically. The flowers pollen did not affect this one, and that is particularly important to note. The middle sphere represents the Veredant Flower. The next one is a Thumarian DNA sequence after receiving the cure. Balanced and whole, this is where I discovered the difference between the same structures in the original and modified timelines."*

The first two holograms disappeared, replaced by two more. Shesain was still bathed in anger, followed by Shenar. At least they were silent.

He pointed out the first one. *"This is a closeup of the individual genome of an infected gene. The next is the gene after the cure, the flower, and the nano-bots. The third one is an example of the same gene before our original trip back in time. Let's drop the infected globe and enlarge the remaining two."*

The specific marker filled both spheres. Robert was just about out of his seat, staring hard at the two holograms. *"Leontul; is this true, or am I seeing things?"*

"It is Robert, and I was astounded myself, and triple checked all my results. I came up with what you are seeing now, and the 'devil flower' is responsible for a suitable part of it. The other components add to the mix, but the flower's pollen unifies the effect."

Vel and Robert got up and dissected the holograms, exchanging thoughts in Telaxue. *"This is a phenomenal discovery Leontul, but why do you need to store live samples if the deed is done?"* Vel asked.

Shesain's anger had subsided, but fear was still there.

Leontul continued. *"Thumarians, for all of their superior health and long life, still succumb to sickness and death. I have one patient in our original timeline that suffers from a rare life-threatening disease. He's sixty-two and looks like he's one-hundred-and-eighty years old. Here is his chart; it's a degenerative disease that will kill him in ten years, and there's no known cure. I ran a computer model of the same chart, after injecting one distilled drop from the flower, and this is the result!"* Two holograms were up now, the untreated disease, and the treated one.

This even got Shesain out of her seat.

"He's cured, there's nothing left, no malignancies, nothing!" Robert got out.

"That is why I collect as many varieties as I can. Different flowers have unique properties. I'm just beginning to discover the possibilities."

Minutes passed before they spoke another word. Everyone

just stared at the holograms. Robert tried to explain some of the intricacies, but only Vel and Jack were grasping the potential. Then the big question came.

Shesain asked Leontul in a controlled voice. *"How large is your collection?"*

He hemmed and hawed, shuffling his feet. It took a gentle mental push from everyone to move him into action. An entire back wall went transparent, displaying at least fifteen different varieties. One example stood out: it had five small violet petals with streaks of white and yellow in mesmerizing patterns. Everyone stepped up to look at it; Shesain was the last. Her hard gaze met his.

"Why is it in a level-eight protective field?" Shesain asked.

He cleared his throat and hesitated before he started. *"I found that one in the Corano Islands. There was a field full of them. After detecting its potency, I only collected one. That one is more powerful than all the rest combined."*

Shesain just stared at him with her arms crossed and lips pursed.

"I apologize to everybody. I should have told all of you what I was doing. But I couldn't, I wouldn't have been allowed to, and this marvelous cure would not be floating in front of you now. I promise all of you now, I will stop collecting samples and keep the entire crew apprised of all of my research."

Shesain shook her head and looked at Leontul, her finger in his face. *"I forgive you for this...this...near disaster, Leontul. Opaque that wall! I don't want to look at...that again. If you ever pull off another stunt like this, I'll skin you alive and then revoke every license you have to practice medicine on Thumar forever, I promise!"* With that, she stormed out, cursing under her breath.

The room emptied, except for Robert and Vel. They turned to him, and Vel thought first. *"Leontul, you're to keep all of your samples under level-eight fields from this point forward. As for any future collections, Qex and Zix will determine that. Also, Robert will assist you on any new research tied to those flowers. We cannot have any mistakes."*

"I don't approve of your methods, Leontul, but I applaud the

results. Another mistake like that might get you lost in a node for good, so keep good on your promise," Robert said before exiting the room.

They left Leontul alone with his thoughts when Shesain re-entered.

"I'm sorry I slapped you Leontul, but you deserved it. You should know better than to put all of your friends in danger. I hope it doesn't hurt too much. Where's your med-kit?"

"That's ok Shesain, I earned it. I was wrong in my execution, but my results speak volumes."

"That was your saving grace. Does this hurt?" she asked as she dabbed a medicated pad on his bruise. He winced in pain as she applied the numbing medicine. *"I still meant everything that I told you. I love you as a dear friend, but the safety of Derak and my children comes first."*

"It won't happen again. I never meant to hurt any of you, I couldn't. I'm sorry I put you in danger."

She embraced him and kissed his good cheek. *"Forget about it."*

Qex, Zix, and Derak popped back to the ship from Telaxia right after the blowup. A sullen mood had taken over the ship. Derak expected a warm welcome from Shesain, but only received an indifferent look before she walked off. He looked at Qex and Zix before following her. He caught up with her in their private room.

"What's wrong Shesain, what happened in our absence?"

"Nothing to worry about, it's taken care of," she responded.

He looked in her eyes after turning her around. *"Everything that happens on this ship is my business. I can't let anything impede the crew's moral or mission and I won't."*

"I...I can't talk about it now, ask Leontul. I'll be all right in a few minutes, I need to be alone now," she pleaded.

Derak contacted Qex, Zix, and Vel. They joined him in Leontul's lab. The four of them walked in and shut the door behind them. Leontul stopped what he was doing and sheepishly looked at them.

"I was expecting you."

"Leontul, what happened while we were gone?" Derak asked.

"Sit down and watch the vid."

Seats came out of the wall and the 3-D vid re-played, down to Shesain's apology. Then they noticed his left check was red.

"That's a good one Leontul," Derak remarked.

"Shesain slaps hard."

Derak caught himself before he laughed, *"I'll remember that the next time she gets mad at me."*

Qex and Zix looked hard at Leontul before Zix started, *"If this had happened on Telaxia, your punishment would have been severe, Leontul. However, I must remember that I am dealing with a compulsive, illogical race. If one of those flower's pollen had escaped inside this ship, we could all likely die. You must examine your selfish motives in this matter, and do not repeat it again, ever. If it does, you will be brought back to Telaxia and tried as one. This is a Telaxian expedition, and therefore, under Telaxian law."*

"I understand, Zix, it won't happen again," Leontul responded.

Qex was next. *"I would like to address your results. They are beyond impressive; your inquisitive mind serves you well. It would be helped with honesty attached to it. Zix and I will inspect the evidence and discuss how to proceed from here; Vel will take care of your cheek."*

Qex left Leontul with Vel. Then he, Zix, and Derak discussed at length the presence of such an extensive collection of live Veredant Flowers onboard *The Shesain.* They emerged to find the rest of the crew getting ready to eat. Everyone was in better moods, including Shesain.

Dinner was served, and the conversation was all over the place, from the visit to Telaxia to the next assignment, to the big to-do that happened earlier. Everyone joked about Leontul's bruise and Shesain's slap. He took the ribbing in stride and cleared his throat. All of them waited for him to start.

"There is one more benefit to the devil plant that I did not discuss."

"Tell us, Leontul," Jack thought.

"I've run the calculations, and Thumarian life spans will average

over four hundred years, plus, when the timeline is restored. That's double what it was in the original timeline."

Everyone just stared at Leontul. *"Are you sure about this?"* Vel asked him.

"I checked it three times. Let me show you." Off to the left of the table, his hologram appeared showing his calculations and bio-chemical markers. Next to that were three charts stacked above each other. Everyone turned their attention to it.

Leontul continued. *"The bottom chart shows Thumarian life spans right after the cure, somewhere around one hundred to one hundred and twenty years. The following charts are one hundred-year cycles. The second chart shows a mean increase of fifty years, as does the third and fourth centuries."* Three more charts popped up next to the first three, showing the remaining three hundred years. *"The last century slows down dramatically. This growth is fueled by the nano-bots, the Veredant plants effects even out and plateaus the growth in the final century. This is unheard of in a normal evolution of a species. Examine my findings."*

Vel and Robert took the greatest interest in his research, dissecting his theorem. They were exchanging thoughts in Telaxue, while the rest of the crew discussed the possibilities.

After they were through, Vel posed a question to Leontul. *"Does this mean that the Thumarians on board will be affected likewise?"*

"I don't know, that's a brilliant question. I can't factor in our individual vectors. I know nothing about the complexities of space-time-dimensional mathematics. Maybe because we're in our own little bubble that we are not affected by the changes we've already made. I'll leave that to you physicists to figure out."

"That should make things interesting when we return to the corrected timeline. If our life spans haven't increased and Thumar's has, how do we make up the difference?" Shenar asked out loud. All eyes turned to Leontul.

"I may have the answer, but I know the Thumarians among us won't like it. Because part of any life extension medicine would include the devil plant. Before anyone complains, our present life

extension elixir contains a derivative of the Veredant Flower, the Pirotane Flower, which is a close cousin. In fact, one third of our most successful herbal medicines come from cousins of the Veredant Plant. Here's the real shocker: there are still active fields of Veredant Flowers in the Lelayan highlands, in our original timeline."

Shesain sat with a shocked look on her face. Then she looked ashamed. "I'm so sorry I slapped you Leontul...I didn't know."

"No worries, Shesain, until now, no one knew but me. I just didn't know how to present the information. I'm Thumarian too, and I was raised with the same fears and myths that you were. I found the results hard to accept at first, but I could not deny the empirical evidence in front of me. I'm filled with some trepidation every time I continue my Veredant research. I would like Vel, Qex, Zix and Robert to double check my data."

"It would honor us to verify your work, Leontul. I believe I speak for all of us," Qex said. "Now we need to discuss your future collection of these plants. It will be done under strict supervision. Robert will assist you in your collection and research. This process must have the highest level of security. Vel has informed me that your samples are under a level-eight field now. That will suffice for the time being. Tomorrow, I will brief you on your next mission." He excused himself and went to the bridge console to link with Terga.

The next morning, they assembled in the great room and waited for Qex and Zix. They entered, and Zix sat down behind him. "This next assignment will provide some excitement. This one involves Frankmur Velmar. They credit him with discovering the Corano Islands. He is primarily a coastal sailor, and has limited experience in open ocean sailing, but enough to qualify him for the journey. He has built a two-masted schooner. The coastal villagers think he is crazy to sail to the southern extremes. Most of his crew have already committed, but he is still short crew members. Robert, Seamus, Jack and Derak will finish filling out his numbers."

"None of us have ever set foot on a powerboat, let alone a sailing schooner." Jack said.

"I have some coastal sailing experience," Seamus added.

"There's more, the four of you will learn dead reckoning, celestial navigation, and the marine sextant. I will set simulations up to give the four of you practice before you start. You will also memorize the northern and southern Thumarian night sky. This mission will last at least three months, real time. You will take vid equipment to record the entire event."

"Since space will be tight, popping back to The Shesain will not be allowed," Seamus inferred.

"That is correct, however, once you make landfall, you can return for brief periods." Zix added.

Training in old maritime navigation techniques was harder than they thought. There were no laser-guided navigation equipment, GPS satellites, or computers to correct human errors. The four of them gained an appreciation of the old manual methods of navigation. In some ways, it was easier; they had the horizon, the sun, and the stars as points of reference. All they had to do now was to determine if a chronometer fit into the existing level of technology used to determine longitude. Time is set to the home port's time, compared to the time of their present position, to chart their location on open seas.

The sextant: or quadrant was used with the sun during the day, and the anchor, or North Star on cloudless nights. The azimuth circle helped to determine quick checks and calculations for the navigator and Captain. They were schooled in these methods, and celestial navigation, guiding the ship by the night sky. The four of them trained on these. Seamus took to the older tech much better than Robert, Jack, or Derak. There was a natural assimilation he enjoyed very much.

After Robert, Shenar, and Shesain discovered that chronometers existed in this timeline, they replicated two, along with two sextants, an azimuth circle, and two compasses to take with them. The more practical part of the instruction was in the rigging and blocking of the projected ship that would use. They also learned how to tie knots and where to tie them.

Period clothing was produced, and they were ready to go after a final briefing by Qex and Zix. They left the next morning after a last dinner the night before with the crew. They would be gone in 'real time' at least three months, and all four of them were already sporting irritating beards, except for Seamus, who was already had one. They popped down outside of the village early in the morning.

Elemure was a quaint, medium-sized fishing village, with a good-sized fishing fleet, and it didn't take long for them to find Frankmur Velmar. He was at the end of a long, newly constructed pier. They moored the larger fishing skiffs down most of its length. The fishermen were loading their boats for the day's sailing and casting a wary eye at the end of the pier at Frankmur's monstrosity. There she was, all ninety-five feet of her. A seaman was painting her name on the aft of the ship in white paint. *The Menarme,* named after Frankmur's mother. Her beam was wider than the usual schooner. She had two masts, the main mast, and the foremast, with a long jib boom they rigged the flying jib to. *They painted the Menarme* blue above the waterline, with a wide white strip painted below the bulwark. She looked seaworthy. The four of them stopped at the bottom of the gangplank.

"Permission to board *The Menarme?* Derak called out loud and clear.

"Who asks?" A swarthy, built man the size of Seamus, with a long black beard answered from the weather deck.

"Hecktur Morkam, Captain, and these are my mates, Rostum, Otur and Chakur. We are hard-working men and adventurers looking for a challenge."

All four men at the top of the gangplank let out a hearty laugh and turned to look them over. Frankmur continued. "If I let you on board and you pass muster from my first mate, you'll get that and more. Any of you sail before, or are you all land scupers?"

Hecktur (Seamus) answered. "I have Sir, fishing skiffs on the east coast of Lelayla."

"North or south?" the first mate asked?

"North, near the tip," Seamus answered.

Cetar, the first mate commented, "There are some rough currents up there, and it looks like you survived. That's no place for a scuper to learn the craft."

"No Sir, I wasn't a Captain or any such. I had a good teacher who taught me the currents, the northern stars, and how to use this." He pulled out one sextant. "I'm no expert, but I can navigate fair enough," Seamus added.

Cetar turned to Frankmur and had a brief conversation and then turned back. "What about the rest of you, scupers? Are you worth your salt?" Cetar asked. "I can use red beard, but the three of you look soft. This ain't no coastal voyage we're taking, it'll be open ocean, and she's a nasty mistress."

Chakor (Jack) spoke up. "Hecktur schooled the three of us on sailing terms, knots and took us on the water before we came here. We heard two villages ago about your voyage and decided to join up, Sir. We got a (sextant) quantar."

The four men conferred more and Frankmur spoke. "Permission to come aboard, all of you. We could use four more hands, if you pass Cetar's muster."

They walked up the gangplank onto the weather deck and stood before the four of them. They cast a careful eye over their size and what they were wearing, down to the boots.

"I'm Cetar, first mate, and this is Yemat, the second mate, and this is Estarbul. He's the chief in charge of deck hands and mid-shipmen. Give him a hard day's work, and you just might earn his respect. This here is Frankmur Velmar, Captain and owner of *The Menarme*. Now, if you don't mind Hektur, I'd like to look at the quantor."

Seamus handed it to him, and Cetar took it out of his hands. He felt the weight and balance, giving Frankmur an approving nod. Then he looked over the mechanisms, testing the smoothness of operation in the index arm and marveling at the micrometer drum. He held the telescope up to his eye and operated it. "I haven't seen one like this before. Where did you get it?"

"They made it under my supervision," Seamus said. "The metal is that new stuff from Ganmer. I think they call it Thumdust or such. Works well, lighter, and stronger than the old stuff. I'm also a smithy. We travel the trade routes and barter for all kinds of odd equipment, besides earning our keep in the villages and towns."

"I like the wheel on the bottom. You get more accurate readings," Cetar said, as he handed the instrument to the second mate. "Got any other useful toys in your bags?"

Seamus looked at Derak and he pulled out an azimuth circle and handed it to Cetar.

"How d'you come by this? You know what it is?" he asked Derak.

"Yes Sir, it's an azimuth circle, you take quick readings with it."

Cetar sized him up again and smiled. "That's a good start. Do you mind if we use it on the voyage?"

"No Sir, that's why we brought it," Derak volunteered.

"What else have you got that can help us?" Cetar asked.

Jack handed over a chronometer, and sextant, and Robert brought out another one.

All four of them were amazed at the treasure now before them. Frankmur asked if he could see one of the watches, and Robert obliged him. The quality of it impressed him, and he worked the adjustments. After his inspection, he handed it back. "Do you know why that is so important?"

"Yes Sir, one has the home ports time, and the other is set to the present location, for longitude." Robert answered.

Frankmur looked at all of them. "This is your property. If you allow us to use them, you're welcome aboard. We could use your muscle."

Seamus spoke for them. "We'll work hard and earn your respect, sir."

"Estarbul, run them through the drill and get them settled in. Call the carpenter and get these instruments mounted. Is that all you've got, or is there more?" Frankmur asked.

"There's one more thing," Derak said, as he pulled out two compasses from his sea bag and handed them to Estarbul.

"These are a far sight better than ours, Captain. You make these too?"

"Yes Sir, Hecktur is the inventive one among us; we just help construct his stuff. I believe there is a liquid the needle's floating in. We haven't had the occasion to test them," Derak answered.

Estarbul handed them to Frankmur and turned back to them. "You're getting your chance now, Rostum. Now all of you show me your hands."

They turned their palms up and he frowned. "Soft hands and booted feet, you will be crying for weeks. Our doctor has some salve to help heal the blisters and splinters you'll get. After a month, you'll get used to it. Any of you four have anything else to add to the crew?" Estarbul Inquired.

Jack answered. "Hecktur taught me how to pilot a skiff. Say's I got a knack for it."

"We could use another pilot. What about you Otur (Robert), what have you got?"

"I'm good with numbers and keeping track of supplies," Robert replied.

"You're our quartermaster. You'll be in charge of the goods and rationing. The Captain likes neat books with no mistakes."

Then Estarbul turned to Derak.

"I've been in some battles, hand to hand combat, and was in charge of a squad for a while. Most of them came home alive. I also read and write. All of us do."

"So, there are some brains that come with the brawn. I'll find a place for you soon enough. Now it's time to show me what you know, I'll show you something on the ship and you name it."

Estarbul walked them from bow to stern and port to starboard. They answered most of his questions correctly, which pleased him. Then they had to tie a series of nautical knots. His overall impression of them improved. He made Derak his first.

"The four of you will start your new responsibilities tomorrow. Until then, we have to finish loading the holds and securing the cargo. We set sail when the highest tides of the season come in. We'll need it all to move this beast of a draft into open water. Otur grab the pad and pencil, get a count, and bring me an accounting at dusk. Chakor, give Otur a hand and Rostum will assist me. Hecktur, give the Captain and the first mate a hand with installing your instruments."

The Corano Islands: 1857, The Voyage

Days were long and hard, and Estarbul was a hard taskmaster. Holds were loaded and secured on the second morning. A crew of twenty-eight tested the sheets (sails), pulleys, and rigging before the evening-high tide came in. Estarbul checked every piece of gear. He tested the four newcomers on their knots and the speed of completion. They had a lot of practice, but needed more. The four senior officers recognized their intelligence, so they tolerated their inexperience in the more practical matters. There were minor rumblings of discontent among more experienced crew members about their quick ascent up the chain of command. It didn't seem to matter that they brought navigation instruments with them. The ones who complained the most didn't read and write. Those who did just grumbled under their breath.

Estarbul took Derak aside after the bulk of the work was done. "There's a problem you will deal with, Rostum. Most of the crew don't like the fact that you're my first. They resent that a scuper outranks them. You don't have near the sea time that most of them do, and some of your skills show it. You've got to earn their respect the hard way. That means no complaining about splinters or blisters and speeding up on your knots and knowledge of the rigging. We say little because most of the crew don't know it all either. *The Menarme* is a new class of vessel. Some rigging and terms are new to me. You will have to exert your will upon them at all times, sometimes against their own. If you don't have the betur to do it, I'll find someone else for the job."

"I won't have a problem when the need arises. They follow orders. I suppose, once we're under way, some of them might get bolder. I'm picking the troublemakers out now and watching them. You've got to know an enemy's weakness before you can prevail. There's a saying where I come from, give a man enough rope and he'll either climb it or hang himself," Derak replied.

"I like that one," Estarbul replied. "Looks like you've got a handle on the issue, but we'll be watching you. Run up the ratlines (rope ladders to the upper rigging) and double check the rigging. We're setting sail in one hour. There's a good southerly breeze favoring us. When I tell you, drop the main fore and forestay sails. Once we're clear of the shoals and under way, you'll open the main gaff, fore gaff topsail and both jibs. We should make good time with these winds. You and your mates can lose the boots now."

"Aye, Sir." Then Derak ordered some men up the ratlines and readied to make way.

The lines were released, and a sizeable crowd had gathered to see if this monstrosity of a ship would even make it out of the harbor. The gangplank was pulled and stored, orders were yelled out and all hands-on deck were at their stations. Derak received the order to unfurl the sails, and the crew scurried to loose the sheets. They were secured as a southerly gust pushed *The Menarme* away from the dock. The bystanders were laying bets as fishing skiffs followed them out to sea. She moved slowly, with the pilot steering her through the mouth of the harbor. Lookouts on the port and starboard side of the ship called out over the shoals. They shouted to the aft deck, where the first mate gave the pilot course corrections.

The entire village stood on the shoreline to witness the event, mostly cheering them on. The skiffs were darting about like Ankora. Once they cleared the shoals, Derak ordered the main gaff, main stay and fore gaff top sails unfurled and trimmed the sheets. They started picking up good speed, and when they were far enough from shore, they released the jibs. The disappearing people on the shoreline broke out in cheers as they moved out into the open ocean. *The Menarme* was reaching fifteen knots; the captain ordered the crew to stand down, and Robert to break out the ale. They passed cups around. The entire crew was in good spirits. Wooden cups were filled, and the captain made a speech.

"To the good crew of *The Menarme*, I'm honored to have you on the maiden voyage of this magnificent ship. We have a long, dangerous voyage ahead of us. Our heading is taking us into the southern seas, past where the currents of the Taburn Ocean meets the Southern. I hear tell that the currents are wicked and high seas are normal. We are the first that I know of to venture into these waters. Here's to *The Menarme* and her maiden voyage!" A raucous cheer erupted from the crew as they raised the tankards and emptied them down thirsty throats.

The days wore on with the crew settling into their jobs. True to the chief's words, the four of them developed blisters on their hands, mostly from working the lines and getting faster at tying the many knots required for a big ship. There were knots the training on *The Shesain* didn't teach. The unfamiliar terms were never ending. Thanks to Derak's photographic memory, he kept them first, and drove them home with practice. Robert drew the long straw with his quartermaster assignment. He spent less time than Jack, Seamus, and Derak did on learning the ropes. His thoroughness in dealing with the cargo and rationing of supplies impressed the officers. His reports were without error.

Jack spent quite a few hours a day learning how to pilot the schooner. His space pilot acumen proved a boon to gaining this new skill. When he wasn't steering the ship under supervision, he was helping the chart master.

Seamus took to the sea like an old lover. He didn't complain once about the splinters or the developing calluses. He started each day with a ready smile and a willingness to learn something new. Estarbul spent a lot of time educating Derak on how a ship's weather deck was run, down to controlling crewmen who get out of hand. As a mid-shipman, he was taught and tested on every part of the ship and how to maintain them.

The sextant, azimuth circle, dead reckoning, and celestial

navigation was pounded into his head, Estarbul expected him to learn it all. He was a quick study, and his knot speed was getting close to a seasoned sailor. None of this mattered much to the rest of the crew. He was still a scuper. They followed his orders because they knew Estarbul would back him.

There was one burly, illiterate seaman disrespectful of Derak during the downtime. Derak let this slide for the moment, but it wouldn't last for long. One evening, while Derak pulled out some new splinters and applied the ship doctor's salve to his feet and the open blisters on his hands, Prack started on Derak again.

"That's what you get when you put a scuper in charge, shoulda left you on the dock. Didn't even know half the ship, and the Chief put him over us."

Derak just cast a wary glance in his direction and ignored his remark.

"What a matter, scuper, rats got your tongue?" he taunted Derak.

"Leave em alone Prack, he's almost as fast as you are now!" Someone else piped up.

"Shut up, imp! He will never match me in anything. Must be a mama's boy, just sits there an says nuthin."

Derak turned to him. Prack had a face only a mother could love. "Maybe if you could read and write, you might make a grade above deckhand one of these decades."

Prack was amused. "Scuper Boy speaks! I don't need that nonsense. I can read a ship better than the first mate. Been on the ocean since I was a kid, and you're all a bunch of f'ter scum, specially him." He pointed a scared finger in Derak's direction.

Seamus looked at him and Derak begged him off. *"This is my battle, Seamus."* The rest of the crew just looked at him, waiting for his next move.

Derak laughed out loud and turned to him. "There's a saying where I come from: 'the pen is mightier than the sword.'"

"What that supposed to mean, scuper boy?" Prack retorted.

"You'll find out." Derak left it and turned back to sharpen his knife.

The next morning, Prack was assigned head duty.

"HEAD DUTY! Fer three days! You're full of it, squibb! I ain't doin any days of head duty, and you can't make me!" Prack shouted at Derak in anger.

Derak stood there expressionless and spoke to him in a threatening, even voice. "You will, or you'll be doing it for a week straight." The deck crew stood around, looking at both of them.

"I will not!" He stalked up to Derak with angry eyes and a mouth half full of gritting yellow teeth. Then he shoved his fore finger into Derak's face. The chief pushed his way past the crew and watched scene unfold.

Prack was violently shaking his finger in Derak's face and raising his voice. "You can't make me squibb boy, go back to your mama's teats!" he yelled.

Before he could blink, Derak grabbed his outstretched finger and bent it back to the point of breaking. Prack's body buckled as he screamed in pain. He landed hard on his knees as Derak bent it back a little more. His agony could be heard all over the ship now. The captain and the officers were in attendance, observing the spectacle.

"You will follow my order, or I will break this one and continue with the rest," Derak ordered "You'll still be required to fulfill your other duties, with no complaints." His free hand shot Derak a crude gesture, and he put more pressure on his finger. Prack was now writhing on the ground in pain and Derak put his foot in his armpit and pulled the arm towards him. "You will clean the heads. Just nod yes, and I'll let go."

He nodded yes, and Derak released him. He got up, massaging his finger. If looks could kill. "Chief, I don't have to do this scuper's job, do I?" Prack asked Estarbul standing in front of him.

"You heard him, deckhand, you'd better get moving. You can start with the Captains and then move to the officers."

"I don't have to take orders from any mama's boy!" he screamed.

"Then you'll be sleeping in the heads with half rations and no ale for a month," Derak said.

Prack's shocked expression and lack of any answer told him he relented. "Your lack of respect just got you four more days," Derak added.

Prack's look pleaded with the chief, to no avail.

"You heard him deckhand, I suggest you move, now!"

Prack retrieved the buckets and cleaning stuff and shuffled off, mumbling.

Derak looked at the rest of the men standing in shock. "What are you waiting for? Get to work!" They left him with the chief and the officers looking at him.

"Looks like you picked a good one, Chief." Frankmur told him as he walked away with the first and second mate.

"What the hell did you do, Rostum? I haven't seen a man his size go down so fast in my life!" The chief asked.

"Just a little trick, I learned. Fingers don't like being bent backwards. The little finger hurts the most. You don't have to break anything, and it gets the point across. However, I don't think he learns; he'll be back."

"You're right. I've seen his type before. If we were making port, I'd kick him off before we docked. Did you mean it when you would make him sleep in the head?"

"Yes, and I can do it too," Derak stated.

"I'm glad you're on our side Rostum, send some crew up to the bridge, it needs sanding and oiling, and get someone up the ratlines to check the rigging."

"Aye, Sir."

Estarbul walked away with a grin on his face. He loved it when he was right.

The days that followed found about half of the crewmen showing Derak more respect. Prack strode about in a foul mood and smelled worse. His week of head duty was just about over and all Derak got from him was scowls and dirty looks. He would sit by himself or with his closest mates. They talked in whispers and shut up when Derak walked by. Derak's constant training was showing. He worked up to a good rating from the first mate on the azimuth circle and the sextant. Jack and Seamus fared better; they didn't have the deck crew to supervise. Robert had the stores, their distribution, and the accounting down to a science.

Seamus had set micro cameras in X-gen mode before they left the dock. They recorded everything. The vids were sent up to *The Shesain* to entertain the crew. When this assignment was over, they could replay the entire voyage.

The Menarme made good speed for three weeks. She had favorable tail winds, and the sea was calm for the open ocean. The four of them had developed thick calluses on their hands and feet by now. Most of the deck crew did not question Derak's authority. There were, however, a few that still bucked it. Prack was their ringleader. His time cleaning the heads only strengthened his resolve to supplant Derak. His rage was silent but bubbled below the surface. Vocal whiners are easy to read and control, it's the silent one's you have to watch.

The middle of the fourth week, they encountered a pod of *Jhakor,* ocean mammals that resembled Earth dolphins. They were one third larger and had twin horizontal tail fins. The fins could be used in tandem or separately. Their noses were longer and more aerodynamic. They slid through the water. This cheered up the ship's crew. The Captain allowed the crew some time off their duties to observe. Even Prack lost his permanent scowl for a couple of hours. The pod surrounded *The Menarme* and shadowed them the entire day. The following day, they were greeted by large *Whandar.* (whale) Some Thumarian ocean mammals were larger than Earths. The Whandar fell into this category. They were almost as long as the ship.

They seemed to enjoy their company, sometimes breaching half of their enormous bodies out of the water. Soon the Jhakor joined them, coming completely out of the water, doing turns and twists mid-air, flying through the water effortlessly in between the Whandar. Both magnificent sea creatures escorted them until sunset, then disappeared. A few days later, the watch noticed a sizable commotion on the water's surface. The water boiled with action. Fishermen recognized the signs. After receiving permission from the chief, they broke out the fishing nets and had them in the water. Seamus was in the middle of the action, joking and laughing with them. This is what he did in his spare time in his home seaside village.

The main school of fish was off the bow on the port side. Then the waters erupted with Jhakor breaching, flipping, and feeding. This lasted over an hour, and then they vanished. The feeding ball was still large, as witnessed by the considerable catch the fishermen were hauling in. The entire deck crew had to help haul the nets in, filled to overflowing with good-sized fish. Then the waters opened up. An enormous tip of a mouth burst out of the waves, engulfing the remaining fish in seconds, before dropping back into the deep.

The entire crew had never seen such a behemoth in all their combined years sailing the open ocean. The reaction was somewhere between outright fear and awe. Whatever it was, it was longer than the ninety-five feet of *The Menarme*. The mouth was wide with sharp white teeth the length of a man's forearm. The sea settled down and they all stood on the weather deck aghast, staring at empty waters where a large school of fish once swam.

The Captain broke the pregnant silence. "Men, that was one for the ages, though I don't know if anyone would believe that yarn. Thank the sea gods that behemoth didn't breach under us. We must be getting close to the southern seas. The winds are picking up and the swells are getting bigger. Get those fish into the holds, and the ones that don't fit, throw overboard. It looks like some rough seas ahead. Secure the cargo, stores, and batten down the hatches. She looks like a big one. Rostum, the oceans going to give you her temper, and she can get nasty, real fast."

The weather turned quickly. The sky filled with large cumulus clouds that turned black. *The Menarme's* bow crested ever larger swells. It required no orders; the crew sprang into action. The holds were overflowing with fresh fish and the remaining half of the catch was cast over the bulwarks and swallowed by the angry seas. Robert secured his stores and joined the crew to get ready for the fast-developing squall. Derak followed orders flying from the chief. With the ship ready, the crew stood by at their posts. The sheets were full, driving *The Menarme* into the storm fast.

Then the fun started. "Pull in the jibs, trim the main sails," this was the start of orders that flew from the first mate and the chief.

The winds picked up and pushed the ship forward without help from the sails. The waves were breaking over the bulwarks, soaking the weather deck. Now Derak knew why boots and shoes weren't allowed. The deck was slippery, even with bare feet.

"Pull in the main sheets, man the bilge pumps!" the chief barked out. Derak was up the ratlines and helped with the mainsail and secured the rigging. The swells were breaking high over the bulwarks now. Everyone was soaking wet and hanging on to whatever was nearest them. Jack was on the bridge helping the helmsman at the wheel to maintain the course setting. The storm raged and grew bigger by the minute. The sky was black in the middle of the day. Up and down, side to side, the ocean was tossing *The Menarme* like a leaf on the wind. She was breaking over fifty to sixty-foot swells and falling down into the abyss in between the next one before cresting again.

The crew was wet, cold, and chilled by the frigid waves crashing over the bulwarks nearly knocking them overboard. The crew hung on to whatever they could find, unless they had to secure a rope or rigging that worked loose. The storm lasted five more hours, *The Menarme* came out of it unscathed, leaving the crew with a stunning red sunset before the stars shone like jewels in the night sky.

After they cleaned the deck, watches were set. Jack and Derak pulled the first. Jack was on the wheel and Derak joined him on the bridge deck. They talked about the last month of learning a new ship and its operations. Even though she was a primitive sailing vessel, they had tremendous respect for her. Conversation shifted to *The Shesain* and their chimera, so far away.

"*The Shesain*? You never mentioned another ship at the dock," Frankmur said as he walked up to the bridge deck while they were talking. "Is she similar to *The Menarme?*"

"No Sir, she's smaller, a coastal vessel, not as grand as yours," Jack answered.

"We're the only ones up now, so you can call me Frankmur. My first mate might not agree, but seeing that you provided our navigation instruments, I can cut you some slack. That was some squall we went through. I think she held up well," he said as he lovingly put a hand on the bulwarks. "Both of you have acquitted yourselves well. In fact, all four of you have. Otur is the best quartermaster I've ever had. Hektur is respected by the crew; even Prack likes him. He still wants your head Rostum, he won't go away."

"I know Frankmur, but most of the crew learned from the first demonstration."

"What will you do next? We need every hand we have and more," Frankmur said.

"That all depends on what he does next. I'll gauge my reaction on his next move. He's got a hard head. Once he's taken care of, his mates will follow."

"That's how it goes with his type. Just try to leave him in one piece. I'm a good judge of character, and my senses tell me you could take him out with no problem."

"I could, but that wouldn't serve anyone. I'll get the point across."

"I'd appreciate that Rostum, according to our latest readings, the storm pushed us seventeen degrees off course. I've got the course corrections Chakor, steer to this new heading. I've got to get some sleep now."

"Aye sir, course corrections made."

"Good job Chakor, I'll see you both in the morning." Frankmur walked down the stairs to his cabin, leaving them alone again.

They had entered the Southern Ocean, and the winds had died. They were becalmed on a sheet of smooth waters. Barely a ripple moved on the water surrounding them as far as the eye could see. *The Menarme* just floated on the still surface. The sky was clear, and the sun was hot, evaporating any remaining puddles of water left over from the squall.

Tempers were getting as hot on the weather deck at noon. Sharp words and insults flew below deck. Prack's insolence toward Derak flared up again in the form of snarky looks. He didn't openly disrespect him, but his posture and the tone of his 'aye Sirs' spoke volumes. It was only a matter of time before he couldn't control the rage burning inside him. Becalmed waters, scrubbing and conditioning the decks only made it worse. Everyone was growing short, even Robert. The fifth day ushered in the inevitable scuffle between Derak and Prack at dusk on the weather deck.

"Hey squibb, I've had enough of you! You're going down!" Prack challenged Derak.

The entire crew gathered around both of them as they faced off. Frankmur gave Derak a don't-hurt-him-too-bad look. Derak turned around to face Prack. Whose face was red with anger and his body was ready to pounce like a cat. One fist was balled up, and the other held a long knife. He was waving it around, taunting Derak.

"What's the matter, squibb, scared of a little knife? I'm gonna gut you and feed your innards to the fish!"

Derak looked at him and started cleaning his fingernails with his own knife. He leaned back against the mainmast and looked at Prack. "Is that all you've got, empty words and a dull knife? You'll need more than that to take me." Words and fists were one thing, but the knife took it to another level, Prack would bleed.

"C'mon you yellow bellied scupper! Defend yourself before I gut you!" Prack screamed in pure uncontrollable anger.

Derak moved away from the mast and spit on the deck. This pissed Prack off even more as he lunged towards him with his blade slashing the air. He screamed as Derak used his martial arts skills to deflect his big body.

Prack fell to the deck and got up fast for a big man. "You fight like a woman f'ter, c'mon, mama's boy." he yelled waving his knife around. They circled each other, and Prack lunged again. This time Derak cut his forearm with the tip of his blade as he passed by.

"Had enough squib bait? You move like a pregnant cow," Derak countered as he took his next stance.

Two of Prack's mates grabbed Derak from behind, trying to hold him fast. "Get him now Prack!" Before they could blink, both of them were on the ground nursing cuts of their own. Prack took his chance and the tip of his blade lightly scored Derak's upper arm.

"So, you bleed rat face! I will finish you." Prack said through barred teeth.

"Too bad you need help to finish your fights. " Derak said.

Prack lunged again, Derak sent him to the deck face first, after lightly cutting him across both of his buttocks as he fell. Prack screamed in pain and Derak had him turned over on his back with his knee driving into his solar plexus. He pressed the freshly cut butt to the deck and the point of his blade pressed into his throat without penetrating the skin. Prack cried out in pain and dismay.

"You can end it now, Prack. Either you yield, or you won't speak for the rest of your life. Do you yield or lose your voice?" Derak demanded.

The pain was causing Prack's eyes to tear up as he showed palpable fear. "I...I yield...Sir."

As Derak removed the knife from his throat, he left a minor cut that bled.

Prack got up and grabbed his butt and throat. "You cut my ass. I won't be able to sit for days!" he said in disbelief. He took his fingers from his throat, revealing blood on his fingertips.

"Just a little something to remember me by, Prack, I could have done a lot worse to you and your mates." Derak bent down and retrieved Prack's knife. "You won't need this for the next two weeks. You and your mates will clean heads. I want to be able to eat out of them when you're done. If I can't, the three of you will. When you're done with those duties, you'll be sanding the entire aft deck. There'll be no complaining, or you'll sand the weather deck at noon, understand?"

Prack nodded his head in agreement and grabbed the two that tried to hold Derak. They retrieved the head buckets and started with the captains.

Derak looked at the rest of the crew standing around and ordered. "Back to work, this isn't nap time!" They scattered faster than wind-driven waves.

The first mate walked up to him. "How's that cut? You should have the doctor look at that. That was some knife work."

"I've had worse," Derak answered. "Looks like the wind's picking up." he said as the flat sheets started filling with the breeze. The first mate smiled and walked off.

"Trim the main sails and set the jibs! We've got a fair wind behind us." Derak ordered as they were under way again.

They had another week of good sailing before the watch cried out. "Sea birds, Captain! Sea birds."

Short-winged birds were flying over the ship, trying to figure what they were. Frankmur and the officers were on the bridge deck. Frankmur took out his spyglass and zeroed in on one of them. "I knew it! I knew it! Land isn't far off, men! Check the depth; we don't want to run aground."

Depth was checked every hour on the hour. The third day after the first birds were spotted, the readings showed they were close. Excitement filled the air. On the fifth day, the watch shouted out: "Land ho, off port side!"

Frankmur was there at once, looking through his spyglass. A large island loomed ahead of them and they could see smaller ones in the distance. He handed it to the first mate and shouted, "Ratour, Ratour!" He slapped his officers on their backs and went into a brief folk dance. "I knew I would find land in the southern seas, I felt it in my bones. A round of ale for everyone and strike up the music!"

"What are we going to call them, Captain?" the first mate asked.

Frankmur thought for a moment before answering him. "Seeing as there's more than one, we'll name the chain after my sister, Corano."

"How about naming this one after you, sir 'Velmar'," the second mate said.

Frankmur smiled. "I like it, mark it, chart master!"

The next day, they lowered the long boats after dropping anchor. They relieved Prack and his mates of their duties and they joined the crew as they made landfall. Strong ale and lively music filled the virgin beach that night around a roaring fire. They roasted the remaining fish from the hold over open flames, followed by a dessert of fresh fruit. Land fall was always welcome after a long voyage. The crew's spirits rose, and Prack was civil with Derak. That evening while everyone slept, Jack, Robert, Seamus, and Derak made for a secluded spot in the thick vegetation. Once they were alone, they popped up to *The Shesain* for a brief visit.

They received a boisterous reception. Shesain and Shenar were aghast at their appearances. Their hair was overlong and the beards longer. Jack's was soft compared to Derak's. Seamus had grown his down to his belt. He was proud of his flaming red mass. Robert shrugged his off.

"You're not getting anywhere near me with...that! Shesain thought to Derak, pointing to his beard. *"Let me check out your hands. Those will not touch this body until they're dealt with."* Then she embraced him and planted a long kiss on his lips.

Jack got the same response from Shenar. They got a proper meal of Telaxian beef and left after briefing Qex and Zix.

They spent two weeks on Velmar Island before getting under way again. The currents were shifting and Frankmur wanted to ride them home. They collected flora and fauna, small mammals, and colorful birds to show as proof. They filled the holds with salted meats and fruits and barrels of fresh spring water. Most of the island had been explored and mapped. The outlying islands would have to wait for a second voyage. With heavy hearts, they left the newly discovered Corano Islands. They raised the anchors, the charts were updated, and a fair wind filled their sails for home port.

The voyage home was not as eventful as the trip down. Prack straightened out his attitude towards Derak and the chief let him call the orders now. The confluence of the three oceans tossed them about good with high seas. Many more large creatures were spotted, including a long serpentine fish with a swordfish bill. The Whandar and Jhakor picked them up halfway home and escorted them almost to the coast. The large mouth fish feeder showed up again, this time showing its entire head. The eyes were as big around as Derak was tall. It was anyone's guess how large it was. They were grateful that it didn't consider them lunch. They wouldn't have stood a chance.

Their welcome at the Elemure docks was a mixture of surprise and disbelief. They had been written off as lost the moment they left. No one had ever come back from the southern seas. They extinguished all those doubts the moment they brought the first exotic bird out of the holds. After that, the crew supervised the unloading. The town's people almost ran each other over to bring out the newest finds. *The Menarme* was unloaded and organized by Robert on the docks in record time. The crew returned home to their families and loved ones. They would be back in the spring for a second voyage, with more men to crew *the Menarme*.

The four of them collected their gear and were getting ready to leave when Frankmur and the first mate approached them. "Where are you four off to?" Frankmur asked them.

"New adventures await us, Frankmur. There's not a lot we can do here, now. We might head up to the mountains. There's news of gemstones lying in riverbeds, waiting to be picked up. We'll find something," Derak answered him.

"Then I suppose you'll want your instruments back," The first mate said.

Seamus answered him. "You keep them. You'll need them in the spring. We can make more of them if we need to."

"You're all welcome back for the spring voyage. It should be easier, now that we have accurate charts and top navigation equipment," Frankmur added.

"Can't say where we'll be next spring," Derak said. "If we are in the area, we might pop in. Watch the confluence, even without storms; it can take you down."

"May the winds be at your back, Rostum, and may you always find a favorable port." Frankmur and the first mate shook their hands and returned to *The Menarme*.

The four of them sailed Thumar's oceans for six months. They tanned their skin a dark brown, and looked ragged. The girls were happy to have them back and even happier when they emerged from the showers, shaved, with clean hair. Shesain prepared Derak's next step. She soaked his hands and feet until they were softer. Jack went through the same, no matter how much they insisted they earned every callus. They used complaints to get pampered even longer. The women knew it.

Qex reported that the resulting time wave was extraordinarily strong, even in a node. The crew reviewed some vids recorded during the journey. Leontul was ecstatic when the Island footage came up, naming every plant recorded. He begged Qex for permission to collect some samples before they left this timeline. Qex gave in when Leontul promised to collect more than just Veredant Flowers. Robert joined him with Vel the next day. None of them ever tired of viewing the footage of the sea creatures, especially the enormous monster that could swallow an entire school of fish in seconds.

•◆•

When the time wave hit *The Mandible*, it rocked the entire moon-size-ship sideways. This sent the Prime Mathematician into an uncontrollable fury. What wasn't knocked over was destroyed by his mental temper tantrum. He was furious. The council would pay for this one, all of them. How dare a rogue agent in one minor ship challenge him? A mere mortal getting the best of him! He would die!

The Cyth, Preparation: 1875

They established a parking orbit in a node. Nodes are where time, space and dimension are one. Time does not exist here, and there are no celestial bodies to orbit around. The entire *Shesain* crew spent three days on *The Menarme* simulation. Re-living the section of the voyage where the feeding ball and the giant beast appeared.

This intrigued Leontul very much. He replayed the vid and froze the program when the beast breached. He telekinetically floated himself out to the hologram, circling it, touching it, and stopping to inspect its eye. After taking readings on its relative size, he returned to the weather deck.

"Interesting," he thought. *"According to my calculations, that beast is somewhere between 150 to 200 feet long. I've studied ocean life in our original timeline and have never come across anything like this. I will talk with Dr. Hensarth about this. He's Thumar's leading marine biologist."*

"That scared the daylights out of me!" Shenar exclaimed, *"Yet it is such a beautiful creature. It didn't seem to me it would harm us, and there was intelligence in those eyes."*

"You saw this twice. Was the second time less shocking than the first?" Shesain asked Derak.

"It was just as startling, if not more so. The second time it showed its eye before sinking back into the depths. Shenar is right, there is intelligence in its gaze, and a gentleness was also present."

"We have such creatures on Telaxia. Sadly, we are too involved in keeping the universe in order. Perhaps this recording might change

that. Mathematics has become our God and only occupation." Qex remarked, and Zix nodded in agreement.

"I wouldn't want to be swimming with that thing," Seamus quipped. *"Show them the sea serpent, Derak; they'll want to see it after this."*

He adjusted the timeline, and they were on the return voyage. A few minutes later, the serpentine monster broke through the waves. The head was twelve feet long with dagger-like teeth extruding from its closed mouth. The eye was three feet wide and as dark as night. *The Menarme* was ninety-five feet long, and the sea creature's body looked to be at least fifty feet longer. It stopped for a moment to study them before it dove back underwater.

"I think they were just as curious about us as we are about them. That was the first time that those beasts and Thumarians saw each other. We used to have similar animals on earth, before we killed most of them off," Robert remarked.

Leontul replayed the vid again, repeating the same inspection he performed on the other whale like creature. *"We need to rethink how we explore our oceans when the timeline is repaired,"* he commented.

After breakfast the next morning, they gathered in the great room awaiting their next assignment. Qex, Zix, and Vel entered, and as usual, Qex gave the briefing.

"Your next mission involves the large predatory bird called a Cyth. Contrary to popular Thumarian belief, this avian exists. They have recorded a few sightings in your original timeline. Combination of disbelief and fear of their size and veracity have driven the government to place them into the unknown and mythological status. Their population in your 25th century are small compared to their original numbers. The Lelayan continental plains were their original hunting grounds.

"The influx of farming communities reduced their population. The burgeoning population of Thumarian people was too great for the Cyth to compete with. This drove them into the mountain alpine meadows."

"That's impossible!" Shesain exclaimed in disbelief. *"Uncle*

*Remor has sent out at least five expeditions into those mountains
and found nothing."*

"How many of those expeditions returned alive?" Qex asked her.

"One, and only half of them returned."

"My point. Most of them were more than likely lunch for the wild
population of Cyth, and the survivor's stories were never believed.
Especially the ones describing the Cyth being ridden by men and
women. Your original history is replete with forgotten or ignored
accounts," Qex pointed out.

"That's preposterous, Qex. If you had seen the artist renderings
of those accounts, no one in their right minds would go anywhere
near those foul beasts," Leontul pointed out, and every Thumarian
onboard chimed in in agreement.

"It has been done and still is today." Qex answered.

"That's pure nonsense," Shenar said. "No one would have the
betur to try such a suicidal mission."

"Derak and Jack did and will, for the first time, again. Your
histories bear this out on at least seven different accounts. They did
it under the names Zeveren and Tyramar; I see that you know these
names well by your reactions."

"They're just a myth we tell our children, and my husband will
not risk his life on such an insane act!" Shesain thought.

I will not lose my chimera to this beast! Shenar chimed in.

Derak looked at Jack and asked him, "what do you think of this
proposition?"

"It looks hopeless, and we haven't even seen what they look
like yet."

Qex was losing control of this briefing and had to get it back.
Shesain and Shenar got up and stormed out of the room. "GET BACK
IN HERE AND SIT DOWN!" He ordered them.

The forcefulness of his thought shocked them all. Shesain and
Shenar blanched and returned to their seats. Shesain sat down hard
and crossed her arms and glared at Qex. Shenar was nearly in tears
at the thought of her Jack losing his life on such an insane venture.
Seamus was shaking his head in utter disbelief, and Leontul was

mumbling to himself. Robert was the only one who seemed to be calm about the entire affair. Jack and Derak were wondering if they could do such a thing.

Qex continued. *"It can and will be done! It is a critical time-fix that must be completed. Otherwise, everything you've done to date will mean nothing. Telaxia Prime will NOT ALLOW failure in this matter. Do you understand me? I mean all of you!"* This thought went out with a force that it could not be ignored or refused.

Shesain and Shenar tried to get over the shock of losing their chimera. Qex and Zix allowed the reality of the situation to sink in. Vel joined the girls and comforted them.

Both of them looked at Qex. *"Can you promise us they won't be hurt or die in the attempt?"*

"No, but I can promise you we will explore all scientific and real time analysis before this undertaking begins." Compassion filled his voice as he answered them. *"I do not want to lose Derak and Jack either. Your histories bear out that not only did they succeed themselves, but they taught the first riders the dangerous craft."* Qex finished.

Jack and Derak sat next to Shesain and Shenar and were embraced in desperation.

Robert picked up the thought. *"Qex is right Shenar, I've looked at all the records. Derak and Jack are the original Cyth riders and taught the first group that followed them. They must complete the mission."*

"Damn the mission, I won't lose Jack to one of these—monsters!"

Robert continued. *"You won't, history bears this out. I might even have come across a wearable saddle worn by the riders, similar to chaps worn by ancient American cowboys on Earth. That and two padded hooks that go into either side of their beaks, something they cannot bite in half. This is how they are controlled in flight, along with signals given from the rider's legs. Some pressure or pokes, that's as far as I have gotten on the subject. You are just going to have to trust us on this one."*

"I don't know Robert, this scares me." Shesain said.

Derak interjected. *"So far in my illustrious military career, the Kek have been the most fearsome enemy I have ever faced and survived. This one has me second guessing my own limits. The Cyth are creatures to be well respected. I will take on the challenge, but only after much study."*

Jack started. *"I've faced similar situations on fighting ships, sometimes in hopeless scenarios. I'll do this with Derak, but we will be prepared for all potential outcomes. One thing we have on our side is the ability to teleport. We're going to have to be much faster than normal."* Jack added.

"Jack is correct. We will improve your reaction time before you start," Zix said.

They broke for lunch and Shesain and Shenar put in long hours working with Robert to collect all the information that could help them succeed.

The next day, Qex continued the mission layout. *"We will first move forward in time to the year 1875. Seamus will deploy his drones in X-gen to locate a population of wild Cyth. Once they're located, I will program the simulator to give an accurate simulation of their size and makeup. Our next strategy will come from Leontul's examination of their physiology. The mounting procedure will be determined and practiced before the actual event. 'The Shesain' will be on Thumar, near to the nesting site in X-gen. The sky-cycles will be ready and on standby. We will take no chances. Zix, Vel, and I are more adept at teleportation than any of you, and one of us will be on watch at all times. Does this ease your concerns?"* They directed this question at Shesain and Shenar.

"A little," Shenar said.

"It's better than nothing," Shesain dryly remarked.

Qex and Shesain exchanged a quick thought before he finished. *"Jack, set a course for the year 1875; the end of summer should do. We will set down in the Lelayan highlands in X-gen and deploy the drones."*

Time travel was now as normal to *The Shesain's* crew as traveling through space in real time, thanks, in part, to the refinements Qex,

Terga and Derak had implemented to the IDMD and the ship's inertial dampers. The only indicator was the counter-clockwise cone they traveled through. Jack set them down on a high mountain alpine meadow on the Lelayan continent. It was a glorious site; multitudinous varieties of wildflowers carpeted the entire field, some waist high. Before the iris opened, Leontul was waiting with his shoulder bag and portable laboratory. They all had a good laugh.

Leontul commented, *"What? This is my professional occupation."*

Robert clapped him on the back before he bounded out of the opening, followed by Vel, who had taken a significant interest in his work. The rest of them walked out into the open air, breathing non-manufactured air for the first time in months, except for Derak, Robert, Seamus, and Jack. This was a crisper air to breathe, even compared to their ocean voyage. They prepared a sumptuous picnic dinner that brought Leontul and Vel back from their wanderings.

They all relaxed and enjoyed the warm sunshine. The trees were like the quaking aspen on earth, only much taller with very thick trunks. The leaves shimmered and moved with the gentle breeze now blowing north to south. The Telaxians were as enamored with the beauty as the crew was, and they commented on how they had seen nothing like this on Telaxia Prime.

Leontul had located a small lake on his previous outing, and they all popped to its location and took a pleasant swim in cold, brisk mountain water. It awakened their senses the moment they entered the water. Derak made it a point to simulate this with warmer waters.

These brief breaks always helped the morale. They could focus on the upcoming mission. This one would test their limits, especially Derak and Jack's.

Derak rarely felt genuine fear in his life, even on the streets of New York City before he met Master Li. This next assignment provoked this specter. He had to be strong, not only for himself, but for Jack. Jack didn't have the benefit of twenty-five years of training with a martial art grand master. Derak remembered a statement Master Li once told him: "Fear is not the enemy, but an ally to temper your actions. Great fear leads you to not underestimate your enemy or overestimate your own abilities."

Seamus released his drones, and they waited with for them to come back or report a sighting. The first results came back the next afternoon. It showed a single Cyth one thousand feet below it. The sight took their breath away and caused some serious second thoughts. They were huge, with about thirty-to forty-foot wingspan. The close-ups were more startling; somehow, they could detect Seamus's drones in X-gen and would not let them come close. Then he sent some out in D-gen. These were more successful, and their nest was located and observed from a respectful distance. Somehow, they were blind to D-gen frequencies.

Their true dimensions and details gave Zix pause. They had enough data to accurately simulate them. Leontul worked hard on this, with Vel and Robert double-checking the calculations. The biggest shock was when, during a close-up scan, the mother Cyth located the drone and ate it in less than a second. They all jumped back in surprise, and Shesain got 'that look' in her eyes. She and Qex had a long-animated thought transfer after that.

If they weren't scared enough at the thought of these birds, Leontul's simulation put a greater fear in them. Robert, Vel, and Leontul programmed a life-sized operating replica of the mother bird. They all stood, aghast at the large model of the Cyth. She had a forty-foot wingspan. Most of the body from the base of the neck to the tail was feathers. The legs, neck and head were covered with reptilian scales. The talons were as long as Derak's forearm and razor sharp. The head was a cross between a reptile and an eagle, with scales and a feathered crest on top of its head. Long magenta feathers thrust backwards toward the back of the body from the crest. The eyes were large, about nine-inches wide, with pupils. The scariest part of the head was the beak. It was three-feet long with sharp serrated edges that could shred prey.

Then Leontul showed them the feet. He brought out a block of the same plas steel *The Shesain's* hull was constructed of and put it inside one claw. *"The feet are ratcheting, like most birds of prey.*

The joints close and lock, preventing the prey from coming loose, if they're still alive. The tighter they grip; they crush anything in its grasp. I brought this block to demonstrate."

He cued the program, and the claw started closing around the block. As the talons sunk deeper into the plas-steel, the block collapsed. When the claw finished closing, the block was in shreds.

Leontul continued his instruction. *"They are very strong, so stay away from the talons, enough said on that."* They looked at the base of the neck next. Where it attached to the body was an extra-large protruding neck bone, and the scales were as hard as steel, yet flexible.

Leontul continued. *"This is where you will sit. Not only is it the strongest part of the neck, but you're also protected from the bird reaching back and chomping you or displacing you. You are also out of range of its talons. Your position protects you and the Cyth. We don't know how the forward neck bones would take your weight yet. This position should carry you and not cause any harm to the Cyth. Any questions?"*

"I do," Jack piped up. *"Why can't we pop on its back mid-flight?"*

Qex answered this one. *"We have to come up with a method to make the riding gear with their existing technology and mount them for this time period."*

"I was afraid you would say that," Jack remarked.

Seamus stepped into the conversation. *"It's my job to make a mounting system that takes advantage of the pliable scales where you will sit. Considering the power of the Cyth, I've come up with a way to slip a ratcheting hook under the leading edge of the scales to help anchor the both of you and not harm the bird. I'll need a couple of days to complete the design. We'll need a couple of Beore (Bison-type mammal) and Menurk, (mountain goat) to make them with."*

"Do we need to kill animals to make the saddles?" Shesain asked in disgust.

"Yes, we do," Vel answered. *"Those who become riders must be able to make their own riding gear. The only thing left is to figure out how to make the beak hooks. We'll need Derak's metallurgic*

background combined with Seamus's blacksmithing experience. We're in null space, so time does not matter. The materials and methods used must be available in this timeline."

"Can we preserve the meat in a 'fresh' state? It might be helpful with the adults. We could use it to help feed their chicks. It could be a peace offering," Derak commented.

"No, we can't," Seamus thought. *"But we can always get a fresh kill when the time approaches. The Beore and Menurk are plentiful enough and are on the Cyth's regular menu."*

"Should we give them just the meat or the whole animal?" Derak asked.

"The whole animal," Leontul answered. *"They use the oils in the skin to lubricate their scales."*

Shesain and Shenar were squeamish during this whole interaction, scrunching their faces in disgust. This was not how civilized Thumarian's acted.

"Must we talk about this f'ter subject?" Shenar complained.

"Yes," Zix answered. *"We must do everything in our power to ensure that your men get home safe."*

"In that case, can we get through this and move on?" Shesain requested.

"I suggest that Jack and Derak study this beast with Leontul, while Seamus finishes the saddles. Everyone else knows what your assignments are," Qex ordered.

Jack and Derak spent the rest of the workday with Leontul and Vel, going over every inch of the simulated Cyth. This did little to reduce their growing fear of the upcoming mission. Seamus continued his work on the mounting gear. It consisted of rugged Beore hide in between the legs, starting at the crotch. There was a flexible saddle like structure that formed to the Cyth's neck ridge ensuring comfort to the Cyth and the rider. The Menurk fur would line the inside and outside of the leggings so that chaffing of the rider's skin or the Cyth's scales could be prevented. They installed ankle locks for the riders once mounted on the bird's neck; they would lock the ankles together to prevent them from falling off in midair. A ratcheting system was designed so that the rider could maintain constant pressure on the Cyth's neck. Sharp spurs attached to the side of the foot. They tested this out, and it seemed to work on the stationary simulation.

The next thing Seamus and Derak worked on were the beak hooks. The metal and its forging were the least of their troubles. They had to figure out what to pad the metal with so the Cyth would accept them, if they would. They would not know until the day came for them to jump on their backs. So Leontul and Vel gave it their best guess.

Leontul and Vel were developing an interesting relationship, and Shesain would talk about it before she went to sleep. She insisted that the two of them were falling in love. It's something only a woman could sense, she always told Derak. The evidence was mounting. Whenever she wasn't attending to Shesain and the unborn twins, she was with Leontul. He acted differently around her. He was softer. Time would tell, but the signs were there.

The saddle was ready, complete with the scale hooks, and it was time to test them. They were awkward to walk in and created a noise that the Cyth would hear with their superior hearing. They were also difficult to manage, and this elicited more than a few laughs. It was nearly impossible to mount them like a horse. They reached the consensus that they would have to jump onto their necks from a higher elevation. Their first attempts were comical. Both Derak and Jack fell to the ground with a thud. They had to close their legs and lock their ankles. This worked fine until Leontul added movement to the mounts.

It bucked them off countless times before they stayed on. Often, they would end up upside down underneath its neck and had to upright themselves. This would pay off during the first flight. After a week, with constant ribbing from Shesain, Derak challenged her to try it. It worked; after that, she kept her chuckles to herself. It took two weeks to get their timing down on locking their positions. Then, Leontul started full muscular movement, complete with aggressive attempts to dash them against the rocks. Their backs were sore and required massage to get them ready for each new day. This gave Seamus time to perfect the saddle design and beak hook.

Qex convened another briefing. *"Significant progress has been made, and we need to discuss the flight portion. It has been called to my attention about the dangers of high altitudes and lack of oxygen. Derak and Jack must deal with this without oxygen masks or any technological help. The riders that will follow you will not have the benefit of such apparatus. If you are close to passing out, you must direct your Cyth to lower altitudes. If you must, use the spurs, but only as a last resort. The Cyth must learn to trust and respect you. How this is to be done, you will find out on the first flight."*

"Old earth aviators had a term for this. They called it flying by the seat of your pants." A round of laughter followed Derak's comment. *"That's what they called it. It was before computers and guided heat-seeking missiles. Your skill as a pilot determined if you lived or died in an aerial battle. This assignment is more like trying to fly a jet fighter plane while riding a raging bull at the same time."*

"That about describes it," Jack commented.

Qex continued. *"Seamus has the final saddle design finished. You will test them out tomorrow. I will now bring up the most dangerous part of your mission. Sneaking up on the Cyth without being detected in real time, no D-gen allowed. It has been suggested that you find an up-wind location to begin from. You will be allowed to teleport to a base camp first. Then after that, you're on your own. After tomorrow's test, you will scout out your approach. That's all."*

After the successful test, Leontul had one more briefing. They started on the simulator. *"You will have to deal with the Cyth's hearing and olfactory senses. Both are far superior to anything I've ever seen before. It is equal to their sight. I estimate by the size and structure of their eyes that they can spot a buck on the ground from at least two miles of altitude. I can't testify to their flight ability. Do not underestimate it at any cost. Vel discovered something else that's remarkably interesting. They may have the ability to locate prey by sonar. This would be helpful for low visibility or night hunting. The other aspect discovered is enlarged glands below the crest. They may have telepathic abilities."*

Qex stepped in. *"Do not calm these creatures with your mental skills. Your success must be repeatable. There is no sign that Thumarians of this time period possess telepathy. Only if the Cyth contacts you first are you to respond."*

"That's all that Vel and I have for now. Good hunting," Leontul finished.

They set base camp up, and Seamus joined Derak and Jack on the scouting mission. He was experienced in hunting and tried to pass on some of his skills. The three of them set out before daybreak, and after locating the nest, they tried to sneak up on them. They were in thick brush when the male let out a warning screech and looked in their direction. They ducked behind an outcrop of boulders. The Cyth stood up to his full height and stretched out to his full forty-five-foot wingspan, raising his head, and sniffing the air. He bellowed another warning and settled down into a watchful stance. Only when the female returned with food in her talons did he take his attention away from them. They took this as a sign to hightail it back to base camp.

After three more attempts, they deemed that this approach would not work. Seamus sent out more micro-drones in D-gen and waited for the results. They could get close enough to locate two fledglings almost ready for their first flight. They had to wait until they left the nest. Chicks made in untenable to approach the birds. In the meantime, they located a cave up wind and within eyeshot of the nest. Jack and Derak could hunker down inside the cave and observe the Cyth's without being found out. Two weeks passed before the chicks flew, and another week before they didn't return, leaving mom and dad alone.

Derak and Jack found out too soon. This did not change their watchfulness.

Vel had an idea that Seamus's drones could monitor their energy output during sleep. This proved to be the Cyth weakness. It was possible to creep up on them during this time. It took three nights of psyching themselves up to attempt it. The first night, Jack and Derak got within twenty feet of them before the female came out of her slumber and looked around. The fourth attempt proved successful. They were perched on a rocky outcrop, right above them, and they could have reached out and touched their feather crests.

The real test came when they had to follow that with the saddles, and beak hooks. They could not make any noise at all. The first time they had the saddles on, they were attached to their legs and back, and tried to walk. They didn't make it out of the cave. They decided that they would put them on when they were in striking distance, which didn't prove fruitful the first few times. Derak thought he had mastered silent movement long ago. This was a humbling experience. The biggest hurdle to overcome was securing the beak hooks, so they were motionless and made no noise. It took them two weeks to stand over the birds in full gear without being detected.

On the way back to the cave, Seamus stepped on a pebble and woke the male, who made a strange low pitch gurgling sound before slipping back into a fitful sleep. They knew that the next trip would be the one. The birds were getting suspicious and one of them was up part of the night for one week before both would sleep together again. They picked a moonless night to make the raid. They would get into position one hour before sunrise and wait until dawn to pounce. This was four days off, so they popped back to the Shesain and waited until the fateful day arrived.

The Cyth Riders: 1875

Jack and Derak spent the better part of the following two days on the Cyth simulation. Leontul had increased the reactions of the birds, based on data taken from their nest. There were rocky outcrops added to the landscape now. They had to learn how to keep from getting knocked off their backs. This included avoiding the rocks, trees, and being eaten. This left their bodies bruised and beaten. It took two days of ministrations to get them ready for the real deal.

The evening before their trials began, they completed preparations. Sky-cycles were prepped, and watches were set to determine their insertion time. The Cyth's didn't return to the nest for three days. This concerned Qex. What if they never returned? They would have to start over again with a fresh pair or site. They could identify the chosen pair anywhere on Thumar.

Much to Qex's relief, and Jack and Derak's discomfort, the Cyth returned on the fourth night, tired and worn out. They lay down and went into a deep sleep. This would work well for Jack and Derak.

Trepidation and fear filled their souls after they popped to base camp with Robert and Seamus following on the sky-cycles in D-gen. Jack and Derak checked and double checked the saddles and beak hooks strapped on, so they would not make a sound. Both of them received loving thoughts from their Chimeras before they set out. Robert and Seamus tried to cheer them up, but the upcoming hours put their minds ill at ease. Seamus and the girls made riding apparel for them to match the timeline. Boots, pants, a riding jacket, and a helmet made from Beore hide. They were lined with Menurk fleece for warmth. The outfits included unlined Beore gloves.

The time had come; they were ready. Thoughts of being eaten by the Cyth crossed their minds more than once. When that happened, Qex would remind them of their teleportation skills, followed by Shesain and Shenar trying to comfort them.

They carried the gear and put it on before they came to the rocky outcrop above the sleeping Cyth. The birds were in a deep slumber and moving their gigantic wings, as in a troubling dream. Derak choose the male which left the large female to Jack. They watched them sleep when another problem presented itself. After they positioned themselves for the jump, the Cyth repositioned their neck ridges, almost as if they knew their intent. Leontul said they might have some physic abilities. Derak hoped that if they did, it wouldn't affect their initial mount. He was never so scared of something in his life as he was now. Only his martial and military training kept Derak from freezing up. He sensed the same thoughts from Jack, only worse, who was already pushing himself far beyond his unusual bravery.

They repositioned themselves three times, almost kicking loose rock on the outcrop more than once. Master Li would be impressed by the silence of their movements now. Ten minutes before the sun rose, the birds settled down, leaving Derak and Jack alone to deal with terror flooding their minds. This would soon be replaced by training that preceded this moment and their survival instincts.

The sun was rising, and they were crouched and ready to jump into the unknown, when Jack's thoughts reached out to Derak in pure terror.

"Derak! I...I...can't do this, I'm going to die!"

"Not today. Buddy," Derak replied, as he used telekinesis to push Jack off of the outcrop. Derak jumped at the same time. Halfway to the targets, he sensed Jack's mind scream in fear before he tracked back to his predicament. They landed with a thud on the solid neck ridges. Instinctively, they closed their legs and hooked their ankles, using the ratcheting gears to lock in the pressure on their necks. This

woke the Cyth instantly; they came to full consciences with the pain from their scales being separated and hooked.

"You will pay for that!" Justifiable anger filled Derak's thoughts.

"I'll take it; we just need to survive the foreplay," Derak responded before his Cyth stood up and flung his neck and head back, trying to dislodge Derak, before letting out a deafening roar of dismay. Jack's female did the same and whipped her neck from side to side. Derak's was doing similar stunts to remove him. They looked like rag dolls stuck to bucking broncos, their bodies being flung in every direction possible and then some. Without the back braces built in into the riding suits, they would have already had broken backs. This was far worse than Leontul's most severe simulation.

Realizing that this would not work, the birds tried to dash them against the rocks. More than once their padded gear protected them as they collided with solid rock. Their helmets were a godsend; Derak would have to thank Shesain for insisting on them. Jacks concentration slipped, and he was upside down, staring at the ground.

"JACK! CONCENTRATE! Get back up and ratchet down twice! Think of Shenar!"

Jack cursed Derak out, righting himself before meeting face first with a boulder. He glared at Derak and sent him another round of profanity before securing his hold. The Cyth's were angry, eyeing the other's rider with small pupils. They had not extricated them by bucking them off, dashing them against the rocks or using tree limbs. The male moved closer to his mate, and she reached out a talon and took a chunk out of the top of Derak's helmet.

"Jack, use your hooks and direct her away from me, NOW!"

Jack pulled his left hook hard, and she screamed in pain as the soft flesh on the inside corner of her beak was pulled. Her head and body moved away from the struggling male. The padded hooks did no harm to their soft inner throat. It painfully reminded them they could be controlled. Their anger hit a new level at this realization. They looked at each other and launched into the air, snapping Jack and Derak back as their helmets collided with the feathery portion of their backs. Their backs were in constant pain now, which increased with every maneuver and jolt the Cyth's performed. They righted themselves only to face a powerful head wind in their faces and buffeting their bodies.

It took all the strength they had to stay upright. The Cyth were trying to use wind force to remove them. They had to ratchet down a little harder with their legs to keep from being blown off.

"I think we'll need eye goggles, Jack."

"Don't talk to me, you f'ter shickster!" He spit back in anger.

Derak didn't blame him. He would pissed if someone did that to him.

"Lean into the neck, Jack; cut down the wind resistance." Jack didn't answer, but Derak knew he heard. He leaned down and could breathe easier. The birds took them to higher and higher altitudes. The air was getting thinner, and their breathing was getting more difficult. They started getting lightheaded and their concentration was slipping. The Cyth sensed this and pressed on further.

"Control your breathing Jack, take in shorter breaths. We can't pass out or were dead!"

"No shit!" he shot back.

They were just about to black out when the birds tucked their wings like hawks and headed straight for the ground at break-neck speed. Derak would guess that they were traveling at 250 miles an hour plus. The Cyth were playing chicken.

"They'll pull out Jack; they won't risk their own lives, just hang on."

"What do you think I'm doing, you shit!"

They pulled out of the dive fifty feet above the ground. The next twenty minutes was a series of dives, rolls, loops, and acrobatics a man-made flyer would not dream of trying. The Cyth were getting tired, Jack and Derak were worn out, every muscle in their bodies screamed out in pain.

"Who are you that you sit on our necks?" Derak's Cyth entered his thoughts.

"We mean you no harm. We want to become your riders." He was picking up a similar thought transfer with Jack and his Cyth.

"We do not need, nor want anyone or anything riding us! I will eat you!"

"There's no need for that. We mean you no harm. We only want to understand life from your perspective. Too many of your kind are being killed daily, We want to change that."

They were in a level flight pattern, one mile in altitude. At least the tricks had stopped, for now.

"If you mean us no harm, pull those nasty things out of our beaks."

"How do I know you will not try another roll?" Derak asked.

"You don't," his Cyth answered.

"Then why should I remove them?"

"I'll kill you quickly then," he replied.

"Sorry, I can't go for that. Here's the deal, you allow us to ride you when we need to, and you remain wild and untethered. Free to hunt, roost and raise your chicks without our interference."

"Why should we? We live free now. We don't need your help," Derak's Cyth insisted.

"Together, we can make an understanding between a precious few of our species and reduce or end the killing," he told him.

"Can I trust you?"

"I could ask the same. We will remove the hooks if you and your mate promise no more tricks."

He looked at her and exchanged thoughts for a quick moment. *"You have our word. There will be no tricks, but a test of your worthiness to ride us will follow."*

Derak sent a thought over to Jack to remove the hooks, and he looked at him like he had just lost his mind. He removed them and clipped them to his saddle. Derak removed his and stored them away.

There was no telling where they were now. These were mighty birds, and they travel fast and far. Both Cyth's flew in formation, taking them through unbelievable maneuvers. When they weren't fighting the wind, their bodies were getting whipped around by the Cyth's sudden moves. The Cyth were worn out and Jack and Derak were ready to fall off their backs. The birds landed on their roost and ordered them off.

"You won't eat us now?" Derak asked the male.

"Not now, though you must pass one last test to live. Get Off!"

Both Jack and Derak realized the futility of arguing the point; they were too tired to fight.

"Lower your necks please, I don't feel like hitting the ground face first," Derak said to the male. He sensed a chuckle of laughter on his Cyth's part; Jack's female followed her mate's example. They unhooked their ankles and released the leg ratchets. Their legs felt like lead, and they had to grab the Cyth's necks to gain their footing. The birds just looked at each other and turned back to them. It took all they had to stand upright, their backs and legs were screaming at every movement. The male turned his eye towards Derak, and the female locked sight with Jack.

"My name is Miron *rider, what is yours?"*

"Derak to you, Zeveren for anybody else."

"What kind of name is that? It doesn't belong to this time!" Miron asked.

"It's not. I'm from the future, and so is my friend, and we must return."

"Not without us! Our union is a lifetime covenant, unbreakable. You are my rider and I your Cyth. Look into my eyes," Miron ordered.

Derak followed his request, and when their eyes locked, they made a mental connection; Jack had made the same wonderful pairing. Each of their Cyth's lowered their heads and the new riders scratched the scales above their beaks. After the Cyth exchanged gentle reminders of their bonds, the female spoke to Jack.

"You will change your mounting gear, what you're wearing hurts us. There will be no more tests, and we will become one in thought, spirit, and flight," Samora thought to Jack.

"We will return with a new design, Samora," Jack assured her.

"Do you intend to teach this to others of your kind?" she asked.

"Only those brave enough to repeat our actions and with the wisdom to know what they're getting into; no hunters."

"One wrong rider and our cooperation is over," Samora stated.

"So it will be," Jack responded.

Derak and Jack could barely walk, so they popped back to *The Shesain*. They were congratulated on their first flight. Even Qex and Zix flashed their toothy smiles.

The celebration was short. Derak requested a hot-jetted bath to relieve his aches. The simulator was ready, and they wasted no time getting in.

"I will get you back for that push Derak." Jack reminded Derak in the tub.

"You wouldn't have jumped if I hadn't given you a hand and you know it. You know we had to complete the task. If it makes you feel any better, I almost didn't jump either."

"What a ride, Derak! That was better than skiff racing! I can't believe the maneuvers Samora was pulling off. I might just be able to figure out a way to recreate some of them in a ship."

"That was the scariest and most exhilarating flight I've ever taken in my life, Jack. I don't think there's a ship in existence that could survive those G-forces. That might be a good challenge for the Mt. Kumar group when we return."

"Speaking of returning Derak, Qex and Zix are mum on the next assignment, more so than usual. After this last one, what could be tougher?"

"I don't know; leave it to a Telaxian to find a way."

They stayed in the jetted tub until their skin wrinkled and were ordered out by Shesain and Shenar. Their next station was a soft medical table. Vel used a muscle regenerator on them and then they received loving massages from their Chimera under Vel's supervision. This healing process was to remind them that only half of their mission was complete.

They consulted Seamus on a new saddle for the Cyth's after debriefing the crew on the entire experience. The natural physic abilities of the Cyth intrigued Zix. Leontul and Vel felt vindicated on their initial observation and worked together to explore this further. It was now all too obvious that Vel and Leontul had connected. Zix was having a hard-enough time with Qex and Terga, and he didn't need this on top of it. He would have to figure a way out to present both to the Telaxian council.

Shesain and Shenar grilled Jack and Derak privately to ensure that their lifetime unions with their Cyth would always be second to them, the children, and extended family. Derak assured Shesain most convincingly. Jack convinced Shenar under Vel's supervision.

It took four fittings to satisfy Samora. She insisted on the comfort of her and her life mate. Seamus was the only one, besides Derak, and Jack allowed near the Cyth. As he had to check the fit and receive instruction from Samora, she drove him crazy. Back at the ship, he complained that she reminded him of his Chimera waiting for him. They all got a good laugh on that one. Miron and Samora established a working relationship with Seamus. They even allowed him to scratch their itches. He marveled at the magnificence of the mighty birds. After the saddles got approved, Jack and Derak continued their daily flights.

Becoming one with Cyth's was more work than they had expected. It took two weeks before they passed their muster. They surprised Derak and Jack one day, when they requested to meet their life mates. Shesain and Shenar were terrified at the thought and had to be convinced by Qex and Zix to comply.

Shenar let out a shriek of terror when they arrived at their nest. Shesain just froze and turned pale at the sight of them. This dissipated after the Cyth's connected with each of them. Derak didn't know what they shared, and Shesain was slow to reveal it to him. They were offered rides, but declined for the time being, the Cyth understood.

Qex determined the order of events that would most likely assure success with any recruits that might volunteer. First, they had to kill a Beore and a Menurk to make their own saddles and beak hooks. Then, they had to go through training on how to sneak up on a sleeping Cyth. They adopted the next step on Jack's recommendation. The recruits would have to catch and ride a wild Antor buck, bare back. This conditions them for the ride of their lives, somewhat. The last challenge would determine if they survived first flight.

In the meantime, Seamus had located the Cyth's vulnerable spot that experienced hunters targeted: The feathered portion right below where their neck scales started. It took much cajoling from Derak, Jack, Shesain, and Shenar to convince Miron and Samora to let them make a protective shield for them. Seamus had to go through six fittings to satisfy Miron and Samora. His last design was raised off of their bodies to allow for air flow between the underside of the shield and the feathers, which they needed to prevent too much heat build-up. The girls agreed to a flight, as long as Jack and Derak accompanied them. Seamus had to make two double saddles, with the usual frustration of dealing with Samora.

The morning of the flight, it took all of Derak's persuasive power to pull Shesain onto the saddle in front of him. Shenar, like Jack, froze when the time came to do it. Derak looked over and Jack shot him a hard gaze. She boarded behind Jack, nearly squeezing the air out of him, she was holding on so tight.

"Be gentle Miron, a level flight should do," Derak instructed.

"I'm not a reckless fledgling! I can read their fear," Miron rebuked him.

Miron and Samora stepped to the ledge and glided into the sky. Both Cyth's took their new charges into account and gave them an enjoyable first flight. Shenar was in delight at seeing the ground so far below. It exhilarated the women when the flight was over, begging for more. The saddles were removed, and they were getting ready to teleport back to *The Shesain*.

Miron queried Derak. *"How do you come and go at will?"*

Derak looked at Miron and scratched his crest a little before answering. *"We have been trained to use our mental abilities. It is called teleportation, moving from one place to another, without moving. The danger is that you have to 'see' clearly, in 'present' time to ensure you don't pop, as we call it, into a solid object. You must master what is called mind sight."*

"You shall share this trick with us. It will be helpful in hunting and not getting killed," Miron insisted.

Jack chuckled out loud and Samora gave him her look.

"We are one Miron, we will share." Derak confirmed.

The Cyth dropped their heads for a good scratch. Upon their return, the flight was all Shesain and Shenar could talk about. That and how gentle the Cyth could be. Jack's bond with Samora differed totally from what Derak had with Miron. Jack's was like being close to a sister, Derak's was more like two warriors respecting and protecting one another. All they had to do was find a Cyth hunt before it left the village. Miron assured him this would not be difficult.

The women no longer feared for their Chimera's lives. After their first ride, they knew they would be safe. The morning of the search, they teleported two live juvenile Beore to the nest. Miron and Samora were well fed before the trek. This allowed for a good clean-up of the roost before they arrived. Seamus, Shesain, and Shenar joined them to see the hunt off. Seamus fitted both of the Cyth with their breastplates, made of six crossed-grained layers of hardened Beore hide. Jack and Derak saddled them and mounted. The new riding gear with a patch over the right chest. The insignia was an opened talon in a purple background.

They were off, gliding down into the valley before gaining an altitude of one mile. They rode the thermals for about one hour before Samora eyed a group gathering in a medium-sized village. Cyth hunters plied their trade at dusk. The change of light caused confusion in the Cyth's sight, but the hunters did not know about their sense of smell or sonar capabilities. They dropped to one half mile, and Miron confirmed that they were hunters.

The hunters were too busy talking to detect the Cyth above. Miron and Samora warned Jack and Derak to hang on. They tucked their wings and nosedived. The villagers didn't know what hit them until it was too late. The Cyth's came out of their dive one hundred feet above the village square and landed in the middle of the group before they could react.

Women, children, and elderly scattered before you could blink, screaming in terror after the Cyth's screeched thunderously. Half of the remaining men cowered in fear and two recovered, they raised their weapons to fire off one round. An arrow bounced off Samora's chest plate and a bullet embedded into the first layer of Miron's. He lowered his head and sounded out another warning. Everyone dropped their weapons in shock and wonderment that the Cyth's had not attacked. Then one of them noticed Jack and Derak sitting on their necks in a saddle.

"There're men riding them!" Someone shouted in disbelief.

"Your right Bechtur! They're devil men! Only the devil can tame those beasts!"

"Shoot em, kill em now!" another cried.

As three of them raised their rifles, Miron and Samora sounded out, causing one of them to run after they dropped their firearms. The others stood frozen in fear. Derak signaled Miron, and he lowered his neck for him to get off, and Jack followed. Derak took in the fearful faces of the remaining villagers, some of them women, and one adventurous boy, peeked around his mother's right leg. Wonderment, not fear was written on his face.

"I am Zeveren, Cyth rider, and my friend is Tyramar. We are men, like you, who have beaten our fear of the Cyth. They are still wild and free and shall remain so. We ride as partners; we ride as one." Miron and Samora raised their heads and bugled in agreement. "They allow us to ride them, and there is no need for mouth bits, for we trust each other and ride the winds as one."

"Impossible, no one can ever tame a Cyth!" one man exclaimed.

"They're not tamed, nor will they ever be. They allow us to ride them after we pass their tests of bravery and endurance. Those who pass live and ride free as a Cyth rider, those who don't, die!" Once again, the Cyth bugled in affirmation.

"Kill them, I say!" An obstinate man in priestly robes bellowed. "Remove this evil from our village!"

"Shut up, Helgur! If they were evil, as you say, we would all be dead by now. You, Zeveren! Is what you say true? We can work with these beasts?"

Samora answered with a warning growl and a nasty stare at the big man.

He lowered his eyes and said to Samora. "My apologies, I meant the Cyth?"

Jack took off his helmet and walked up to him. "Yes, it's true. We stand before you now, flesh and blood. Look," he said as he took out his knife and scratched his skin; the blood dripped and hit the ground. "We are the first Cyth riders, Zeveren and I. We are looking for fearless, like-minded men and women to join our ranks. It will not be easy, and not all shall make the first flight, but those who do will forever have their lives changed. We seek an understanding between Thumarian's and the Cyth, a balance. The two can live together in peace."

"I cast thee out, oh devil among us," the deranged priest cried out. "leave us now!"

Miron lowered his head in front of the man and growled deeply, sending him running away like a scared child. This caused a round of laughter in the remaining crowd.

"What must we do to ride these...Cyth?" one asked.

Derak continued. "You must face down death and walk away. Once you commit to first flight, there is no turning back. We must establish a new home, one Cyth riders can call their own. Your old life will be gone forever, family, friends, and village. Who answers this call?" He and Jack re-mounted the Cyth and waited.

Half of the crowd dispersed, grumbling underneath their breath. The hunters left. About a dozen individuals remained, shuffling their feet, looking at each other. One after another hesitantly stepped forward. Five in total presented themselves, looking back at the village. Two of them were women. One of them had the curious child.

"I wanna ride one of those," he told his mom, tugging on her shirtsleeve.

"When you grow up, Vetur. First mommy has to pass their test."

"Syrah! You can't, think of Vetur!" Someone cried out.

"We have nothing here Wanfur, no family, no farm, and no future. No one here can give me that. How can I resist such power and beauty?" Syrah reverentially spoke as she eyed Samora.

"Meet us in the meadow at mid-day," Derak said. "Two miles

northeast of this village tomorrow, to start a new life. Bring what you need, you must carry what you bring to your new home."

The next morning, they met seven brave souls. Two wives had joined their husbands. They were heavily laden with household goods, clothing, and cooking gear. The spokesman, Artir, presented the group. He was tall and fit. Most of all, he possessed a fearless attitude.

"We are ready! Lead on Zeveren," Artir stated.

Seamus had joined them under the name of Arimus. He would teach them how to construct the saddles, riding gear, and beak hooks. They split the provisions up, and set out for their new home on foot. Basic Beore-hide-covered huts were already set up and waiting for them; they would have to do the rest. A day out, a scout caught a young boy following them. They brought him into camp and questioned him.

"Why did you follow us?" Derak asked him. He must have been no older than twelve. "Your family will miss you; you need to return to the village."

"Please mister Cyth rider, don't make me go back. I have no family and the villagers just make fun of me and feed me their scraps."

"What's your name, son?" Derak asked him. He looked scared and the single mother of the other boy comforted him, sitting him down on a fallen log.

Derak knelt down and faced him. "What's your name?" He asked.

"Cirith, Sir, an I wanna be a rider like you."

Derak looked at the woman and she smiled before she spoke. "Tis true, rider, his folks died in a flood two seasons ago. The village didn't take too well to putting him up and he's been barely surviving ever since."

Derak looked into her kind eyes and asked her name.

"Syrah, and this is my son, Vetur. I'll take charge of the boy, he's my son's age, and they shall be brothers."

"Fair enough, he shall be taken care of by all of you. You're all family now and will act accordingly. No one person among you will ever go without, understand?"

They chimed in agreement and Cirith joined the small band of the future Cyth rider community. Four days later, they arrived at their new home in an alpine meadow. There were enough huts for everyone to have shelter, with a few left vacant. A central square held a meeting hall, and there was enough fresh meat to last a few days. The new recruits would have to forge their own future now.

Derak gathered them together in the big hut and gave them their orders. "It's high summer now, and pleasant, but the winters are heavy, so hunting parties will bring back Beore and Menurk for now. Small game will help too, they have soft pelts. These will be used for making your saddles and riding gear. Each man or woman who challenges a Cyth in first flight must make and maintain their own gear. Second, pelts will be needed for the winters to keep you warm. You will gather herbs and roots for salves and food. Use the empty huts to store them in. You will build a large sturdy corral, strong enough to hold a wild Antor buck. We will return in seven days, and training will begin."

They split up into groups, and the new village was empty by the time Miron and Samora descended from the sky. They rode bareback to *The Shesain* to complete the plans. The saddles made the ride more comfortable. Seamus was allowed to ride on Miron. After Seamus dismounted, he assured Derak and Jack that he was ready to commit to first flight. He wanted to be a Cyth rider. After considerable consultation with *The Shesain's* crew, Qex approved it.

They returned in seven days, and training began. Miron and Samora located a Cyth big enough for Seamus. Eight weeks of hard training culled the candidates down to four villagers and Seamus. They had all ridden the wild Antor's bareback and were ready to track their own Cyth, Syrah was the lone woman who would impress.

After tracking and observing their Cyth's sleep habits, the group held a celebratory dinner the night before they attempted first flight. One Antor was killed and roasted with a fresh batch of ale some men brewed up. The other bucks were set free. The following day, prayers were said, and the new riders were off. The wait was long and nerve-wracking back at the camp. Jack and Derak were concerned about Seamus. They could not afford to lose him. He had to be present for the last time fix. Miron and Samora had been tracking the progress of the five brave souls and sent confirmation on each of their completed first flights: all five bonded with their Cyth's.

A feast was prepared and made ready. Miron and Samora bugled each of their arrivals, one at a time. Five happy, dazed and worn out new Cyth riders stumbled into camp. They were attended to and enjoyed a merry feast. The next morning, they fit the new Cyth's with riding saddles and chest armor different from first ride gear; they strapped it to the neck for mounting from the ground.

It was time to leave. Derak gave them last instructions, including recommendation to trust their Cyth's on weeding out those who would never ride and hunters tracking down their camp. They left Artir and Syrah in charge. They had made a powerful bond already; everyone could see it in their eyes.

Miron and Samora instructed the newly flown Cyth's on their responsibilities. Artir's Cyth, Beron, was chosen as the alpha male, and Syrah's Arana, the alpha female.

Seamus's, Borath, would come with them, back to the future with Miron and Samora. It was an emotional goodbye, knowing they would never see them again. Yet they would be immortalized in Thumarian history.

The three riders glided to the ground in front of *The Shesain* in X-gen. They had to show the Cyth's a lengthy demonstration on the safety of being reduced to pure energy in the transporter buffers. After Derak, Jack, and Seamus did it themselves and came back whole, the Cyth agreed. And only after Terga confirmed their safe keeping many times did the three riders feel a little less uneasy about the procedure. They didn't have to endure another time wave, as they were at its point of origination. They packed, lifted off, and made their way to a node to receive instructions on the last time fix.

•◆•

The Prime Mathematician was knocked out after he was thrown across the room from the time wave. He woke up with a pounding headache in a murderous mood. He was about to scream for Councilman Number One to take him apart limb by limb when the sound stuck in his throat. He was no longer aboard *The Mandible* with its innumerable resources. In fact, *The Mandible* was nowhere to be found. It had been catapulted back to the twenty-fifth century by the time wave's change, and he was alone on his cramped Telaxian ship.

Thumar: 1814

Qex gave the crew a lengthy period of free time. They took advantage of it at first but were getting suspicious. Qex, Zix, and Vel were in conference a lot, and Zix and Qex had teleported back to Telaxia several times, not saying anything upon their return. They were nervous and hesitant when asked about the last mission. Derak confronted Qex at the end of their second week.

He caught him alone with his usual long thought transfers he and Terga had on the bridge. *"When are we going to be briefed on the last assignment, Qex? Everyone is wondering what's up. Your silence is speaking volumes."*

"You will not like it very much."

"Like we bought into the last one without a fight. What could be worse than riding a Cyth?" Derak asked him.

"Your next mission. I do not look forward to dealing with Shesain and Shenar. They will pose the largest obstacles."

"You need to get it over with, Qex. We all want to go home. Almost two years of ship time is wearing thin. The simulations are great in helping our morale in the short run, but we long to step foot on Thumar, in real time, 2414."

"Tomorrow morning, 0900 hours, we'll meet in the great room. That is all for now."

Derak left Qex alone with Terga. He would need it before facing the reaction to his orders.

After clearing the bridge, Derak contacted Terga. *"Terga, what's so radioactive about the last assignment?"*

"You will have to hear it from him, Derak. You and Robert will agree with the logic, the ends will justify the means. Shesain and Shenar will make it almost impossible to start. That is all I can tell you. Just try to understand it from Qex's point of view. They will require you to complete the mission, whether you like it or not."

The next morning, Qex entered and started. *"We would like to congratulate you on the completion of the last mission. We realize that it took a great amount of bravery to face the Cyth and prevail. The next assignment will require all of you except Robert to face yourselves, to challenge you beyond what have experienced to date. Your last mission will be to stop yourselves from starting your original visit in the year 1814."*

"Wait a minute, Qex, how can we stop ourselves unless we..." Jack asked.

"Face yourselves," Qex finished.

"You can't face your past or present selves without dire consequences. That could destroy the whole timeline. This is getting confusing," Robert said in surprise.

"Normally it would, but in this case, it is required," Qex stated.

"That will take some fancy calculations, Qex. It's not as if our two-year goal hasn't required considerable brain power from your home world. Now they want us to go where no one has gone before," Seamus added.

"We have the required data with us now. Zix and I brought it back on our last trip from Telaxia. Facing yourselves in the flesh is the simple part, what comes afterwards will be the most difficult action. We must eliminate the original crew and The Shesain *from this timeline and universe."*

Shock silenced all of them. No one knew how to respond. The look on Robert's face told Derak that he was calculating the consequences in his mind. He was the first to respond.

"What do you mean by eliminate, Qex?" Robert asked.

"They must be physically removed from this universe and timeline."

"How do you propose we do that, short of ending their lives and

destroying the original Shesain?" Derak asked in an incredulous tone.

The silence answered the question and Shesain jumped all over Qex. *"How can you expect us to kill ourselves? Are the Telaxians crazy!? Of all the things we've had to do, this is the most outrageous request yet! Would you kill yourself, Qex!?"*

He responded, *"Technically, you are not eliminating yourselves because your present incarnations will still exist. Your copies, the original crew and ship that caused the time-space paradox in the first place will cease to be, leaving only one* Shesain, *not two. Two representatives of the same being cannot occupy the same universe together without dire consequences. Since this crew is educated and aware of the trouble the original crew started. We saddled you with fixing the paradox. You have the knowledge to complete what you started, not the first* Shesain *and her crew."*

Derak butted in. *"We go back in time 600 years, thanks to a Telaxian operative in the Mt. Kumar group. We mitigated the plague of 1814. Now we have to physically face and stop ourselves from starting the original assignment your government sent us on. Aren't the calculations required for this last fix a stretch for even Telaxians?"*

"It challenged us at first, but the formulas were calculated by our top minds and deemed acceptable after many simulations," Qex answered.

Shesain had calmed down a little. *"Where did we go wrong the first time, and how are we going to fix it?"*

"Without going into too many details, you were one day early in a successful inoculation. The result was one man that had to die, lived. This event changed your original timeline."

"Then why didn't we just fix that and be done with it?" Robert queried Qex.

"Because your genetic markers were found on the previous missions."

"Who was the individual that had to die of the plague?" Leontul asked.

"Shamur Andehar, of Shesain and Shenar's family lineage."

Shesain's anger reignited. *"You expect us to let one of my family line die? If Shamur dies, then who will carry on our family name!?"* Her eyes were flashing red now.

"I, in all consciousness, cannot allow this to happen! I will not!" Shenar stood up in anger and started to leave the room.

"ENOUGH, SIT DOWN!" They all quaked at the sharpness of his rebuke. After Shenar sat down, he continued. *"Tukar Andehar, the one you helped to locate the Cave of Lights, carried your lineage forward. There are brothers that continued the line as well. It is Tukar that establishes the main Andehar family name. His discovery of the caves placed him in the pinnacle of your society, past, present, and future. You saw firsthand how Shamur's life disrupted the continuum, he must die."*

Shesain and Shenar sat, arms folded in silent protest. The rest of them didn't argue anymore; it would have done no good. They had to accept the assignment and see it to completion. The Telaxians would take no less. This pushed Derak to think of ways, besides death, to remove the original crew from the universe. After a lengthy period of total silence, an answer came to him.

"Qex, what if the original crew and The Shesain *are sent to an alternative universe? Would that be an acceptable compromise? If there is not a compatible one, then perhaps one they could mold into a similar Thumarian type of civilization. Both Ships have timing capabilities, and they could use null space to stretch out their years,"* Derak suggested.

Qex stopped and thought for a moment, then turned to Zix, and Vel for a thought conference. *"That may be an acceptable counter offer. I must clear it with the council. They will not like having to waste any more time on this mission. But, considering the sacrifices you have made, they might consider it. If they approve your idea, we will have to spend more time in the node to allow for the final calculations to be run. If the entities they report to agree. Is this acceptable to you?"* he asked Shesain and Shenar.

Both of them unfolded their arms and looked at each other before

Shenar answered. *"If it is the only alternative, it's better than dying. Can you do the same for Shamur?"*

"No Shenar, he must die to preserve your original timeline. Remember, if the original crew does not agree to this, they will cease to exist with The Shesain. *The stability of this universe comes first to Telaxians, even to an individual's life. Zix and I will command the assignment from start to finish. If we feel we have to, we will end their existence."*

"Now you're beginning to sound like the Syndicate," Jack commented.

"Not even close! If we were the Syndicate, we would have not told you, or we would have eliminated them behind your backs!"

"And I thought it couldn't get worse than the Cyth," Jack rebutted.

"We will consider your counter proposal and get back to you this evening. That is all for now." Zix said before he, and Qex exited while Vel comforted Shesain and Shenar.

Qex and Vel came to them after dinner. *"Derak, your suggestion received full approval from the Telaxians and their superiors. The equations are being worked through now. It will be two day's ship time until we receive the final calculations. Until then, you have time off before we start,"* Qex reported.

Shesain and Shenar spent the next day in nasty moods, grousing over the fact an Andehar had to die, and the original crew was being sent off to an alternate universe. They felt that there had to be another solution, but Qex and Zix would not move.

The second day found them on *The Menarme* simulation, approaching Velmar Island. They lowered the longboat and made landfall. Leontul, Vel, and Robert trekked inland, while Derak, Shesain, Jack and Shenar lounged on the pure white sands. The scouting party returned with Leontul almost skipping across the beach. Robert and Vel, in deep thought conversation, followed him out of the trees. Leontul could not stop marveling about the wonders of this undiscovered land.

The information packet arrived from Telaxia the next morning. Qex and Zix went over the equations in private, while the rest of crew continued optic training. They also spent several hours a day perfecting telepathy, telekinesis, and teleportation skills, in the form of games in the simulator. Adding fun to the practice helped them advance much faster.

Qex got them together to instruct them on the last mission. *"In three days, the six of you, without Robert, will teleport down to Thumar in the year 1814 in X-gen. We've tested the D-gens capabilities to detect X-gen and found one to be invisible to the other. When the original crew lands and disembarks, you will put them to sleep and attach this red band around their wrists. It has two purposes: the first is to distinguish this crew from the original, and the second is to allow me and Zix to act, if we feel you are in any danger. Jack will explain the situation and conditions to the original crew. They will have to make their decision based on this."*

"Why don't we take two vid records with us? One showing Thumar's original timeline, and the other Thumar in the modified one. Pictures speak louder than words. The vids won't go past Thumar or include the Altairian footage," Leontul suggested.

"We will include your suggestion Leontul" Qex thought. *"Jack will take point for this crew, to prevent any unnecessary confusion between the crews. There will be one spokesman for the original crew. You will separate the crews and maintain distance for the entire encounter. Should they agree to the terms of relocating, we will give them optic AI's and any data that will assist them. We have located an alternate universe. It is one they will have to form to their liking. We have approval from all participating parties. If the original crew does not agree, or tries to escape, you know what will happen. If you need a demonstration to drive home the point, Zix and I can provide it for you.*

"After they leave, you will repeat your assignment in curing this plague, one day later. Remember, Shamur Andehar must not survive the plague. If we have to adjust the entry point by another day, we will. We will confirm this from Telaxia by the time you teleport. You will take orders from The Shesain"

The six of them were grumpy for the three days leading up to the assignment. Shesain and Shenar were in foul moods. Derak felt the heaviness of having to make a hard decision.

The morning of the departure for the planet's surface, they were given Telaxian styled clothing to help distinguish them from the original crew. They had the red wrist bands and were told that if they didn't put them on, Qex would. He was very aware of their reticence about what they were about to do. Derak detected sorrow in his thoughts, with a determination to complete this task, no matter what.

Armed with sleep darts, wristbands, and phase pistols set on minimum stun in case things got out of hand, they popped down to the glen. Shesain and Shenar objected when Zix handed Derak, Jack, and Seamus the pistols with instructions. Their arguments fell on deaf ears. All of them were in X-gen and would switch to D-gen when all the original crew was slept. Then, Jack would try to convince them to consider their alternative, hopefully, they would agree.

They waited only fifteen minutes before the first *Shesain* appeared one hundred feet above the glen. They were given firm orders to wait for everyone to exit the ship. Derak had to be among them, or there would be trouble. *The Shesain* landed, and the iris opened. Leontul was the first to emerge, with his usual look of wonderment at the local plant life. Then Shesain and Shenar came out, followed by Seamus and Jack. This was getting more confusing by the moment. It was one thing to imagine facing your doppelganger. It was another when it was happening. Even Derak was having serious doubts about completing the task. Qex picked this up and reminded them of the alternative. With heavy hearts, they proceeded with the plan.

Everything was going as planned until someone from the time team shot their sleep darts early. Seamus and Jack hit the ground asleep, and then Leontul, Shesain, and Shenar followed.

"Who shot those darts!? Now you've caused us a big problem." Derak asked.

"We did, Shesain and Shenar responded. I couldn't wait any longer and got it over with." Shesain's impetuousness was strong in the reply.

299

"If this had been a real-life mission, both of you would clean heads for a month! What an idiotic reaction!" Derak responded.

"We're not in the military, Derak!" Shesain shot back.

"This IS a military operation! You will follow orders or face the repercussions! Do you understand!?" he barked back.

"Yes, Sir!" Shesain returned the threat.

"I'll deal with YOU later!" Just then, the original Derak stepped out of the iris to find his crew down and went into combat mode. Avoiding the real Derak's sleep dart and disappearing into the trees. *"Now you've done it, Shesain! This should prove interesting."*

"Let's just flush him out and ambush him," Shenar suggested.

"None of you even realize who you're dealing with," Derak warned them. *"He could take all of you out in less than a minute. Leave him to me. NO ONE, and I mean NO ONE, even tries to enter this fight. If you do, the worst rebuke from Qex will seem like child's play after I dress you down!"* It worked; even Jack shrunk back from the order, and Shesain's eyes were wide with fear.

Derak (D2) sensed that the original Derak (D1) was activating his DNA strands. He finished with his third and was activating his fourth, D2 couldn't let this happen. So, he switched to D-gen and stood in front of the ship, ready for anything. Derak activated his second and third strands to match him. That halted D1's fourth strand from coming on line.

He stepped out of the trees in shock. "What in the hell is going on here, why is my wife and crew slept? Who are you!? Wait... impossible...this can't be, how can you be me?

"Because I am," D2 answered.

"NO, NO, this could destroy the timeline; Go now!" D1 pleaded.

"Your actions already accomplished that. I'm from the future and have spent the last two years, ship time, fixing what your crew messed up. Stand down and you'll get a complete explanation."

D1 evaded another sleep dart. His reaction was a lightning quick charge with an activated light sword. D2 responded just as fast, blocking his thrust. Both swords sparked and popped on contact. Two more darts flew, barely missing D2.

"Whichever f'ter idiot is trigger-happy, STOP! Before I sleep you until we return to our original timeline! Jack, get that P'tah in line, NOW!" This momentary delay cost him. He parried D1's thrust. Both of them were in full combat mode now. It was almost impossible to tell them apart.

Two sword masters put on a show. The battle grew fierce. Both light swords turned into a blur of light beams arching in complicated patterns and crossing with crackles and pops of converging plasma beams. This was turning into a stalemate. Blow for blow, block for block. These were dangerous weapons to fight with. If either of them made contact, the damage would be severe. Qex might have to eliminate D1, something had to be done fast.

"Use your telekinesis and teleportation," Qex reminded D2, not wanting either of them to get injured or die.

It was difficult at first, fighting a physical fight with telekinesis at the same time and not losing concentration on either. He knew what he had to do. He activated his fourth strand. This would be an excellent test for his control. He was fighting with both now. Their swords would cross, and D1 would have to duck a small rock flying at his head. His desperation was growing. He was getting sloppy. D2 hit his legs with a small branch, taking them out. D1 recovered and took a tiger stance. D1 charged and when he would have struck a killing blow, D2 disappeared, and his plasma sword cut through thin air.

D2 popped behind him and injected his neck with a dart; D1 hit the ground. With significant effort, Derak shut down his fourth strand. It was such an intoxicating feeling of oneness with everything. Only after he received powerful orders from Qex and Zix did he put it to sleep. The second and third followed much easier, leaving him furious. He switched to X-gen and faced the shocked crew in front of him. "WHO DISOBEYED MY ORDER!?" Everyone, including Jack and Seamus, wilted.

Shesain dropped her head and spoke. *"I...I...was...just trying to..."*

"Trying to get me killed! This isn't a diplomatic mission where you walk away with bruised egos! You either live or die on this field! You nearly got me killed out there! If Qex had not reminded me of our

mental abilities, one of us would be dead now! He shook his head in anger and was ready to continue."

"Shesain doesn't have military training Derak, and she was trying to help you out of love." Jack reminded him. *"Look at her."*

Shesain fled into trees.

"All right Jack, move the original crew next to the ship. Bind the other Derak, his hands and feet. I don't want him getting loose again. Make sure all of them have the red wrist band on. Set up our demonstration while I talk to Shesain."

Jack got the rest of the crew on their assignments while Derak located Shesain. Shenar was giving him a mean look, he ignored it. Derak tracked Shesain down and popped in front of her. She let out a shriek and backed against the nearest tree.

"Shesain." Derak said gently.

"Get away from me you... you... monster, I don't know you! I know the kind hearted Derak, not this!" she spit out in fear.

"Welcome to my world," he informed her. *"This is what I have been trained to do from six-years old on. I'm still the best black ops agent in the galaxy. What you witnessed wasn't even scratching the surface of what I can do. To operate as one, your mindset has to be directed. Any interruption can get you killed, fast!"*

She wasn't so fearful, but still crying. *"Why...why didn't you stay in X-gen?"*

"Because the other Derak was about to activate the fourth strand of his DNA. What I did distracted him long enough to prevent this. He doesn't have the control I have over mine. There's no telling what kind of damage he would have caused. The last time I lost control, hundreds of seasoned Kek warriors died by that sword. I decapitated most of them or cut them into pieces. I almost had him backed down when you fired your first dart, and the other two didn't help much."

"I'm sorry my Chimera, it won't happen again," She said.

"All is forgiven," he thought as he helped her up.

"I get myself into trouble sometimes, don't I?" she lightly remarked.

"Yeah, you do, but you're worth the trouble, my love." She laughed and kissed him before they popped back to the original *Shesain*.

When they returned, they had sequestered the original crew in their space, and the time crew had theirs. Now the real challenge began. They had to convince them to take the alternative choice or sentence them to death. Neither was good. They set the vids up in X-gen, and used the hyper sprays to wake them without the usual headaches. The looks on their faces were priceless. First, at waking and then looking at themselves fifteen feet away. Derak (D1) woke in a fighting mood and found himself bound hand and foot to a solid chair. He struggled until he realized it did him no good.

"What's going on here?" He said as he looked at D2 and remembered the sword fight. "I thought I was dreaming, but I wasn't. Are you me, or am I you?"

"You're right on both counts, Derak," D2 answered.

"I'm looking at myself, I think." The original Shesain asked. "How are the twins?"

"The twins are fine." Shesain answered. Each of the crew exchanged a similar greeting. It took a long moment to assess the situation.

D2 continued, "To keep the confusion of this moment to a minimum, Jack will speak for us. He'll explain why we are all here. You must pick a spokesman for your group."

The original Derak, D1 had calmed down by now. He looked at the rest of his crew, and they nodded approval for him to represent them. They had decided beforehand not to tell them about Shamur. It would have complicated an already difficult task.

Jack, J2, addressed the original crew sitting down, looking at him with questioning gazes. "First off, only me and your Derak shall speak. Once I finish, you can discuss your questions and comments among yourselves, then Derak will speak for you. This is how our dialogue will be conducted." He was in command mode now. "Your arrival here in the year 1814 was engineered by others. Once here, you discovered you arrived in the year of the great plague that took so many lives. Through research, persistence, and some creative work on Leontul's part, you helped stop the plague. This was meant to be, but you completed the cure one day early. The result was a modified timeline when you returned to the year 2414. After returning, you realized what had happened and sought Robert's help, which explains our presence.

"I can't go into any more detail. It's confusing enough as it is. Here's the quandary: there cannot be two of each of us in the same universe and timeline. As your Derak could tell you, the results could destroy the space-time continuum. There is no merging the two teams, one of us must leave this universe and timeline and never return. That would be you, all of your original crew and the ship, Derak."

"Why us, why not you? You could tell us what to do to make it right." D1 queried Jack.

"It has to be this way," Jack answered. "I can only give you specific information and allow all of you to decide."

"Between what?"

"Life or death, the terms are not set by me. You will notice red wrist bands on your arms. Should any of you try to change the situation in the slightest, they will receive a quick, painless death. I have no choice, so it will do no good to negotiate."

"Can you at least release me from my bonds? I won't try anything. You have my word." Derak requested.

"If you do, you will be the first." Jack removed his bonds with his mind. They fell to the earth, and Derak quizzically looked at Jack.

"I can do a lot more. We've had mind training in the last two years. Your second choice is to move to an alternate universe and timeline. The one that fits is not as advanced as your original one. Its technological level is like this timeline. However, with *The Shesain's* ability to transcend time, space, and dimension, you could mold it into your version of Thumar. You will receive help from others who will make themselves known to you once you enter their universe."

"How do we even know what you're saying about an alternate timeline is even true?" The original Shesain butted in. She received hard looks from Jack and her Derak.

"That's why we've set a demonstration up for you," Jack said before the vids came out of X-gen. Jack looked at Derak. "We've upgraded the D-gen. We call it X-gen. The vid to your right is the original timeline. The left is the modified one. Watch them. They are original and not edited." Jack turned them on.

The expressions on their faces for the next hour told the story, from disbelief, to horror, to dismay, to resignation and regret. Derak asked for some time with his crew in private. The time crew left them alone for over two hours before returning. They were sitting in front of the iris, waiting.

Derak spoke for his crew. "We watched the accounts again and determined that they're real. We have chosen the alternate universe and pray that the help we will get shows up. We don't know who you work for, but I'd like to lodge a complaint about our choices."

"It will do you about as much good as it did us," Jack countered. "We complained to no avail. It relieves me that you choose life. The journey shall be long, but you will have time on your side, lots of it. Where you're going, time does not exist; you don't grow old, get sick, or die. You'll be able to move from this place to mortal time and back at will. This is one way to make a great society. We work for the Telaxians, time, space, and dimension Sentinels of this universe. Their word is law. They are not monsters or unfair, just strict. Their counterparts will meet you in your new universe. They have promised to work with you and guide you as needed.

"They will upgrade your Shesain with optic devices that are teachers. Terga and her full abilities shall be uploaded. Representatives from the new universe will move you through developing your mental abilities and teach you their language. All of our *Shesain's* improvements and upgrades shall be uploaded to your Terga. You will also have the vids of our time fixes. By the time you get to your new home, you will understand. This is a one-way trip. Any attempt to change your course will cause death. When you reach your new home, all the data that got you from Thumar to your new universe will be forever lost. You cannot cross into this universe again."

"Or die," D1 commented. "How much time do we have to prepare to leave?"

"Take as much time as you like as long as you lift off after sunset. You should at least see it one last time. It promises to be glorious today. We are so sorry we could not offer you more. It's only because of our crew that we could get you the concessions you received. Telaxians are normally not so generous with those of us they call mortals. This crew has been and promises to be the only non-Telaxians to ever receive such compensation. Consider yourselves fortunate."

"One more thing Jack, how will we know when these upgrades are complete?" Derak asked.

"You'll be ready for liftoff in two hours. Enjoy your remaining time on Thumar. Even with the simulator, you can go stir crazy in ship time. May you always find a safe port."

"Keep our Thumar green and thriving, and may our twins bless your lives," the original Shesain said through tears.

"I will, we will, and I'll think of you when I look into my daughters eyes." Both Shesain's embraced and touch foreheads before parting.

D2 walked up to D1 and extended his arm in a warrior's grip. "I never want to fight myself again; it's too much work." D2 said in jest.

"It was interesting. You're still telegraphing your kunjar strike a little."

"And I thought I broke that years ago, I'll work on it," D2 said.

The others exchanged farewells before they returned to their *Shesain,* which landed two hundred feet away in X-gen.

The time crew spent the remaining days in the year 1814 duplicating their original efforts under Qex and Zix's supervision. The events unfolded as they previously occurred. Down to the last mob that Seamus and the earth settlers rescued them from.

They found out what happened to the bodies. They were buried in a mass unmarked grave. They allowed Shesain and Shenar to bury Shamur with Thumarian customs. It took them awhile to identify his body, and they beamed it to a secret location. They left it unmarked with an electronic tag in X-gen that would last one thousand years.

The Shesain set course for Telaxia Prime. They would node hop, cutting their travel time down to five days. The Telaxians plotted a space time course that would put Shesian back on her normal pregnancy cycle. The children would go to full term and they would be born before the next Festival of the Lights.

The Prime Council: Telaxia Prime

The celebration was muted. Knowing what they did to themselves dampened the overall success of their last time fix mission. Seamus, Jack, and Derak checked on the health of their Cyth. Terga assured them they were healthy and would beam out in one piece. Life onboard *The Shesain* got back to normal, as normal as two years of ship life could be. They relaxed for the rest of the time it took to travel to Telaxian space.

They received the usual reception from the same Telaxian Commodore that treated them so rudely the first time. He picked up where he left off, mispronouncing their races, and gritting his sharp teeth. Zix did not put up with his behavior this time. He moved in front of the viewscreen and had a scathing thought transfer with him. Derak didn't know what bothered him the most, a racially charged Commodore or the syrupy sweet apologetic attitude that followed his rebuke. Either way, he could live without him.

His battle group escorted them to the home planet, and they had to close all the portals and windows again. Qex guided *The Shesain* to the surface and parked the ship in their windowless hanger. Derak thought he knew about the hidden cameras, but chose not to say anything. There were no guards that ushered them to their living quarters or their back-and-forth movements from the ship. But Derak knew that if they tried to leave the building, they would be stopped.

They were allowed three days to assimilate to Telaxia again. No finger nails, skull caps, chin beards, daily shaves, or the restrictive dresses for Shesain, Shenar and Vel. This ended on the fourth day. The same females with their kits followed Zix and Qex, and they fit their skull caps. There would be no removing them at all. Last but not least, chin beards and fingernails with rank were put on. Derak's were one inch longer.

They prepared Shesain and Shenar for public presentation. They removed facial makeup, including lipstick. Female Telaxians followed this with equally bland clothing.

They hoped that this visit would be shorter than the last one. It was nearly impossible to eat with four-inch-long fingernails that had to remain in pristine condition at all times. Seamus had come up with a solution. During their time away, he designed extended flatware for them to use amongst themselves. Jack and Shenar's chaperone did not approve of them. They tested out Seamus's knives and forks. It took them a brief time to adapt. They were better than what was left for them to use. They found out how the highest ranking Telaxians dealt with this inconvenience or any physical work. They had servants with short fingernails to serve them and it looked like they would receive the same treatment. The entire time fix crew would have a private dinner with the Valuk-Manou.

A private audience with the Valuk-Manou required the highest level of social practices. Shesain, Shenar and Vel received a temporary reduction in their breast sizes. They would be restored after business on Telaxia was concluded. The men went through treatments removing all body hair, except the chin beards. The Telaxians left their teeth alone. Their successful restoration of the time line allowed them this minor concession. Afterwards, they could mingle with a very select portion of the population.

The day arrived when *The Shesain's* crew was to be de-briefed by the Prime Council on the two-year mission. This included Zix, Qex, and Vel. They were ushered in and stood and waited for the Council Members and the Valuk-Manou to enter. They were clothed in attire for their new elevated rank. Shesain and Derak wore white semi-adorned robes, while Jack, Shenar, Robert, Leontul, and Seamus were given light gray robes. They wore individual insignia according to their contributions.

The seven of them had risen to the pinnacle of Telaxian society. Shesain and Derak made the top tier. This was the first and last time any non-Telaxian ever achieved this in their multi-billion-year history. Their fingernail length and chin beards, with their indicators of privilege, bore this out. Being de-briefed by the Valuk-Manou and the Prime Council confirmed this. It is a rare occasion for most Telaxian citizens to be accorded such an honor.

Derak suspected that their completed mission would not be their last, as did Jack.

The Valuk-Manou entered after the council members and signaled the seven of them to sit.

She started the meeting. *"I would first like to congratulate you on the successful completion of your mission. Qex, Zix, and Vel performed superbly in their duties and have been promoted. There is much information that we will give you that could not be previously released, because of its sensitive nature. I will start with the last two years, ship time. The space-time continuum has been ninety-nine-point five percent restored. The point-five percent left uncorrected can be adjusted from here. One key difference in the point-five percent is the extended life expectancy of the average Thumarian. It has doubled to four hundred and fifty years. Those of you who require this life extension will receive it before you leave our space. Derak and Robert will not need this procedure, as their life span exceeds that number. We can allow other subtle changes to fix themselves over the following centuries.*

"Shesain's unborn twins have done well during this time. They will be very special children. Both of them shall understand the inherent nature of time, space, and dimension from birth. With proper Telaxian training, they will navigate all three without the need of any ship or external travel apparatus.

"We will send Vel and one other female nanny back with you. Their appearances shall match Thumarian standards. Both shall be with the children at all times until they pass the tests that shall earn

them independent status. The twins will be required to complete all their training. Their abilities will put them in a unique category. They could do great harm to the timeline without knowing it.

"Derak, you must know about your son, Calvin. He is a second generation of the same experiments that you resulted from. He has three strands and is developing a fourth in his DNA. His presence has been foreshadowed by our equations. He and his mother must live on Thumar and go through Telaxian training.

"Calvin is slated to accomplish great things for us, we must prepare him. Tom Morton will have to be brought into the fold. We will calculate his contributions. Derak, Qex shall be your 'Telaxian Shadow.' We cannot allow another accident to occur. Zix will take Qex's place as Robert's chief science officer on Altair. He shall be known as Terenber.

"Derak, your accomplishments for an individual happen once a millennium. They shall be long spoken of after your presence in your galaxy will no longer be felt. You now hold the rank of full Zenex, Admiral, in the Telaxian Navy. Your military experience shall help us understand mortal thought patterns on this subject.

"Shesain, you will be the mortal race's Ambassador to the Telaxians. Robert will develop technology for our operations in your galaxy, with Zix's help. Seamus shall continue as a planetary engineer. Leontul's developments of new herbal medicines will continue with a Telaxian doctor, to be assigned to him later, and Shenar will monitor all communications between Telaxia and Thumar.

"We, the Telaxian Prime Council, would like to offer the crew of The Shesain an advisory role. Your responsibilities will be to experience and report the effects of time, space, and dimensional travel from a practical point of view. Jack, you will be the chief pilot and navigator on the missions, with the rank of Tenart, Senior Captain. Do you accept our request?"

Their choice did not take much thought transfer between them to approve. Excitement could be felt throughout the room. To have the chance to expand their travel in these realms put a big grin on Jack's face. Derak acknowledged their heartfelt acceptance.

"Zenex, I am the Minister of Defense, what is the completion date of your new ship, The Aries?*"*

"Defense Minister, Robert would know more about that than I would."

"Robert, when will The Aries *be finished?"* he asked.

"Defense Minister, she should be ready for trials in six months."

"That is not acceptable at all. We need her to base our operations out of in three months. The time line must be moved up!"

Robert was unperturbed by his attitude. *"Only if we get help. Our crews are handpicked and already working three shifts, twenty-eight-hour days, eight days a week."*

The Minister engaged in thought transference with the council and the Valuk-Manou before replying. *"We will send a contingent of Telaxian scientists, engineers, and technicians to assist in a completion time of two months. I will instruct our citizens to work without prejudice with yours."*

"We'll accept your offer. I can give your chief engineer all the specifications and plans they require. They will have to consult with me and Derak on all work performed or recommended," Robert answered.

After another few moments of council deliberation, he said. *"That is acceptable to the council. We will meet after this debriefing to complete the details."*

The Valuk-Manou continued. *"Thank you Minister, Zenex, you will meet with the Council of Zenex's after this and the rest of you will be individually briefed on your responsibilities."*

"The crew of The Shesain *will join me for a private meal this evening. I will give you the protocol and dress before you are shown to my private residence."*

They rose from their seats in unison as she signaled the end of the meeting. They escorted the time crew to their individual appointments. After the briefings, they all met back in their quarters.

They relaxed around an afternoon meal and regaled each other about their new duties. The most exciting revelation was that they would continue their space, time, and dimensional travels. Shesain and Shenar started going over Thumarian history to determine a schedule to be presented to the council. Derak was interested in the evolution of the Cyth.

Qex, Zix, and Vel showed up. All three of were in high spirits. The further adventures of the time crew excited them. The servants wasted no time getting started. They worked in a fast, concerted manner. In no time, fingernail extensions were stripped and re-painted with more ornate markings. The men's bald plates were polished to a dull sheen.

The chin beards were attended to. They were longer and more decorated than before. It was weird to look at Shesain, Shenar and Vel with flat chests and no hair. Like all Telaxians, tall genetically engineered agents or short nationals, their teeth were not capped at home.

Their clothes arrived: Shesain and Derak had pure white robes. The others graduated to off-white. After they were dressed and instructed on the evening's protocol. They would feed themselves. Servants would serve them, fill their plates, pour the drinks, and wipe their mouths. Qex quelled the complaints with a stiff thought.

Next on the list was to practice of eating with the utensils that would be provided. This proved challenging with their extended fingernails. Vel stepped in and got them up to speed with some 'cheater moves.' Qex and Zix just frowned and looked the other way. Shesain did her best not to spear the food with her nails. Qex told her that the last female to do so ended up losing them and was working in the mines now.

At six pm, their escorts arrived. They were led to the Valuk-Manou's personal transport. Rank had its privileges. It was large enough for the seven of them and their official escorts. The outside design was like the aero-dynamic lines of *The Shesain*. The interior was as luxurious as Derak's air car on Thumar. The upper class lived differently than the common folk. Some things never changed.

They left the windows open as they glided through the downtown district of their Capital City. Buildings rose no higher than four stories in the city proper. Taller structures could be seen in the distance. The orderly rows of businesses and houses looked the same, square with a dull gray finish. The population reflected the housing. Diminutive hairless Telaxians clothed in the same dull gray color. The only differentiation that separated the sexes were the chin beards on the males. Otherwise, they all appeared the same.

The Valuk-Manou lived in a spacious lake front house, more like a palace. This almost felt like Thumar, large spans of green lawns with sculptured hedges and manicured trees. Colorful flowers filled deep beds in between and around the trees. They coated her palatial estate white with royal blue trim and the front doors rivaled the polished bronze doors of Shenmar's main Temple.

The air car set down on the wide graveled, circular driveway surrounding a fifty-foot-tall, ancient deep orange tree with large white leaves. Leontul reverted to his excited discovery state as he tried to approach the tree. He was stopped in five steps by three very mean-looking Telaxian guards. The official guide stepped in to assure the guards they meant no harm. He informed them that Leontul was Thumar's leading herbal doctor and an expert on plant life. After they stood down, he explained the security requirements concerning the tree.

"This is the Antexeral tree. It is our oldest and last living example left on Telaxia. We estimate its age in the billions of years. An accurate age cannot be determined, as they allow only three Telaxians near it, the Valuk-Manou and the two gardeners. Next to the Valuk-Manou, the Venexara, gardeners are the most treasured citizens in Telaxian space. Because of the reverence given to it, we cannot test it for an accurate age. You should feel honored to set eyes on it. Only a rare few Telaxians have been given this privilege," he informed them.

"Please accept my apology," Leontul thought. *"It is such a marvel to behold, I was compelled to get a closer look."*

"The Antexeral tree is what you mortals would refer to as our 'most revered' gift from the gods. Now let us proceed to your dinner."

Their guide led them to front doors made from the wood of the Antexeral tree.

Considering the previous conversation, Leontul politely asked the guide. *"Why are these doors made from such a prized wood?"*

He stopped and thought for a moment. *"Since you know about the Antexeral tree and its importance, I will tell you a little of the history of these doors. Long ago, when the Antexeral tree grew in groves, our predecessors built these doors to honor the gods. Since then, the Antexeral tree has become a rare sight and protected to preserve the species. Our calculations predict that an outsider shall show us how to extract its seed pods without endangering the tree. This knowledge to extract the seed pods was lost eons ago. The last known gardener with that knowledge went home to the gods over three hundred million years ago."*

The doors were about twenty-five feet tall and twenty feet wide. They opened in the middle and had an arched top. An Antexeral tree was masterfully carved into each of the two panels that met in the middle of the door. They carved a grove of the same trees in perspective, leading back to a horizon point. Telaxian figures were seen tending the priceless groves with the Valuk-Manou supervising. Master Altarian craftsmen could only dream of matching the craftsmanship that stood before them. The beautiful doors silently opened into a grand entry, large enough to swallow the giant doors without taking up any room from their presence.

Seven vaulted arches met at the top of the roof: forty-five feet high. A gigantic chandelier hung from the center twenty feet down. It was an elegant statement of Telaxian right angle architecture made of pure hand carved optical quality natural crystal. They were led to an equally opulent parlor with the Valuk-Manou surrounded by about twenty guests. Qex, Zix, Vel, and Bel were present. In Thumarian gatherings, they relaxed formal titles. It seemed at first glance that this was not the case here. Rank and formal titles were still used and the Valuk-Manou was held in the highest regard. They gathered around something, waiting for their arrival. To Derak's surprise, abundant, comfortable seating was available and occupied. Standing only was not a requirement here.

The Valuk-Manou approached them with a male partner. *"I would like to introduce my 'Cherixtou,' the Maluk Venar."*

He was slightly taller than she was, five feet, two inches. The only difference between the two of them was his long chin beard and squared off fingernails. His bald plate was polished to a shiny gloss. He bowed his head slightly and greeted their party. They returned the gesture.

The Valuk-Manou continued. *"Let me introduce you to the finest wine produced in Telaxian space. I understand that Shesain's father is a vintner of the highest quality."*

"You are correct, Valuk-Manou. Andehar distilled beverages are the finest in the galaxy. It would be an honor to partake of yours," Shesain answered her as the Valuk, and her husband led them to the bar.

The Valuk-Manou telepathically ordered nine glasses of a blue blush wine. Then Derak thought to himself that they had three bottles of Rhemar's 05 on board *The Shesain.* In an instant, he teleported a bottle to his right hand.

He politely interrupted. *"Valuk-Manou, may I introduce you to Rhemar's famous 05 Brandy? It is very prized in our galaxy. May I pour you a taste for your enjoyment?"* he thought as he reached for two glasses. The look he received would have withered a Kek. *"Pardon me Valuk-Manou; it is our custom to pour out the first taste."*

"Not ours. You may refer to me and my husband by the first part of our titles here. Instruct the Extebar on the pouring instructions and it would please us to sample your offering," the Valuk answered.

Derak sent the instructions, and the Extebar handed them the glasses. The Valuk and Maluk eyed the dark color and sniffed the aroma before taking a sip and rolling it on their tongues. Then they drained their glasses. They smiled and exchanged a thought before the Maluk responded.

"An exceptionally good...brandy, rich and full flavored. My compliments to your father Shesain. Perhaps we can work out a trade agreement to receive this fine vintage."

Shesain smiled. *"It would please my father to fulfill your request. He would love to have his brandy universally popular."*

The Maluk continued. *"Now it is time for you to try our vintage."* As the seven of them were handed a glass of blue wine. They followed the example set by the Valuk and were pleasantly surprised.

Shenar was the first to comment. *"What an excellent vintage, light, fruity and fulfilling, Maluk. My father would love to know the secrets to this delightful wine."*

"Perhaps we can come to an agreement on both vintages," the Maluk answered while guiding Shesain and Shenar to the front window to discuss the matter further. They made more introductions; Seamus, Robert and Leontul started conversations with Telaxian equals in each of their professions, leaving Jack and Derak alone with the Valuk.

She engaged them in further thought transfer. *"I would like to discuss what we would require from your future missions. We have a unique situation in which our two races, immortal and mortal, can exchange valuable information. Telaxians have only data retrieved from our agents to base our mortal calculations on. I would like your ongoing missions as an advisory council to help us understand mortal thought patterns in all areas. This will allow us to calculate the structure of your universe to more exacting standards. In return, we will allow you to keep all Telaxian modifications applied to your ship. We will add more to guarantee your success. Qex and Zix will allow some of our technology to be shared with your Mt. Kumar group and Altairian factories. It will be only minor technology advances that will not be construed as Telaxian.*

"Most help will apply to the completion of The Aries. *It is critical that we complete it in two of your months. It will serve as our mobile base of operations in your galaxy. The Orion Syndicate is strong and getting more dangerous by the year. We can discuss the details later, before your departure. Now I have something to show you, Derak."*

She led him through the crowd to reveal an Earth grand piano. It was black and looked to be older than his, it was. The Valuk informed him it was an early nineteenth-century original Steinway.

"I understand that you play very well Derak, it would please me if you played for us," the Valuk thought with a smile.

"It would be my pleasure." The area around the piano cleared, and every available seat was taken. Shesain sat next to the Valuk, waiting with a bright smile. Once he figured out how to play without damaging his nail extensions, he played for one and a half hours. The crowd was appreciative and demanded an encore. The concert cemented the partnership better than anything else they did as a team beforehand. Then the call to dinner came. A spirited dinner cemented relationships that started earlier in the day.

After all the other guests had left, the Valuk took Leontul to the Antexeral tree, close up. He was like a kid with a new toy. She allowed him to touch the bark and hold a pure white leaf. Because of his previous research, she let him keep one leaf. She asked him to help the Telaxians to extract seed pods, so they could replace the long-disappeared groves. He was also given ancient Telaxian religious text to help his understanding. They were flown back to their quarters and rested for a busy schedule the next day.

They were up at four am and out the door by five. They led them to a room with seats for everybody, including the Telaxians. After the usual protocols for the Valuk-Manou's entrance, they were all instructed to sit. Two mental stenographers were present to record the meeting. They would cross check one by the other for an accurate accounting. They bred these citizens for perfect memory recall. Not that the normal Telaxian didn't have this capability, this class of individuals was made for this purpose only. They would know nothing beyond endless proceedings and mental play back for millions of years.

It made Derak wonder if they engineered their entire society for specific tasks. Having been in contact with them for a brief period, it wouldn't surprise him if they did. His humanity, engineered as it was four hundred years earlier, left him wondering if not only their Antexeral tree, but also their society was in serious decline. Perhaps the introduction of the seven of them was a calculated alteration of their society by their masters, or gods. Dealing with the relationships between Qex and Terga, a conscious AI program, and Leontul and Vel would push the limits of their boundaries.

They cut his ruminations short by the start of an early meeting. After introductions of the presiding Telaxian members, they stated the purpose. The contractual negotiations for the exploratory crew started. Even though the Valuk-Manou had ultimate power, dissention was in the air. This put her in a foul mood. She was too used to getting her way. The chief managers of Telaxia's primary industries and her Prime Council were at odds on giving the seven of them such a high ranking and broad latitude of action. This was not what bothered them the most. The aforementioned relationships pushed hard at their sensibilities and interpretation of Telaxian law.

While the members argued Telaxian precepts, the seven members of *The Shesain's* crew elected Shesain to head their delegation. After what seemed like an eternity for Telaxians, the Valuk-Manou turned to them.

"We have been discussing the merits of your team continuing your time, space, and dimensional missions. Our industry leaders needed to be convinced of the necessity of such action. We have worked out our end of the negotiations. I will now transfer to your lead negotiator."

Shesain looked at Derak before she put on her Ambassadorial face and addressed the Valuk-Manou. *"I will represent this crew, Valuk-Manou."*

"I was hoping it would be you, I have seen the results of your negotiated treaties and agreements. I look forward to this." She smiled.

Shesain gave Derak's hand a squeeze and started. *"Shall we begin?"* The Valuk-Manou returned a toothy smile, and the sparing began. This was a chess match not to be missed. Two grand masters going at it with sometimes veiled threats delivered with a little honey. They enjoyed crossing their diplomatic swords a little too much. Both of the women's eyes could stop a battalion with just a glance.

This was Shesain's battle mode, one Derak was glad he was never on the receiving end of. The two women went back and forth on every issue. The six of them and the other Telaxians were witnessing a historic event. Both sides of the table exchanged more than one look for three hours before they declared a recess.

During the break, Shesain collapsed into Derak's arms. *"I thought the Reptilians were tough to deal with. She's a hard nut to crack, but I think I have her figured out. The Katkurn's will seem like a vacation after this. We got through most of the stipulations. There is one more. This one's big, and I don't think she will bargain at all. She's calling us back."*

They took their seats and waited for the Valuk-Manou to start. She and Shesain spent the better part of the hour completing the previous three. Then the hammer fell, and it stunned them to utter silence. The Valuk stated her last requirement. The length of the contract would be for five thousand years, with an option for renewal for another ten, a short time period for Telaxians.

There would be no movement or negotiation on this term. Seeing that this would take much consideration on the crew's part, she declared a recess until six am the following morning.

It was an interminable night. They all stayed up discussing every angle. The most talked about subject was watching families and loved one's growing old and dying. Knowing they would outlive their great, great, great grandchildren. They all decided before they slept fitfully for two hours. They would see if the Valuk-Manou would agree to their request.

Back in the council room, at six am sharp, the Valuk Manou entered alone.

Shesain stated that they would accept only on the condition that they would include their immediate spouses. Since Shesain and Derak were the only ones expecting children, this meant future husbands and wives. Jack and Shenar were easy. However, Seamus was another story altogether. His fiancé was still on Thumar and had nothing to do with their time fix, and Robert was not engaged. Leontul was a special case, as he and Vel were in love. The Qex and Terga situation did not present life expectancy problems. Leontul and Qex were to be dealt with in Telaxian council. Shesain ended with a non-negotiable statement of intent.

The Valuk gazed at them for a long time before replying. *"That is acceptable. As for Qex and Leontul, further considerations must be made. You will have our decision in one of your hours."* She rose and left the room.

The time passed in silence. Had they made the right choice? They agreed on the terms and if they accepted, the time crew had to comply with their end of the bargain. They were all alone in their thoughts. Was it too late to turn back?

The Valuk returned with the Prime Council. *"We have come to an agreement on the contract. All terms spoken and recorded shall bind the Telaxians and your time crew. We have worked out the conditions for Qex and Terga. We shall allow Leontul and Vel to marry, according to Thumarian standards, with a Telaxian chaperone until the wedding day. The same shall stand for Qex and Terga once we place her consciousness in a suitable organic form. Your presence and acceptance now make this contract legal and binding. We shall tolerate no breaches from either party. You will remain on Telaxia for three life extension treatments.*

"You will receive eight. Your physiology will only allow for three now. Derak's and Roberts will be painful, considering the existing four strands. Derak, you will return with a detailed report on four strand technology for your doctor. He will be pleased with our thoroughness," the Valuk-Manou finished.

The meeting ended, and they wasted no time implementing their procedures. They all cursed the moment they agreed to this, but it was too late. Shesain's treatment was gentler, with the twins still in her womb. She lay awake many a night wondering how they were affected. They would find out soon enough. Derak and Robert went through a living hell from the moment it started to the very end. Their DNA structure posed more problems than the Telaxians expected. An anomaly reared its head during their procedures. The combination of their four strand DNA and the Telaxians treatments doubled the target life spans. From twenty-five hundred years to five thousand.

Three months passed before any of them felt anything like normal. Four months saw them in training to learn how to shape change at will. This would prevent the Telaxians from having to tend to their appearances again. They thought Qex and Zix were tough instructors. They were kind compared to native Telaxians.

By the time they declared the time crew fit to travel, they were more than ready to leave. All of them received much more than they could have dreamed of or imagined from their two-year adventure. They started as mortals who needed help to fix their own mistake, then moved into developing advanced psychic skills for mortals. They agreed to sign a possible minimum fifteen-thousand-year contract with the mathematicians of the universe, the Telaxians.

What had they done? Did they go from bad to worse? It was too late, for it was done. What kind of life did Derak doom his unborn children to? To cast more doubt on the deal, it included as well Calvin and Tara. Nothing could be done to change their actions and most of them had two-thousand and five-hundred-year life spans now. This was only after three treatments.

The Shesain was recognizable from the outside only. They did things to her that would take years to learn. They left terga alone at Qex's request. Telaxian scientists finished Qex and Terga's formulas for her body. This could not be accomplished until they commissioned *The Aries*. They would build the required technology into her. Qex, Robert, Jack and Derak were taught *The Shesain's* new controls and technology via thought transfers. They were cleared to leave Telaxian space, to everyone's delight.

Homeward Bound

There was one more matter to clear with their new employers. Shenar had become a master librarian and researcher. This skill would prove invaluable in the centuries to come. The entire crew wanted to 'time it' on the trip home. After days of discussion, they settled on tracking the evolution of the Cyth from the beginning. Shenar completed the research and calculations. She had become an expert on Derak's 3D model of the fifth dimension. All they needed was permission from the Prime Council. Qex verified Shenar's work and gave it his stamp of approval. They set a meeting up, and they would convene the next morning at 5:30 am.

Valuk-Manou chaired the meeting. The conference had an air of equals gathered to go over a well-conceived plan, far from the judgmental attitude of their original briefings. The council heard their request and told them that their answer would arrive the next morning, after a team of scientists verified the calculations.

The answer arrived the following morning with Zix. They received approval with a few minor adjustments to the math. Shenar received a commendation for a complete report from a non-Telaxian. It was short and curt, but getting a nod from a senior council was rare for even a Telaxian. *The Shesain* was packed and ready to launch. Last-minute adjustments were seen to with Jack and Derak receiving instructions during the pre-flight check.

Before boarding, they received a surprise visit from the Valuk-Manou. She cleared the hanger before addressing them. *"You performed beyond our expectations. I charge you with a vital, long-term mission. What you have received has never been done before, nor will be again. Only my efforts as the Valuk-Manou made it happen. Disappoint me and the cost to each of you will be great. You cannot hide anywhere in time, space, or dimension from our Zextur, Telaxian black ops. Ask Derak if you have any doubts. He has trained with them for two months. You will be dealt with, if you violate your end of the contract. With compliance, the rewards will be as pleasant.*

"*Seamus and Robert, once you have found a suitable partner to share your lives. They will be transported here and treated with the respect and honor equal to your rank and standing in Telaxian society. Their treatments will be as painful as yours, but they shall receive the finest care in the universe. This shall happen before any children are born. They shall also be trained as you were. Since time is of no consequence here, their training could take years of your time. You will always be free to visit them with proper notification.*

"*Shesain, the final calculations have been made and loaded into your ship's computer. You will return to your corrected timeline at the exact moment you left. Your pregnancy shall proceed to a normal Thumarian full term.*

"*Vel and Bel will accompany the twins at all times until we deem it safe for them and the universe. The daughter shall give you the most trouble. She seems to have inherited your precocious personality. Your son will follow in Derak's footsteps, but do not underestimate him. They will know time, space, and dimension from their birth. After they are born, you will have no end of predicaments raising them.*

"*Derak, you have the most responsibility as Commander of this crew. You also have the most to lose. We would not have put this mantle on you if we did not feel that you could carry out our orders. For the rest of you, you know your responsibilities. They are as important as any given to the others. Only as a team shall you return our investment. Be well and have a safe journey home.*" She came to each of them, taking their hands and touching foreheads with a momentary thought transfer. After she finished, she smiled and left.

324

They all stood silent for a moment, taking in the last private instructions. Derak for one would do everything in his power to please the Valuk-Manou of Telaxia. He received a confirming thought from everyone present. In a way, he would miss Telaxia. It would not last for long though. The crew would make regular flights back here to report to the Prime Council. One of his final private orders was to build personal ships like *The Shesain* for each member of the crew. This would only happen after they commissioned *The Aries*. This ship would only be built on *The Aries*. Not even Remor's vaunted navy would see them.

Derak broke the silence. *"Everyone aboard and to your posts, we have the past to visit."* They all entered *The Shesain* to a magnificent surprise. She was vacant except for the modified helm.

"Welcome back!" Terga chimed into all of their minds. *"Do not worry about the interior; I shall set it before liftoff."*

"I've missed you so much, Terga!" Shesain thought back.

"I've missed you too, Shesain. How are the twins?"

"They're fine, in the pink of health according to Telaxian doctors."

"Jack, pre-flight is complete, get ready for liftoff," Derak ordered.

"Aye sir," He responded. He and Qex moved forward to the bridge. *"Quasi-dimensional generator engaged."*

It populated the interior with every comfort that they would require. Everyone headed to their private rooms. Leontul made haste for his laboratory followed by Vel and their Telaxian chaperone, Darexvanor, Dar. In his excitement, Leontul took Vel's ready hand, only to be reminded by Dar of Telaxian courtship protocol. They would get away with nothing for ten months. Robert's future chaperone, Aliaxmur, Ali, shadowed him. There was an unusual glint in her eyes when she looked at him. Shesain caught it and grinned at Derak. She might just prove to be more than a chaperone. Robert didn't seem to mind the company.

Jack received clearance for takeoff, and he guided *The Shesain* out of her hangar and gained altitude fast. Berona, Telaxia's capitol city spread out before them for miles on end, with the government buildings sitting in the outskirts in its own protected district. They had all the windows and portholes open this time. Telaxia, for its obvious uniformity, had a beauty that none of them had seen before. Once they were in space above the planet, their now friendly Commodore escorted them to the edge of Telaxian space. He sent a pleasant note of departure and left.

Qex left them with last instructions before Jack started the new, highly modified IDMD. *"We can now take on our Thumarian bodies."*

Whoops of joy erupted as their outward appearance changed in an instant. Seamus was sporting a long red flaming trimmed beard, Robert and Leontul let out a sigh of relief.

The only ones who did not change were the new Telaxians. They had looks of bewilderment on their faces. Vel transferred the information for them to shape change. After they did, bewilderment turned to surprise. Vel, Shenar, and Shesain led them to a mirror. They stood before it, taking in their unknown forms until smiles crossed their faces. Ali's glint returned to her eyes as she glanced at Robert. He didn't miss the gesture and blushed at the look with a wicked smile.

Derak broke the reverie. *"Jack, take us home, 127 million years into the past. We have the Cyth to track down."*

"Aye Sir."

What originally took months to travel was reduced to days. Derak would have never imagined he would ever cross the universe, let alone a galaxy in mere days. This would make their job much easier. Just how much could they teach the Mt. Kumar group?

Halfway to Thumarian regular space, Shesain grew pale, groaned, and sat down fast, holding her belly. Vel and Bel were there in an instant, with the rest of them crowding around.

"Get back everyone, give her some space!" Vel ordered. *"What is happening, Shesain? Tell me!"* she insisted.

Shesain took a minute to catch her breath before she thought. *"The twins are trying to pop out of the womb. Stop, you two!"* She ordered. Vel and Bel placed their hands on her belly and took charge.

After a few minutes, Shesain regained her composure. She looked at Bel and Vel. *"Will I have to deal with this for nine more months?"*

Bel answered her. *"I think our presence in null space is triggering this reaction. Once we are in regular space, it should calm down. You will stay out of null space for the rest of your pregnancy."*

"If this is what I have to put up with, I'll comply. That f'ter yellow touch pad. We must keep Ariana on a leash!" she replied.

"We can make one before she is born," Vel said with a smile.

They all broke out in laughter. Shesain gave them a serious look before she joined in. The ship calmed down and Derak brought her some tea. *"I think we will need an army of Telaxian nanny's if they're trying to pop now."*

"I think you're right, my Chimera," she responded.

The X-gen had been upgraded to N-gen, the capability to generate a portable node where time, space, dimension, the future, past, present, and future exists in the same instant, a timeless place. They were left optics to instruct them on how to generate the same field for themselves with their minds.

They emerged into Thumarian regular space. Their approach to Thumar was slow. Once they established orbit, new scanners verified they had entered the corrected time line, 127 million years into its past. During the scans of Thumar, Jack picked up a momentary energy spike traveling through the outer part of the solar system. It was too fast to be a natural occurring celestial event. Derak's inclination was to follow the reading, but it was gone before they could get a fix on it.

"We can come back later and investigate. You need to complete this mission and get you home," Zix informed Derak.

Shenar was on a 3D/5D hologram and located the first known predecessor of the Cyth. Their instructions were to deploy Seamus's modified drones to observe only. They would operate in X-gen and send back detailed data. They could leave them and move into the future to collect data later.

Thumar was far different from what they were used to. The continental drift that formed the planet in the year 2414 was happening. A super continent was breaking apart and the Corano Islands had not formed yet.

An enormous desert occupied the center of the supercontinent, with the coastal regions bearing most of the plant life. They located the specimen on the eastern coast of this continental mass. They sent probes to explore the entire planet and take atmospheric readings. The probes could teleport to any region of the planet, either by instructions or an alert from another probe.

Their specific drone arrived in a patch of thick rain forest. The fern leaves were as wide as Derak was tall. They were looking for a large raptor type of bird and were perplexed by its absence. The probe was showing the subject was three feet away and to the right. The camera was pointing its lens straight at it. They couldn't believe their eyes. It was a small, feathered prehistoric bird no larger than a Thumarian Kecten. It didn't look dangerous at all. Then the camera panned back and picked up a reptilian creature scavenging the forest floor. In a flash, the bird took to the air, swooped down, and clamped onto its prey with a beak filled with pointed teeth. In an instant, lunch was over.

Then the camera zoomed into its eyes. They were the same as those of a modern Cyth, only much smaller. Satisfied, it flew off, straight into a spider's web. A four-foot spider dropped down and made quick work of the struggling bird. The crew jumped when the spider came into the frame. That spider could take one of them down, another reason for the probes.

They had to catch one of the Proto-Cyth's sleeping. They could shoot a tiny dart into it and receive biological data. Leontul was running this show. He was the expert. They sent another round of probes down to study the plant life, with another 3D/5D hologram tracking the information.

They shifted to different parts of the planet until they observed a large herd of Mastodon-type grazers with four long upward arching tusks, two on each side of its mouth. They were heading to a small lake for a drink of water. The adults were twenty feet tall.

The herd stopped about twenty feet from the water's edge, sensing danger. After a few minutes, a brave few meandered in for a drink. One particular juvenile, about twelve feet at the shoulder, warily approached the water's edge. It sniffed with its pig-type nose before drinking. Its eyes darted back and forth when, in a flash, a reptilian mouth full of back-facing teeth clamped onto the beast's neck. It bleated wildly as six-foot-high coils wrapped around its body. The crew jumped at the sight and felt sick because they could do nothing. It cried out for help that never came. The rest of the herd, along with the grieving mother, backed off and drank from a safer vantage point. Within minutes the juvenile was dead, the life squeezed out of it by a giant snake.

Leontul was the only one not grimacing at the sight. He was too busy up-loading data to size the snake. It left them wondering how the snake would swallow such a large meal. Its next move answered the question. It let go of the dead mammal and uncoiled. The rest of the body came out of the water. All of them were glad to be in orbit now. The snake recoiled its long body around the entire mammal, head to tail, with one coil wrapped around the base of its tusks. With three mighty contractions, the mammal's body was crushed into a four-foot blob of skin, muscle tissue, shattered bones, and blood. The tusks were snapped off at the base in one contraction. Then the snake swallowed its meal and disappeared under water again.

"That snake had to be at least sixty-five to seventy feet long," Leontul informed them. *"What an amazing sight! I hope they don't live in our time."*

The rest of them were still in shock, so they followed the herd out to its feeding grounds. They spread out into family groups and other mothers consoled the mother bereft of its young, while the males smelled a female ready to mate soon.

"Just like men, they take what's ripe for the picking," Shenar retorted.

"It's the females that allow intercourse," Jack countered.

"Just how it should be," Shesain added.

All of them were wondering where the apex predators were. They should be present with such a full dinner plate in front of them.

They weren't disappointed for long. A mid-level probe scanned an incoming life form. It was a flying reptile with a fifty-to sixty-foot wingspan. It had bat-like wings, a long tooth-filled beak and powerful legs with long talons that resembled a Cyth's. The probe darted the winged reptile, and the markers matched some modern Cyth's, another piece of the puzzle. But how did a little hen-sized bird and a monstrous flying reptile come together to make a modern-day raptor? This left Leontul puzzled.

The reptile was gliding, circling the herd at about a thousand feet and then it went into a quick dive and snatched a newborn before anything could be done; not even a warning bleat from a lookout. The speed of the kill surprised them all. It was far too quick to be attributed to an animal that size. It must have been warm-blooded to move that fast. Scenes from the oceans and waterways confirmed the previous data. It was time to jump forward thirty million years. They hoped that the probes would live up to their hype. They tasked specific drones with following the two flying specimens that fit the Cyth markers. They allowed the other drones to roam about.

With the modified IDMD, traveling through time was like moving through regular space. Their bodies registered no ill effects or queasiness. The twins didn't act up again. Perhaps Bel was right about null space. Thirty million years ushered in dramatic changes. The super continent had partially split up, isolating multiple species to develop into modern Thumarian mammals, sea life, and avian populations. Some were recognizable, and some were still a mystery. They collected the probes, they performed better than expected. Some of them failed, but only a small percentage. Seamus went straight to work on fixing the problems experienced by the beta versions.

Leontul saved thirty-million years of records and took a quick look at the data. Terga took over and isolated the markers for the two avian subjects. Over the eons, their first feathered proto-Cyth had grown larger, while the reptilian flyer had shrunk in size by fifty percent. Both of them were close to the same size now. Over half of the species previously observed had gone extinct. Because of the land mass breaking apart and the reduction in the food supply. Some, like the twenty-foot-tall four-tusked mammal, had been marooned on a much smaller land mass and its size had evolved to its surroundings. Adults were as tall as the juvenile that became the giant snake's meal.

The snake had evolved to a third of its size, responding to the evolution of its prey. Vids of the smaller reptile still scared them as much as its predecessor. Their feathered friend had grown to achieve a wingspan of twelve to fourteen feet. It had a beak similar to the modern day Cyth. The scaled neck and legs were not present yet. They were just as fast and fierce as the smaller versions and populated three continents.

After Leontul finished the massive downloads, they maintained a standard orbit for a week, observing the differences that thirty million years made. They jumped forward another forty million years, Seamus sent down fresh drones. He had corrected the faults that caused the previous ones to fail, doubling their data storage and life spans.

Moments before Jack broke orbit, sending them back to the future, the same energy spike occurred again. They were being followed through time, but by whom? Qex and Zix couldn't account for any Telaxian patrols this far back. This time was too primitive to bother with. Seamus sent deep space probes to the outer solar system in N-gen. Perhaps they could glimpse these interlopers next time.

Forty million years later, they were in for more surprises. Before attending to the planetary drones, they retrieved the deep space probes data. Terga zoomed through the data and found no anomalies. Either they detected the probes, or they only showed up when they did. How could they track them in N-gen? They were invisible. They did not exist in regular space.

The three continents were almost in place now. The North Pole was a frozen wasteland, as was the South Polar Region. Air was breathable now, but still a little too rich in oxygen for their physiologies. Life had transformed; the little proto-Cyth had evolved a thirty-foot wingspan and was still full feathered. They were the apex predator from the air now. They had come into their modern form, sans the scaled neck and legs. Leontul traced the origins of the two behemoth sea creatures recorded on the Corano Island mission.

A large black cat, six feet at the shoulder, appeared on some vids. They were lucky enough to catch a rare hunting sequence. The forest was dark, and a Surgant was scavenging for food on the forest floor. Light patterns appeared at the edge of the small opening. The Surgant grunted at the sight and kept feeding until curiosity got the better of him. He approached the changing patterns, grunting and stopping many times, always moving towards the source.

At the forest's edge, it stopped, sniffed the air, and squealed in terror, turning to run away. Fifteen feet into the clearing, the pitch-black cat pounced and sunk its long fangs into the Surgant's neck, breaking it. The cat lifted its neck and looked around, almost as if it detected the probe in N-gen. Its eyes glinted; its growl was spine tingling. Looking at this display through a camera lens sent waves of fear into the crew. Leontul glanced at the bio-data the drones dart returned.

He let out a long whistle. *"These cats have a built-in bio-luminescence, much like some deep-sea species we've discovered."*

The black cat picked up the dead Surgant by the scruff of the neck and disappeared into the forest without making a sound. They all just stared at the footage and replayed it with Leontul tracking the math on the 3D/5D hologram.

The next stop would take them to the point when the Corano Islands were created, twenty-five million years into the future. Special care had to be taken this time. A three-mile-wide asteroid would strike the southern polar region, eliminating over seventy-five percent of the species on the planet. Somehow the Cyth survived the apocalypse and thrived. On Earth, after a six-mile-wide rock hit, all the large animals perished. How this raptor lived through it might be solved. This time they set deep space probes in N-gen. Perhaps they could see the elusive visitor this time. Jack set the co-ordinates without even blinking. His mastery of time, space, and dimensional navigation was awe-inspiring. It would take Derak some time to catch up to him.

The planet was in its present modern day form, and the continents had settled into place and the atmosphere was breathable. The asteroid was being tracked at the edge of the outer asteroid belt. It had not been dislodged yet and was over three times the size of the rock that decimated Thumar in 2414. The last drones they deployed at the edge of the solar system did not record any action from their friends yet. The next time they would use D-gen mode. They were placed, and they set their sights on Thumar itself. This gave them time to outfit probes to record the strike and the aftermath. They had six days before they had to retreat to a safe distance.

They spent most of the time retrieving data from the planetary drones they left twenty-five million years in the past and tracking the asteroid. On the day they started the recon, the target rock was hit by a larger one, breaking up into three pieces. Two stayed in the belt, the third headed for Thumar.

The Cyth and the reptilian flyer had changed little in twenty-five million years. So, their convergence must have taken place after the strike. Their days were long and busy uploading all the information from the planet. They now had one hundred million years of planetary evolution on record. Who would believe it if they told them?

They were orbiting Thumar's first moon four hours before doomsday. The rock passed their position close enough to record its true size and composition. They all watched in horror as it entered the atmosphere and lit up the day brighter than the sun. The explosion was blinding from their position. The mushroom cloud penetrated space. It instantly destroyed their probes near the impact site. The further away from the South Pole, the greater the chance of survival. They stayed around long enough to send in more probes before they flew into the future. Ten million years.

Derak took *The Shesain* into the next time line. He needed the practice. Jack gave him some pointers, and Derak did the rest. Thumar recovered to a recognizable view. They collected the deep space data and were almost finished reviewing it when they got a hit.

"I've got him!" Jack thought. *"It's not much, but I've seen nothing like it. I'll bring it up."*

A blurry image showed up on the 3D/5D hologram in front of everybody. Only the sun's light reflecting off of its many faceted sides gave the image shape. It looked like a huge crystal. The Mt. Kumar optical group could fine tune the image.

The signal went off showing a location of the raptor and another avian in the same airspace. The hologram showed the vid in 3D, and they waited. The Cyth came into the frame followed by the reptilian flyer in tow, mostly covered in feathers now, except for the head, neck, and legs. Leontul jumped out of his seat. The next few minutes excited him even more.

The camera panned out, taking in the surrounding landscape, sky and the two birds. One was chasing the other. It didn't take long to recognize that this was a mating flight. Leontul let out a cheer. They watched the entire spectacle in rapture.

The next-to-last jump would take them to four hundred and fifty thousand years before the original timeline. Shenar traced the beginning of bi-pedal Thumarians to an exact time. They jumped and could hover over the targets, this time on Thumar. Two Bipedal ape-like creatures emerged from the forest and walked to the nearest waterhole. What happened next shocked them all, and it took a lot to surprise a Telaxian.

Four crystalline entities appeared before the bi-pedals out of thin air. Before the native species could react, they were put to sleep. Two of the alien life forms split off to attend to the male, while the other two saw to the female. They bent over them and spent the next hour working telepathically, never touching their subjects. After the four gathered in a group, they looked straight up at them, before they teleported to who knew where. The crew was astounded and hovered, silent for over one hour. The implications of the event they just witnessed could not be calculated. Qex had a strange look on his face, one of utter contentment. The cameras recorded just the bi-pedals, not the aliens.

"Did they speak to you, Qex?" Derak asked.

"Yes, they spoke to all of us. When the time is right, you will remember. I can say no more," Qex answered.

After finishing the information retrieval and setting fresh drones, they set sail for one last jump before they went home to the year, 2414.

Their next destination was to the year 1875. The crew wanted to witness the first Cyth flights from a bird's-eye view. After facing themselves in the year 1814, this would not seem strange. Their presence would not even be felt. They watched Derak's jump onto its neck and the subsequent ride that wore both of Jack and Derak out. Training the fresh recruits was skipped to view Seamus's first flight. They were all glued to the spectacle. The dives, dips, sudden turns, and rapid ascent to higher altitudes had them all spellbound. After it was over, everyone, including the riders were impressed with the feat. They recognized it that only a chosen few would ever hold that honor.

After they established a parking orbit, they enjoyed a flavorful meal. The men cleaned up and a good night's sleep was in order before they returned home. They had one more surprise waiting for them. Just before they engaged the IDMD, the crystal ship de-cloaked in front of them, they were all left speechless. The 3D/5D hologram appeared, independent of any command from the crew, or Terga.

The head and shoulder of a crystalline entity filled the space. They were clear and when thoughts were transmitted, white and blue cloud like striations flowed through the body. The featureless form stayed with them for only a few moments that felt like forever. Then it was over. Empty space and Thumar's first moon filled their view. They were held in individual trances as telepathic information flooded in. Derak felt a pleasurable tingle the entire time his mind was locked with the crystalline entity.

Moments felt like hours. None of them were sure how much time elapsed until Seamus looked at the chronometer on the bridge. Two hours had passed. Where had they taken them? What did they do? Qex summed it up. *"We will all know in our own time. The Telaxians have heard only the rumor of these beings. They were a myth to our civilization until now. There is a purpose for first contact. We have not seen the last of them."*

They mulled over the incredible encounter before *The Shesain's* IDMD was turned on. It was time to return home. Would life be boring when they got back to business as usual? How would they top the last two years? Qex shook Derak out of his reverie with a thought. He assured him that if it was excitement he wanted, his future assignments would provide plenty.

"Jack, take us home, we have a planetary survey to complete." Derak ordered.

"Aye sir, with pleasure. IDMD engaged in 5,4,3,2,1." Jack responded with a wide smile.

In a moment, they were back to where it all started, hovering over the ground on the Anean continent.

Qex approached them. *"This is where we leave you until you return from your planetary survey. We shall return with Robert to Altair, and I shall once again be known as Petemar. You started with six and must return with six. It has been my honor to serve with you, Derak Andehar and your crew. I will be in contact soon."*

Qex, Zix, Vel, Dar, Bel, Vir and Robert were gone in a wink of an eye.

Back to Normal, I think?

The survey was complete with a few more minor time travels. They worked out allowable ventures into the past. The future was off limits. *The Shesain* touched down at Derak's estate and was parked in its secure hanger. Technicians were waiting for them and ready to service *The Shesain*. They weren't surprised to see Petemar as the lead engineer. Dr. Maritak was there also, he was in charge of the programming crew. Telaxians were an efficient race.

The six of them entered Derak's huge parlor to find a welcoming party waiting for them, complete with Tenara, Seamus's Chimera. A long banner hung on the opposite wall congratulating Shesain on her pregnancy.

"Twins, I'm so excited!" Temela, Shesain's mother beamed with an infectious smile. "Have you named them yet? If you haven't, I've got some excellent candidates for you." She continued non-stop as Shesain and Shenar joined cousins and aunts by the front window.

"Save me Derak, please," Shesain transferred a pleading thought in his direction.

As he was moving toward her, he got shanghaied by Remor, Rhemar, the Mayor of Shenmar, Tom, and the entire male side of the Andehar family.

"I see you wasted no time," Remor said with a wide grin, "Twins, no less."

"You can blame Shesain for that. She planned everything, down to the last detail," Derak said in response, as he took another drink of Rhemar's 05.

"So Derak, what are the names of my grandchildren? I hope you two have picked out some good ones. You know Temela will have to approve them." Rhemar added.

"We both know that you can't get anything past her. We've decided: Ariana for the girl, and Tomas for the boy, leaving the middle names for Temela to decide."

Rhemar thought for a moment. "That just might work. The two of us have been discussing the matter and decided to give you a little latitude on the first names. A toast to the happy couple and grandchildren we can spoil."

Rhemar and Remor shared a laugh as glasses clinked. Then they looked at their sons with questioning glances. Derak never saw grown men find an excuse to retreat so fast in his life. Rhemar and Remor laughed before joining their wives.

Shesain joined Derak and shared that her mother approved of the first names but insisted on picking out the middle ones. Temela was not to be trifled with on this matter. That was until Derak's mother got into the game. Before long, the both of them were congregating with Tranoka and Betrawn on fitting middle names.

The party went into the early morning. Both families, Tom, and Tara remained. Therese and Karn joined them later in the afternoon and hung around. Tony and Teren were smitten with each other. Derak heard that they were giving Tony's shadow and Teren's mother a run for their credits. He could tell by their looks and abbreviated physical contact that their wedding night would be a very active three days. Shesain saw it too and giggled at the thought.

"She will tear him up," Shesain sent Derak's way.

"He's younger than me by fifteen years. I'll put my credits on Tony."

"You're on! We'll work the wager out later."

At the end of the party, Tara and Shesain spent over an hour together. They had grown close. Shesain and Shenar declared Tara their long lost sister, with Temela's approval. Therese, Karn, Tom, Tara, and Calvin stayed the night and Shesain ambushed Derak before they slept.

The time crew stayed over too. They had the onerous task of finding a home for the Cyth. There would be no telling what kind of mood they would be in when they were beamed out of the pattern buffers. Tenara left to visit her sister in Shenmar. After an excellent breakfast with the rare appearance of real bacon Tom brought from earth, they all split up for the day.

Remor showed up before they took off and cornered Derak and Shesain. "What happened on your survey? Both of you, including the rest of the crew, are different."

"You'll get your answers soon enough, Remor. After we finish the day and arrange our schedules. You might have to clear out a day or two," Derak replied.

He gave them both a knowing look before he left for Shenmar.

Shenar located a known Cyth colony in the Lelayan highlands. This spot was avoided at all costs by both outsiders and hunters alike. *The Shesain* popped there in less than a second. They had teleported into a deep alpine valley rich with fresh meat for the bird's first meal. A large clearing stood before the ship. They stood ready while Terga beamed all three Cyth's back into solid form. Each Cyth locked eyes with their riders and gave them a good chewing out before declaring that they were hungry. It nearly blew all of them to the ground when three mighty Cyth's downdrafts hit them. Their flight was awe-inspiring. After gorging themselves and then washing in a cool mountain lake, they returned in better moods.

Miron spoke. *"We are being watched from the cliffs behinds us. They almost sent a patrol to scare you off before we appeared."*

"Shall we pay them a visit?" Derak asked.

"After our itches are scratched," Samora stated.

Shesain and Shenar laughed before all six of the time crew attended to them. They craned their necks and pointed out every spot. Their utter satisfaction was made known after the women oiled their scales. Leontul made the final check, and he gave them his approval.

Samora, the alpha female spoke to him. *"You show the bravery to ride us, Doctor."*

He smiled at her. *"I'm brave enough to tend to you, that's as far as I go."*

"Then you may tend to us anytime."

"It would be my honor, Samora."

The saddles were found, and put on the waiting Cyth's. They were itching for a good flight to stretch their wings. Derak, Jack, and Seamus waved before they were airborne. The exhilaration of Cyth flight returned, and the three of them were enjoying the freedom. Miron, Samora, and Borath took them through some dives, rolls, and other acrobatics before heading to the colony. The entire Cyth population bugled their arrival. They landed on a large outcrop of rock. The colony, birds, and riders were in a semicircular ring before them. Miron, Samora, and Borath announced themselves.

A Thumarian male approached them with his life-mate. "I am Keruk, and this is my life-mate, Cerrum. We ride the alpha male and female, Verum and Hekphor." The Cyth bugled their name recognition. "How may we assist you riders? Your birds are large; we've only heard of wingspans that big. Our history places Cyth your size at least three centuries back. Our largest known male on Thumar today only has a thirty-five-foot wingspan."

"May we confer in private?" Derak asked.

"Follow me," Keruk replied.

"Just you and Cerrum please; the information I have is very sensitive."

"As you wish. Aren't you…Derak Andehar? You look a lot like the man the vids have shown," Keruk said.

"I am, and I will explain everything as soon as we are alone."

His look of puzzlement grew as he looked at the crests on the riding jackets. Once they were alone with Keruk and his mate, he asked them. "How did you earn Zeveren's crest? Only one rider is allowed to display it."

"Who bears this crest now?" Derak asked him.

"I do. It takes a lifetime of service and bravery to earn the right, and yours is fresh. Is it a forgery, a joke from Meterak?" Keruk demanded.

Derak didn't let his rising anger affect him. If he were in his place, he would feel the same way. He brought out a portable 3D/5D hologram. "This will answer your questions, I hope. Just watch it, and we'll talk afterwards."

The vid played back Derak and Jack's first ride, and then Seamus's. It showed the training and preparation that the first riders went through. Their three faces looked just the same now as they did over five hundred years earlier. After playback finished, Keruk and Cerrum took a deep drink of ale before they found their voices.

"How come you by this trickery? You could not be the same men in those vids. You should be long dead!" Keruk demanded.

Derak looked at him. "Zeveren and Tyramar were the first riders of the Cyth in the year 1875. They stopped an organized hunt in the village of Hanshurt. A small group of brave individuals followed them into the highlands of Anea. They trained for eight weeks, including the riding of Antor bucks, bareback. If they failed here, they went no further. The first riders after Zeveren and Tyramar were Artir, Syrah, Veronn, and Kylar. Their Cyth in order: Beron and Arana, the alpha male and female, then comes Porath and Jorshah. Seamus, here to my left is Arimus and his Cyth is Borath. Two young men followed from the original group, Vetur and Cirith."

"You know the beginning as only the eldest do! How come you by that?" Cerrum asked Derak.

"By technological time travel, we, the three of us here and a few more made it possible. I cannot go into details now. Zeveren's Cyth is Miron and Tyramar's is Samora. You must trust us that what we have shown you is truth and fact. We could not recite precise history otherwise."

Keruk was dumbstruck. "I can't deny the pictures or history. Only a handful of elders know even parts of the histories. How can we help the great Zeveren and Tyramar?"

"Do not refer to us with those names again outside of private meetings. Only you two know the truth. The bearer of the Zeveren crest will only receive this knowledge. I am Derak Andehar, Tyramar is Jack Morgan, and Arimus is Seamus McGrue. We need a home for

341

our birds. Not an established one, but a new one. We do not seek to displace any alpha male or female. Miron and Samora were already a mated pair when they were ridden. Maybe an old, abandoned colony with some willing followers. Our Cyth's won't displace your alphas, but they will be respected for who they are. Our duties do not allow us to live as full-time riders, so we will be in and out. Perhaps Miron and Samora's offspring can strengthen the resident population."

This pleased Keruk. "We will make a home for Miron and Samora. Perhaps Borath could fly the next colonies mating flight. I'm sure he could out fly any modern Cyth. His wingspan is at least ten feet longer than the present record holder," Keruk said. "This way we can spread this lineage much faster. Another thing, I would cover your crests up. Not all alpha riders are as patient as I am. Plain saddles would work better from this point forward. Once you and your Cyth are settled, you will receive a new crest."

"I agree, we will fly our Cyth to our ship and send them back up. I will instruct them to not take over alpha duties until they settle the new colony. They must be shown due respect. I will know what Miron knows." Derak said.

They hammered the last aspects of the agreement out and prepared to leave after a filling meal of Antor meat and fresh vegetables. The outcrop was empty except for five Cyth, and riders, their three and the colonies alpha pair. They were shown the secret Cyth riders greeting, and farewell and they were off.

When they returned to the ship, Shesain and Shenar wanted to have a flight of their own, and Jack and Derak grew concerned. Shesain and Shenar were pleading with them, and Miron and Samora assured both men they would be safe.

"Shesain is pregnant with twins. If anything happens..." Derak started.

"I already know," Miron answered him.

Shesain walked up to Miron and gave him a loving scratch on his crest before climbing into the saddle. Shenar climbed onto Samora after a good scratch, and they took off and didn't return for an hour. Shesain and Shenar were exuberant afterwards, and they all wished the Cyth well before they returned to the colony. *The Shesain* popped back to Derak's estate unseen.

Qex popped in after announcing his intent. Robert and Ali joined him, who showed her intent on snagging Robert. He warmed up to the concept.

They communicated in Telaxue. One of the efficient habits they practiced when in the company of known agents. They set a date for Remor's briefing. Tom would be present also, considering his daughter, Tara, and his grandson, Calvin, were now part of the contract. Qex indicated two more agents would be present. Derak forwarded the date to Remor, and they included Rhemar, as it involved his daughters. He confirmed the date for the next day.

They all met at Derak's estate to ensure total secrecy. Thrashur Katur, the best Thrashur black ops agents who received advanced training from Master Li, guarded the meeting. For every visible Thrashur Katur, there were four more in X-gen backing them up. The large parlor was scanned and determined clean of any eavesdropping device before the meeting convened. To be sure, Qex and Zix installed advanced Telaxian detection devices. The secrecy of the incoming visitors had to be protected at all costs, even by deadly force if required.

Dr. Centur and Nurse Teren would present a part of the day's briefings. Derak gave the doctor the Telaxians findings on his DNA. Dr. Centur was giddy with delight before he ran off to his research team to decipher the information. He now had a full understanding of its complete structure. This would be the most important meeting in the galaxy in modern times. The outcome would affect every known inhabitant of the Milky Way Galaxy. The physical presence of Telaxians outside of Telaxia had never occurred before in all of their eons of existence.

Temela, Tranoka, Tara, and Derak's mother were the only non-Thrashur women present, besides Shesain and Shenar. They directed the food, beverage, and comfort of all the participants. Temela had no problem gaining the immediate respect of the Thrashur. She would have made an excellent one herself. The preparations were complete and Tom, Remor, Rhemar, the doctor, and nurse Teren were delivered by Jack in *The Shenar.* Shenar insisted on flying herself, under Jack's supervision, with the time circuit turned off.

All of them entered the parlor engaged in animated conversation at eight am. They started at the breakfast buffet and were served by Thrashur Katur. They brought in comfortable chairs and the central 3D/5D hologram was set up. Remor noticed that there were more seats than were required. Derak informed him that others would show up. Remor gave Derak a strange look.

Five minutes to nine, Derak asked those present to take their seats. He remained standing. "In a few moments, the rest of the participants will arrive, so please remain seated and keep the center of the room clear." He sent Qex the signal to pop.

The party teleported into the middle of the room, causing those not used to such a thing to jump out of their chairs. Some chairs were knocked over. It was more their instant presence and not the size of the party that overwhelmed them. Qex, Zix, Vel, Bel, Ali, Robert, Leontul, Seamus, the Telaxian Ambassador with two grim looking body guards and two stenographers. To Derak's surprise, Demar, the high Priest of Thumar, Danella, the High Priestess, and Master Li were with them. After regaining his composure, Remor shot Derak a questioning look.

"Sorry, I couldn't tell you." Derak apologized to Remor.

"We'll discuss this later. Who are they?" he replied.

"I believe introductions are in order. We are all familiar with Dr. Leontul Bundett, the foremost herbal doctor on Thumar. Dr's Centur and Bundett exchanged greetings. Next is Seamus McGrue. Robert Jamar, CEO of my three corporations, Air Car, Sky Cycle and Gel Tech Computers. Petemar shall make the remaining introductions," Derak finished. The Telaxians were wearing their teeth caps.

"Petemar is my assumed name that I use in public. It is to be used by all present outside of this meeting. My correct name is Qextenar, or Qex; I am a Telaxian, a mathematician of the universe. Aside from the previous introductions, the rest of us are all Telaxian. For time's sake, I will use our short names until I get to the Ambassador.

"This is Admiral Zix of our Royal Navy, next is Vel and Bel, Vel is a nurse and research scientist, and Bel is a medical doctor. Ali's profession is comparable to your T-K agents. Paxtarentex Borinuragesh is the Ambassador assigned to Thumar and the mortal races." Qex finished.

Remor and Rhemar were shaking their heads in disbelief. "Your race and function in the universe have been nothing but an outrageous rumors for eons of time."

Qex continued. "That is how we maintain it. We keep the universe in order by our apparent absence."

Tom started to make a comment and stopped short. Qex encouraged him to continue, he did. "Qex...right?"

Qex nodded.

"There are ancient tablets on Earth that mention aliens. They say that, that...race...enhanced our early bi-pedal ancestors to push Earth's evolution forward."

"We do not intercede or interfere in mortal affairs, Admiral," Qex responded. "There is another race of crystalline beings that we Telaxians have known about, and have confirmed their existence. They would be the most likely source. As you all know, *The Shesain* and her crew embarked on a planetary survey. The completed survey was far from ordinary. We shall view a vid recording of their entire two-year mission. I represented the Telaxians on the mission for the entire time." Qex left one of the largest chairs for the Telaxian Ambassador and then instructed Remor to sit beside him. They were all seated. The room darkened, and the vid replay began.

Qex and Terga had edited down thousands of hours of footage to four hours. The final vid had to be approved by the Valuk-Manou and the Prime council. You could see looks of surprise, shock, disbelief and surrender to the facts. The Thumarians knew this video to be true and sat after the curtains opened and the lights came up.

Remor turned to Derak and Shesain sitting together. "I knew something was different about you two, I just didn't know what it was."

The vid left out a lot that would be revealed to individuals later.

The lunch bell rang, and everyone stood up and stretched before eating a light lunch. Rhemar's 05 was the most requested beverage. The Telaxian Ambassador enjoyed it very much.

"Rhemar, this vintage is everything and more than the Valuk-Manou, our head of state, raved about," the Ambassador said.

Rhemar looked at him, wondering how his 05 got so far afield.

The Ambassador continued. "We brought our top Blue Blush Wine for your pleasure. The Valuk-Manou would like to open a dialogue with you on trading these superior vintages. Please taste our offering." Then he handed the bottle to a Thrashur-Katur to open and pour. The T-K showed no emotion as she complied.

Rhemar took the glass and put it to the test. After tasting the blue blush, he smiled. "This is superb, Ambassador; it would be my pleasure to open negotiations. You should try this, it's made by Admiral Morton, the finest pear brandy in the galaxy." The T-K handed the Ambassador a snifter. He swirled it, sniffed it, and took a sample sip, rolling it on his tongue.

His smile told the story. "Admiral, this is a magnificent blend, you shall be included in the negotiations. How rare is this pear brandy?" the Ambassador asked.

Tom answered with a grin. "Because of the lengthy process to perfect this liqueur, too few bottles are available each year. I can explain the process to you after our business is taken care of."

"You and Rhemar can fill me in on a walk of these grounds. We have little property on Telaxia so landscaped," the Ambassador remarked.

"Ambassador," Remor started.

"Pax is suitable in private," he interrupted him.

Remor continued. "Pax, if you like these grounds, we can assign you a similar setting for your residence."

"That would please me very much Remor, we need to get back to business."

They were all seated, and Pax took control of the meeting. "This meeting establishes Thumar as the point of contact between Telaxians and the mortal races. Telaxians live many millions of years. Qex is tens of thousands of years old, and we do not consider him a full adult yet. That title comes only after fifty thousand years and extensive testing. I am seventy-seven thousand years old. Our head of state has to be over two hundred thousand. So, when I say mortal races, you now know the reasoning behind the statement. Qex will serve with Derak, Zix will assist Robert on Altair, and Vel and Bel will attend to Shesain for the rest of her pregnancy and beyond.

"Dr Bundett will have a Telaxian scientist assigned to his team to help and monitor all of his future research. Remor, I would like to place an agent in your office for your protection. We already have two in the Alliance President's office; his life is in danger. The Orion Syndicate has plans to assassinate him and place the Vice President, who they control, in his place. Stable governments must stay in place. Telaxians are very strict about adherence to their calculations. We demand nothing less from ourselves. Derak's original time journey and its subsequent failure required us to help fix the paradox."

Pax gave them a moment to absorb his words before continuing. "I also propose to assign a psychic combat instructor to accompany Master Li in training your Thrashur Katur. Derak has been through two of your months in instruction with our military on Telaxia. He knows how helpful and difficult the training is. You will need such skills. We have contracted the crew of The Shesain to serve as an advisory council to our Prime Council. Their purpose will be to report the operational side of time, space, and dimensional travel. They have the required experience to carry out this assignment. Qex and Zix will be our representatives on their missions."

"Pax, when would your physic combat instructor arrive?" Master Li asked.

"He can be here as soon as Remor agrees. He will adjust to your mortal capabilities. They must be tough for what is coming," Pax said. "There is one more thing. Derak's first son, Calvin, has very special abilities and must be trained by Telaxians. This will require that he and his mother Tara live on Thumar. Admiral Morton's service is being considered as well. This would make your presence on Thumar helpful, Admiral. To highlight the science behind this, Dr. Centur and Nurse Teren will present the evidence."

Dr. Centur and Nurse Teren presented his team's medical research amended with the Telaxian data of Derak's family's DNA structure. Then it went into Tom's genetic code, ending with Calvin's growing from three strands into four. The new revelation astounded Tom. He had to ruminate on the information for a few minutes.

Tara wasted no time. "Calvin and I would love to re-locate here. He could be close to his father, and I would like to finish my college education. I knew Calvin was special, but not that much. He would also enjoy time with Uncle Jack."

Jack and Shenar smiled at the thought, and Shesain spoke up. "My household and family would welcome them, and they could live here."

Tom butted in. "It looks like there's a mutiny on my bridge." he delivered with a warm smile and laughter followed. "I seem to have no choice; my crew has made it for me. I must split my time between Earth and Thumar. Perhaps Rhemar would like to join me on my next trip. Maybe in one of Derak's new ship's, I've only heard about."

Derak looked at Pax and Qex and exchanged a thought transfer before replying. "That can be arraigned, Tom. There's one being delivered this week. Since your inclusion into our group is official now, you will need a ship assigned to you, with a trained T-K crew."

Tara smiled and gave her father a big hug and kiss on the cheek.

Pax continued. "The time crew of *The Shesain* shall have personal ships built for each of them after they complete *the Aries*. How is the time line proceeding on her construction, Robert?"

"She's one month out, Pax. Your Telaxian work crews are making marked progress on her and both races are working well together," Robert reported.

Pax nodded in confirmation. "I believe we have covered enough for a first meeting. We will agree on the details in the formal negotiations. We will meet here at 0600 hours tomorrow morning to complete our cooperative efforts."

They all got up to stretch, and smaller groups formed, with Pax to get a tour of Derak's grounds with Remor, Rhemar, and Tom. Tara. Temela, Tranoka, and Derak's mother caught up with Shesain to work out Tara and Calvin's living arraignments. The rest of the time crew congregated to talk about future missions to present to the Telaxians.

After dinner, Jack, Seamus, and Derak cornered Pax, Qex, and Zix. *"Pax, we have one more inclusion for our contract."*

"What would that be, Derak?"

"It concerns our Cyth. The giant raptors we rode in the year 1875."

"I'm familiar with them, by sight, fearsome looking avian. What is your wish?" Pax inquired.

"Riders establish a lifelong bond with their birds. That is why we brought them forward with us. Since our life spans have already been enhanced, and will increase with further treatments, we would like to include our Cyth."

"We expected this, and the council is considering the matter. We will get back to you once we have deliberated. How will they take the enhancements? They are not painless, as you know," Pax reminded them.

"That is where the challenge comes in. The Cyth are not tame and must be held motionless for the most troublesome parts of the transformation process. Leontul has some ideas on how to do this."

"We will consider this," Pax said before tracking down Remor and Shesain.

The official governmental negotiations started at 0700 sharp the next morning. Remor and Shesain led the mortal side and Pax headed up the Telaxian delegation. A Navy Admiral, Army General and Pro Counsel representing the Valuk-Manou, and the Prime Council joined him.

Both sides fought hard for their side and a diplomatic chess game played out. Remor proved to be a match with Shesain at the negotiation table. The process took two-and-a-half days to complete. Both parties were satisfied, and each signed the accord. Tom would serve as the primary mortal military liaison to the Prime Council and Zenex Council on Telaxia. He wouldn't live there, but he would report to Telaxia Prime. His prime responsibility would be to command *The Aries* after they completed her.

The meeting never happened to the eyes and ears of the known galaxy. After every detail was taken care of, the entire contingent went back in time to the evening before the first introductions and briefing. Only those present would ever have knowledge of the event. The Mt. Kumar group would receive technological improvements agreed upon.

They all signed a typical Telaxian contract, complete with the life extension treatments. They received the usual declaration of what would happen to anyone who breached their agreement. Derak found out that Master Li, Demar, and Danella were already agents. The Telaxian psychic combat instructor arrived after the accord was signed. Derak knew him well, after spending two months training with his unit.

Tony moved into the T-K program, along with the human black ops agents who rescued Derak's family. Bull was in for a hard time. Master Li was tough, Ter could be terrifying. Jack, Seamus, and Derak were ordered to complete the course from the beginning.

Derak was still expected to serve in his post as Ambassador in between strenuous daily mental and physical instruction. He would often sleep through trips to another system and could not fall behind the class, no matter how long the diplomatic mission lasted.

Jack, Seamus and Derak were given no special treatment because of their previous experience with the Telaxians. They spent three torturous months in boot camp before they could spend time with their chimera.

Derak grateful to be home, he was sore and worn out physically and mentally. Shesain was the cure he longed for. Her baby bump had gotten more noticeable while she grew more beautiful. Their first night alone in three months did not disappoint.

Three Weddings and
The Festival of Lights

Derak was home for one week after two months of specialist school. He adjusted to Telaxian time, four hours of sleep per day. In between the class work he brought home, catching up on the latest diplomatic news, and working with Vel and Bel on controlling Ariana and Tomas. His days were full, and he wouldn't have it any other way.

Halfway through the week, he was woken by Shesain's cry for help. Ariana was getting adventurous again with Tomas following. Vel and Bel were instantly there, with their hands on Shesain's bulging belly. It was taking longer to quiet Ariana down. She would prove to be more than a handful after she was born. Tomas had a quieter side, but he would have to be watched as much as his sister.

"That jartor yellow touch pad! I hope you can come up with some type of leash for Ariana, Vel," Shesain thought in exasperation.

"We will have to Shesain, I will contact Telaxia on this matter," Vel responded with concern.

The rest of his leave went smoothly. Ariana settled down to minor infractions. Bel or Vel always accompanied Shesain, sometimes both of them.

Derak returned to the new moon base. He was moving up in both learned techniques and complexity. More was demanded from him than ever before. He knew that a commander must embody all of the cumulative knowledge of his unit, with the sternness and wisdom to carry out orders, the higher the stakes, the rougher the training.

Every two months, they were given one week of leave to maintain their sanity. All the recruits were instructed to separate their military state of mind from normal living. Because of his previous martial and black ops experience, Derak was monitored more than most. A delicate balance had to be established, as this type of training permanently changes the mindset of the person. Time at home, away from exhaustive training schedules helped out greatly.

Due to Derak's knowledge and the lessons he acquired during the two-year time fix mission; he completed his first level of instruction early. He was home for the duration of Shesain's pregnancy and the upcoming Festival of Lights. She had not been bothered by any more of the twin's antics since the last one. Vel and Bel seemed to have worked out the proper mental leash to keep them in the womb. Shesain had three months left and couldn't wait to give birth. Temela, Tranoka, and Virginia were going through their own school. One of them was always with Vel or Bel, learning how to mentally quell the twin's eagerness to teleport from Shesain's womb early.

A wedding invitation arrived one day. Seamus and Tenara had completed their ten-month engagement, Seamus called it an ordeal. It was to be a simple village wedding with no royal treatment.

His and Tenara's love of the sea and sailing prompted Shesain and Derak to book a grand adventure on Harlome, a mostly ocean planet with climate-controlled weather to prevent major squalls. Both of them refused the wedding gift at first but conceded when a Presidential decree followed. They thanked them profusely and requested that they be in the wedding party. Leontul would serve as Seamus's best man. Any outside interference in the wedding plans was strictly forbidden by Tenara's mother. The men would be provided with suitable village finery. Terena and Petar were on top of it.

The day of the wedding saw five local villages joining forces to set the stage for a joyful celebration. Derak and Shesain's presence sparked an uptick in the preparations. The central square of Tenara's coastal village looked like a miniature version of the Temple complex in Shenmar for their wedding. Streamers, multi-colored flags, balloons, and fireworks to start the party in the evening. The entire time crew showed up to celebrate Seamus's wedding. The men from the time crew made up half of his wedding party. Shesain, Shenar, and Vel helped to fill out the bridal party.

Shesain was mobbed by the women upon their arrival. They complimented her on her dress and pregnancy. The bridal party left laughing and giggling with Shesain egging them on. The men laughed, shook their heads, and headed to the nearest mug of ale to catch up. This promised to be as equally festive as Derak's wedding.

Tenara's dance company had a new show to be debuted on her wedding day. Tenara had been briefed on Seamus's doings during the planetary survey, his real duties, and rewards, including his extended life span and the need to match hers with his. She balked at first, wondering how she would handle watching her loved ones die, while she lived on. In the end, she agreed and took an extended trip to Telaxia to receive her treatments. Seamus nursed her through the procedure and the long mental training required for her new position, flying her back and forth on his private ship.

Merriment abounded both inside the bride and grooms tent and the burgeoning crowds gathering outside. Jumar was there with his berry pies and had them specially delivered to both tents. Ever since Derak's wedding, his pies were now spread throughout the known galaxy. His wealth was close to a founding family by now.

Seamus was dressed in a very colorful tuxedo, styled after the local customs. Petar, as usual, out did himself.

Terena designed Tenara's wedding dress, with a removable skirt that revealed a shorter dancing skirt underneath. Tenara relished the royal treatment, enjoying Telaxian blue blush wine. The vintage became immensely popular in a very short period of time, and Rhemar appreciated the wine as well as the profits.

Terena wore an engagement necklace now. Unbeknownst to Derak during his training, Terena and Petar's son, Porthaim had shared the tea cup ceremony. Terena and Petar collaborated on a new youth line that was doing very well. Their clothing lines were a hot item on Earth and her colonies.

Shesain mentally hailed Derak. *"I hope you don't mind my Chimera; I've enlisted Betrawn to split her time between you and*

Paulos for the fast jigs. Oh! Those little rascals, they're up to it again. I'll see you soon my love, Vel!"

Derak laughed to himself. The music started. Seamus and Tenara were guided by her family to the altar. It was apparent that they would not get away from all royal involvement. Demar and Danella would perform the ceremony, and Remor and Tranoka stood in for Seamus's parents. It was a beautiful ceremony. Derak loved witnessing the outer provinces customs, they told so much about the diversity on Thumar.

They followed the lead set by Derak's wedding. Both of them wore Thumarian and Earth symbols of wedlock. Temela designed the broach and necklace, and Remor had the rings commissioned by the finest Thumarian goldsmiths. After the formal ceremony was complete, the party began. It was dusk when the first lively jig was struck. Seamus and Tenara choose this one for their first dance. Betrawn danced with Derak on the opening number and then Paulos stepped up for his turn, Derak immediately had another partner. He must have danced with half of the village's women, to their delight and his, the slow numbers were for Shesain only.

Fireworks went off, giving them all a spectacular show, then the bride and groom were shuttled off in a new air car, provided by Robert. Ali was at his side at all times now. She positively glowed in his presence. Robert was close to a tea cup ceremony, but not until Ali was comfortable with Robert being around other women or working with them. The party lasted until the early hours of the following morning. Shesain turned in early. Betrawn and Derak closed the party down to the last jig.

They were there to greet the married couple after the three-day wedding night. They both looked spent and very satisfied. After the customary breakfast, they were off to Harlome in Seamus's new ship, *The Veelar,* named after Tenara's mother.

The planet's attention was now turned to Jack and Tony's wedding. Royal pomp and circumstance would define this double wedding in Shenmar's Temple complex. One month remained on Jack and Tony's engagements.

Seamus and Tenara returned from their honeymoon tanned and gushing with many thanks. Tenara started on a special presentation for Jack and Tony's ceremony. Seamus was off to Telaxia for a briefing and Tom Morton was commissioned a full Admiral. He worked well with his Telaxian counterparts to complete *The Aries* and see her through space trials. It was one thing to command an Andromeda class cruiser, but that barely prepared him to take control of a moon sized ship. The officer corps was still being set. Getting Telaxian approval was daunting, to say the least.

Derak's mother, Temela, Tranoka, and Betrawn marshaled an army of volunteers. Betrawn kept Paulos, Demar and Danella busy with preparations in Shenmar. Petar and Terena worked day and night on the brides and grooms apparel. Their assistants finished the wedding party's suits and dresses.

Teren was Shesain's second cousin, and her family owned controlling interest in a global food distribution corporation. Their ancestor started one of the Founder's families, twelve in total. They were all part of Tukar Andehar's original crew that discovered the Cave of Lights. Teren's mother, Perana, took a regularly active role with Temela in the wedding arraignments.

Jack was used to the rituals of being tied to the royal family, after twenty-two months of courtship with Shenar. Tony, now a full Lieutenant in the T-K special ops unit, was used to a simpler way of life. He was just now getting acclimated to his elevated status. Remor put forth a bill to give the Jamar family registered royal status according to Thumarian law. This would be a first in their recorded history. If it passed, it would surely be signed by Remor and celebrated by the Thumarian population.

Tony was given a leave of absence from his T-K duties and Jack was kept home with *The Morwen*. Both of them were busy with fittings and last-minute preparations. Derak was Jacks best man, and Yuratan, Tony's best friend in the T-K service would serve as his. Both Shenar and Teren were always present at their chimera's fittings but forbad them to have even a glimpse of their wedding dresses. The carriage that Shesain and Derak used would carry both couples to the Temple. Temela single handedly made sure this day would be as special for Shenar and Teren as it was for Derak and Shesain. The street boxes that separated the crowds from the horse drawn carriage would be used. Once again, the call went out for a mass engagement ceremony before the wedding.

Jack's fame insured that this would be well attended and broadcast across the known galaxy. Tony was having as much trouble as Derak did dealing with his rise in Thumarian popularity.

Shesain was kept at home during the last two weeks of her pregnancy. The twins knew the day was close and tried on a daily basis to leave early. Their mental/psychic leashes were fine-tuned, and Shesain had to deal with only minor rumblings now. Thumar and the galaxy's press reported daily on her progress. Remor's press secretary worked overtime to keep rumors out of the daily vids.

Shenmar started filling up with guests, luminaries, and the press one week before the due date. By the time she was days away from delivering, the crowds had overflowed onto the Ganmer plains. They would stay for the double wedding and the final preparations for the Festival of Lights. The newlyweds would return from their honeymoons in time to attend this year's festival.

Shesain delivered two days later at her estate. Her water broke in the morning, and after hours of labor; Ariana's head appeared, followed by her wriggling body. Both children were fully aware before they made their appearances. Ariana let out her first cry before her umbilical cord was cut. Tomas quickly followed on her heels, literally. His first cry was heard throughout the house, and it was clear that he had a healthy set of lungs. Tears of joy were shed by everyone, none more so than Shesain and Derak. After they were cleaned, Dr. Centur and Nurse Teren put the two babies into Shesain's waiting arms.

Shesain looked like an angel, lovingly cooing each in turn as they settled onto her milk-filled breasts and fell asleep. Tears flowed, and her smile lit up the room. Derak gently stroked the sleeping babes and gave Shesain a tender kiss. Champagne corks were popped, and a quiet celebration ensued in another room. Virginia and Temela were adamant that they could not wake the children.

One or two at a time, everyone got a chance to admire the children. They woke up screaming for food, and Shesain satisfied them until they burped and fell back asleep. Vel and Bel put them into their cribs. The children were taken into an alcove with a one-way silence barrier. Friends and family milled in and out of Shesain's room before Doctor Centur ordered everyone out.

"Congratulations Shesain, your children are beautiful and healthy," Terga thought.

"Thank you, Terga! Aren't they little angels, and in perfect health. I can't wait until you can see them," Shesain joyfully responded.

"Very soon Shesain. The transfer is almost complete. I will have a body in time for the festival. Qex has been so good to me, they had to finally kick him out. He was told to wait until the process was complete. Three more days, that is what I am told," Terga thought.

"I can't wait to see your new body. I'm sure you're going to be stunning."

"Not as beautiful as you look now."

"I love you so much, Terga."

"I love you too, Shesain."

Shesain promptly fell asleep. She looked angelic, totally at peace. She had given birth to two healthy children. Temela, Tranoka, and Derak's mother, Virginia, turned into drill sergeants, ordering the party to move to the front of the house, far away from mother and children. They attended to both children, with Vel and Bel.

Shesain could not attend her sister's wedding after the birth of Ariana and Tomas. She was disappointed. Therese would stand in her place. Her children were now the center of her life. The three of them would be cleared to attend the Festival of Lights. They would be expected by the adoring masses in attendance.

Therese and Karn decided to eschew the royal treatment for their wedding. It would be a large affair and would take place before the Festival of Lights. Ariana and Tomas's birth dates, time, and names were all over the galactic vids the same day. Within days, two large spare rooms were filled with gifts and well wishes from more sources than either Derak or Shesain knew existed. Ariana and Tomas would not go without anything, judging by the endless delivery of gifts. The staff relocated the cache, after sorting, recording the sender and sending out prompt thank you packages.

Well-wishers streamed in and out of Derak's estate, monitored by female T-K agents. Derak's father took four weeks off work to spoil his new grandchildren, and Tara was constantly at Shesain's side. A regular routine was quickly set by the Telaxian guardians and Derak was freed up to get back to the double wedding.

The day arrived with much hoopla. Tents were set up outside of Shenmar proper for the brides and grooms and the crowds were boisterous. Once again, the plains outside of Shenmar turned into a city itself. Shenmar was decked out and the procession wound its way through adoring crowds to the Temple after a mass engagement ceremony took place in front of the Temple. Robert and Ali shared the tea cup ceremony as the lead couple, along with Derak's sister Catherine, to a leading Senator.

They were dressed in finery, waiting for Jack and Tony to arrive by carriage. Bets were made on who would or would not last the three days of their wedding night. After making a grand entrance into the Temple, both grooms made it to the waiting room. They received congratulations and a lot of ribbing. Both Jack and Tony looked dashing in their military dress uniforms. Tony's had a few new ribbons earned from one of his latest assignments. One last toast and it was time to begin. The wedding party took their place in the naves of the Temple and watched as the two couples slowly walked to the altar.

Derak joined them and the long ceremony commenced. To his delight, he saw Qex sitting with Terga, now in an organic body. She must have patterned it after the women which she frequently saw him with in the past. She was almost equal to Shesain, almost. No woman in the universe would come close to Derak's chimera.

Teren and Shenar looked absolutely stunning. Both of them glowed with love for their soon-to-be husbands. Calvin was the ring and necklace bearer for Jack and Tony. Teren's niece served her and Shenar. Seamus and Tenara had returned from their honeymoon, and joined the wedding parties.

The Alliance President attended with his wife and the five outlying sectors were well represented. Remor would entertain them all, including his fellow Galactic Senate colleagues. The ceremony was a fabulous affair. Calvin looked as princely as he did in Derak's wedding. After the vows and declaration of marriage by the High Priest and Priestess, the roar of approval erupted from the Temple to the plains of Ganmer.

After walking down the aisle as married couples, they presented themselves to the rapturous crowds gathered outside the Temple.

They emerged again after the women changed into their party dresses to a sumptuous lunch supervised by Danella. Derak got his chance to get Jack back for his best man speech, and he got him good. Yuratan had them in stitches when it was his turn. After all, what are best friends for at a wedding? Derak could see Tony cooking up a suitable response in between the laughter. The brides didn't get off easy; their maids of honor had the guests rolling in the aisles.

The lunch was delightful, and the invited guests would take their serving sets home with them. Remor made the same arraignments for the cake cutting ceremony. This time, there would be two cakes to share.

Tony, Teren, Jack, and Shenar greeted the joyful crowd, anticipating the cutting of the cake. Both men got a face full of cake and a tender clean up afterwards. Judging by the mental repartee Shesain and Derak shared over a year ago, what Tony and Jack were giving and receiving must be downright inappropriate. The grins and lusty looks from all four verified this. The cake and champagne were served to orderly crowds until it was gone.

At dusk, the single men and women smothered the dance floor for the bouquet and garter toss. The men got their women back for the cake smash. Both of them took a long time, teasing them with well-hidden tongue tickles and mouth nibbles on their toes, sending obvious shudders of delight through both women. After the garters were caught, the four lucky recipients received hugs, complete with pictures.

The dance floor cleared, and the music started. After the wedding parties dance, the floor filled with guests and spectators that snuck in. If one couldn't fit on the enormous dance floor, the streets served just as well.

Betrawn kept Derak busy, along with many women he had never met. Shenar and Teren gave Derak serious competition on a few very spirited jigs. Derak met his match with Tenara, she wasn't even breathing hard when it was over.

They hugged before Derak returned Seamus's wife to him. "I feel sorry for Seamus if you treat him like this on a dance floor. He must be twenty pounds lighter by now."

She giggled, "I give him a break. It's not the dancing that's trimming him down." She winked at Derak before taking Seamus's hand.

He laughed out loud and returned to the head table. Temela was Derak's slow dance partner. Therese and Terga were allowed to butt in, that was it. Shesain had a vid hooked up for the wedding, she didn't miss a thing.

"My credits are on Teren and my sister; would you care for a wager, my Chimera?"

"Prepare to lose again. After T-K training, this will be a walk in the park for Jack and Tony."

The time had come: the fireworks were lit, and the happy couples were ushered to their waiting air cars. Derak hoped that Tony and Jack were ready; otherwise, their wives were going to really give it to them. There was no sweeter surrender. After the farewells, Derak returned to his beloved wife and their two beautiful children.

Clean up was light for the city. Final preparations were being made for the Festival of Lights. Many of the decorations were added to and Jumar had prime real estate again. Vendors and pavilions sprung up all over the city and countryside.

There was one last wedding to attend to, Therese and Karn's. It was quiet compared to Jacks and Tony's, but no less elegant. Derak's estate was ground zero and the wedding crew saw to the details. Shesain was in shape to be Therese's maid of honor, and Derak was in Karn's wedding party. Demar and Danella performed the ceremony and his mother, Tranoka, and Temela organized the feast that followed. His piano was moved outside, and he played for hours, Jazz, twentieth century Earth rock and roll and Thumarian ballads. The symphony lent him some talented musicians to accompany him. Therese and Karn were effusive in their joy. They would be back from their honeymoon in time for the festival. They were both deep into the T-K program.

Shesain was on maternity leave from her Ambassadorial duties, and Derak returned to T-K advanced warfare training. Jack, Tony, and Karn returned from their honeymoons. Derak saw them occasionally during exercises.

Two weeks remained for the festival to kick off. There was a lot to celebrate this year, bumper crops from the agricultural sector, a larger than normal take from the fishing season, three notable marriages, and the birth of Ariana and Tomas.

One lazy afternoon on Derak's front porch, while they watched the twins playing, Qex and Terga popped in after announcing their intention. Qex and Derak caught up on the latest news, while Shesain and Terga admired each other.

"Shesain, you look marvelous! you've lost almost all of your baby weight, and the children look great," Terga complimented her.

"Terga, I must say, you could give me a run for my credits. How did you come up with that figure?"

"Derak! And yours was my true inspiration. We wanted to visit while Derak was home. We would like to perform the tea cup ceremony. The details have been worked out with the Prime Council and they are going to allow us to use the Thumarian timeline for the engagement period, with a Telaxian chaperone. It is such a strange sensation, for me to feel these feminine desires, but I do enjoy them," Terga confided.

Shesain laughed with a twinkle in her eye. *"Wait until you share them in ten Months! there is nothing more fulfilling. I'll give you some pointers to reduce Qex to mush. We have to get you a proper engagement dress. You're close to my size, let's take a look in my wardrobe."*

Both of them disappeared into the house and returned with Vel, Bel, and Derak's mother, who smelled another wedding. Temela, who was visiting, walked out with a tray holding a single tea cup, filled with kava tea and an orchid floating on top. Terga wore an eye-popping dress. The skirt was cut above the knees and her waist was accentuated. The white form fitting blouse was tied off below her décolletage, showing off her cleavage. Her sculpted neck bore the tell-tale pink scarf as she sensuously approached a smiling and speechless Qex.

His eyes glinted in desire as he accepted the tea cup from Terga and sipped it. He handed it back and their eyes locked in loving thoughts as she took her sip and handed the cup to Temela. Then they shared a long lingering kiss. Shesain pulled out a necklace and a lapel engagement broach. She clasped the necklace around Terga's neck and gave her a big hug. Then she pinned the broach on Qex, giving him a hug of congratulations.

Shesain started. "Ok Qex, you must wear this at all times…"

"I'm familiar with the protocol, I'm sorry Shesain, I must remember, this is not a mission. Thank you very much for doing this for us. We have to meet our chaperone and receive a Telaxian briefing." He rolled his eyes.

"Oh, the travails we go through for happiness," Shesain jokingly replied.

He smiled and gave Shesain a goodbye hug, then exchanged a few operational thoughts with Derak before he and Terga popped to their next meeting.

"I'll never get used to that teleportation," Temela said. "I'm happy for them. Do you think they'll let us plan their wedding?" she asked Derak's mother.

"I hope so," Virginia answered as the two of them walked into the house already ahead of the game.

Shenmar was decorated and ready for the opening of the three-day

Festival of Lights. Intergalactic governments and cultures were well represented. This promised to be the largest Festival of the Lights in recorded history. Presidents, Prime Ministers, Kings, and Queens had sent their advanced support teams to set up accommodations for them. The President of the Alliance of Planets and his family would stay at Derak's estate when they arrived. Tom and the representatives of three admiralties would stay with Rhemar and participating members of the Galactic Senate would be hosted by Remor and his children. Every prominent family on Thumar jockeyed for positioning to house and entertain any prominent VIP.

Petar and Terena relocated their individual pavilions to a primary corner location that intersected the men's and women's haberdashery districts, with a new store on the corner in between them. It carried their new line of youth and infant clothes.

Their most popular line was based on the fashions they personally designed for Ariana and Tomas. Shesain was adamant that her children would be the best dressed children in the galaxy.

To no one's surprise, Tenara, Shenar, and Teren were expecting. Jack, Seamus and Tony were beside themselves with joy.

Upon hearing of Qex and Terga's engagement, Leontul and Vel requested a tea cup ceremony at Derak's estate. The entire time crew and Leontul's family were present for their betrothal. The evening concluded with a party for Qex, Terga, Leontul, and Vel. Neither couple looked forward to the ten months of strict Telaxian engagement standards. Yet, they knew the rewards would be worth it.

The good news was mixed with the bad. Remor had to draft Shesain's help to get his recent bills through the legislature. The fight was fierce. A new progressive party held an effective minority in the senate that worked to stop any laws Remor tried to push through. It did not matter how beneficial it was to the populace, they were against it. Their leader, Senator Kamar, was a charismatic and influential man. Now that Catherine was engaged, Remor convinced her chimera, a senior senator to lend a hand, for a fair trade. In the end, the progressives lost more than the vote. Their party was severely damaged. Remor could be a nasty opponent, as Senator Kamar found out.

Shenmar and the plains of Ganmer were filled up once again. Shesain, Shenar, Jack, and Derak walked through as much as they could. Being the luminaries that they were, even with a T-K guard, their exposure was limited. Popularity had its downside. Two years ago, any of them could do the same without the hoopla that followed them now.

The city and the plains were one enormous party. Jumar's berry pie pavilion quadrupled in size. Even with a full staff and alternates, he was still running his feet ragged. He had no complaints; his profits were swelling as well. Jumar had expanded his operations to include six satellite locations on the Ganmer plains. They were just as swamped as his primary location. Festival set up was complete and the Andehar family hosted a private party with Paulos and Betrawn for the galactic potentates and their entourages in the Temple proper. The affair was well attended, and many galactic diplomatic negotiations were finished over Rhemar's offerings, Tom's pear brandy or Telaxian blue blush wine. All three vintages were in high demand and trade agreements were signed that made all three vintners very happy.

The twins made a brief appearance at the party. Shesain and Derak presented them from the altar. They were quiet for a short time before Ariana started itching for some action. Tomas was better behaved, but an adventurous side of his personality was starting to show up more each day. Vel and Virginia took them away to calm them down.

By this time, they didn't cry to be feed, they sent a thought to whomever was closest to them: *"I'm hungry!"* When it was time to change their diapers, they usually communicated the need, followed by the scent. They kept everyone on their toes. Derak rarely changed diapers, not from avoiding the task. Willing volunteers got to it before he could.

When opening day came, Shesain and Derak were in the receiving line. Even with the improved shape and strength he developed from T-K training, his arm felt numb after shaking so many different hands.

Shesain poked fun at him while they received the dignitaries. The VIP pavilion swelled with invited guests before Paulos and Remor announced the beginning of the Festival of Lights. The ceremony was slightly different this year. Shesain and Derak would follow Remor with the twins for their official presentation. Temela and Betrawn rocked them before handing them off to the parents.

Paulos introduced Remor, after quieting the crowd, he started. "I would like to welcome you, one and all, my fellow Thumarians and our guests and participants from across the galaxy. We have had a prosperous year on Thumar; our global rebuilding efforts are well ahead of schedule..."

Senator Kamar sat with his progressive party, grousing about their recent defeat in the senate, glaring at Remor in the middle of his opening speech. *You may have won this time Remor! But the next round belongs to me. You and your old ways will be replaced. I will see to it!* The Senator thought, as he robotically applauded at the appropriate pauses.

"...and now I proudly present the newest members of the Andehar family, Ariana Velore Andehar and Tomas Tukar Andehar, born to Derak and Shesain Andehar one month ago today."

The applause was deafening long after they stepped up. Fortunately, the children held up to the noise and thousands of cameras and vids. Afterwards, Vel and Bel whisked them away and gave them to their grandmothers.

Remor finished, "I now declare the beginning of the Festival of the Lights!"

The tens of thousands that packed the Temples main circular front courtyard roared in approval. The sound of raucous cheering and celebration echoed out to the plains. An air of excitement ignited as strangers in the avenues hugged and greeted each other. This was truly the festival for all peoples. All citizens were on the same strata for three glorious fun filled days, with a few exceptions.

Under guard by Telaxian and T-K trained troops, Shesain and Derak were allowed to tour the courtyard with Ariana and Tomas. Viewing was permitted at a safe distance only. The paparazzi were not allowed to monopolize the picture and vid sessions. Silent cameras with no flashes were tolerated. This type of demonstration helped to bring the everyday populace closer to their beloved leaders. The children were handed off to Vel and Bel while Shesain and Derak took a photo op enjoying one of Jumar's large piping hot berry pies. Laugher ensued when the juice dribbled down their chins. Both of them unceremoniously wiped the juice off with their fingers and finished the last of it with their tongues. This was followed by a public kiss, then they were taken back to the heavily guarded VIP Pavilion.

Derak surprised the expectant crowds at the Barquete match. He wanted to play the whole game but was only given permission to participate in the second half. He repeated the red team/green team split to the delight of the athletes and the crowded stadium. Unknown T-K agents roamed the field with him for two quarters. He was on the losing side this time but didn't mind at all. He loved playing the game.

Thus, started three days of unadulterated joy, even considering the constraints put on Derak and Shesain's public contact. Despite the twin's rambunctious nature, they enjoyed every moment of the festival. Shesain, Ariana, and Tomas were the center of Derak's life. He could not imagine living without them. He would have to thank Tom the next time he saw him. Without posting him on Thumar, he wouldn't have the blessings he now enjoyed.

Epilogue

The Prime Mathematician woke up with a blistering headache and a bruised right arm. His foul mood grew even darker when he realized where he was. He was back in his small square Telaxian cruiser. Back to ship's rations and confined space. He checked the rest of his body for further damage and found none. After a hot cup of gexturon, Telaxian coffee, he tried to contact *The Mandible*. After hours of fruitless labor, he gave up. Where were they, it was like those shicksters to abandon him after all he had done for them.

After a dull meal, he returned to the bridge to track down the data from his last day. The last thing he remembered was enjoying fresh Tex worms wriggling in his mouth before he chewed the life out of them, the savory juices dripping down his chin. He remembered how he broke in the fresh recruit from April's Pleasure Palace. She was a tough one, screaming about the injustice of being removed from a senior science post and being dumped into April's for the life of a sex slave. He went painfully slow and steady, whipping and beating her down to her new station in life. He left her sobbing, broken, bloody, and well aware of her fate.

Then the time wave hit, and he woke up here, alone on this tiny ship again, without another ship in hailing distance. There should be standard shipping routes, even out on the rim of the galaxy. Yet he picked up no traces of any ship activity. Where was he? What timeline was he in? This would take time to figure out. He had developed the mortal shortfall of impatience over the tens of thousands of years he had spent with those useless dogs. All mortals needed to be tied up and beat into submission. They had to learn who their real god was and serve Dex, in all of his benevolence.

They would learn. When he caught up with *The Mandible*, he would teach the entire moon-sized ship's crew the cost of failure.

He checked and double checked his ship's sensor logs and communication records. No data transfers were found. It was as if *The Mandible* never existed. How did the Prime Mathematician remember the name of a moon-sized ship? This threw him for a loop he could not figure out. His anger flashed for a moment before he took control of his mind again. A laziness set into his habits from long millennium of direct contact with the cursed mortal races. It would take precious time to reconfigure his thought patterns to efficient Telaxian standards again.

One mystery that his ship's external sensors recorded was seven-time waves. Why would there be time waves, he asked himself. Who would toy with time changes and why? He wished he could remember. There was key information missing that he needed to find. Perhaps a recalibration of his thinking processes would turn something up.

He moved the ship into a node and recalled meditations and exercises to sharpen his mental skills. Weeks passed until his thoughts began to resemble Telaxian thought language. Now he could look at the numbers and get an accurate interpretation of the data, but his research turned up more questions than answers. One constant was the name Derak Jamar. Who was he, and what did he have to do with his present predicament? He would find out when Derak Jamar's time and place were determined.

After much time, he determined that he was in the year 1480, deep in the Pegasus sector. He looked for any habitable planet within one hundred light years.

One piqued his curiosity: Thumar. After setting course for the planet and establishing a parking orbit, he scanned the planet. This Jamar fellow could not come from this time. He would go forward in time until his presence was detected. If this man was responsible for his present situation, he would make him pay dearly.

Glossary

3-D Holo-screens - Three-dimensional holographic images

3-D/5D Holographic Display - Fifth-dimensional images displayed in a three dimensional holographic format

Admiral - The four highest officer ranks in a navy that can be achieved, equal to a General in other services, denoted by one to four stars

Aft Deck - The stern or rear of the ship when the frame of reference is within the ship

Antexeral Tree - The holy of holies on Telaxia, the last living tree given to the Telaxians by the gods

Air Car - A flying car that uses anti-gravity

Alliance Treaty - A trade agreement between Earth and Thumar

Altair - The home planet that Derak Andehar's three companies are based on

Altarian - Anything that originates from the planet Altair

Altarian Tablets - Very ancient stone tablets found on Altair by Derak Andehar years before they stationed him on Thumar

Anea - A continent on Thumar

Anean Light Caves - The caves that have the glowing crystals Tukar Andehar discovered in the year 1852

Ankora - Small, quick sea birds

Antanob - Thumarian card game similar to cribbage

April's Pleasure Palace - the top-rated house of prostitution on *The Mandible*, the mobile home of the Orion Syndicate

Artificial Gravity - A generated gravitational field in zero gravity

ASP - Advanced Science Protocol

Asteroid Belt - The asteroid belt is the circumstellar disc in the Solar System. It is occupied by many irregularly rocky shaped bodies called asteroids or minor planets.

Azimuth Circle - A device for measuring azimuths, consisting of a graduated ring equipped with a sighting vane on each side, which fit concentrically over a compass

Barquete - A physically demanding sport played by the Thumarians. It is similar to a combination of rugby, soccer, and cricket

Bashk Ball - The predecessor to Sheshk Ball, introduced by Derak and Jack in the year 1917

Becalmed - To make a ship motionless on a body of water for lack of wind

Bengal Tiger - A large fierce Asian cat from Earth with an orange and black stripped coat

Beore - Bison-type of mammal

Beshkebar - Bullshit

Betur - Balls

Berona - The capitol city of the Telaxian system on Telaxia Prime

Bi-locate - The mental ability to project a believable copy of oneself in a second location.

Bilge pumps - A water pump used to remove bilge water

Bulwarks - A wall that is part of a ship's sides that is above the ship's upper deck

Celestial Navigation - Also known as astronavigation is the ancient and modern practice of position fixing that enables a navigator to transition through a space without having to rely on estimated calculations, or dead reckoning, to know their position

Chambar Valley Offensive - A key battle fought in the Voeleron War

Chart Master - Charts and tracks all, essential cartographic reference detail for cruising, sailing, and fishing: port plans, safety depth contours, *marine* services, tides, currents, and *navigation* aids

Chimera/Chimera-te - Thumarian terms of endearment

Christian - A member of the Earth-based religion, Christianity

Cloaking Device - A technological device that hides an object in the third dimension

Commander - A Naval senior officer equal to Lieutenant Colonel in other services

Corano Islands - The southernmost inhabitable island chain on Thumar

Cyth - A giant predatory raptor with wingspans that starts at thirty-five feet. Larger birds can reach forty-five feet

D-gen - A portable dimensional generator based on Quasi-Dimensional Theory

DNA - Deoxyribonucleic Acid, the building blocks of all life

Dead Reckoning - The process by which a ship's position is deduced or computed trigonometrically, in relation to the known departure point

Deckhand - a sailor who performs manual duties

Detarch - Smart Ass

Dolt - Idiot

Earth - Home of Derak Andehar, Jack Andehar, and Seamus McGrew

Elemure - Frankmur Velmar's mother's name

Emperor Ming the Merciless - A reference to a twentieth-century Earth film's iconic villain

Etag - Thumarian currency

Extebar - Telaxian Bartender

Fahrenheit - A temperature scale that defines freezing at 32 degrees and boiling at 212 degrees

Festival of the Lights - A major annual Thumarian planetary celebration. It celebrates the discovery of The Cave of Lights, found on the Anean continent on Thumar. The light emitting crystals fueled Thumar's technological advancements

Festival of Prosperity - A festival that celebrates the past years prosperity

First Generation - A pure blood that goes back to Earth's twenty-first century super soldier genetic project

Five Card Stud - An Earth-based card game, also known as poker

Flash Gordon - A reference to a twentieth century Earth film iconic heroic character

Flora and Fauna - Plants

Flying Jib - The outermost of two or more jibs, set well above the jibboom

Founders Day - A festival celebrating Thumar's founding fathers

F'ter - Shithead

Galactic Senate - A legislative assembly representing the known galaxy

Gamma Ray Burst - GRB, a by-product of a Super Nova, gamma radiation traveling at near the speed of light

Gangplank - A movable bridge used in boarding or leaving a ship at a pier

Ganmer - A continent on Thumar

GDP - Gross Domestic Production of a country or region

Gel Tec Computers - Advanced computers built by Derak Andehar's company

Gexturon - Telaxian Coffee

Head - A toilet on a marine or space going ship

Helmsman - One who steers a ship

Hyperspace - An alternate dimension that can only be reached by traveling faster than the speed of light

IDMD - Interstellar Dark Matter Drive, using dark matter and energy as a fuel source

Ion Plasma Beam - A generated plasma beam

Jim Beam - An ancient liquor produced on Earth in the twentieth and twenty-first centuries

Jhakor - similar to Earth dolphins

Jinourka - The cover village of Seamus and Leontul in the year 1852

Jesus - Jesus Christ, savior of the ancient Earth based religion, Christianity

Katkurn - A silicon-based race that chews on rocks for snacks, the denser the better

Kectur F'ter - Fucking shit head

Kenmar Braid and Medallion - The highest galactic honor given for heroic action during combat actions, given by the Galactic Senate. Derak Andehar was its first recipient

Kek - A barbaric warlike reptilian race who occupy a rocky home world at the edge of the rim of the galaxy

Kexinshar - Telaxian Air Car

Kinitar - Thumarian horse-drawn carriage

Lelayla - A continent on Thumar

Lesk - A tip off that determines who controls the ball in the game of Bashk Ball

Light Speed - The speed at which light travels, 670,616,629 mph. It is the constant used to measure astronomical distances

Light Swords - A sword whose blade is an ion plasma beam in a force field

Longitude - is given as an angular measurement ranging from 0° at the Prime Meridian to +180° eastward and −180° westward. The Greek letter λ (lambda), is used to denote the location of a place on Earth east or west of the Prime Meridian

Long Jib Boom - A *boom* is a spar (pole), along the foot of a fore and aft rigged sail that improves control of the angle and shape of the sail

Marine Sextant/Quadrant/Quantar - A doubly reflecting navigation instrument that measures the angular distance between two visible objects. The primary use of a *sextant* is to measure the angle between an astronomical object and the horizon for the purposes of *celestial navigation*

Math Mode - A mental state in which math is the understood language

Matter Transfer Technology - The ability to transfer matter from one point to another via an energy beam

Menurk - Mountain Goat

Micro-jumps - A small controlled hyper-speed jump

Moratain Falls - A twenty-three-hundred-mile-long waterfall on the continent of Lelayla

Mt Kumar - Thumar's tallest mountain

Modernists - A movement to eliminate Thumar's old ways and replace them with modern rules

N-gen - A third-generation portable dimensional generator based on the Quasi-Dimensional Theory

Nano-Bots - Nano level self-replicating robots

New York City, Earth - A major city on Earth that is the center of the planet's black market and is a part of the URNA

Number One to Nine - A Numerical designation of prime council members in the Orion Syndicate

Node - A bubble in the physical universe where time does not exist. Time, space, and dimension exist in one place at the same moment

No-see-ums - Small bugs that cannot be seen and irritate to no end

Null Space - Where time, space and dimension occupy the same moment, a timeless space

Null Space Generator - A generator that puts the user in a space where the past, present, and future exist at the same moment. Time does not exist here

Orenbar - The village that Dr Bundett claimed to be from when the time crew were in the year 1814

Organic Nano-Bots - Self-replicating nano-sized robots made from organic material

Paradox - A statement or situation that seems contradictory but may be true

Passive Wall Technology - Walls built and infused with nanotechnology, with the ability to achieve any form with a command sent by thought

Pegasus Sector - Home sector of the Thumarian system

Petak - Similar to Earth's Cockroaches

Pfizer - An Earth-based pharmaceutical company

Phase Pistol - An energy pulse weapon used in warfare

Pheteberal - Poison

Pirotane Flower - A flower in the family of the Veredant flower that caused the plague of 1814

Plague of 1814 - A plague that nearly wiped out every male Thumarian above the age of 13 on Thumar in the year 1814

Pocket Watch, Chronometer - A marine *chronometer* is a timepiece that is precise and accurate enough to a portable time standard; it can therefore determine longitude by celestial navigation

Port side - The left side of a ship

Portable Dimensional Generator, PDG - A small, wearable dimensional generator

Portuma - A village on Thumar in the year 1917

Psychometric Training - A type of ESP training

P'taw - Quack

Quartermaster - A senior soldier who supervises stores and distributes supplies and provisions. In many navies, *quartermaster* is a non-commissioned officer (petty officer) rank

Quasi-Dimensional Generator, QDG - A generator that increases the inside of a space, while not changing the outside dimensions

R&D - Research and Development

RMT - Reverse Magnetic Drive

Ratlines - Lengths of thin line tied between the shrouds of a sailing ship to form a ladder

Ratour - Hurrah

Ratubla - Similar to Earth's Raccoon's

Recon - A military term for a reconnaissance, a fact gathering mission

Renbar - Thumarian Horse

Run aground - For a vessel to be immobilized by water too shallow to allow it to float

Scotland - A country on Earth

Scuper - Land Lubber

Self-aware - When an AI, artificial intelligence computer, becomes independently aware of its surroundings and is free of its initial programming

Senate - A legislative assembly representing a government

Shabul - The village where the cure of the plague of 1814 originated from

Shadow - A female chaperone assigned to a male after an engagement is started

Shenmar - Thumar's and Ganmer's capitol city and home to Thumar's main Temple

Sheets - Sails

Sherka - Thumarian Horses

Shesk Ball - A primitive sport played on a large open field that preceded Bashk Ball

Shoal - A place where a sea, river, or other body of water is shallow. A sandbank or sandbar in the bed of a body of water, one that is exposed above the surface of the water at low tide

Simulation - Similar to star treks holo-deck

Sitan - Damn

Skiff - A small coastal water craft

Sky Cycle - A covered flying motorcycle; also referred to as a 'Flyer'

Squibb - A derogatory term used to insult fellow crew members

Stellar Class Cruiser - A spaceship the size of a medium size moon

Surgant - Wild Thumarian Boar

Supreme Council - The ruling counsel of nine for the Orion Syndicate

The Aries - A moon-sized, stellar-class ship registered to the War Alliance

The Corano Islands - The southernmost habitable Island chain discovered by Frankmur Velmar, in the year 1857

The Mandible - A stellar class cruiser registered to the Orion Syndicate

The Menarme - The ocean-going schooner, Frankmur Velmar used to discover the Corano Islands

The Orion Syndicate - A 240-year-old organization dedicated to conquering the known galaxy. Their aim is to control by fear and strict marshal law

The Pamella - Tom Morton's personal space ship

The Prime Mathematician - Head of the Orion Syndicate

The Tiger Shark - A Battle cruiser registered to the Orion Syndicate

The Shenar - A smaller sister ship to *The Shesain*

The Shesain - A medium class war cruiser built by Derak Andehar and home to the time crew for over two years

The Veelar - Seamus McGrew's personal space ship

The Void - A timeless place in sub-space that one cannot escape

Taburn Ocean - An ocean in the southern hemisphere on Thumar

Tea Cup Ceremony - The official method that women use to start the ten-month engagement process on Thumar

Teeth Caps - Faux teeth caps worn by Telaxian infiltration agents when they are on assignment to the mortal races that covers their shark-like teeth

Telaxia - Home world to the Telaxian race of immortal time lords

Telaxian - Anything attributed to Telaxia or the Telaxian race

Telaxue - The official language of the Telaxians

Telekinesis - The ability to move solid objects with your mind

Telepathy - Extrasensory thought communication between minds

Teleportation - Instantaneous travel or movement of self, or an object by extrasensory ability of the mind

Tele-vid Program - Televised news and entertainment for the masses

Tenart - Telaxian Naval Captain

Terag - Thumarian language

Terelians - A hybrid reptilian race that borders Thumarian space

Terrestrial Engineer - A multi-talented and trained engineer, involved in planetary level projects or terra-forming

Texas Hold-em - An Earth based card game, also known as poker

Theth Class Cruiser - A new class of war cruiser built with Derak's and Telaxian technology

Thumar - The second planet in the Thumarian system in the Pegasus sector, home world of the Thumarian system

Thrashur Katur - Highly trained Thumarian black ops

Thumdust - A soft rock that turns regular steel into a super metal, only found on Thumar

Thought Control - The ability to communicate and control the external environment with a thought command

Threngar - People

Time Parallax - The apparent change in position resulting from a change in the viewers position

Time space fabric - The fabric of space-time is a conceptual model combining the three dimensions of space with the fourth dimension of time

Time Vortex - A counter clockwise whirlpool that indicates time travel

URNA - United Regions of North America, founded after the second great American civil war, in 2175, on Earth. It is made up of the former countries of Mexico, the United States of America, and Canada

Veredant Flower - Cause of the plague of 1814 that nearly wiped out Thumarian males. Also known as Plantara Eusipiodus

Venexara - Telaxian Gardener

Venerians - A multi-armed and breasted race. The women have more than two breasts and the men's organs are just as astounding. They are the most popular male and female prostitutes in April's Pleasure Palace

Vorturak - A town on Thumar in the year 1835

Wanderers - Gypsies

Weather Deck - An upper deck on a ship having no overhead protection from the weather but sheltering the deck below

Whandar - Similar to Earth's whales

Wild Antor - Large deer

X-gen - A second-generation portable-dimensional generator based on Quasi-Dimensional Theory

Xerubtilominite Beetle - A poisonous Telaxian delicacy eaten to keep their shark-like teeth sharp

Zenex - Telaxian Admiral

Zertha Braid - The highest honor for heroism given to Derak Andehar from the Voeleron war

Xextufuquel Beetle - A voracious beetle used for execution on Telaxia

Zextur - Telaxian Black Ops

Characters

Admiral Morton - Admiral, father of Tara Morton and grandfather to Calvin Morton

Aliaxmur/Ali - The female Telaxian assigned to Robert Jamar

Allen McGregor - Seamus McGrew's cover name in the year 1817

April - Owner and Madame of Aprils Pleasure Palace; on *The Mandible*, home base to the Orion Syndicate

Artir - A member of the first group recruited to be Cyth riders in the year 1875

Arimus - Seamus McGrew's cover name in the year 1875

Arana - Syrah's Cyth

Avutar - A Bashk Ball player and Portuma villager

Belantorex/Bel - The Telaxian nanny assigned to Shesain Andehar's first born twins

Beltur Fractum - A member of Keltur Shenmar's crew in 1817

Betena Parkur - Wife of Vendell Parkur in the year 1814

Betrawn Rhebold - Wife of Paulos Rhebold, the Mayor of Shenmar, the capitol city of Thumar

Beron - Artir's Cyth

Borath - Seamus's Cyth

Calvin Morton - Derak and Tara's son, grandson to Admiral Morton

Captain Peter Robinson - Captain of the stranded Earth colonists on Thumar in the year 1814

Cerrum Satoreb - Wife of Keruk Satoreb, Chief Cyth rider

Cetar Lorkam - First mate on *The Menarme* in the year 1857

Chakur - Jack Andehar's cover name in the year 1857

Charlie - A Bashk Ball player and Portuma villager

Charlie Thompson - Commander Thompson, Captain Thompson; commander of an elite assassin corps in the Orion Syndicate

Cherixtou - The Valuk-Manou's husband

Cirith - A member of the first group recruited to be Cyth riders in the year 1875

Commodore Xetackir - A senior Telaxian naval officer

Councilman Pevutamet - Telaxian elder on a senior science council

Dr. Centur - Thumar's leading doctor and surgeon

Dr. Cilenture - A Telaxian scientist who supervises Derak on Telaxia

Dr. Elias Vander/Vander - A founding scientist and prime council member for the Orion Syndicate

Dr. Endell - Physician of record that crafted the cure for the plague of 1814 on Thumar

Dr. Frank Thorsen - An early scientific mentor to Derak Andehar

Dr. Leontul Bundett - Thumar's leading herbal doctor, and time crew member

Dr. Maritak - A Telaxian agent assigned to Thumar

Danella Shodurn - Thumarian High Priestess

Debra Joshekur - A female seeking the heart of Tukar Andehar in the year 1835

Dedore Thuber - Leontul Bundett's cover name in the year 1852

Demar Zatain - Thumarian High priest

Derak Andehar - Earth-based Ambassador to Thumar and the husband to Shesain Andehar

Dermot - A Bashk Ball player and Portuma villager

Dorack Herbicke - Seamus McGrew's cover name in the year 1852

Dreck - A transient con artist in the village of Portuma in 1917

Estarbul - The Chief on *The Menarme* in the year 1857

Frankmur Velmar - The mariner that discovered the Corano Islands in Thumar's southern seas in the year 1857

Felain - Seamus McGrew's shadow

General Xextuct - A Telaxian general

Hartakale/Hart - A female Telaxian assigned to the time crew.

Hecktur Morkam - Seamus McGrew's cover name in the year 1857

Hekphor - Keruk's Cyth

Herculean Yiskurak - A Bashk Ball team captain in the year 1917

Jack Andehar - Husband to Shenar Andehar, sister of Shesain Andehar. He is Derak Andehar's best friend and brother-in-law

James Jamar - Derak Andehar's father

Jorshah - A Cyth

John Roberts - A stranded Earth colonist from the future on Thumar in the year 1852

Jumar Quentel - Maker and seller of the best berry pies at Thumarian festivals, and Shesain's favorites

Karn Honara - Shesain's former bodyguard, and husband to Therese Honara

Karuk Phrelbar - A legendary Kek commander

Keltur Shenmar - Founder of the city, Shenmar in the year 1817

Kethela Erenger - A female seeking the heart of Tukar Andehar in the year 1835

Keruk Satoreb - Chief of the Cyth riders in the year 2414

Lt Granger - Shift officer in the ASP room, on the Orion Syndicate ship, *The Mandible*

Leyla Voxmur - Shenar's cover name in the year 1817

Master Li - A martial arts grand master and mentor to Derak Andehar

Mikail/Mik/Technician Peterson - An Orion Syndicate operative manning a science ship

Miron - Derak's Cyth

Mutah Shakur - The Prime Mathematician, supreme leader of the Orion Syndicate

Nafka - A transient con artist in the village of Portuma in 1917

Otur - Robert's cover name in the year 1857

Paul Rankin - A stranded Earth colonist from the future on Thumar in the year 1817

Paulos Rhebold - Mayor of Shenmar, the capitol city of Thumar

Paxtarentex Borinuragesh/Pax - Telaxian Ambassador to Thumar

Petar Frankil - Derak Andehar's pseudo name in the year 1814

Petar Wolmneb - The Andehar's family's personal tailor

Petemar Vorshock - The Altarian name for the Telaxian, Qex

Pikurtinele/Pik - A female Telaxian assigned to the time crew

Porath - A Cyth

Porthaim Ventana - Terena Ventana's husband and Petar Wolmneb's son

Prack - A crass vengeful crewman on *The Menarme* in the year 1857

Prime Mathematician - The dictator of the Orion Syndicate

Qextenar/Qex - A Telaxian covert agent to the mortal races, also known as Petemar Vorshock on Altair

Remor Andehar - President of Thumar and husband of Tranoka Andehar

Rhemar Andehar - Brother of Remor Andehar, the President of Thumar, husband of Temela, and the father of Shesain and Shenar Andehar

Robert Jamar - Brother of Derak Andehar and CEO of his three galactic corporations

Rostum - Derak Andehar's cover name in the year 1857

Torimere Eshimar - Leontul Bundett's cover name in the year 1817

Rothure Beliminde - A Thumarian scientist in the altered time line of 2414

Samora - Jack's Cyth

Senator Kamar - A Thumarian senator who opposes Thumar's traditional ways.

Seamus Mcgrew - Retired chief master petty officer, and time crew member

Shamur Andehar - A predecessor to the Andehar family in the year 1814

Shara - A transient con artist in the village of Portuma in 1917

Shenar Andehar - Daughter of Rhemar and Temela Andehar, sister of Shesain Andehar and wife of Jack Andehar

Sherese Navollo - Shesain Andehar's pseudo name in the year 1814

Shesain Andehar - Daughter of Rhemar Andehar and niece of President Remor Andehar, wife of Ambassador Derak Andehar

Syrah - A member of the first group recruited to be Cyth riders in the year 1875

Susan Anderson - Science officer with the stranded Earth colonists on Thumar in the year 1814

Tara Morton - Admiral Morton's daughter, Derak's former lover, and mother to their son, Calvin Morton

Temela Andehar - Wife of Rhemar Andehar and mother of Shesain and Shenar Andehar

Teren Berel - The chief nurse to the Andehar family, and wife of Tony Berel

Terena Ventana - Maker of Thumarian top female fashion, Shesain's favorite

Terenber - Zix's Altairian name

Terga - Derak Andehar's former AI computer

Teruxankor/Ter - A Telaxian combat instructor

Therese Honara - Derak's Thumarian Shadow, Shesain's first cousin, and wife of Karn Honara

Tony Berel - Derak Andehar's brother and husband to Teren Berel

Tranoka Andehar - Wife of Remor Andehar

Tsuris - A transient con artist in the village of Portuma in 1917

Tukar Andehar - The discoverer of the cave of lights in 1857

Tyramar - Jack Andehar's name as a Cyth rider

Uncle Vemur - Remor Andehar's mother's brother

Valuk-Manou - The Telaxian head of state

Vendell Parkur - Dr Endell's host when he served as Shabul's village doctor in the year 1814

Velumtebar/Vel - Shesain's Telaxian nurse

Verum - Cerrum's Cyth

Vetur - A member of the first group recruited to be Cyth riders in the year 1875

Vortan Turbul - Derak's Andehar's cover name in the year 1917

Villumn Shatnar - Jack Andehar's cover name in the year 1917

Virginia Jamar - Derak Andehar's mother

Yemat - Second mate on *The Menarme* in the year 1857

Zenar - A prostitute on *The Mandible,* in April's pleasure Palace

Zenusha - A Venerian whore from April's Pleasure Palace

Zerick - A citizen of Vorturak in the year 1835

Zeveren - Derak Andehar's name as a Cyth rider

Zixunaxe/Zix - A Telaxian general and cultural consultant to the time crew

Printed in the United States
by Baker & Taylor Publisher Services